CHRONICLES OF ASTORIA

By M R Shields

Part 1

DELTA

To Hayden enjoy, happy Reading from M R Shields

PROLOGUE

High above the earth, just on the edges of the atmosphere, High Commander Vorador surveyed the planet's surface below. He shook his head in disbelief at the purple mass that now covered the once beautiful blue green world. There was a time that he had longed for nothing more, than to view the world from such a high orbit, safely aboard a star ship, with a viewing chamber that would allow him to admire its intricate land mass and colourful oceans, to look down upon the vast mountain ranges from a perspective few could have shared. He now had such a star ship to his command, and the viewing chamber he desired, but unfortunately the scene that expanded before him was anything but pleasurable, and his mind tired at the thoughts of how it had all come to this.

He stood there on the bridge of his flagship, the 'Exodus' wearing his full military attire, coated with all the medals of honour and valour he had earned over his 60 years of service. His uniform was pristine white and had gold trimmings made of a simple thread. He wore his hat squarely on his head.

He looked down at his antique watch, it was a simple timepiece that also bore multiple faces within the larger face, each face would depict the date, the day and the time.

He noted that the mission was almost complete and in the allotted timeframe, 18; 47 Sunday 11th march in the year 2599. He took a moment to glance around the room, sparing a thought for each of his command staff on the bridge. Were they going through the same chain of thoughts? This had been their world too; their homes and now they too had the burden of guilt to bear upon its desecration.

His uniform felt tight around his neck and he could feel a bead of sweat forming on his temple. This was a mission that he never thought he would ever have to embark upon. He knew he had to remain strong, keep a united front for the sake of the men and women serving beneath him, but he wanted nothing more than to yell out his frustrations at the complete waste, that was now their home.

He straightened his posture and held himself in check. He had a duty to perform, and perform it to his best he would.

High Commander Vorador was a powerful man, having spent ALL his years in service to the Federation. Once he was promoted above the rank of Master General, his voice could now be heard loudly and across the entire senate. When the decision had been made to evacuate, it was to Vorador that they turned for planning and execution.

"Corporal Lament report, have all ships made safe evacuation?" he said to the young adept at the console next to him. The Young gentleman had been in the service for almost 6 years, and had progressed quickly through the ranks of the core due to his hard working and attention to detail. Vorador liked this man, mostly because he reminded him of a younger version of himself. He liked the way the boy conducted himself, and most of all, he enjoyed the respect that he received from him. The Corporal would go far in the military, and he aimed to give him all the right chances possible, to ensure that one day he may command a ship much like this one.

Corporal Lament was almost thirty years of age, but to the High Commander, whom had only just received him onto his flagship the year before, he was still relatively new and therefore young in his eyes.

The young gentleman ran his eyes over the data screen and ran some quick diagnostics. He then looked up and met his High Commander's eyes.

"No sir, we are one short, Arcology 137 sir is still grounded."

The High Commander scratched his chin in thought. All ships should have reached orbit by now, for this one ship to still be grounded, was a bad omen. Each Arcology was a city size ship, easily 40 miles tall and each floor could house up to 90 thousand inhabitants. With over 10 grand floors throughout the massive ship, and not to mention the massive cargo storages and engines housing, the ship was basically a small world capable of sustaining nearly a million lives.

'A million lives' he thought as a grim feeling overcame his focus.

"Hail them, find out what the delay is" he barked toward the Corporal.

"Yes sir" he replied.

The next few moments passed painfully slow. From the other viewing consoles, the High Commander could see hundreds of the city size Arcologys breaking the earth's atmosphere and heading on their way. There massive engines firing at full capacity to achieve light speed to reach their intended target in a much more desirable timeframe. The High Commander found himself nodding in appreciation, at each ships success as they broke orbit.

The flagship, the 'Exodus', Voradors prize ship, stood sentinel on the fringes of the earth's atmosphere to ensure they all escaped safely.

'Escaped' he thought again, another phrase that he never believed he would be using in regards to his home world. Voradors attention was turned back to the Corporals after a small bleep on his console indicated a response from the grounded ship.

"Sir it seems there has been a revolt, fighting on all decks"

"Rebels? Mutants?" Vorador asked. He had asked the question but he was almost already certain of the response.

Before mobilising for the mission, Vorador had followed the news updates carefully, taking particular interest in the various factions that had sprung up in the aftermath of the tribinium outbreak. He had made note of one of the main faction's leader, Mobeus, and had committed such details to memory, details including his main conspirers, what they looked like, what their gifts were. All information on these mutants was vital. Although truth be told, hijacking one of the Arcologys did not seem to fit the mutants' profile. The mutants longed to have the world to themselves, once the population had left, they would have such a goal, disrupting an evacuation ship did not make any sense, if anything the mutants would want to hurry the craft on its way, a disruption like this one, stank of an entirely different faction, and this worried the High Commander more so.

He had heard rumours, rumours of a secret faction of mutants. Individuals strategically positioned high up within the ranks of humanity and the federation, whom kept their allegiance to the faction a secret. It was said that their leader was very powerful, invincible, and had already lived for hundreds of years. The rumour was, that this leader was a megalomaniac, visions of grand domination and coupled with the knowledge and wisdom to bring those plans to fruition. Vorador was unsure if this was just another urban myth, and yet, here and now, on this day, he was unwilling to take the risk.

"Unsure sir, I will try and contact the bridge"

Vorador pondered on this once more, *a revolt inside one of the Arcologys? Perhaps they intend on an alternative destination, away from Alpharus prime. Make their own way in the universe?*

"Sir I have a link to the bridge" the Corporal said.

"Put us through""Arcology 137, this is the High Commander Vorador requesting immediate response on the nature to your disturbance" there was a short pause and some static before a response could be made clearly.

"High Commander, this is Commander Vega, our ship is over run, there is fighting on all decks, We have sealed off the upper levels for our safety but I fear the worst"

The High Commander listened intently. Something about Vega's words did not seem genuine. He did not sound as panicked as the situation should have incurred. A strange notion, although he could not recall if he had ever met this Commander Vega in all his years' service, well he couldn't recall if he had met him in person, but he had certainly heard of his endeavours, endeavours that at times, seemed to baffle all those that had read about them. Stories of hopeless battles against unfathomable odds, against guerrilla terrorists in the Middle East, entire platoons wiped out by photonic explosions and yet, this Vega would always walk free from the wreckage, with some heroic tale of courage and luck.

Some admired the man. Others, like the High Commander, became weary and hearing his strange voice over the link did nothing to stow those doubts.

He replayed the words back in his mind and wondered if this 'strangeness' in his voice was perhaps just the way the man conducted himself, was he truly fearless, was he maintaining a complete calmness in the face of certain danger, perhaps this man did deserve to be commended, perhaps he had underestimated his bravery, he decided he would give the man the benefit of the doubt for now.

"Is the revolt mutant based?" Vorador asked.

"Erm...hard to say" Vega responded. The hesitation in Vega's voice irritated the High Commander further. It now seemed very odd to him, that this braveness had quickly been coupled with hesitation, almost as if he had been caught unawares of the question and forced to quickly produce an explanation. Surely the explanation was simple, surely it was fact, they were either rebels with weapons, rifles, or mutants with all manner of powers. The Commander of the ship should be direct, should be straight talking, yes or no answers, it baffled Vorador to have heard anything in-between. The High Commander suddenly felt like he was being lied to, and there was nothing that he disliked more than a liar.

"You would know dammit, did they display any powers from their extremities?" Vorador barked.

"Erm no sir they...well" none of this reassured him and most of it pointed to a swift and certain outcome. Again the hesitations in Vega's voice sent the High Commanders choler through the roof and raised his suspicions even further. Something was not right here and he was going to get to the bottom of it.

Vorador cut in

"Well how on earth have they managed to overcome your guards with no weapons?" Vorador said. Cutting to the chase.

A silence fell. Broken only again by Vorador

"Commander Vega, who else is on the bridge with you?"

"Corporal Borealis, Lieutenant Kleinman..Captain..."

Vorador cut him off mid sentence, he had heard enough.

"Corporal Borealis, initiate contingency 151" and within a mere three seconds, a large shot was heard as the Corporal had followed his orders expertly and executed the pilot with his bolt gun.

Each Arcologys control handles were pre-programmed on this mission, to accept only the neural handprint of the designated user. If the pilot was eliminated, the ship had been effectively neutralised. It was the only clinical way the Federation had, of ensuring no undesirables made their way off the planet to infect their intended new home world.

Cut off the head and the body wont function, that was the general idea with regards to disabling these massive ships.

A few more shots could now be heard, followed by angry shouts and screams. A silence fell followed by heavy breathing, the sound of very deep and weathered breathing. It sounded very menacing, almost as if there a great anger only just being held in check by the smallest of wills.

Vorador was left in no doubt as to the taint that had infected the bridge of that particular Arcology, he had dealt with it swiftly and cleanly, as he had been instructed to by his peers. The action itself did leave him with a small level of remorse, for he knew that by eliminating the pilot, there was no other possible way that ship could leave the ground. A million lives had now all been perished. It was a heavy burden to bear.

The silence was broken by a voice, a very different and very angry voice that still yet unmistakably belonged to Commander Vega.

"THAT WAS MY SON YOU JUST EXECUTED!!! YOU HAVE DOOMED US ALL TO THIS FORSAKEN PLANET VORADOR!!"

"Your ship is clearly not under your control Commander, we cannot allow any mutants to follow us to Alpharus prime. It will be our fresh start, sadly not for you"

"THAT WAS A FOOLISH MISTAKE, I WILL FIND A WAY, I WILL AVENGE THIS I SWEAR ON IT"

"That much I really doubt Commander. Corporal Lament, please make ready the E.M.P cannon, target Arcology 137, render it, and all its life systems inoperative" The High Commander said.

The Corporal frantically pressed a few buttons on his data screen as he followed his High Commanders orders to the letter. A small vibration could be felt humming through the floor of the bridge. This was an indication to Vorador, that the weapon was ready. Other ranking officers present on the bridge turned and watched closely. Vorador could feel their eyes burning on the back of his neck, he could feel their anticipation, not anticipation based on pleasure, more like dreaded anticipation of what they were about to bear witness to.

High Commander Vorador took a deep breath before speaking, his eyes never left the view screen.

"May god have mercy on their souls...FIRE"

CHAPTER 1

399 years later...

"Those that have power, must protect those that have not"

This was the opening line in the book of Astorian law. It was a simple notion, the line itself having been written in an entirely different time and for an entirely different purpose. It did however, have precedence here in Astoria, where power, true power could be harnessed by individuals.

Astoria was located in the centre of the one remaining continent that was free of the toxic tribinium crystals. Over the years, information regarding its exact location had been lost. Reference texts and maps had been damaged, and without access to any orbital satellites it was no longer possible to pinpoint its exact location. It had been passed down, much like Chinese whispers, that Astoria was located in the 'Rican' continent of the planet although this had never been confirmed nor had any of its citizens bothered to research it since the entire planet was swamped in toxic crystals, and left uninhabitable bar the area Astoria occupied.

There were not many weapons in Astoria, well no clear weapons anyway. The time of visual deterrents was long gone. Weapons could be wielded, as some chose to do so, but there was no real need to any longer. Weapons were one of the few links back to the Age of Technology, a time that had long since passed and left in its wake a new understanding, that technology had eventually been recognised for what it truly was, a burden on the pursuit of life.

That is not to say the Astorians were not technologically advanced, far from it, they had just ascended to a life where vintage methods were more desirable and technological short cuts frowned upon and only used when absolutely necessary.

Astoria had been built during the golden age of technology, a time when the people of the world put their every effort into developing tools and devices to make their lives easier. There had been deemed no limit as to how far they were prepared to go. Astoria had become a symbol of this, a monstrously big, and yet aesthetically pleasing city of Angels (as it would later be referred to).

Within the super hardened stone walls, lay secrets and methods that had long since been chosen to be forgotten.

Astoria was perfect, its every structure, uniquely designed to withstand all manors of precipitation, temperature and debris. Each building was shaped precisely to capture the hot sun's rays and distribute the energy throughout the city. The waterways had natural filtration systems in place to cleanse and purify the rain water that fell from the sky. Even the sewers were very unique, in that they were inhabited with bacteria consuming creatures whose very existence ensured a clean and healthy environmental city.

Astoria was unique in many ways, standing out from all the other bastions in the land, and the only area that was regularly referred to as the 'city of Angels', this title was mostly down to the rise of the Allfather, whom to this very day, ruled over the area firmly but fairly.

The Allfather was just a man by his birth right, and yet he had grown very quickly into a symbol of so much more. It was he who had written the book on Astorian law, the very essence of nobility that his now great people adhered to.

The Allfather was a gentle, fair and kind man whose wisdom had gathered him much respect upon the occupants of the city. Along with his excellent qualities as a man, the Allfather also had powers, REAL powers that his body could generate at his will. It was never clear exactly WHAT the Allfather's gift was, but what powers he had, he always used them for the good of the people.

From an early age he had recognised that there were others like him, those that possessed powers beyond any technological means and, with the help of his brother, Ganon, he united them all for the purpose of building a safe and secure, happy way of life.

He had a vision, where the gifted would be viewed as Angels, pure of heart and protectors of the city. They would encourage the regular people to be better people, to do good where they could, safe in the knowledge that their wellbeing was being looked after.

His vision, he ensured, was brought to reality.

To say this journey had been difficult would be an understatement. Betrayals and treachery could be found in the purest of hearts and this had puzzled the Allfather for many years. He had been known to lock himself away from his wife and child for days on end pondering such a conundrum.

This issue had caused great friction between the Allfather and his brother Ganon, who was his most trusted counsellor. Ganon believed that the people should be ruled with an iron fist to deter any such treachery, But this was not part of the Allfather's vision and would not entertain such ideas.

"Even the best of the good, can turn to bad"

His second chapter in Astorian law.

What scared him the most about betrayal, was the blindness that fell before it.

Even he had been blinded to an obvious betrayal, the pain still cut him deep, deeper than any wound he had received banishing the Sarfan Lord, an act that inexplicably opened his mind to the possibilities of the dark gods, Beings of such immense power, whose sole purpose was to create chaos and anarchy wherever there was peace and harmony. The dark gods were to be feared and never trusted, they had been known to seek out weak minds, control them, and go to any lengths to destroy something beautiful.

Astoria was the ideal target.

Realising this, the Allfather erected a psychic shield, an invisible barrier dome around the massive city limits, an impenetrable barrier of pure energy that protected its people from the perils of wave space, the realm that the dark gods resided.

Without the evil influence or the lure of darkness being able to penetrate the shield, the Allfather had eventually restored peace, harmony and fairness to the land.

Astoria had become famous for more than just its beautifully stunning architecture, its Angelic protectors and its fair ruler. Astoria was also famous as being the host of the 'Superfuse' world championships, a game in which drew the attention of all the inhabitants from across the ravaged world.

The game appeared simple, a table top game of soccer, with each side taking control of eleven inanimate players. Along the side of the table there were five handles, and on each handle the eleven players were distributed in respect to their position. The object being to manually control the handles which, in turn, would animate the players in an attempt to get the small Lastic ball into the opponents score box.

This simple game however, had the added bonus in that it had no technology sanctions, and so the handles that aligned the side of the table were littered with tiny neural connectors that would bond with the player grasping them, transporting them onto the board itself in tiny form to make the shots. The technology for *Superfuse* had been originally designed for military use. The basic Avatar design, would allow a General to drive super heavy battle tanks onto the field of battle and command them, from a safe distance, miles away from harm. When the world had been evacuated, such technology was deemed useless. With no war to fight, there was no need for tanks and so the technology had been converted into a game that the inhabitants of Astoria could enjoy.

The game would be played with two players, one on either team. The player, using only their feet to hit the ball, would grip the handles of the table, these handles had neural projection points that would in turn, catapult them down onto the table itself in mind only, becoming the inanimate little man and attempt to score points. The player could at all times feel the original positioning of their hands on the neural bonds, and so a simple release of the handles would instantly return the player back to full size and into the orbital view of the gaming board.

Due to its popularity, Astoria has an entire quadrant dedicated to the sport itself. With training halls, practice arenas, mini stadiums as well as full size stadiums for the larger tournaments that would draw the attention of people from far and wide.

Down in the practice arenas, Angel Chance was found at one of the practice tables, training her young aspirant, Gregor, to hopefully one day take her crown as champion of Astoria.

Chance's title of 'Angel' signified her role as one of Astorians grand protectors. The Angels had the ability to produce and control all manners of vast powers, powers drawn from within their body, and loosed upon the world in the form of impressive energies and forces. It was powers such as these that stood them higher in the community, making them awed and admired by the very people they had sworn to protect.

The powers, or gifts as they were referred to, would become prominent during their youths and trained throughout their teens to ensure they could control and unleash them safely, causing no harm to anyone around them. It was never clear why these gifts appeared, some kind of mutation perhaps from proximity to the toxic crystals that had engulfed their world, or perhaps they were chosen by a higher power, selected by the gods to make them stand out for whatever purpose they had planned, either way, the Angels of Astoria were set apart from the regular people, and in this segregation there had been an understanding, as written in chapter one of their law, "those with power must protect those that do not"

Chance herself was beautiful. She was the only daughter of the great Allfather, and was much considered the princess of Astoria. She had beautiful blue eyes and in all her eighteen years, she had kept long golden, blonde hair that she would wear in all manner of different style depending on her mood. She was relatively small in height and had a beautifully slender body that was certainly well toned and maintained. On this morning she wore loose, white cotton trousers that allowed her to move freely around the tables, small open toed sandals and a pink sleeveless top. She liked her arms to be free to move when she was competing.

On the other side of the table was young Gregor, he was barely 9 years old and was a very keen learner. He wore simple red trousers, he wore no shoes, as the floor was cushioned, and his t-shirt was blue. His hair was a mousey ginger, his eyes were a deep dark brown and he was rarely seen without a smile on his face.

Little Gregor idolised Chance. His plan was to one day grow up, win the *Superfuse* championship and then repeatedly win it year after year and hopefully break her record of most consecutive wins. It was a modest dream but a dream nonetheless.

"You need to relax your hands more, drop your hips and keep your eye on the table" Chance was telling him. She loved nothing more than a good competition, to play and play hard to win, but there was something even more enjoyable that she found in teaching this young boy, to pass on her talents and see him succeed. In his young eyes she could see the same determination that she once had, that eagerness to be the best and win, a quality she admired.

On the bleachers sat Raphael patiently. As always, wherever Chance went he wouldn't be far behind. Raphael was of similar age with Chance and was wearing white cotton trousers also, simple open toed sandals and a yellow cotton t-shirt. He was tanned skin with dark short hair and he had dark brown eyes that seemed, to most, to hide many dark secrets. He sat there casually, watching the lesson before him.

He had a quiet way about him, almost as if he preferred to observe the world around him rather than partake in it. He wasn't rude by any means, just reserved in his approach to the crowds of life. There was a deep mystery that surrounded him, only a select few seeming to know his real character, and the rest were left guessing. For the most part, the citizens of Astoria were weary of him. His coming to Astoria, although a long time ago, brought with it some very dark times and it was not uncommon for the good people of the city to walk the other way upon his approach. Had he been a louder character he may have been able to voice his defence, win them over with the good deeds that he did daily, show them a side to him that they would not fear. As it is, he tends to keep his head down and mind his own business.

As he sat there, watching the lesson before him, he stretched his arm around his back, as he returned his hand back to his lap, he had within it, a deliciously green apple, which he had seemingly produced from thin air. Feeling a little famish, as he regularly was, he took a large bite from its centre and began to chew it quite loudly. He had been carrying a cold of late, and had been feeling under the weather. His nose had been blocked up now for days and as much as he tried, it just would not clear, forcing him to eat much of his food with his mouth open allowing him to breathe at the same time.

14

The slurping and chomping of the apple as his jaws masticated it into tiny pieces made quite the sound, and it took no time at all for that sound to travel to more mannered ears.

Chance stopped mid sentence from her lesson, straightened her back, turned slowly and gave him a stern look. Nothing quite irritated her more than the sound of a noisy eater. There was many a time in the main banquet hall, which she found her choler rise at such a sound, and had even gone as far as to get up from the table and leave, creating as big a statement as possible to the importance of good table manners.

This was not the banquet hall, but she would stand her ground on the subject nonetheless.

"Oi Chomper Chops! Do you mind keeping down over there" she shouted across.

Raphael merely raised his eyebrows and then slowed down his chewing, ensuring he was closing his mouth each time he turned the delicious fruit over in his mouth. His cold had shown no sign of passing and so keeping his mouth shut during eating was difficult, but at the same time he dare not risk the wrath of Chance.

She turned back to her apprentice and continued with the lesson.

"Okay you need to focus, when the ball hits the mid line.. THATS when you zoom in, don't do it too early or you'll miss the ball" she explained. Gregor had been finding this part difficult, his timing was always off and he was forever being scolded for using his right hand on the left handle.

"Can I not play it off the middle man and then zoom in?" Gregor as always would try and negotiate a way to make a difficult situation suit him better. A natural businessman in his own right, Gregor was a master at getting his own way, although with Chance he quickly realised there was never any give, and that she too liked to get her own way. As young and defiant as he was, he chose to accept his position as student to the teacher and fell silent, allowing himself to listen more clearly to her instructions, she was the champion after all.

"That will take too long, look, left hand here-" she indicated to the correct handle-" play the ball then zoom in" Chance was always firm with him, patient but firm and her training methods seem to be paying off, as he was slowly starting to get the hang of it.

After around twenty minutes, Raphael had slowly laboured his way through his apple while keeping his chewing decibels to a minimum. He sat there as he did before, casually on the bleachers, the core of his apple still in his hand.

He looked around puzzled, a real confusion on his face as to what to do with the apple core. There were no bins and certainly no animals to feed it to. He looked down at the core closely, the flesh of the fruit had been stripped from it and all that was left was the harsh rusk centre. He raised his eyebrows, shrugged his shoulders and launched it in his mouth.

He immediately regretted doing that, as he chewed seed after seed and swirled it over in his mouth, the shards of apple core were cutting deep into his cheeks and he was forced to swallow hard to dispose of it. A sour look crossed his face throughout the act. There was many a time that he had regretted his impulsive behaviour, regularly choosing the path of least resistance only to find a far less comfortable fate at each turn. As he turned the last sharp pieces of apple core over in his mouth, he was once again reminded of his folly. He swallowed one hard last time, and finished the apple. His eyes were a little red from the exertion but he had survived it nonetheless.

Down on the table, Gregor's lesson was almost complete.

"Okay are you ready..try it again GO!" Chance said encouragingly.

Gregor followed her instructions to the letter. He played the ball forward and ensured he kept his right hand gripping the handle. He waited for the ball to cross the mid line and then he took his left hand and grabbed the handle.

Instantly he was projected down onto the table. He was tiny and felt helpless from his upper body as it was strapped to the gaming pole. He watched as the ball passed by his side. He lunged forward, catching the ball just on the tip of his shoe and sending it in toward the goal.

He watched on in delight as the ball went into the goal and fireworks went off on the mini table he was playing on.

He released the handle and smiled, as he zoomed out and returned to the side of the table, the fireworks vanished and he was met with a massive hug from Chance.

"YOU DID IT!" she exclaimed.

Gregor went slightly red at the volume of attention he was receiving from his idol. He was young but it hadn't escaped his attention that she was beautiful and he always faltered when she praised him. He chose to remain silent as he really did not know what to say

"Well done Gregor I am proud of you" she added, affectionately patting him on the back. Gregor smiled and made his way over to get his shoes, knowing that the lesson was now concluded. He packed up his things quickly and headed for the door.

As Gregor left the area, Chance turned on the spot and pirouetted on one toe, a huge smile had crossed her face and she had 'smug' written across her forehead, well she might have had as her expression was nothing short of it. She made her way slowly and playfully over to the bleachers where Raphael sat.

"Yes very good" Raphael said before she had an opportunity to open her mouth. He then reached down into his trousers and produced his token card which she swiftly removed from his grasp in a snatching movement. The token cards were the way in which Astorians gave and received payments, a simple device no larger than the palm of their hands, barely a millimetre thick and rectangular in shape with a small lip down one of its sides.

Chance too pulled out her own token card, and held them close together. With one sure swipe she ran the two cards edges together and a small sound, like the dropping of metallic coins could be heard.

"You said it couldn't be done" she exclaimed after the first swipe.

"And in one day" she added as she swiped again, the same sound of dropping coins could be heard upon the cards making contact.

"And with his left hand" she added making a third and final swipe with his card before returning it to his grasp. She turned her head sharply and in victory, turning on the spot and taking two steps forward.

Raphael eyes remained on his card that was now emitting a small robotic voice

"TOKEN EXPIRED" it said, and then the entire card disintegrated into flakes of dust right before his eyes. He dropped his head slightly in defeat, raising it again only upon hearing the short giggle from Chance.

"Lucky for you my father is on dinner tonight, or you'd be going hungry" she said laughing.

"Everything's a competition with you hey" he said, a statement more than a question but she answered all the same.

"Of course, I love winning, love beating you even more though" she finished her sentence with a wink. "And do you remember the wager?" she asked.

"Yesssss" he said long fully. His eyes rolled up in his head slightly as he said it.

"Good, well grab my laundry by noon, oh and take my shoes to get polished, I want to wear them to the banquet tonight" she added.

"It will be done my lady" he jested.

Out on the dusty sandy plains, a small group of people made their way on foot toward the great city led by a weary figure in a black cloak.

His dark boot crunched down hard onto the remains of an old sand scarab shell and the shattered pieces were pressed deeply into the ground beneath his foot.

He held a staff of unknown metallic origin in his left hand which he used to steady himself as he surveyed the area.

The desert wind was light and barely blew any sand much higher than his heels.

He had grown weary, his body starting to feel the full effects of age upon him now. Under his black cloak he wore simple grey fatigues, they seemed loose fitting although they were never always this loose. Time had not been kind to his body and as it deteriorated, his clothes hung from him. His hair had grown thin and was very grey; patches of baldness littered his skull now. His hands were all bone and resembled claws more than anything else. They looked weak and incapable of gripping anything for any period of time. His eyes however were something spectacular. They were forever changing colour. It is unclear if they changed with his mood or if they just refused to remain a set shade but his eyes were a wonder nonetheless. He leant heavily on his staff as he paused to catch his breath.

The next few days were going to be very difficult he knew that much. He would have to call on his gift once more, of that he was sure and he knew that to flex more power, in using his gift would make his condition all the worse, but he wanted his revenge, it was all that drove him on now, pure, dark and evil revenge.

His teeth blackened at the very thought of it and he began to salivate in his dirty mouth.

'Revenge!! Sweet revenge!! And then I'll have my cure' he thought to himself. He was so close now; the great city walls were in reach.

Astoria, the great and famous Astoria, its mere perfection disgusted him. He eagerly anticipated the anarchy he was set to unleash on this righteous set of vermin. Their arrogance and higher right of living angered him. He took pleasure in the simple notion that soon; his actions would show that the Astorians were no better than the rest of them. They would all be found corruptible!

He turned to regard his pathetic entourage labouring behind.

A being as powerful as he was had now been reduced to leading a drove of peasants, a fact that only pressed his anger and lust for vengeance to whole new levels. His mystical eyes remained on his slaves and watched on as they slumbered their way slowly in his wake.

They looked exhausted from hauling so much equipment over such a large distance but he was not going to cut them any slack.

As they neared the old man, he began to bark orders to them. Tired or not they would fulfil their duty. Never before had he felt like a god amongst insects.

"Set up camp here, I want clay domiciles here, here and there" the old man pointed with his claw like hands.

"My lord" a brave tired male peasant asked "Shouldn't we seek shelter within the city limits, the sandstorms will.."

The man didn't finish his sentence; he was never given the chance to. Not a single one of the slaves bore witness to what happened, nor could they lend an explanation as to their companion's fate, it was as it happened.

The questioning peasant merely dropped to the ground, his eyes white in their death throws and his limbs went limp as the last remnants of life left his body. From his chest there was a dagger protruding from a wound, a sizeable wound that was surprisingly not venting any blood and this all happened in the blink of an eye. Not one of the other slaves had seen the old man move, nor did they see him impale the peasant swiftly, ending his life.

"Our orders are clear, outside the city walls" the old man growled.

In that moment, he aged again.

Pepsy made her way down toward the market as she did every day, stopping to ask the locals if they knew the whereabouts of her most troubled friend.

She moved swiftly between the regular faces at the stalls, asking the same question over and over, and each time the answer was the same. She found no success.

Standing on her tip-toes she peered down the length of the market, her eyes darting between the stalls, looking for the tell tale stagger that her friend would no doubt have adopted by this time in the day.

After a few moments she concluded that she'd have no further luck here and so 'shifted' suddenly to the palace courtyard gardens, a popular place to find her troubled comrade.

Pepsy was beautiful, there was no mistaking that, she wore tight fitting black trousers that showed off her slender physique perfectly. On the top she wore a long sleeve green blouse, which had a pattern stitched into its middle. Her hair was long and golden, and today she was wearing it straight, a sign that she was in a good mood.

To those that didn't know Pepsy's gift, it could seem quite confusing. She could be picking her favourite white Lillie flowers in the palace gardens, peacefully humming away a little tune to herself and then in the same instant, she would be high up in the palace walls carefully arranging them into beautiful displays, almost giving the impression of being in two places at the same time.

To those that knew her, they would be well aware of her gift of teleportation.

For the most part, she didn't like to use her power too frequently, preferring to use the brisk journey between errands as her exercise quota for the day. Her teleportation took her dangerously close to *Wavespace*, a realm that was inhabited by undesirables. Her quick shuttles through this realm rarely attracted any attention but she had been warned of the risks.

As much as she tried avoiding the use of her gift, there were times, such as when running late, she would had no choice. For an individual with the power to travel great distances in the blink of an eye, lateness should never be an issue.

Should never, and yet in Pepsy's case it was all too often.

Pepsy continued to scan around the palace gardens, hoping to catch a glimpse of her, would be, intoxicated comrade. She decided to walk slowly along the perimeter wall just behind the palace section, and her change of route had paid off, there she found her friend lying slouched against the perimeter wall, a near empty bottle of slogan juice in one hand, the lid sitting precariously in the other. Pepsy walked right up to him and kicked his feet.

"Come on Jeremy wake up" she said.

Jeremy had once been a fine and upstanding Angel of the community. During his school years, his 'gift' which was quite simply accuracy, allowed him to excel at all sports and he quickly became the high school jock alongside his best friend Lucas. Between them, they led the school team to countless *Bruteball* victories. Everyone loved him and he would be welcomed by cheers everywhere he went.

Upon leaving school, he quickly found the cheers stopped. Without a match to win he was no longer a match winner. He was no longer the younger ones hero. When he at last gained the ultimate honour by ascending to the status of 'Angel', Jeremy quickly found this was never enough, and after the death of his best friend during the bone war, he quickly turned to the bottle and had been drinking ever since.

Pepsy had made it her sole task to try and bring him back to his former greatness, this task had been difficult and tedious thus far.

"Jeremy, get up!! I need you sober for the banquet!!"

Jeremy merely grumbled and then burped. He slowly opened his eyes and upon seeing Pepsy, a cheeky smile crossed his face. Jeremy was wearing the tattered remains of an old light blue suit. Once upon a time, this suit may have looked smart but here, hanging off Jeremy's drunken shoulders and covered in various patches of dirt and dust, with a tie that had been poorly put on, the suit looked awful. Pepsy could make out two clear smells that were all too common around Jeremy. One was clearly the slogan juice, both drunk and spilled upon his self, the other was the distinct smell of mint. She could never understand why this was but whenever she was around him, there was undoubtedly the smell of mint.

Jeremy's eyes slowly blinked and began to resemble a modicum of sense of both his situation and his surroundings.

"Ah you found me...took your time" he said as if his disappearance had all been a game.

"This isn't funny Jeremy, that's the fourth time this week you've gone missing!"

"And it's the fourth time you've found me" he burped again "Although your getting slower each time...I must be getting better at this"

Pepsy shook her head and hauled him to his feet, taking the remains of the bottle out of his hand which Jeremy reluctantly let go of.

"Now come on let's get you cleaned up."

CHAPTER 2

The banquet hall was grand indeed. Its ceilings rose higher than the eye could see and were lit up with a strange, light emitting paint. No bulbs or candle wicks were needed for this paint; it was a marvel chemical mix from a time long forgotten, and it gave the room a magical feel to it.

The main floor area was aligned with rows upon rows of large and thickly set wooden tables; each could easily sit twenty occupants if needed. The room contained around fifty of these tables, spread right down to the far end of the hall where two, ceiling tall double doors completed the room.

At the top end of the room lay a raised stage area where a simple speaker spot sat in the centre, this was usually occupied by the Allfather when addressing the audience before him.

Slowly, the sound of bustling crowds and conversation of many kinds began to pour into the room, as the cities key members began to take their seats.

At the far end of the room, the Astorian guard, the top two hundred elite within them, took their seats now near the large doors. For the Astorian guard it was an honour being invited to such a banquet, as it showed testament to their adoration to duty. It was but a minor achievement, but something to strive for nonetheless. They all wore their light armour, plates of shiny golden metal that covered their bodies. Light shoulder guards hung off their necks and they all wore their hair in the same slicked back manner.

The next ten tables were occupied by a group that would no more than look at the food before them, than ever attempt to consume it. These tables were occupied the praetorians of the Lastic guard, the elite of an army of drones created by the Allfather to assist the Astorian guard. These Lastic troopers armour was made from a special blend of leather and Lastic, giving a flexible yet sturdy defensive layer. These troops were immune to corruption, since they had neither personality nor even a soul. They all had an almost silver complexion to their bodies, and yet consisted of no metal parts whatsoever.

They sat there, ever still and observing the occupants of the room.

The next ten tables were then occupied by the key vendors in the cities market. As key visual figures seen by the public every day, the Allfather deemed it important that they should be made aware of the entire goings on in the city and to act as ambassadors between the regular townsfolk and the armed protectors. It had proved quite successful and was welcomed by all. Each vendor had come dressed in their best garments, looking as clean and pristine as they could, impression was everything.

There was a table that had just twelve occupants at it, ten of those wore blazing orange coloured armour with similar coloured shoulder guards and large tribinium fuel tanks on their backs, complete with flame rifles stowed at their sides. At the head of this table sat the Angel Fern, for the other ten were her Phoenix guard.

Fern wore a bright red and short dress. It was by no means fancy, and she wore it with simple flat red shoes. Her eyes were a blazing orange colour and her red hair was tied back in a simple pony tail. She sat there with a serious look on her face, as she always did.

The rest of the hall tables were then filled with the protectors of the city, the Angels.

One such Angel made his way through the crowd to his special designated and reinforced chair. He was the only Angel to have a set seat and this was due to the fact that he was easily larger than any other person in the entire city.

His name was Wallace, and he stood a modest 6ft 2, but he was almost as wide as he was tall. His skin was a dark brown and his teeth were a gleaming white, perhaps contrasted even whiter against the brown of his skin and he was rarely without a smile. In each ear he wore a hooped earring and his dark hair was always cropped short against his head. He was so large, that finding clothes to fit was at times very difficult and so Wallace tended to go for dark clothing with Lastic stretching waist bands.

This evening he had however made an effort and put on his best and brightest shirt, which was a combination of yellows and greens and resembled a contemporary artist's masterpiece. Others may have described it as a mess of colours.

Wallace was definitely one of the crowds favourite, a jolly fella that adored his food, as his belly would prove testament to. He had self appointed himself market controller, but that was mostly to sample the foods coming in each day. Food had a real precedence in his life.

He sat down heavy into his chair and gave the occupant of the chair next to him a playful slap on the back.

"Argh, I've been looking forward to this all day, my belly has been rumbling" he said through his loud booming voice.

The recipient of the slap was none other than the Angel Quincy. Quincy was a mischief character at times, playing pranks on those around him to lighten the mood where possible, his gift was the power to conjure up electricity, and channel it through his hands in various watts and voltages. It was not uncommon to receive a friendly jolt from him when in proximity, a reminder that he refuses to grow up, and still lives the life of the school boy.

Quincy had short blonde hair and a medium muscular build. He was an expert with a sword in hand and yet rarely carried one, concluding that his hands are mightier than the sword. His eyes were a solid green colour and his cheeks sported two dimples on each side, when he smiled it were hard to remain angry at him. Unlike his larger friend, Quincy had put on his best evening wear, a tight fitting black sleeveless shirt and black trousers. He wore a yellow tie that was testament to his electric personality.

Recovering from the thundering backslap he had just received, he spoke with Wallace.

"When is your belly not rumbling WalRUS" Quincy deliberately mispronounced his name as to stick in a little fat jibe to his remark.

"Ah my little sparkplug, your remarks are lost on me, a good woman respects a good, and well constructed power belly, it gives me strength" Wallace needed not stick his belly out with the remark as it

26

was already pouring up onto the table edge, but he completed the gesture anyway, rubbing it at the same time.

"I don't think Astoria has a woman desiring a man of such strength" Quincy countered, his wit was sharp as it ever was.

"Grrr one day ill have you and I locked in a room with rubber flooring... we shall see true strength then boy"

Wallace would always turn the conversation toward a little aggression if he felt he was losing out on wit. As friendly as he was, Wallace was actually quite nervous around people, and found it difficult to think quickly, a trait that proved perilous when arguing with the likes of Quincy.

Instead of replying, Quincy simply looked away and waited a few moments, waiting until Wallace seemed satisfied that he had won the exchange and had turned his attention elsewhere. That was when he slid his hand under the table and slowly began to conjure up his gift.

The food from the banquet was now beginning to be served out in large, shiny metal trays and placed on each table. On each tray there was massive servings of wildagoat and various other desert dwelling animals. Salad bowls were placed on each table at regular intervals and there were large rolls of bread placed on fine, shiny metal dishes. Glasses were sat at each seat placement and bottles of slogan juice were abundant across the banquet hall tables.

Quincy conjured his gift further in his hands that were still hidden beneath the table. He then carefully allowed his gift to be unleashed, into a constant flow, into Wallace's side who, at first, felt nothing.

Wallace slowly began to grow...he grew a little more. His eyes were fixed on the food being served out and his tongue began to lick his lips, salivating at the forthcoming meal.

He again grew a little more, as Quincy increased the flow of electricity into his side.

Wallace turned back and realised that he had grown exponentially big now, and the reinforced chair was straining under his weight. His bright coloured shirt had now burst at the buttons and were it not for the Lastic waistband on his trousers, he was sure they would have burst also.

Before he could issue a curse toward Quincy, the chair snapped under his weight and his sheer monstrous size dropped onto the floor. Wallace was now easily 8ft tall and just as wide again. His body was filled up with an explosive amount of potential energy just waiting to be released.

"Wallace!" the voice of the Allfather could be heard "If you please" and the Allfather gestured toward the door.

Wallace turned to Quincy "Had I not the manners, id unleash this right back at you"

Quincy merely smiled as Wallace made his way to the grand doors, his hungry belly would have to wait. He needed to unleash this built up energy safely and in the open where nobody would be hurt.

That was Wallace's gift, his body could absorb any kind of energy; it could be absorbed, built up and unleashed back. An unfortunate side effect of such a gift, was that he grew in size with the volume of energy being stored, there was many a time that he had burst his clothing while using his gift.

Further up the banquet hall, the Angel Chance made her way into the hall and floated through the crowds. With one finger resting on her chin, she looked around the room, deciding where to sit. Raphael stood, as he always did, just behind her.

Chance was wearing an immaculately white, long floaty dress that was open shouldered and ran the length of her body and even trailed slightly along the floor. Although the floors to the banquet hall were cleaned regularly, such a dress would always be at risk of getting dirty as it trailed in her wake everywhere it went. To avoid this, she spun on the spot as she often as she could, the momentum kept the tails of her dress aloft. Chance was forever seeking the attention of those around her and so spinning and careering her way around a room was not uncommon, in fact it was almost expected of her.

Her long blonde hair was tied up and fastened with a little silver tiara, and around her neck she wore a beautiful heart shaped necklace that was made from a very rare metal, that shone beautifully in the light. There was no other person or Angel in the entire land that had a necklace quite like the one she wore, the metal being so rare, it was basically one of a kind and this appealed to her vanity perfectly.

Chance's eyes fanned their way slowly around the room, as she tried to decide where to sit. She took her time doing this, she never felt hurried or rushed, she was the unofficial princess of Astoria, and such a title lent her certain privileges, and one of these was time and patience.

Scanning around further, her eyes eventually caught a frosty set of blue, amongst a table of orange, that were looking directly her way.

Chance held the gaze for the briefest of seconds before looking away, making a note to avoid that particular table, and sat down at the table nearest her whilst ensuring her back was to that direction.

The table she sat down to was occupied with Pepsy at the near top end, with Jeremy the drunk swaying next to her. Pepsy wore a stunning long red dress that clung to her slender body at every contour, finished off with cream shoes and a matching cream bag. She wore her hair both up and down, as part of it was fastened up with a golden clip, allowing the rest to flow down her back beautifully. Jeremy had made a minimal effort as always. He did wear a suit although once again, his shirt was a crumpled mess, and his tie need not have bothered been worn as it was so badly fastened.

Spanners sat at the head of the table reading from a data slate as always, never to be found without some form of tech that he was uniquely allowed to have. He wore his standard dress fatigues, black trousers ironed to perfect, a white shirt also ironed perfectly. He wore his shirt open at the top, and his muscular chest could be seen through the open space.

Spanners was quite a unique individual, with his gift linked directly to the use, and manipulation of machines, he was virtually Astoria's head technician, and would forever be found with his head in some damaged tech-engine or reading diagnostic outputs from data slates. His personality matched his gift, as he came across very cold, unemotional and not at all unlike the machines he was gifted to repair.

The bottom half of the table sat Quincy, and beside him there was a space, where Wallace had just vacated.

Just as chance felt the comfort of the seat beneath her, she turned to her left where Raphael, who had taken the seat adjacent, had also sat down. She then observed him turn and make a gesturing smile toward the person with the frosty eyes, before returning his attention back to the table. Chance was less than pleased with his manners.

Raphael wore light blue dress trousers, and a black open topped shirt like Spanners, and he too openly displayed his muscular chest. Chance was about to say something to him regarding the frosty eyed person in question, but she chose not to. Anything she would say would more than likely come out all wrong, and give the wrong impression. She instead began to make origami shapes with the napkin in front of her.

Behind them, amongst the sea of orange of the Phoenix guard, was Crystal, with whom the frosty pair of beautiful blue eyes belonged to. Crystal looked a lot like Chance, in fact so much so that they were often mistaken for one another when seen at a distance.

Crystal, like Chance, had very slender figure, both were equal height and both had a beautiful white and welcoming smile. Where Chance's hair was long and golden, Crystal's hair was of medium length and slightly more platinum in its blonde. They both had blue eyes and yet Crystal's blue eyes twinkled like diamonds, a testament to her ability to harness and manipulate ice. Crystal wore a medium length, tight fitting blue dress. Her body was regarded, by many, to be perfect and this blue dress did it every bit of justice. It was open necked and strapless, and she wore it with a pair of white stiletto heeled shoes that had diamond encrusted straps.

Since early into their school years, Crystal and Raphael had become friends when all others stayed clear. There was a definite chemistry between them both, although it is unclear as to which party carried the flame. It did seem to others that Crystal was the more eager, although this would never be admitted.

From two tables away, Crystal stood up slowly and made her way across to where Raphael sat. She slowly walked down the line of the table, gliding past the backs of the seated Angels. Her beautiful looks never failed to turn heads and she gained a lot of attention from this simple and short walk. Along with Chance, Crystal was clearly the most sought after girl in the whole of Astoria. Young girls would groom their hair and wear similar attire to dream of one day being even a small fraction like Crystal.

As she passed Raphael, she placed her small, soft gentle hand over Raphael's shoulder and into his hand. She held it there for a brief moment, depositing something into his grasp before continuing to walk on and complete her cycle back to her table, where she gently sat down, keeping her eyes on Raphael the whole time.

Raphael felt embarrassed, the entire table's eyes were now burning down upon him. He dropped his hand into his lap, opening up his palm to examine the contents of his hand.

In it sat a small butterfly, carefully and meticulously carved out of ice. It was very small but the detail was excellent, each little curve and ring of the butterflies wings was carved into the small ornament.

Raphael craned his neck round to Crystal's table, met her eyes, smiled and then mouthed a thank you.

Chance's choler was visibly growing.

From his drunken disposition at the table, Jeremy piped up

"Awww it's a little butterfly frozen in time" he said rather mockingly. His drunken demeanour often led him to insult others around him. He cared not.

"Yes, it's a butterfly, a symbol of life" Raphael said smiling, refusing to allow the happy moment of receiving a gift to be ruined by his mockery.

Chance by this stage was fuming. She simply spread the palm of her hand wide, stretching the fingers as wide as she could and then clenched into a fist where she sat.

The ice butterfly broken into multiple pieces.

Raphael's look of sorrow and confusion made Jeremy laugh.

"Still just a little boy inside hey Raph" Jeremy mocked.

Raphael looked up and around the table, confused as to what had just happened and a little saddened that his gift had met such a fragile end. He dropped his eyes down upon the broken pieces of ice within his grasp. A look of sorrow crossed his features again as he turned his hand slightly and allowed the broken pieces to fall to the floor.

"Awwww does Raph want to cry?" Jeremy mocked further. Raphael ignored his comments and kept his eyes down.

Chance felt a little bit agitated about Jeremy's remark. It was a witty remark, but Raphael was her plaything to tease and she didn't appreciate others jumping on the band wagon. She eyed Jeremy closely and felt a rising irritation at his drunken demeanour. *Had he no shame coming to dinner in such a state* she thought. Watching him for a mere moment longer she decided she wanted to take him down a peg or two.

"Oh Jeremy" Chance called out;" fancy a little game?"

Jeremy laughed and swayed left to right, slightly exaggerating his condition but still indicating that he was perhaps a little too intoxicated for games.

"Well a game of accuracy?" Chance followed up with.

Instantly Jeremy's eyes lit up, this was a game he could win, put some points in the bag against the little Astorian princess!!

"You are on!" he stated and then burped as the contents of his stomach rumbled.

"Ok the rules are, we flip a coin, heads is me tails are you, and whichever side it lands on goes second. We throw these bottle lids to land on the top of the bottles down the table. Last top left standing wins?"

Pepsy eyed the exchange wearily from her position further up the table. She wasn't sure she was going to like the way this game was going to go as it was well known to all Astorians that Chance had a competitive streak. She certainly did not like to lose. It was also well known that Chance would not take on a competition unless she was almost certain she would win.

Jeremy was a little confused but agreed nonetheless. As drunk as he was, he was still a little wary that she would choose a game that would suit his skill set, he knew that it wasn't really in her nature to give her opponents an advantage and yet surely he could not lose at his own game.

Chance took out the coin and flipped it, the table watched as it landed on heads. She was to go second. She nodded to Jeremy who then picked up one of the bottle lids that sat next to the open bottles and hurled it down the table.

Naturally, with his gift, it landed perfectly on top of one of the slogan juice bottles. A massive arrogant smile crossed his face, his eyes rolled slightly in his head as a small amount of dizziness overcame him.

Chance merely returned the smile, took a lid that sat next to her, closed one eye and aimed. She then threw the lid which then knocked Jeremy's off the top of the bottle and left hers sitting neatly on the lip.

Chance 1 Jeremy 0

Almost immediately frustration stretched his face. He couldn't believe what had just happened. He had clearly been tricked somehow. He naturally found himself sitting more upright and shaking his vision clearer and trying to do all he could to sober up and focus on the task at hand. Keeping his eyes fixed on his opponent and watching carefully for any signs of trickery, he awaited round two.

Chance flipped the coin again and again it landed on heads, she was to go second once more. So again Jeremy hurled his lid and it landed perfectly on the next bottle down, and again Chance's return shot knocked his off.

"Arghg this is a fix" he growled.

"What's a game without a little...chance in it" she smirked as she toyed with the coin in her hand. Jeremy snatched it out of her hand and flipped it, convinced that she was somehow flipping it in such a fashion that it would always land on heads.

 Again the coin landed on heads and he was to go first. And again the same outcome occurred.

His anger grew now even greater. He was positive the trickery was linked with the coin itself, concluding that the coin was perhaps loaded to land on heads, with this outcome in mind he demanded they switch, that he be heads and she be tails.

Chance just nodded in agreement as it mattered very little to her. He flipped the coin quite high into the air and it landed hard on the table with everybody's eyes looking at it.

Pepsys eyes immediately rolled in her head as it landed on none other than tails. Chance was to go second again!!

"I'm beginning to lose count of the score teehee" she giggled.

Jeremy was furious and rummaged in his pockets and produced a dirty old coin. Flipped it into the air and once again landed on tails. He didn't even play the round. He stood up in utter disbelief and stormed out.

Pepsy went to call him back but in that moment the Allfather stood up to make a speech and Pepsy was forced into silence. Chance sat a little more comfortably in her seat now having bagged a small victory. She was more than willing to sit back and remain quiet for the rest of the banquet having had her fill of glory for now.

The Allfather stood there all resplendent in his immaculately white robes. He had a short and well maintained beard and combed over hair on his head. His eyes were a light friendly blue and he stood there waiting patiently for silence. There was still murmuring and chatting going on around the hall and so he remained silent for a few moments more.

From the doorway a small white rabbit came hopping in. It hopped forward a few steps and then stood up on its hind legs and surveyed the area. Its little pink nose was sniffing rapidly and never stopped. Its long white ears were perked up as her head darted from left to right, looking for something. It looked sharp to its left.

Then to the right

Then to the left again.

Its eyes eventually locked on to Pepsys table and it sniffed the air a few more times before hopping down onto all fours and began to make its way into the room and heading straight for the table. It was so white and fluffy that it looked like it should have came out of a hat. It hopped right up to Pepsy and stopped for a moment; it crouched even lower and then sprung up high onto the table in one bound. Pepsy got a small fright as she hadn't seen it coming but then shook her head with a giggle when she recognised the bunny.

"Oh Harmony, you don't half know how to make an entrance" Pepsy said and observed as Harmony turned on the spot and headed for the salad bowl where she pulled hard on some grated carrot that sat on the edge of the bowl. Her little mouth began to chew really quickly as she yummed up the thin strips of carrot.

"Now now Harmony shouldn't we be using cutlery" Pepsy exclaimed. The rabbit made a strange growling sound and then hopped between Pepsy and Spanners at the table.

 Spanners eyes never left his data slate.

The rabbit continued to make the same strange noise as it then appeared to grow. Rapidly grow and its paws became hands and legs that stretched out to the floor. Within an instant the rabbit was now a fully grown Angel of Astoria, sat there quite happily chewing the carrot on the edge of the table.

"I really thought that carrot would taste better as a rabbit" Harmony said. Pepsy just laughed at how comical her friend was.

Harmony like some of the Angels of Astoria was dual gifted. She was the only serving apothecary in the city and with her gift of instant healing she was very useful if anyone got sick, hurt or injured.

 Her second gift, which unlike other dual gifted Angels, she had actually mastered and could change her form into any animal she pleased. It puzzled Pepsy that she never chose more impressive beasts like lions and tigers. Instead Harmony liked to change into birds and rabbits, possums and other small creatures. During a prank once she turned into an elephant and soaked a crowd of naughty children that had refused to go home to their beds past dark, So Pepsy knew she was certainly capable of becoming much larger beings she just simply chose not to. A curious use of her gifts Pepsy thought.

Harmony turned to Spanners with eager eyes.

"And how are you today Joshua?" Harmony was most probably the only person in the whole of Astoria to call Spanners by his proper name, she refused to give him a nickname the way that a love interest refuses to do the same. Harmony was wearing a short and sparkly black dress. Her figure was far more voluptuous than any of the other Angels and she wore clothing to accentuate this. She had long dark hair that she chose to wear straight this evening and in her ears she wore little heart shaped diamond earrings that caught the light and sparkled here and there.

Spanners lifted his eyes from his data slate and produced a smile at her, then went back to his readings.

It was clear to all in Astoria that Harmony had an interest in Spanners. She was attracted to his cold ways and emotionless manner and she found something very masculine about the way he went about his business. It can only be assumed that she longed to be the one that warmed up his very cold and emotionless heart.

Her eyes dropped to the gap in his shirt and she smiled on the inside at the sight of his muscular chest.

Distracted briefly, she gazed at him vacantly; having to shake her head to bring herself back to reality where she then returned his smile and hopped down onto the chair that was sat next to his. She would always have a habit of finding reasons to converse with him and some believe that her persistence was paying off for Spanners rarely conversed with anyone and yet he was slowly speaking more and more with her. He certainly never displayed any sign that she irritated him in any way.

"ANGELS, AND OTHER FINE UPSTANDING PROTECTORS OF ASTORIA, PLEASE BE SEATED" the Allfather boomed out in a loud voice of authority. The room instantly became silent. He paused a moment before continuing.

"Our world has been ravaged, mistakes made by our fathers before us, and here we stand, defiant against its encroaching purple mass of tyranny. We stand strong and united; at peace with ourselves and doing all we can to maintain peace with others. I see around me here, gathered today some of the finest individuals that I have ever had the pleasure to serve with. Were it not for your honour, your pure hearts and dedication to our goals, we would not have all that we can merit ourselves with today. So let us first toast to the present!" the entire room raised a glass to toast. The Allfather continued.

"All our work is a continuation of work done before us, for without the sacrifices made by our predecessors, we could not possibly have the ground work to build upon that we do today, let us toast to fallen comrades, to heroes past and to lost souls" the room raised their glasses once more. A few heads fell around the room, deep in thought.

Quincy's head immediately dropped as his thoughts fell upon his fallen hero, the idol of his childhood. He recalled the events leading up to his death and how he had watched it all, his champion, the peoples champion yet another casualty of that damn bone war. Although it was all so long ago, the wounds still cut him deep. Quincy's eyes looked around slightly and met those of Pepsy's, her eyes were red and daring to bleed tears. Although he was too young at the time to know for sure, Quincy got the impression that there had been romance between his champion and Pepsy. He knew better than to assume anything purely on 'prom dates' but there was something about the way they had looked at each other that said there was a lot more going on. Quincy dropped his eyes back down as the Allfather continued.

"And one particular fallen Angel I will mention in detail, for his heroics are still unmatched and unforgotten. He was our champion, YOUR champion, the peoples champion.."

Tears flowed down Pepsys face by this stage, she had been pre-warned that his name would be mentioned but this did nothing in the way of stemming the flow or reducing the hurt, the guilt that she felt.

"He showed courage and honour and he stood his ground against an entire platoon of skeletons soldiers, he held his ground when others had fled in fear, he held it fast so that others may make it to safety. He was the founding member of our Phoenix guard and always at one in our hearts. Let us toast to the great Lucas and all his triumphs!"the Allfather said. Cheers went up from Fern's table where the ten Phoenix guard members shouted in unison "for Lucas"

Quincy felt a small bit of courage and drive build up inside him. Talk of his hero always had this effect on him. Lucas truly WAS as great as they all said he was, he knew this as he was there and had witnessed this all for himself. There was no myth to his legacy, only fact.

"And here with us today, we have a new and recently ascended leader of the Phoenix guard, and to our dear Fern, I offer you a sacred artefact, one that signifies strength and trust, devotion to the protection of Astoria. To you I present the *FIREBLADE*...the sword of Lucas!" the Allfather said.

The entire room gasped in awe, mostly because they hadn't been aware that anything had ever been recovered of Lucas's body. To have his sword, here in Astoria once again was a good omen.

 The Allfather walked out with the magnificent sword draped across both his wrists. It had a keen blade with a Phoenix engraved on its inner side. Its pommel was shaped like a globe and the guard resembled a claw that protected the wielders' hand expertly. Through the middle of the blade there was a thin strip cut out, it ran the length of the blade itself giving it an even greater uniqueness to it, as unique and brilliant as its previous owner.

 Fern had by this point stood up from her chair and made her way to the main stage, where she stood before the Allfather awaiting her reception of the sword. Upon taking the blade from the Allfather, she activated her own gift, sending a wave of torrent fire through the blade and igniting its ornate surface. The spectators of the banquet hall looked on with exasperation and immediately realised where the *Fireblade* has got its name from. Fern swung the blade from left to right and found that its balance was perfect in every way; she deactivated her gift and then bowed before the Allfather before returning to her chair. Just as she sat down, the other ten members of the Phoenix guard stood up in unison. Their military precision was remarkable. They all spoke simultaneously to pledge their allegiance to their new leader.

"We follow you as we followed our Lucas..through the fires of hell!!!" they all then sat down after Fern nodded to them each individually in appreciation. Crystal then smiled across the table at Fern, who then for the first time that evening returned a small smile.

The Allfather allowed the moment to settle before addressing other matters on his agenda.

" In other matters, we have the *Superfuse* championships arising soon and I require an Angel to take command of security detail".

As soon as the word 'command' had left the Allfather's lips, Quincy made a dive under the table. He hated any form of command and avoided it at all costs. Hiding was the only way he could be sure he wouldn't be selected.

The room remained silent at first, with nobody willing to take up such a mundane task. Eventually Crystal broke the silence and volunteered herself.

"I will take the command" she said in her soft spoken yet voice of authority. Before she had even managed to finish her sentence however, Chance had stood up for all to see and spoken over her.

"I shall take the command, it is after all my area of expertise" she said with an ear-ear smile across her face. She held both her hands behind her back and began to sway left to right around in a semi-circle repeatedly.

"You cannot take the security detail if you are in fact competing my dear" the Allfather interjected.

"I have been contemplating retiring" Chance said and there was a gust of air all around the room as everybody breathed in deeply at once. Chance had been Astoria *Superfuse* champion for the past ten years, she was virtually unbeatable. Her potential retirement could open the door for an all new, exciting tournament with a whole new champion. The buzz of anticipation could be felt around the room.

"My rule stands, if you take the detail you cannot compete" the Allfather said, all too aware that Chance can be very specific with her choice of words at times and had only said 'contemplating' "

"Then I shall take the command" Chance said turning her swaying axis slightly to regard Crystals table. Her eyes met the beautifully frosted blue of Crystals. Crystal gave her a warm and genuinely caring smile as Chance returned it with a hollow equivalent which was immediately dropped as soon as her head turned away. Chance then sat down carefully in her seat to a murmur of excitement from all who were in the room.

Quincy remained down under the table where it was very cramped. He had to curl himself into a little ball to fit under nicely without giving himself away. The tables were very sturdy and made from thick wood and so the legs were equally as thick, swallowing up the majority of the floor space under the table. Quincy cared not so long as he was hidden.

A few moments passed and he heard the pattering of small feet. Above the tables he heard the Allfather continuing to speak and dish out command positions. He was sure he only had to wait another few moments and they would have moved on to a different subject.

As he lay there crouched, he heard the pattering of feet coming even closer now. He looked up.

"You've goat to be bleating me!!" he exclaimed as he came face to face with a little white goat that instantly licked his face. Its velvet tongue made Quincy screw his nose up as it tickled him.

"Harmony buzz off!!" Quincy growled as he tried to push the goat away from him. The goat vanished quickly and was replaced by a little flying love bug, perfectly white also

"You really shouldn't give me ideas Quincy" Harmony said in a tiny little voice as she flew around his ears irritatingly. Quincy started to swat his arms about as the buzzing of her wings tickled his ears also. It all became too much and Quincy forgot how near the underside of the table top was to his head. In his irritation to swat away the bug he foolishly attempted to stand up.

A huge bang was heard that echoed around the room, magnified by the thickness of the wood within the table he had struck. The sound drew the attention of everyone in the banquet hall as Quincy's head collided with the underside of the table. Realising he had been rumbled he shamefully made his way out from under the table and back to his seat. He made no attempt to find an excuse as to why he was under there; he just continued to grumble profanities toward the little love bug that flew its way back towards the top end of the table.

"And thank you Quincy, you can make the necessary observations of the recycling centre and try get to the bottom of the blockage there" the Allfather said, his attention having been drawn to Quincy position mere moments before with the bang on the table.

'Blockage' Quincy thought, 'this sounds delightful.'

A small errand civilian entered the banquet hall through the side door and made his way to the Allfather's side. The civilian was no more than 20 years old and his task was to deliver messages around the city in replace of the much frowned upon tech systems that would have previously relayed messages much faster and electronically.

The new system, without the use of tech, had proven to be very useful and allowed for more jobs to be created within Astoria. The system relied on good verbal communication between all of its citizens so that the whereabouts of an Astorian would be known most of the time. When a message needed relayed, a messenger would run the words, on foot, directly to the person wherever they were dwelling. Most messages were passed around between the key people in the city anyway who were always quite easy to find and on this occasion the young man knew exactly where to find the Allfather to deliver the message, minimising the lag time between time of event and the delivery of the news.

 He reached the Allfather side and spoke quietly into his ear. The Allfather was nodding as he was receiving the message and then his eyes lit up slightly followed by more nodding. The errand civilian then turned on his heel and sped off. The all father addressed the crown again.

"My apologies to all here this evening, it seems out tech sensors have picked up another disturbance that I must attend to. Please enjoy your meal and the rest of your evening, I thank you for your company. Spanners, can you accompany me please"

Spanners merely nodded at the Allfather before standing up and heading out with him.

Harmony's eyes watched him long fully as he left the hall. She then turned her head around and her eyes met Pepsys who were looking at her with a scornful playful look.

"One day Pepsy. He will be mine" Harmony said and they both laughed together.

The bottom doors to the banquet hall opened once more and re-entering the hall was the unmistakably large frame of Wallace, plodding along with real purpose in his step. He returned to his space where his chair would have been and then he produced a steel bench that he was carrying in his other hand. Quincy's eyes never left Wallace but Wallace refused to be goaded. He just wanted his dinner. He sat down on his makeshift seat, brushed down his damaged bright shirt and grinned as he could finally set in about his evening meal, a large smile reaching ear to ear.

Mean while, just outside the hall, the Allfather made his way down towards the main gates, Spanners following closely behind him.

The evening air was cool and light mist had descended onto the ground within the city walls. After fifteen good minutes of brisk walking, the Allfather could see a few of the Astorian guards who had been standing sentry, holding a small group in the inspection bay. The bay itself was simply a small area within the clearing that had a slightly different coloured stone floor, the guards used this space to herd suspicious visitors or cargo until they could be properly examined. There appeared to be no immediate threat or evidence as such, and so the Allfather slowed his pace slightly to arrive a little more composed.

He approached slowly and this allowed him to size up the cause of the disturbance that had pulled him away from his evening meal. It was not uncommon for the tech sensors to detect such a highly dangerous reading of equipment, the sensors themselves were very sophisticated pieces of technology that were programmed to scan for elements of explosives, electrical currents or standard mechanical potential. It was uncommon however, for this to occur as late into the evening as it had. Those trying to gain entrance to the city by darkness usually had something they were trying to hide.

The Allfather cast his gaze upon the occupants of the inspection bay. Before him sat a very old man in what appeared to be a hovering chair. At his side, there were three skinny looking servants whose clothes had seen better days, and who's faces looked gaunt, sand struck and malnourished. The Allfather stood before them, eyed them closely and then turned to address the two guards that had noted the alert readings.

"Are these the individuals in question?" he asked the first guard, the guard nodded. It was very obvious to everyone present what had set the sensors off and that particular question need not be asked, but the Allfather did have an interest in their business here, and also to how an apparent scruffy old man, could have acquired such an expensive piece of tech.

"What is your name and state your business here in Astoria?" the Allfather stated with a level of authority. They were, after all, in HIS city.

"My name is Kane, and I plan to spend what remaining days I have left in my weary old body enjoying the pleasures and sites that your great city has to offer."

The Allfather drew a puzzled look across his face.

"Kane?? I knew a Kane once, strange that in a land where names are not shared, that I should meet another" it was true enough that in Astoria, not one single person shared a name with another. As the population had dwindled, names had become unique, slight deviations had been permitted but on the whole it was one person to the name and no more.

"I assure you I have never met anyone else by my name, perhaps the spelling of your FRIEND'S name differs from my own" the old man replied.

"I can assure you that the Kane I knew was no friend of mine. Hmm but I will concede that I was not purvey as to the correct spelling of his

43

name, How and where did you acquire this chair and for what purpose?"

"The chair I acquired in Sanctuary in a game of chance. Its purpose is quite obvious" the old man lifted his claw like hands; they shook where he held them as he indicated the frailty of his health.

As the two men conversed, Spanners walked his way around them, scanning the chair himself and trying to discern its inner workings. Something was tugging at his gut instinct about this chair but he could not quite put his finger on it. He left a puzzled look openly across his face in the hope that the Allfather may pick up on his instinct and perhaps act for him, however the Allfather didn't even seem to notice.

"How many are in your party?" the Allfather asked?

"A little over ten" the old man replied.

"Let them know they can get refreshments from the east end of the market in the morning, it's where they stock the little extras for travellers and passersby. Fresh water can be acquired there also. Welcome to Astoria"

Seemingly happy with the investigation, the Allfather nodded at the old man, turned and walked away. Spanners followed him quickly behind, a feeling of unease still flowing through him.

Raphael sat on the stone wall just outside the banquet hall next to Pepsy, she seemed really worried and was unsure of what to do.

"Do you think he is ok, I feel like this is my fault, I should have put him straight to his bed" she said.

Raphael put an arm around his friend, he had a special closeness with Pepsy, she had always looked out for him and had been kind to him, she had even seen through the awful rumours regarding him and the bone war, seeing the good in him and had trusted him when all others had grown weary of him. For this he was forever grateful.

It seemed to Raphael though, that Pepsy was forever worrying about everyone else and never making time for her own troubles or problems. There were times when she would take on somebody else's problem and do all that she could to fix it, and all the while she would be carrying a burden of her own that she chose to keep silent on. Knowing this, and knowing his friend well, he then took it upon himself as his duty to worry about her.

He looked at her closely and she returned his gaze. His soft brown eyes diffused her stress almost instantly.

"Do you remember the time we tried to surprise Harmony on her gift day, and we took her to the circus on the other side of the city?" he asked her softly.

An Angel's gift day was a celebration of the date in the year that the person first discovered their special gifts and powers. In some ancient cultures, the populace would celebrate the day in which they were born, or dates that they became married to a partner. In Astoria, the regular people would celebrate 'Allfathers day' or the day in which the Allfather took power and the Angels would celebrate their 'gift' day.

Raphael knew Pepsy so well, and over the years he had found that distraction was the best way to distress his friend.

Pepsy instantly smiled and then laughed out loud as she recalled the day.

It was about 5 years ago and they were celebrating Harmony's gift day, or the date that she had first shown her gifted abilities. Pepsy and Raphael had decided to take her to the circus, see some exotic animals, some tricks, and have some fun. Well UN be known to Pepsy or Raphael, Harmony had a phobia of clowns.

"Ahahaha and then she turned into that crazy little chiwawa dog thing and wouldn't stop barking" Pepsy was giggling hard now.

"Yes and then you tried to 'shift' her away but she kept running back through the portal and going for the clown's shoes." Raphael added.

"I'd never seen her so wound up before" Pepsy laughed "she nearly earned herself new red armour" she added. They both laughed together.

"And it took Jeremy to throw an orange, all the way from the palace walls, through your portal, and hit Harmony on the head to calm her down" Raphael added. They laughed even harder.

"Those were good times, back when Jeremy was motivated, now I just don't know what to do with him." Pepsy said

"You'll find a way peps, you always do" Raphael said as he hugged her gently.

As they both embraced, Crystal then made her way out of the banquet hall and joined them on the wall. She sat down softly at Raphael's side and they smiled at one another.

Pepsy, sensing she was the third wheel stood up.

"Id best go find him before it gets too late, will speak soon darling, and goodnight Crystal hunni, your shoes look amazing by the way" Pepsy said. Crystal returned the smile and watched as Pepsy turned to walk away.

Pepsy's mind wandered to Lucas briefly as she turned to leave. Something about seeing the way Crystal clearly cared for Raphael stirred old memories in her. She remembered a time she had the same care for Lucas, that same deep devotion. Her mood sunk slightly as she then teleported away, leaving a small shimmer or purple matter floating in the spot she had previously been, it lingered for a moment or two before dissipating into nothing.

Raphael broke the silence.

"I broke your butterfly I'm sorry...I must be stronger than I thought" he said softly.

"It's ok, I can always make you another one" she replied. She reached forward and took one of Raphael's hands and turned it over, she observed the heavy burn scarring on his palms and thought back to the time that he received this. She gently rubbed his hands for a moment, enjoying his touch against hers. Raphael looked up into the clear skies and observed the stars. He could feel her fingers running over the scar contours that coated his hands and found her soft touch comforting. As his eyes remained high, there was massive flash and then a huge ring of blue white light that emanated from high up in the sky, making its way down to the earth below. It headed straight for Astoria and the sight truly was magnificent and beautiful. It flowed down slowly, its bright throbbing light making a perfect ring ten yards in diameter all the way around. Its descent toward the earth was slow and aesthetically pleasing, and all who looked upon it marvelled in its beauty. As it eventually hit the ground somewhere around Astoria's perimeter, it dissipated into the earth and the bright light was gone.

Raphael broke the silence first as he pondered the event before them.

"Do you ever wonder where it comes from?" he asked, referring to the great halo that drops upon the whole of Astoria three times daily and at irregular intervals. Some of the civilians worshipped it as a divine act and would drop to their knees in prayer upon setting eyes on it. For Raphael, it only stirred curiosity within him.

Crystal continued to massage his hand within hers; happily enjoying the beautiful moment that she was sharing with him.

"I heard Spanners once suggest that it is in fact a solar flare, although I am unsure as to what that is exactly" Crystal said. Raphael took in her words but shook his head in an unconvincing manner.

"All our lives it has fallen from the sky and yet we know very little about it. Is knowledge THAT powerful that it needs to be guarded from us?" he pondered aloud. Crystal remained quiet and continued to caress his hand with her own. It wasn't often that she managed to find alone time with Raphael anymore, and so cherished each and every second she could with him. And in this moment, under the great halo, divine or not she felt happy and content beside him. Raphael's focus however was elsewhere as he continued to play over the mystery of the halo in his head.

"Have you ever heard of Alpharus prime?" he asked her.

Crystal shook her head. She had never really taken any notice of the science of the skies. With no way of getting off this place she didn't feel the need to tease herself. She had heard that there were star maps somewhere deep within the palace libraries that she could have access to if she so desired, but she never felt the need to be fulfilled and so had never explored such avenues. There were millions of stars with millions of names and she could reach neither of them, so to her it seemed like pointless research.

"When I was young I heard my father speak of an Alpharus prime, a place where everybody went. The entire world's population left this place and headed there to start again. He once told me that Astorians were mans unwanted children, that they were all left behind here" Crystal just listened on intently; she loved how Raphael's mind wandered to strange places and ideas. She could sit and listen to him for hours talking of unforeseen possibilities.

"I asked the Allfather once about it and he chastised me, he told me that such words were heresy, that it could cause unrest amongst the other children. He made me promise never to tell the other children"

"Why are you telling me this now?" Crystal asked, with genuine interest.

"Because I kept my word, I hadn't told any children, but we aren't children anymore and I feel I need answers" he replied.

Crystal thought about this once more. She sat there with her hand still clasped in his and she caressed his gently, trying her best to send him a signal to show she cared. His eyes never left the stars.

 A moment later their comfortable silence was broken as Chance exited the banquet hall. Crystal immediately let go of his hand.

"Come on, we need to go, and carry these for me" Chance handed Raphael a tray of various fruits that she had decided to take home with her. She gave Crystal a small smile as they passed, knowing full well that she had interrupted a quiet moment in a very LOUD fashion.

"Good night Crystal" Raphael called out.

"Good night Crystal" Chance mocked in a quieter voice as she teased Raphael on the walk home.

The next morning, Chance got up early and headed out into the city. An eerie fog had descended over the desert plains blinding everything from view. Its cold grey matter blanketed the desert and made it impossible to see the ground below unless you got down on your hands and knees to be really close to it. This same fog had drifted into the city and was having a similar effect there also.

Bouncing her way around the city in her enlightened mood, it was clear for all to see that she had enjoyed a long and restful sleep, feeling invigorated and fresh as she hopped and danced her way around the streets. She passed other citizens and smiled, giving her morning greetings, determined to share her good feelings with all that she came across. It would be fair to say that Astoria loved its little Angel Chance, a celebrity to all and a villain to none. She made her way through the bustling crowds that gathered around the market area.

After a few moments, Chance became aware of footsteps following in behind her, she turned slightly and could see that Raphael was, as always, following in behind. He was rubbing his eyes free of sleep and she grinned that she had outsmarted him this morning by a good nine minutes. Another sweet victory in the bag she thought.

There was an unusually high gathering of crowds this morning and it attracted her attention, she immediately began to scan the area with her beautiful blue eyes. She could feel the commotion and excitement from the people but could see no obvious source.

With no clear attraction in sight Chance decided to bounce a little closer to investigate. Raphael followed silently behind as he continued to rub his eyes and scratch his head. His sleep had clearly not been as deep as his blonde comrade.

Raphael had a quiet way about him the majority of the time, he only interacted with a set group of friends, friends whom he knew well, trusted and held close to his heart. To others he would just be reserved, observant and mindful.

Chance on the other hand was playful with all whom she came across, seeking new pleasures and games wherever she could. A new face meant a new challenge and someone new to beat so she made a note to speak to all that she came across. In doing this she learned so much over the years. New languages, new games and new tricks. Her intelligence bellied her playful demeanour. Her outward approach to everyone was a polar opposite to the reserved approach of Raphael's and so off she bounced, weaving her little self through the crowd and drawing ever closer to the source of the crowds focus.

As she neared, she slowed her bounce into a short tap step. Carefully and methodically removing her designer sunglasses from her head and casually dropping them over her shoulder.

Swiftly and smoothly, Raphael lunged forwards and caught the glasses just short of an inch from the ground.

"Diva" he was heard muttering as he returned the glasses to their soft leather case that he had produced from what seemed like thin air.

Chance took no notice, she knew in her head that she was in no way a diva but enjoyed this little game of making him sweat to keep her happy. She made a mental note to throw the glasses harder next time and really make him work.

The dullness of the morning gave Chance focus to push on to the root of this colourful distraction. Slowing completely now to regain her composure, she tip toed around the epicentre of the event. Raphael followed as ever closely behind.

At the centre of the crowd, was a carefully placed hover chair. Not a large hover chair by any means, but not a small hover chair either. Upon that chair sat, what appeared to be a very old man, A very very old man by Chances estimations.

Immediately Chance began to size this old man up. His long withered grey beard covered half his face; she would hazard a guess that there were a good few weeks of lunches still embedded within that beard.

His shoes were fashioned from some animal skin that she had never set eyes upon. His hands were old looking, resembling more like claws than anything of basic use. She then realised why his beard was such a mess, she doubted he could grip anything for very long.

Her gaze was almost immediately drawn to the eyes of this old man. Eyes but not eyes, more like socketed spectrals into a world she had never seen. Like a moth for bright colours, Chances focus drifted deeper into that world...

A small pinch brought her back to reality. A pinch, to her alarming realisation, made upon her derrière. She turned to find the crowd had parted and Raphael, as always, remained.

With the reflexes of a cat she gave him a short swift slap across his face, so fast that it made the perfect 'snap' sound as her skin connected with his. Raphael took the blow stoically, saying nothing merely nodded her attention forwards. She turned back with a small feeling of confusion and sorrow as she was not entirely sure it had been him that committed the crime.

'*Oh well*' she said to herself '*no freebies on this ship*'

And with that she re-tuned her attention into the old man that sat before her. She suddenly became aware that the bustling had come to a stop. A deafening silence had cascaded over the area, a silence broken only by the heavy breathing of Raphael behind her. She cursed him again for forgetting his inhaler. He should know better than when he is unwell with a cold that he should carry his damn inhaler. Must she remember everything for him?

Raphael eyed the old man carefully, there was something about him that was stirring deep inside Raphael but he could not quite put his finger on it. He felt like he recognised him but was not sure that he had ever come across anyone such as this before. He found it difficult to shake the feeling of association he had toward this strange old man in the chair. Raphael had always prided himself on his exceptional memory, capable of recalling facts and events from as far back as his very early childhood. He could remember names, faces and even the dates that certain events occurred and yet here he was, with this nagging sensation inside him, screaming to his senses that he KNEW this person and yet he couldn't put a name to him.

Unwilling to disregard his instincts and yet without facts to explain his ill-feelings toward the old man, he chose to remain silent until he could conclude his investigation.

There was a silence between the old man and Chance as both eyed each other up warily. Inside her head, she played a small game as she always did, taking victories where she could. The silence that had befallen between them only built the suspension of victory. As the old man spoke Chance smiled inside at the small victory she had taken from their unsaid game of silence.

"I know you little one, I have travelled far and wide to find you"

"Wh...." Chance's attempt at conversation was cut short with a wave of his degrading, sorry excuses for claws.

"The where's and whys will be answered later" the old man stated. There was something strong and powerful about his words and Raphael was quickly getting the impression that there was a lot more to this old man than met the eye. A LOT more.

"All you need to know is that I have taken a keen interest in your endeavours and I wish to...test myself against your set of skills" the old man said. Raphael immediately got his back up and went to move forward. Something about the old man's behaviour made Raphael feel threatened and he wasted no time in moving to protect Chance right away.

Chance sensed his movements coming forward and placed her hand out to the side to stop him. She turned her head slightly and met his concerned brown eyes. She gave him a strong look that told him to back down and after a brief moment he receded back to his place behind her.

"And what shall I call you?" Chance asked in an attempt to try and take control of the situation.

"My name is not important, for now you may simply call me the 'old man'" he replied.

"Well if the face fits...although I think you'd suit the name 'Grand wizard' better, we could get you a pointy hat" Chance said mockingly. The old man sat there quietly, completely unfazed by her comments as he chose to remain silent.

"Oh you are a serious one, ok Grand wizard what do you want to test me against?" Chance asked, eagerly awaiting the potential challenge.

"Perhaps a game that an old man like myself would be capable of playing, a game that requires speed, skill and intellect" the old man trailed off at the end of his sentence, letting the idea linger with her for a moment. A coy smile could just about be seen at the corner of his lips.

Raphael shook his head, he could see she was being led into this and for what purpose he was unsure. It took every ounce of his will power to remain where he stood. His eyes then focussed back on the old man. There was definitely something about this man that was familiar but he really could not put his finger on it. The familiarity without recognition was irritating him.

Chance had her finger on her chin, pondering the various games they could partake in. Her eyes lit up and she concluded the best option for her.

"Ok, well I have thought of a game, it involves speed, skill and intellect. Have you ever heard of *Superf*"

"*rfuse*... no I have not. This game sounds perfect" the old man said as he finished her sentence for her"

Raphael was fuming by this stage. Never heard of the game and yet finished its title before she did. Sometimes her blondeness baffled him. He clenched his knuckles in frustration. He had a feeling that today was going to be a bad day.

"Oh perfect, I'll explain the rules to you and then we can play" Chance said. She was all excited now at the prospect of playing her favourite game. The onlookers began to murmur and talk amongst themselves. Only minutes before Chance had arrived that morning, the old man had taken centre court with the inhabitants of Astoria. He had stated that he was going to dethrone the champion of Astoria at *Superfuse.* He had stated this with such a degree of certainty that the crowds had amassed quickly and with a keen interest had observed the exchange.

They all made their way over to the gaming quadrant and on the way Chance explained the rules to the old man whom was still playing 'babe in the woods' with regard to his knowledge of the game.

Raphael followed closely behind. The volume of crowds gathered worried him slightly, mostly because no great announcement had been made and yet the crowd gathered was massive and the feeling of anticipation was ever growing. There was clearly something about this old man that the crowd knew that he was not purvey to.

They reached the table and Chance made her way to her favourite side. She was about to speak but the old man waved her quiet again dismissively with his claw hand.

"I do believe that if we should play this game, there should be some kind of wager" the old man stated.

Raphael ground his teeth in irritation. *'This man's done his homework'* he thought. There was nothing that would capture Chances attention more than a wager. This really was going to be a bad day he thought.

"Oh I thought you'd never ask" Chance said, The excitement growing inside her by the minute.

"If you win, I will retire here in Astoria and become your faithful servant, of course my old bones limit me to many tasks, but what errands I can run I will run for you. What is a princess without a servant" he said.

"And if I win" he paused "you are to be banished from Astoria completely for one year. To live a life wandering the dusty planes as I have had to endure" the old man barely had the opportunity to finish his sentence before Raphael burst through the crowd, ready to grab him by the scruff of his fatigues. Chance reacted quickly, turning on the spot she threw her hands out, emitting a small portion of her gift and force pushed him. Raphael was sent flying through the air where he landed heavily, crashing through some slogan juice barrels some ten feet away. He slowly climbed to his feet, his deep brown eyes looking directly back at her.

"What IS the matter with you today?" she shouted at him. "Do as you are told and stand where you belong...BEHIND me!" she added. Raphael dusted himself off and walked over slowly. The onlookers watched him warily, unsure of what had just happened but in all appearances it looked as though he had just aggressively launched himself at the weak old man. Some of the people shook their heads in disgust.

Chance turned her attention back toward the old man.

"Ok grand wizard you are on! Remember the rules though, no gifts allowed on the table"

"Of course not my dear" the old man replied, although he was not entirely convincing in his response.

Chance took hold of a small Lastic ball and then dropped it down into the slot.

The game had begun and already it was flowing fast. Chance was using every ounce of her speed and skill, playing the ball forward and then zooming into the board to make the shots on goal. Each attempt though was foiled by the old man whom had chosen to simply remain on defence with his goalkeeper. Again Chance tried another angle of attack, playing the ball wide then gripping the attacking handle, zooming in down onto the board. From down here she could see all the possible openings; she turned slightly and kicked the ball with all her might. She released the handle at the same time and appeared back up again above the board only to see the old man somehow get his goalkeeper into the way in time.

It was impossible. There was no possible way that he could have managed that, he would have had to move at incredible speeds to accomplish that particular move.

She continued on, trying lots of different tactics. Playing a through ball and then hitting the shot from above instead of zooming in.

Again the old man seemed to block the shot just in the nick of time.

She looked closely at his claw hands and was bewildered that such things could move at such speed. Her eyes rose slightly and she looked at him closer.

'Had he gotten older in the time they had been playing? He looked at least twenty years older than when they started. He had more bald patches and his body seemed all the more frail' she thought. Her eyes drifted to the game clock; there was barely ten seconds to go. She took the ball and played it wide. She spun the handles profusely and with added vigour. She was running out of time.

7 seconds to go. She played the ball through.

6 seconds to go. She passed it wide again.

5 seconds to go. She zoomed in.

4 seconds to go. She swung her leg back.

3 seconds to go. She swung forward.

2 seconds to go. She kicked the ball.

1 second to go. The ball sailed toward the open goal. Chance zoomed out to what she thought was certain victory. Goal sirens went off around the arena. A smile crossed her face in the close fought victory. Her eyes were drawn to the scoreboard and suddenly she frowned. She looked again and rubbed her eyes. It just wasn't possible, surely a mistake.

The scoreboard stated she had been beaten 1-0

"What???"She shouted aloud. The old man had an evil smile across his face as he rummaged in his cloak. The crowd were going crazy. They had never seen her beaten before. The sad part was that even SHE hadn't seen herself beaten. She didn't even see the goal. She couldn't understand it.

"But how? " her face was in absolute confusion. The old man stood up from his hover chair, turned to the side and then pushed the chair toward her. She fell upon the chair and as she did so it began to transform into a small flying capsule.

Raphael was quick to react. He dashed from his position as fast as he could. What happened next seemed to occur in the blink of an eye. Time appeared to slow down completely as the old man pulled a device the length of his forearm, concealed from within his cloak. At the end of this device were four long prongs' which he immediately placed against Chances head.

Raphael's run seemed in slow motion. Each step was taking an eternity to land. He drove his arms through the air and bounded off one leg and sent himself hurling towards Chance.

The pronged device against Chances head spun rapidly, withdrawing a red glow from her head that generated into a perfectly round orb within the four prongs. The old man pulled the device from her head and kicked out with his foot. By now the hover chair had transformed completely into a small launch capsule. The old man's boot connected with the launch button and sent the capsule sailing off into the sky. Just before it left the ground, Raphael landed hard onto its outside and gripped on with dear life.

All of this happened in the mere blink of an eye.

By the time the crowd had refocused on the gaming board, Chance and Raphael were in fact long gone, leaving only a small trail of exhaust fumes in their wake.

The old man grinned. He aged again.

CHAPTER 3

Spanners made his way down toward the main gate. Awaiting him there was the same guard whom he had spoken with the previous evening. A nervous looked was worn across the guards face at the puzzling news he was about to break to him. Spanners stopped directly in front of him, almost invading the man's personal space. He did not do this deliberately or to intimidate the man in any way, it was just the way Spanners was. He liked to get up close and personal to truly read a situation. He took the data slate from the guard and skimmed through the information quickly. The guard looked on anxiously. A puzzled look then crossed Spanners face about halfway down the information he was reading. He paused, straightened himself out, and then giving away no emotion whatsoever he looked up and spoke directly into the guard's eyes.

"I am authorising your men to make use of their thermal imagining devices. I feel it is only logical that these tech-readings are a result of smuggling, and by the looks of your findings here, smuggling on a grand scale. I also want you to double up the men sentries around the perimeter and tell them to keep their eyes open for any suspicious behaviour." Spanners said quite methodically. The guard nodded, turned and made off to complete the orders feeling quite glad that his attention to duty wasn't being called into question here.

As Spanners watched him leave he looked down again at the information on the data slate. By the tech-sensors calculations, there had been a further 500 devices smuggled into Astoria since the previous evening. The sensors indicate a small reading, holding only for a fraction of a second and then vanishing, gone almost as quickly as it had appeared.

Spanners pondered this one intricately. For what purpose would such devices be needed? With those numbers it could easily be weapons? He concluded it would need to be small arms as a quantity of 500 of anything large would surely be noticeably found right away. He turned and headed for the palace to report to the Allfather right away.

Pepsy had been 'shifting' about all night, she was exhausted and yet still she could not find him. She had asked around everywhere and nobody had seen him. She had searched all the usual bars, she had checked the palace flower gardens, and she had checked the market, the slums, and the sewers, she had checked everywhere and each time she came up short. The more tired she felt the harder it became to 'shift' accurately. Her last teleport she landed straight on top of a lamp post, she had to quickly grip on so as not to fall. She held on tight and gazed into the lamp head and on the inside she could make out a couple of glow worms wriggling about inside. She shuddered at their forms and slid down the pole. She was still wearing the same dress she had worn to the banquet and so she had to be careful to remain ladylike when descending the pole.

From the bottom of the pole she started to wander aimlessly through the streets, scuffing her good heels as she went. She began to calculate the amount of time she had spent in the last year looking after or pulling his sorry self out of sticky situations. She could hear Raphael's voice in the back of her head telling her to 'make time for herself, too busy helping others to help yourself' he was right but Jeremy was her friend and he was capable of so much more he just needed to focus again and find a new purpose. If she could only help him achieve this then maybe she could have her normal life back again, for at the moment it felt like she was babysitting a social hand grenade that could go off at any minute.

She did feel rather responsible for Jeremy. He had never turned to drink until Lucas had died. Although it was by no means her fault, she felt that if she had been faster she may have been able to save him. A guilt that she has every day since been trying to repay through helping Jeremy.

She turned down another street and discovered a small bar that she didn't know existed until now. The bar was called 'peppers pot' and she laughed at the similarities to her own name. *'Surely he wouldn't be hiding in here, right under my nose'* she thought.

She pushed her way in through the double door and the inside of the bar was painted with bright colours, glaringly bright colours on each of the different walls. It was actually a bit of an eye sore, so bright that it almost gave Pepsy a headache. She made her way to the bar and sat down on the stool.

A very large plump woman came out from the back room. She was fairly grim looking and never said a word; she just eyed Pepsy up mockingly.

"Found yourself in the wrong place have you?" the big woman asked.

Pepsy refused to be lowered to her standard. This woman clearly needed some exercise and lessons in manors, a smile now and then wouldn't go a miss either but it wasn't her place to say so she held her tongue and remembered her purpose.

"I am looking for my friend"

"You have friends do you, lucky you" the woman said. Pepsy wasn't sure if she was being sarcastic or actually meant what she said. She decided to ignore the comment.

"My friend is tall, skinny and is forever pacing back and forth between his front and back leg?" Pepsy said.

"Ah you'll be looking for Jeremy then, he sure is a grumpy chap"

Pepsy thought to herself sharply 'that's rich coming from you'

"Do you know where he is?" Pepsy asked?

"I don't know where he is but I do know where he is heading" she replied.

Pepsy waited a moment.

She waited a moment longer and then realised that this old fat grump wasn't going to be spilling anything in a hurry.

"Well would you mind telling me where I might find him, I am worried about him and he is not himself, I need to find him" Pepsy said.

"Must be nice to have someone come looking for you" the woman said. Pepsy rolled her eyes; this woman wasn't half hard work.

"Okay okay how much will this information cost me?" Pepsy began to reach into her little purse that she pulled from her bag. When she looked up she could see that the woman had welled up in the eyes. Large plumes of tears had now filled her face.

"I am so sorry, have I said something wrong?" Pepsy suddenly felt terrible. She had no idea what she had done or how she had upset this woman. The woman sobbed some more, and as she sobbed she named her price.

"Ill tell you what you need to know if you will maybe help me with my wardrobe" the lady sobbed harder. Pepsy rolled up the bottom of her dress and hopped the bar, she knew she was fairly strong and this woman looked like she could shift heavy things so between the two of them she was pretty sure they could get this wardrobe moved in no time, a small price for the safety of her friend.

Pepsy put a hand around the woman's back to console her tears and then asked her to direct them to this wardrobe. The woman led them through the back of the bar, down a long passageway and into a large dressing chamber. Once inside, Pepsy turned on the spot and laid eyes upon the task at hand. Before her, in the centre of the room was the wardrobe, and it was massive., almost 7 ft tall and twice as wide. Pepsys eyes grew wide in astonishment; she almost wished she had Wallace with her for this endeavour.

She took a breath and tried to remain calm to think logically around this problem. She could always teleport out and bring Wallace back here to move it, how far did the woman want it moved? She didn't know. She decided to find out the smaller details.

"So erm, where would you like it" Pepsy asked

"Where would I like what? It's there!" the woman sobbed and flung open the cupboard doors. Inside were all manners of old fashioned dresses and gowns, all covered in dust as they hadn't been worn in years. Some of the gowns looked ancient. Pepsy looked on with a little confusion.

"Do you want it emptied? Is that what you need help with?" Pepsy asked, still a little baffled as to what this woman had wagered on.

"Sniff, no...I want to look as pretty as you...but I don't have the wardrobe..." she sobbed.

61

Realisation started to set in. This woman needed not her muscles or her strength and certainly NOT Wallace's input. She needed style. Pepsy began to nod as a smile crossed her face.

"Don't you worry darling, ill sort you out, hold on tight we are going somewhere...fast" and with that, Pepsy teleported the woman away.

The old man crept his way to the cities edge. The recent use of his powers had made him grow weary and he had even aged a little bit more. He had perhaps underestimated the girl's potential, having not foreseen the requirement to use such a level of power in the match. No matter, soon he would have his cure and soon he himself would be restored to greatness.

Once outside the city walls and free from the tech-sensors, one of the old man's peasants approached and handed him a small device.

"My lord, as you requested" the slave said. The old man gave no thanks and took the device in his claw hand and used his other hand to dismissively wave him away.

He turned the device over gently and then flicked a small switch on the underside. Almost instantly the small oval shape sprouted wings and began to hover within the palm of his claw. A small red light also started to blink on its surface.

"Now fly my little beastie...attract your friends...blanket the sun and cause anarchy" the old man gestured the device into the air and it flew off high into the sky. He watched with malevolent eyes as it took off into the distance.

....Chance awoke and opened her eyes, and yet it was still dark. A strong hazy feeling overcame her, she instinctively found herself reaching for her face, using her little hands in an attempt to gain some sort of orientation on the situation. After exploring her face she confirmed what she had known earlier, her eyes WERE in fact open and yet she could not see a single strand of light.

The room she had found herself in was made of stone, of that much she was sure, it was cold and rough to the touch, the air was stale and she could smell a slight musky stench floating around the area. She had no recollection of how she got there, nor even where she was, or if anyone was...wait, was she alone?

"Hello" she ventured out with a quivering voice into the dark, the sound dissipating into the stone. She found it difficult to determine the size of the room; she couldn't see, there wasn't a single sliver of light and there was no echo to the words she called out. Where was she?

She ran her hands up and down her body, she was dressed at least, one less problem to worry about. Her trousers felt soft and comfortable, made from a material that allowed her fingers to glide over its surface with ease, had she been in a less alarming environment, she may have found their touch quite comforting. Her top felt loose, sleeveless and open necked, and she felt something hanging around her neck, something hard and durable. She played around with it in her fingers, turning it over and over, running her fingers tip along its smooth edge. It seemed to be of a heart shape, it was quite small, and as she ran her thumb over its surface, she could just about make out small engravings, tiny cuts that had been scraped into its design, but she had no clue as to what they were or what they meant. She tugged on the chain slightly and found that it was very durable indeed, clearly made from a strong metal ore, she imagined it would be quite valuable.

She ran her hands over her face again, gently investigating all her features before continuing on and into her hair, which she now realised was tied up with a small clasp.

She was absolutely baffled. Where on earth was she?

"Hello, is anyone there" she called out again, although she was not entirely sure why. Did she really want company in this deep dark place that she had found herself in? Unless the company had a light or some kind of illuminating device then she wasn't interested.

"I guess I'm alone then" she said aloud, her morale dropping slightly in realisation of her lonely predicament. Her knees began to ache from their position against the cold, stone floor. She pressed her hands above her head, ensuring the area was clear, before adjusting her position and climbing to her feet. Once her feet, she gapingly waved her arms around herself, trying to determine her proximity to her surroundings. A few tiny steps later she found herself in contact with a cold stone wall, she suddenly thought she had heard a noise. Holding her breath and listening hard, she remained quiet for a few seconds, straining her ears for any more sounds, once again she heard a sound, a muffled sound, but from where?

She pressed her ear to the cold stone of the wall in front of her; the muffled noise could certainly be heard more strongly from this wall.

She held her ear to the wall, pressing it as closely to the source as she could, just then, a loud thump shook the room, and in particular the wall from where she had stood.

Blindly she jumped back in fear.

The muffled noise grew slightly louder, sounding more like a voice, and a familiar voice too and again there was the loud thump followed by the trickle of small stone rubble that traversed its way down the wall.

Her heart began to race and she instinctively raised her little punchers up in defence, what she hoped to achieve with them against a creature that can rattle stone walls she had no clue, but raised fists she adorned nonetheless.

An even LOUDER thump this time, followed by what she could only describe as an anguished shout of pain. What on earth was going on??

 She began to take slow steps backwards; the mystery of the dimensions of this room would be a mystery no longer as she carefully made her escape away from whatever was trying to get to her.

Punchers still raised, a bead of sweat running down her forehead, she realised that she had in fact stopped breathing, holding her breath subconsciously. She had to push hard to let out a breath, feeling slightly light headed from the exertion.

The thumps became louder as more rubble could be heard trickling down the wall.

A tiny spot of light appeared in the wall. It shot a sharp lance of searing hot light through the room where she was cornered.

Another thump

More rubble coupled with the muttering cursing of her pursuer.

Another thump and then...silence.

By now there were at least 20 tiny little beams of light protruding into the room that she could just about make out its rough dimensions.

'It wasn't very big' she thought, not even half the size of her dressing room.

Her hands began to ache, she realised that while holding her boxers stance, she had also been squeezing her tiny little fists, clenching her knuckles so hard that they were starting to hurt. She couldn't see to confirm but she was sure her knuckles would be whiter than white from the exertion.

Still the silence, or was there? She could make out the light padding of feet. The sound seemed to be getting quieter, almost as if it was moving away from her.

'Thank goodness', she thought, 'it's left me alone and'...

There was a sudden loud shout!

What was said was not very clear but it was followed by the thundering of heavy feet. The noise was getting louder...

No, not louder she realised but NEARER.

If she didn't know better, she was sure her heart had actually stopped.

What on earth was happening?? This was not how she wanted to go out, squished by some rampaging demon in a cold dark stone room. It was too dark to even make out her clothes. Was this going to be her end? Wearing soft cotton trousers and a strappy top? She didn't even know if she was colour coordinated. Oh the thought was unbearable to her.

The thundering beast was so close now. She pressed her back against the wall and squeezed her eyes shut as a HUGE crash was heard all around as she felt something career its way into the room. Rubble was strewn everywhere and the dust was rising and filling the room quickly.

Chance tried to open her eyes but a massive white solace of light engulfed her vision.

She stood absolutely still as she could hear the continued mutterings of her assailant.

As the dust started to clear, she was suddenly aware of a familiar smell, a scent, a boy's scent. She realised that her hands had relaxed all of a sudden.

She became aware of a figure within the room that appeared to be attempting to remove dust from itself.

"Hello" she said calmly.

At first there was no answer except from the sound of patting skin against cloth. Before she could speak again the figure spoke.

"Quite the pickle we are in this time missy" the voice said. It was definitely a guys voice. It sounded so familiar to her and yet she had no recollection.

"Where are we? How did we get here and who are you?" she had so many questions that she needed answered that she blurted it all out into one big rambled mess.

"Ha ha tongues tied are we? Shoe on the other foot this time hey?" he replied.

She had no clue what he was talking about but cared little for his cheek in this situation. She wanted answers, no she NEEDED answers and so far he was the only way to get them. So she cut to the chase.

"I just asked you three questions and you answered none of them!!" she displayed a little irritation in her voice. She was still not entirely sure whether this guy was friend or foe, she only had a "feeling" and that was certainly not enough for her right now.

"You did" he replied

"Well don't you think it is polite to answer them?"

He considered her comment for a moment and then calmly said

"Are you being serious? You don't remember how we got here?"

"Yes I am being serious! Do I look like I'm in the mood for joking around?" Chance replied. The dark cave they occupied was now slightly lit up with the beams of light from which he had crashed his way through. Chance stood there looking him up and down. To her he looked like a monkey. He was powerfully built and yet seemed athletic with the way he held himself. He had bushy dark eyebrows, dark hair and really tanned skin. She was pretty convinced that if she gave him a banana he would do anything she wanted.

He looked at her closely before replying.

"No I guess not, you look like you are in quite the mood today!"

"I'll have less of your cheek and more of my questions answered please! And who are you anyway?" she countered. Irritation was now at the forefront of her emotions.

"Wow you really have forgotten me, ouch! Hmm I wonder how this has happened" he pondered. Chance gave him a very serious and unimpressed look as he had still not answered any of her questions. She tapped her foot and he got the hint.

"Okay okay, my name is Raphael, I am your "friend" "he said indicating inverted commas around friend.

"We crashed here in the tail end of nowhere in a modified escape pod that some old man used to banish you from Astoria"

"What's an Astoria?"

"It's where you live, your home. He used some dirty trick to beat you at a game of *Superfuse and.*"

"Oh *Superfuse* I like that" she replied quickly. Raphael looked at her closely, this time it was he who adorned the unimpressed look.

67

"Really? You remember that and not me?" he shook his head and continued. "It seems this old man must have taken your memory somehow before he banished us."

"Wait a second there monkey boy, are you telling me some old man beat me at *Superfuse*?" she asked. Raphael nodded slowly. She burst out laughing.

"And this old man took my memory?" she asked.

"It would seem so yes" he replied.

"Why?"

"Well that is the part I do not know but I will make sure that we find out" he said confidently.

Chance's mood dropped. She had lost her memory, it was gone and she might never get it back. She had no idea who she was, where she was, who she was with. She had some memories, really odd ones like the game of *Superfuse,* she remembered she had style and she remembered how important looking good was to her. But she couldn't remember anything else.

Nothing.

Raphael sensed her sadness, he knew her well enough to recognise that look that had now crossed her face. He looked her deep into her little blue eyes.

"There is nothing that's lost that can't be found" he said, trying to comfort her over her lack of memory. The statement raised her spirits slightly and she held herself a little taller.

"Now Can we please get out of this dusty room now as it's not good for my lungs and I've lost my inhaler" he added.

Chance shook her head dismissively and followed the light out of the engineered hole in the wall. The world she emerged into seemed so bright in comparison to the room she had just occupied.

Upon reaching the outside she took a look at the hole that had been made. She looked around for any sign of battering ram or wedging tool but could see none. No tools of any kind could be seen. She looked her rescuer up and down; she glanced back at the hole,

"How did you..." she trailed off on her sentence as she realised that nothing really made sense today.

Chance stretched up as tall as she could and instantly felt a twinge in her back. Within a flash her "friend" was at her side offering her assistance.

"Do you want me to crack your back?" he said

"Do you want to do what to me??" Chance responded in alarm. Automatically adopting her defensive position once again she took a few steps back. He eyed her defensive position briefly before shaking his head.

"Suit yourself" he muttered and turned to walk down from the rubble and towards a makeshift fire he had constructed from...well she couldn't actually discern where he sourced the wood from.

'What an odd character' she thought to herself and made a note to keep well clear of his creepy advances.

She stood as tall as someone of her stature could. She took her neck in both hands and proceeded to yank her chin up, cracking her neck to relieve the pressure.

She took in a few large lung full's of the crisp air and then looked around, taking in all her surroundings.

There was the rubble ruin from which she had emerged. A small grass hill that eventually levelled out into a plain which then stretched for as far as her vision allowed her to see. As she scanned left she passed over her "friend" who was crouched by the fire doing, well she couldn't actually make out what he was doing from her sunny disposition. As she continued her analysis she realised that at least he was telling the truth, this place really was the tail end of nowhere.

'Perfect' she thought, 'I'm stuck in the tail end of nowhere dressed in sporting gear with a creepy back snapping chimp that calls himself a friend, and no recollection of...well anything at all really'. She thought to herself.

Just before the disparity of the situation really set in, a delicious smell wafted its way through her nostrils. Instantly her mouth was saturated with saliva. Food!!! She thought, her third favourite thing!

With such incredible speed that surprised even herself, she was over to the fire to see what was cooking.

Amazingly enough, her chimp had somehow cooked up some chicken kebabs on sticks served up with a small purple fruit drink from a Lastic bottle.

"How did you..." she trailed off again as he shot her a puzzled look and yet still he said nothing.

Well she wasn't going to stand on ceremony so Chance helped herself and started wolfing it down where she stood. All intentions of being lady like went out the window. She was hungry and besides she wasn't trying to impress this loser!

A couple of minutes later, Chance had finished her kebabs, her belly full, she felt good. She actually felt really good, taller too.

'Taller?' She thought to herself and then looked down to find herself standing on the point of her toe on both feet.

That actually looked quite incredible she thought.

"Woo check me out" she called out.

The chimp just looked up, shot her a small smile and then started shaking his head.

A little scorned that he wasn't impressed, she let herself back down.

'Stupid chimp boy' she thought, she had barely known him five minutes and already she was bored of him. She started to look around once more in the hope of seeing something remotely interesting but to her sadness there was nothing. Her shoulders sunk and she found herself staring aimlessly into space.

A moment later, Raphael casually lumbered his way up to where she was. Still a little wary of this backslapping chimp she kept her distance but her eyes were instantly drawn to what he held in his hand.

From what seemed liked nowhere, the chimp had produced a large a3 map, folded twice.

"Where did you...." she started to say but then was instantly drawn to the various amenities littered across the page.

At the top of the page was simply "LOCAL ORDNANCE MAP ASTORIA" Chance looked at it closely. It seemed to her that Astoria was, as he had said, her home, and it was very large place at that. It seemed the entire area had been dubbed 'Astoria' although only one city shared its name. On the map she could make out another large bastion on the opposite side of the map titled 'SANCTUARY' and its relevant size on the map looked like it rivalled Astoria in its dimensions.

The chimp began to point out another location on the map and Chance instantly recognised that he bit his nails.

' Hell this boy must be hungry by the state of those bad boys' she thought and made a further note never to let him come near her with those paws.

"I judge our location to be approximately here-which is only a few hours walk to Sanctuary. Once there I can ask King Tut to help me contact the other Angels to come and get us" he said.

"Angels?" she questioned as she raised her eyebrows.

"Never mind" he replied.

Ah this guy was already starting to irritate her with the volume of unanswered questions she now had with him

"I am definitely dropping this loser at the next port" she thought.

In pure politeness she nodded, although not fully understanding what he had just explained.

"It's not a long hike, "he began "But it will be very dangerous so stay close"

'Whatever chimp boy, how are you going to protect me' she thought but politely nodded again instead. And with that they got themselves together and off they went.

Ferns fiery gaze was locked high in the sky on a black mass that had gathered not far from the city limits.

She stood just outside the city walls, her Phoenix guard stood alert, as always, around her.

Although Fern was the only Angel amongst her guard, wielding the power of fire, the Phoenix guard had been trained up to make excellent use of tribinium fuelled flame throwing weapons. Her Phoenix guard were one of only a very few that openly carried weapons of violence. It was true that the regular Astorian guardsman carried staves of various lengths but they were mainly for marshalling crowds or reaching high places such as straightening the tapestries in the palace, they were never held with any kind of malevolence.

The Phoenix guard however were clearly geared up for war. The very training that they undertook each and every morning was a clear indicator of this, rehearsing battle formations over and over, sparring at each and every opportunity. It seemed like a great insult then, that the Allfather regularly called upon the guard to partake in menial farming duties such as the blazing of the harvested fields and also the cleansing of certain areas to kill off the pestilent flies. These duties, Fern ensured she took to with as little reluctance as possible but she was finding it harder and harder each time to hide the disquiet of the men, although her alternative was war, and even Fern in all her ill-tempered ways would not wish that upon the city.

Ferns gaze remained locked on the swarming mass above, was unsure if it was heading toward the city, into her jurisdiction or not.

"It's a very large swarm indeed, and heading toward Sanctuary" a voice spoke. Sanctuary was Astoria's sister city. It was not as grand or as technologically advanced as Astoria was, but some citizens that chose not to live the life ruled by the Angels had left and created their own city 30 miles away from the city of Angels. Relations between the two cities were always strained and trade had been encouraged as much where possible to build bridges between them.

Fern turned and her eyes widened in surprise to see that the words had in fact come from the Allfather himself. A little surprised that he was outside the city walls she remained silent for a brief moment.

The Allfather spoke again.

"A swarm that large may devastate the harvest in Sanctuary, hunger and famine may become rife, perhaps you should take your guard and make your way over there, show them that Astoria still cares for the people of Sanctuary" he said.

"Yes Allfather, an excellent idea, I shall leave immediately" Fern returned, still a little bewildered by his intrusion. The Allfather had always been nothing but kind and fair in all his teachings and dealings with Fern, but there was something about him that made her feel the need to shy away. He held some unseen power that few could understand, but what was clear was that he radiated strength in levels beyond all others and it was this strength that made Fern, who feared no one, fear him.

"Oh and Fern, it is maybe advisable to take Crystal with you, just in case anything gets out of hand. Can't have Astoria being blamed for any...damage"

"Of course Allfather, I shall fetch her right away"

And with that Fern barked out a few orders and two of her Phoenix guard were jogging into the city while the rest were jogging with her toward Sanctuary.

The Allfather watched her leave and then turned and began to walk away; each step he took was placed directly in front of the other, carefully and meticulously, almost feminine in nature.

Slowly his dust robes fazed into a long black dress and the disguise vanished as quickly as it had been conjured. The female that remained smiled.

Out on the desert planes and on route to Sanctuary, Chance and Raphael were making good time. Raphael had chosen to remain virtually silent for the journey. He was still dealing with an inner anger at her for her antics that got them into this mess; she never listened to him and this time it had got them into really deep water.

Raphael thoughts drifted to her loss of memory and pondered this puzzle further. He could not understand why the old man robbed her of her memory? What purpose did it serve? He scratched his head as he played out the possible outcomes in his head.

Chance followed behind and had been feeling an inner boredom for the last few miles. Trying to spice the journey up a little she attempted to coax her trail leader into a game of some sorts to pass the time.

"What about a game of something?" she asked.

"No" was his simple reply.

"Oh come on this is tiresome and your chat is non-existent" she said. He remained silent.

"Ok, how about the first person to spot the city gets..."

"Nope" was his solid reply

"What about eye spy" Chance countered

"Nope"

"What about the guessing game, ill think of a number and you've to guess what I..."

"Nope" was his reply each time.

Chance was so bored. This stupid chimp wasn't any fun and they had been walking for what seemed like forever.

Her little feet were starting to get sore and she was positive she would have blisters.

"So who is this king tut?" she asked. She conceded to settling for general conversation, although she secretly made a game to herself that, since he was being so quiet and evasive, she would earn points every time she got an extended answer out of him.

'Ha it was genius' she thought, *'he wouldn't even know he was playing.'*

"King tut is also known as king of the Jamheads" he responded

'Damn', she thought, *'not a long enough response, mmm come on Chance you are smarter than this.'*

"What are the jam heads?" she asked.

"People with jam on their heads" he responded, still no points. She would have to try a different tactic.

"Can you please explain it to me please as my head hurts and Chance is tired" she deliberately put the cutest voice she was capable of on and then fluttered her blue eyes into his, carefully speaking of herself in the third person.

He paused and gazed at her, and for a split second she saw empathy in his eyes.

'.ha sucker 'she thought,*' got you!'*

"King Tut lives in Sanctuary and rules this section of the domain. He has a nose for making money and is well known for being really stubborn in his ways. He commands a large guard that keep the peace there but every now and then he likes to stir up trouble by increasing the trade value of his stocks. Much to the dismay of the Astorians"

Chance 1 chimp 0

"But pretty please tell me about the jam heads, what are they" she countered, again being all coy and using her beauty to her every advantage.

"The Jamheads are the slaves with which the King uses to run his land. Swarm flies are rife in this area so he has his people smear their heads with strawberry jam to attract the flies and therefore take the flies AWAY from his more privileged dwellers"

Chance 2 chimp 0

"But why use strawberry jam, I don't understand please help"

'Absolute *sucker chimp boy'* she thought!! *'Now I know why I keep you around'*

"Because strawberry jam gives off higher levels of pheromones from the sugar and the swarm flies can smell it from miles off"

Chance 3 chimp 0. Game, set and match.

She sniggered which then progressed into a loud "Ahahaha" style laugh.

He stopped in his tracks and turned to face her. His look of frustration was undeniably clear

"I know that laugh!" he said "did you just beat me at something??"

"Ahaha ahah ahaha" She laughed again quite uncontrollably. This chimp was good, she will give him that much.

She was about to make further comment when his demeanour changed altogether. His face was suddenly one of the utmost sincerity.

Chance looked right at him.

' Oh no' she thought,*' chimp is really going to smash my back....'*

And before she could even conclude that thought, the chimp lunged at her. Her world was instantly turned upside down and was being shoogled violently.

Her brain felt like it was being flipped from within her skull. Could she see? Yes? Light black light black light black.

She suddenly became aware that she was in fact hanging off the chimp and moving very quickly!

He must have thrown her over his shoulder and made a run for it...yes that's what it is; she was running, or being run.

' Wait a second', she thought, *'oh no get my face out your ass chimp boy.'*

Chance's positioning over his shoulder meant that she had the delightful view of his rear end as he made his way across the plain.

"Woooo why are we running chimp boy" she suddenly realised that her inner monologue had just become public.

'*Oops*' she thought.

There was no response. Probably from his exertion which, to be fair to the boy, they were travelling fairly fast.

Quite impressive actually, she made a note to commend the boy on his effort.

Dark light dark light dark light....that was all her vision would allow for now. Being upside down gave her a whole new perspective on the world she had found herself in today. It also gave her an increasingly sore stomach as her abdominals were pressed even harder against his toughened shoulder.

She suddenly caught sight of something.

Something very, very dark.

Chance strained her neck to get a better look without straining to close to his derrière. Yes definitely dark, like a large dark blanket covering the sky. Whatever it was, it was huge and was slowly blanking out the day's sun.

She strained her eyes to look closer and could see that although it was a huge mass, it was in fact made up of millions of tiny smaller objects bundled together, millions upon millions of them.

Her curiosity suddenly turned to dread when the penny finally dropped.

"Swa swa... SWAAARRMMMM" she screamed and used the full force of her abdominals to push herself upright. She then strapped her legs around his waist and found herself facing directly towards him as he powered onwards.

From her new position she could now make out the full extent of their peril. A swarm that thick would suffocate them both without a doubt.

Once again she craned her neck toward their destination. Her little heart sank. The city walls were now in sight but were still too far away. She couldn't see how they could possibly make it.

The swarm grew ever closer, a titanic mass of dark death, looming closer with every second that passed.

Wrapping herself tight around his body she could feel his every muscle pumping desperately to get them to safety. His heart was racing at alarming speeds. Chance found herself wishing she had a whip in her hand to push him on faster, at least she would feel like she was helping. She wasn't sure if he would appreciate that though but needs must!

The swarm's position now had started to block out the sun itself. Like a doom curtain closing in on them, the swarm came ever closer.

Chance craned her neck toward their goal, still too far.

'Come on' she thought.

She looked at the ground passing beneath their feet. She was pretty sure that he was still travelling faster than she could alone and she didn't want left behind so getting down was not an option.

The swarm above them had now formed the shape of an arrow head and she could just about make out its new direction which, to her peril, was aiming down towards them.

She looked hard at her muscle steed. From her position on his waist she could see he was starting to wane slightly. The poor boy was trying but it wasn't enough. She turned her head again and still the city was just out of reach.

She had to think and think fast!

And suddenly an idea played into her mind, it was not her style but if it kept them alive she would play helpless.

"Please, go faster I'm scared" she said into his ear.

As soon as she heard the words leave her lips, she felt quite pathetic and inwardly laughed at all those damsel in distresses that called out to their would be heroes in such a manner. She played the words over again in her head and she cursed them. Yeah she was scared but it just wasn't her style to show weakness. Well, she figured they won't have long to live now anyway so what the hell.

Remarkably though she felt him tense up just a little harder. Looking toward the ground she reckoned he HAD sped up. They were running faster... quite a bit faster...they might actually make it.

She kept her eyes dodging between the flying black hulk above them and the city walls in front.

Almost

Almost

Almost there.....

She could hear his breathing blasting out his mouth now. It sounded like more air was leaving his lungs than could ever have possibly fitted in.

The swarm above them, making full use of its arrow head formation, had begun to dive bomb at great speeds towards them.

Just about there.

She held on tight now, gripping him around the back of his muscular neck. She realised that her grip must have been leaving marks on his skin as her panic had truly set in now. She closed her eyes and hoped for the best.

To her absolute relief, this moment of vulnerability came to a crashing end as they burst through a small wooden door that was set into the city walls.

The swarm could be heard buzzing on over the top of the city walls as it went searching for jam. They had made it and were safe as they tumbled to the ground, their pace bled to nothing.

A few moments passed and nothing was said as they both lay in silence. Chance became suddenly aware that she was pinned beneath her steed. Breathing dangerously heavy, she allowed him but a moment longer to relax before she would hurl him off her.

She leaned her head back to free herself, straining her neck muscles hard to put some distance between them and then with two hands she pushed gently on the top of his chest to indicate it was time for him to move.

For a brief moment her eyes met his and she found herself curiously looking deep into them. In that moment she felt a flash of something, something warm and familiar but she immediately dismissed it.

"There's a good boy" she said mockingly tapping his head, "Now now, why didn't you just run that fast in the first place?" she said.

He rolled his eyes instantly and toppled off her and lay on his back. His chest was heaving dangerously hard.

Chance climbed to her feet and began to asses her surroundings. It looked like they had arrived in some sort of cellar. There was another wooden door at the far end of the room, and the floor was littered with old barrels and wooden crates.

The room smelled old and dusky, kind of like the way a cellar should smell she concluded.

She looked down at her clothes and realised she was absolutely filthy. The floor of the cellar had been covered in dirt and dust and in her few moments of lying in it had completely taken away her style. She cursed herself for allowing such dirt into her life.

She turned her gaze back to her wounded steed. She angled her head so she could meet his eyes.

His eyes were blood shot, his face was shot red and there was a small trickle of blood coming from his nose. He wasn't in good shape. He was still breathing dangerously heavy and it sounded like one of his lungs had been damaged as with every breath he took a deep whistling sound could be heard.

He looked at her long and hard, trying to regain some level of composure, and as if sensing her need to go, he waved her on without him.

That suited her, she preferred to do things alone anyway and besides, she HAD made a promise to drop him at the next port and here they were.

Sensing that awkward moment of goodbye, Chance turned casually and headed for the far door. She didn't even look back.

CHAPTER 4

After helping out her new friend Paula, whom was affectionately known as Pepper, Pepsy then discovered that Jeremy had in fact packed his bag and made his way to Sanctuary.

She calculated that from his rough time of leaving, to now that he should have arrived in the sister city already and so she 'shifted' straight here to cut him off.

Teleporting to Sanctuary was less than easy to her as it was a route through wavespace that she had embarked upon many times in her past, this journey was no different as she 'shifted' straight into the middle of the busy market where the civilians were going about their way. It had been a long time since Pepsy had been to Sanctuary, a long time indeed. The occupants here often viewed Astorians as too righteous or up their own egos. There seemed to be a class difference between Astorians and the Sanctuary inhabitants and as much as the Allfather tried to bridge this bond, it seemed to be forever out of reach.

Pepsy turned and started to walk to the north end of the market, an area that she knew quite well to have a few bars and drinking establishments. She was pretty sure these were the places Jeremy would head to first upon his arrival to quench his insatiable thirst. His habits had become predictable over the years at the very least.

 The market dwellers instantly recognised Pepsy as an Angel of Astoria and eyed her both suspiciously and amazingly. It wasn't too often that an Angel would visit the city and on many occasion it would be to meet with the king or perhaps a meeting with Ganon the master of magnetism. It was very rare to see an Angel wandering the streets without an entourage, very rare indeed.

Her wandering took her up past the north end of the market where she checked the bars there but to no avail. She stood at the top of a tall set of stairs and surveyed her surroundings. Her eyes then caught the unmistakable form of another Angel, her beautiful blonde hair flowing in the light breeze as she made her way along the side street.

Pepsy eyes went wide as she rushed down to meet this Angel.

She wove her way through the streets of Astoria delicately and meticulously. Taking her time and enjoying every moment of the chaos she was causing. Here and there, where she could sense the works of the anger pheromones was at its strongest, she would stop and gently whisper into the ear of the nearest Astorian.

"They are all going to leave you.... leave you in this city to rot" she whispered.

She walked on, a cruel and arrogant smile playing across her lips. She marvelled at how effective Kane's devices had been at spreading fear and panic amongst the city dwellers. A simple work of chemistry and suddenly the people were just as vulnerable to corruption as any other.

She ensured that she added to this panic as much as she possibly could as she travelled her way around the busy areas, her gift allowing her to float relatively unseen, spreading her whisperings like hypnotic suggestions. These suggestions were setting fear deep into the hearts of its dwellers and she could see that the devices smuggled into the city had worked perfectly. They had been secreting a small amount of neural calming inhibitor pheromones into the air. Once inhaled, these pheromones reduced the person's ability to remain calm or think rationally, blocking out the sense required to remain patient and instead allowing the persons natural animal instincts for survival take over, it was in effect a riot causing device and it was working like a dream she thought.

She walked on, running her fingertips unseen along the backs of the shoulders of one broad man before stopping at his ear and whispering.

"They will not protect you..Their loyalty is only to themselves." And then she walked on with a creepy smile across her face.

This kind of work had been Childs play for her. Everywhere she looked she could feel the tension in the people's hearts. She could see the anxiety building in their faces and their need to unleash it in bouts of shouting and angry explosions. She could hear their teeth grinding in an attempt to hold back their frustrations. She passed a woman standing near a stall; already this woman had the stink of anger around her. She was complaining to the market vendor about the quality of the fruit there. Complaining? It was such a strange concept for an Astorian. She crept past her slowly...taking extra special care on this suggestion.

"The big one eats all the good fruit, he greedily takes and samples what is rightfully yours...What you work hard for and PAY for..And he takes it for his greedy self...he thinks because he is Angel he can, but what has he ever done for you?"

She allowed the thought to linger before moving on. The carnage that she was causing with simply a thought was extraordinary. Today was going to be a very good day she thought as she walked on through the crowds, spreading 'her word'.

Gregor quickly gathered his things together as he glanced briefly at the time. He knew he had to get down to his 'spot' just in time to catch the market dwellers as they leave after the morning shop. Already he was running late. He looked at all his equipment before him and took quick stock before heading off. He had his bagpipes, his credit token card and also a stand to hold it on. He also had his lunch ready in a small bag that his mum had pre-prepared for him. He had planned a long day busking and didn't want to have to leave his location for any reason at all.

Once satisfied that he had everything he needed, he set off out the door and made his way down the main habitat walkway. His hands were full, and so he had to hold his bagpipes up high on his little chest, almost obscuring his vision as he hurried along the pebbled street.

In his mind he was fantasising about what he was going to spend his hard earned credits on. He really wanted his own pair of *Superfuse* gloves, specially designed to enhance the neural connection speed between the player and the table's handles. He had read all about them in his monthly subscription to 'Sport Astoria' and had been

84

eager to get a pair ever since. They were however, quite expensive, and he did wonder how he was going to justify this to his mother. Perhaps he would hide them from her? Hide them where though? Under his bed? Too obvious, behind his wardrobe perhaps? Not easily accessible.

Gregor hadn't even realised that he had started into a small run. He was late, and earning enough credits for his gloves was all dependent on catching the early marketers as well as the late afternoon lot. If he didn't make swift progress now, he would miss the morning group entirely and so he picked up the pace as much as he could. The increase in speed however did cause him problems with his line of sight, as the various artefacts that he was carrying continued to bounce higher and higher within his grasp.

The route was familiar to him, having walked this route many times before in his young life, he could have virtually have made the journey blindfolded, that is, until somebody got in his way, and just when he turned the corner, this was the exact obstruction that foiled his pace.

He managed but a brief glimpse of their face at the last minute, through the obscured view between the various sprouts of his pipes, he saw a beautifully tanned face of a girl, but it was all too late. He dug his feet in hard to the ground and braced for impact.

Strangely, no collision ever came, and the simple act of digging his heels in had actually sent him off balance, crashing embarrassingly to the floor. He landed hard, face first down into the pebbled street, spilling his stand, his pipes and his credit token card halfway across the street in a calamity of noise that echoed off the stone walls of the buildings around him. His palms were red raw from the slapping motion he made on impact with the ground, and he felt his knee ache, as it must have struck the unforgiving surface.

"Hey where are you going in such a hurry?" a soft voice asked. Gregor turned his head and was slightly bewildered by what he saw. Standing above him was a beautifully tanned girl with deep dark hair tied up in a bun on top of her head, she was displaying the whitest set of teeth that he had ever set eyes upon. She had pretty brown eyes, or were they dark green? He couldn't make them out clearly from where he was lying, but he stared on regardless, he stared mostly because she was there...but she wasn't there.

85

He shook his head and then rubbed his eyes with both hands. When he opened them again, she was still standing over him smiling, and the effect was the same. It was like she was some kind of ghost.

She stretched out her hand, and Gregor noticed that each of her nails were immaculately maintained and coated in a shiny red paint, on her third finger she had a small symbol feature, as he looked closer he could just about make out the rough shape of a love heart, carefully painted in pink amongst the border of red.

He reached out and tried to take her hand, but his attempt failed, his hand grasped thin air and he slouched forward slightly as the weight of his upper body fell through the motion. He tried again and once again his hand fell right through hers. He looked up at her confused. She laughed.

"I'm sorry I always forget "she said and then a moment later she was completely there before him. The ghosted visage was gone.

Gregor rubbed his eyes once more, ensuring that he had not struck his head in some way when he had fallen, but true enough, there she was in front of him now, and in full colour. He saw that she was wearing black stretch trousers and a loose fitting sparkly blue top that came off at her shoulders, all of which were no longer ghosted, no longer a mirage against the backdrop of the building. She was definitely there now, there was no doubting it.

She leant down further and helped haul him to his feet. His eyes never left hers. He was truly amazed, he found her beautiful.

"Are you one of those gifted?" he asked her, as sense slowly returned to him. Gregor had learned very quickly over the years, that there were many strange anomalies in Astoria, weird, peculiar and truly amazing incidents that were witnessed everyday by the good people there, and in all cases, the explanation would always be related to one of the Angels and their powers. She smiled at him further.

"Yes I am gifted, my name is Ariana, and what is your name?" she replied.

"Gregor" he answered quickly, he had little interest in talking about himself; he wanted to know more about her, she seemed AMAZING.

From where he was now standing, he estimated that she must have been in her mid twenties. He had grown quite a skill for determining people's age, taking the time to analyse their eyes, their skin and their complexion before making his estimations. Nine times out of ten, he was spot on, much to the dismay of his mother, whom hated nothing more than to be reminded of her age.

"Do you get to go in to the palace then? Like the other Angels?" he asked, his curiosity for Angels was grand. He had only ever met a few of them, and none of them were as fascinating as this Ariana before him. There were always stories going around about the Angels, their latest endeavours and adventures, and Gregor ensured he listened intently to them all, never missing any piece of vital information.

"I am sadly not an Angel little Gregor, so no I don't go in to the palace" she said.

"But you have gifts...doesn't that make you an Angel?" confusion crossed his little face. He thought that anyone with a gift would be an Angel.

"I chose not to be. My gift is, well, not that helpful really, so I opted out of graduation" she said, a small look of sorrow crossing her beautiful features as she reminisced to her old hopes and dreams, which still remained unfulfilled. Gregor watched this happen and realised that she didn't suit an unhappy look, although he didn't know what to say or do to change it.

"But your gift is amazing, you can go...you can be...you can" he struggled to comprehend exactly what her gift was. It seemed to him that she seemed to ghost out of thin air. He couldn't touch her, but he could still kind of see her. His smile dropped from his face also, as he realised that she was in fact correct, what really COULD she do with a gift like that.

He fell silent and she looked him up and down closely.

"You never told me where you were going in such a hurry?" she asked him.

"Oh it doesn't matter now, I am too late" he replied and placed his hands into his pockets.

"Late? Where were you going?" she asked him. She knelt down slightly to peer under his saddened drop of his head. She gazed into his little brown eyes with her enchanting gaze; he couldn't hold her look for long, he found her so beautiful and her direct attention was intoxicating for the young boy, he quickly went red faced with embarrassment and looked away as he replied.

"I was going to catch the marketers as they left the morning trade, but ill have missed them by now. I wanted to play my bagpipes and make money"

Ariana stood up straight and regarded him slightly.

"Market dwellers hey, they will head to the north exit, out by the Angel dwellings. If we move fast we can still make it" she said rather confidently.

"The main market will be packed and I am too little to get through. I won't make it in time" he said. Sadness was evident in his every word.

"Trust me little guy, you'll make it through. Get your things and then take my hand. There is but one use for my gifts today" she said.

As Gregor placed his little hand in hers, she activated her gift, making her entire body ghost out. The gift then stretched on and over Gregor's body also. He felt a warm tingle run through and over his chest and then down each of his limbs, it was a sensation he had never felt before. Within a mere moment they were both standing where they were, but resembled a light shimmer of their normal selves. Ariana looked down at him and winked.

They took off on a run, hand in hand, and started to pass through all obstacles that came in their way, boxes, crates, animals, people and ghosting their way straight through them. A huge smile now crossed his little face. He was going to make it in time.

High up in the palace observation chamber, the Allfather stood by the huge open window looking down upon the whole of Astoria. In his left hand he held a cup of dungletea which he had barely drank. His mind was deep in thought, attempting to solve the mystery of what was unfolding before him. Even from high up in the palace, the Allfather could 'feel' the change in the mood of the city. It wasn't something tangible that he could reach out and touch, but it was definitely there.

He watched as the Astorians hurried about their business. To him they all seemed a little bit more aroused today than usual and he just could not understand why. He witnessed something that, to others may have just been a simple act or accident, but to the keen eye of the Allfather he knew there was something sinister to it. He had watched as one Astorian had made his way across the plaza and virtually shoulder charged his way through the crowds and headed off toward the gaming quadrant.

No apology was given whatsoever. The man had barged his way through and then kept walking, he didn't even look back.

The door to the observation chamber slid open behind him and Spanners made his way into the room. He walked slowly up to the Allfather's side and shared the viewing portal of the great window. The familiarity between these two was so great that they didn't even turn to address one another, even though protocol dictated that the Allfather outranked Spanners and therefore should be addressed face on.

"Sir we have had more tech readings entering the city although I am now having trouble pinpointing them. It's almost as if the devices are somehow hidden from the type of sensor we use" Spanners reported. The Allfather merely nodded to confirm he had heard it all clearly. He then took a small slurp of his tea, all the while keeping his eyes fixed outside the window.

Spanners waited for a moment and then took the Allfather's silence as a queue to continue.

"Also sir, I have detected a pollutant in the air, its nature is unknown along with its origin. It would seem some parts of the city are more infected than others" Spanners added. With that the Allfather furrowed his brow and turned to face him.

"A pollutant? Is it toxic? Dangerous?" he asked.

"It doesn't seem to register as toxic, our sensors are programmed to recognise any pollutant that is directly hazardous to our health as toxic therefore I would logically assume that any danger may come from its after effects ON the city itself. It could be perhaps some corrosive pollutant that would weaken the walls without harming flesh? I hypothesise this conclusion, as it is around the perimeter wall that the readings are at its highest" Spanners replied.

"Hmm, weaken our walls, perhaps a pre-cursor to an attack? Where are the Angels? I have not seen any of them this day?" the Allfather asked.

"I have not seen them either sir. Not a single one"

"Finding the Angels is a priority one and get them to garrison and patrol the perimeter walls. See if you can locate these tech-devices. I feel there is a sinister plan at work here" the Allfather replied. Spanners nodded, turned and made his way out of the chamber. The Allfather continued to stare out of the window.

The room had become chillingly cold. Almost as if a gust of evil cold air had blown in from an open window, except this room had no windows. The clay domiciles that he had erected outside the city were designed to retain heat at all costs. Candle light was required to illuminate them as leaving open spaces for windows reduced insulation.

The candles flickered and the old man raised his head from the table, instantly sensing the change in ambience of the room.

He scanned the room slowly, peering to each of the dusky dark corners, noting the volume of cobweb build-up in each section, and making a mental note to chastise the peasants, whose duty it had been to clean the domicile.

He was by no means a meticulous man, but he loathed laziness wherever he saw it, the cobwebs reflected that crime, reflecting the inattention to detail and he made a mental note, to plan a suitable punishment.

For now he was intent on finding the source of his disturbance.

The room was by no means large; it had a single desk upon which the old man worked, a large bookcase stacked with volumes of dusty books, which had been written in a time long since forgotten. There were no skylights or slits for any light whatsoever bar the heavy wooden main door, and it had certainly not moved, for opening that door would have given noise to a cacophony of loud creaks and squeals from hinges long past their worn use.

To his conclusion, the room was empty, and yet he still felt a strong sense of unease course through his old bones.

This unease quickly turned to dread as the silence was broken.

"You have remembered our...." there was a pause, the cold speaker delivering its words carefully "arrangement"

The question was reciprocal and the old man considered the nature of the intrusion. He had no need to set eyes on the intruder, nor had he any wish to, he instantly knew who they were and chose to keep his fear in check.

He replied slowly as to display a modicum of calm.

"I would hope you would be pleased with my progress thus far father?" the old man replied.

"Hope" it paused "is the first step on the road to disappointment...do you plan to disappoint me?" its words cut like a cold blade straight through the old man's resolve.

He averted his gaze down, overpowered by the presence that had ghosted its way into his chambers.

"No father, I plan to honour"

"Honour?" the cold, careful voice cut in once more, the question needed not to be answered, the sincerity in the voice, reminded the old man of his place in this scheme that was far from honourable.

A silence drifted between them.

He was unsure if the voice had left the room or if it had even entered it in the first place. His gaze remained submissively looking at his desk.

The silence was deafening now but he dare not look up, he had borne witness to this beings power, and knew it was enough to strike fear into the very heart of his soul.

He held his breath.

After what seemed like an eternity, the voice spoke again.

"The swarm was a mistake..." each word was spoken so calmly and carefully "it could have jeopardised my plans" it continued.

The old man stowed his head, his old claw hands beginning to shake. He could feel the level of choler that was aimed toward him, which this being was barely keeping in check.

"Tolerance is a sign of weakness..... Do you think me weak?"

To answer anything short of no, would have certainly guaranteed his doom. In reality, this being had once been epically powerful, causing havoc amongst these lands and creating fear wherever it stalked. It had eventually been banished, and so in all respects it HAD been 'weakened', but he dare not hint at weak.

"No father" the old man replied, sorrow creeping through his voice. His claw hands were shaking violently now.

"Then heed my warning....I will tolerate no more failings" "transport the orb to me...ensure it arrives here quickly"

"Yes father, how will they know where to look for it?"

"The...Siren...will deal with that" the voice ghosted off toward the end.

The candle flickered once more and the presence was gone.

The old man exhaled.

He stood up, dusted down his robes and called out to his peasant servants; he felt angry, he felt debased, and he aimed to transfer

these feelings of disgrace upon his weak followers, he had some
retribution to dish out.

CHAPTER 5

Chance wandered around Sanctuary with the pace of an awe inspired explorer, taking in all her surroundings and enjoying all the new smells and sounds. She would be forever turning on the spot and marvelling at some new sight that passed her by or some strange looking person that caught her attention. She found herself people watching constantly, and sometimes the people would watch her back. Some appeared disinterested in her and would look away; others would gasp almost in recognition, and then point toward her, she smiled every time this happened, was she some kind of celebrity? She was clearly well known but for what reason? She smiled as a list of potential identities flowed through her mind. Maybe she was a famous entertainer? Maybe she was royalty? Whoever she was, it was clear that the inhabitants of Sanctuary were shocked to see her simply wandering around these parts, and this excited her even more.

The further into the city she walked, she found the dwellers all the more exciting. Some wore strange long cloaks that hid most of their bodies and faces; others wore simple, flesh bearing garments that would show off any body art they had inscribed onto themselves. Here and there she passed what seemed to be the local enforcement in the area, as there were guards wearing rusted metal armour, some carrying long staves with mechanical tips; others carried no weapon at all.

As she turned around the next corner, she heard a voice call her name; just as she turned she got a sudden fright, as out of nowhere there was a blonde woman standing directly next to her.

Had she crept up on her? Impossible, it was a fairly open area and she had been looking around constantly, and yet here this lady was.

"Chance sweetheart how are you?" the lady said. Chance was a little taken aback. The lady was smiling and seemed friendly, but she had somehow sneaked right up on her and she didn't like that one bit.

"Erm do I know you?" Chance replied, a genuine question in her response.

"Haha you are a funny girl. Where is Raphael? You haven't seen Jeremy have you? He is winding me up the wrong way today, I've been looking for him everywhere.." the lady had bombarded her with so many questions all at once, that she wasn't sure which one she should prioritise and respond to.

"Errr... Jeremy?" she answered, furrowing her brow in a puzzled look. The lady seemed not to notice that she had in fact, no idea to whom she was referring. The lady spoke on anyway.

"Ah you haven't seen him either; oh that boy is in big trouble! Oh wait here...give this to Raphael, if he keeps losing it HE will be in big trouble too, and you can tell him that from me"

The lady handed Chance a little blue inhaler, it was a small Lastic 'L' shaped device and fitted neatly into her hand. She looked at it for a moment, realising that she had in fact planned to abandon the chimp boy when they arrived here, it would be unfair of her to take his medication that was intended for him, if she wasn't going to see him again. She held her hand in the same position, stretched out in front of her, before speaking.

"Erm well actually I wasn't planning on seeing him again, so I'd be the wrong person to give this to" the words had barely left her mouth before the lady drew a puzzled look and then burst out laughing.

"Oh Chance, you are so funny sometimes, you nearly had me there" and then the lady playfully tapped her on the shoulder.

"No really I..." Chance tried to say but the lady's attention turned towards an old man that walked along the causeway, she completely turned away from her to greet this newcomer.

The old man was wearing a long, silver cloak that stretched down toward his ankles and covered his feet. His hair was white and cropped short upon his head and his face was covered neatly in a thin, white beard. He had old and brown caring eyes and he walked with a pace that bore no stress.

"GANON! HOW ARE YOU?" the lady said and embraced the old man in a hug.

95

"I am well young Pepsy and how are you? I see little Chance is here also, and what do we owe the pleasure of such Angels here in Sanctuary" Ganon replied.

"Well, I have been hunting high and low for that little monkey Jeremy, have you seen him?"

"Ha-ha, has he eluded the great teleporter yet again?" Ganon replied.

"YES and this time for longer than usual" Pepsy looked to the ground as her mind tried to deal with the fact she had been outsmarted since the day before, it had been the longest that he had ever managed to evade her for, and it didn't sit well with her.

"Ah well my dear, I am sure the fool will be down near the liquor quadrant, he likes to get a skin full I am told" Ganon said.

"Thank you and once again it is great to see you"

"Send my brother my best" Ganon shouted.

"I will, listen I've gotta run" Pepsy said, "oh and Chance, take this, it's a homing beacon, if you want a 'shift' home just hit the button" she threw her a little silver crescent shaped artefact, before turning and rushing down the street for a few yards before vanishing before their very eyes.

Chance looked on bewildered; the nice lady had literally disappeared, leaving behind a mere purple cloud of smoke that eventually dissipated. The sharp departure seemed abrupt, but it did explain how she had managed to sneak up on her.

She looked down into her hand at the little silver device she had been given. It was fairly small, fitting neatly into the palm of her hand, and along the edges were small red lights that pulsed ever so slightly. In its centre, there was a clear and distinct button about the size of her fingertip; she surmised this button would activate the device. Placing it safely into her back pocket along with the little blue inhaler, she turned to look at Ganon carefully; he drew a big smile and outstretched his arms, requesting an embrace. She reluctantly declined.

"Are you ok little one? Not going to give your uncle a hug?"

"My uncle, I don't know you?" she replied, her head was beginning to ache from all the excitement and wonders that were occurring all around her. Now she was face to face with her uncle and she didn't even recognise him, if he was in fact her uncle at all.

Ganon looked very puzzled, he knew she was a practical joker at times, but he found something very honest and sincere about her response today.

"You aren't joking either are you little one?" he said more seriously this time.

"Nope" she said, shaking her head. Ganon scratched his well kept beard, trying to logically understand the situation.

"Has something happened that you are aware of, that has caused your memory loss?" he asked her.

"I think so, the chimp boy told me an old man must have taken my memory, and then he banished us from a place called..ermm"

"Astoria?"

"That's the one, but he didn't say much more. He doesn't say much at all to be honest. Pretty useless that one" she said and her mind wandered to the journey across the desert, when her chimp boy was refusing to tell her anything.

"And where is, your 'chimp boy'...Raphael now?" Ganon asked, immediately knowing to whom she had been referring to.

"Erm I don't know actually, I ditched him earlier on, some old cellar in the city walls"

"I see" "and does he have the same memory loss that you have?"

"I don't think so, he seemed to know things" Chance replied.

Ganon pondered all that he was taking in. He walked closer and leaned in close to her, speaking slightly quieter so as what was said would remain between them both.

"Chance darling, I am your uncle and I care about you very much, this situation is as much alarming as it is puzzling but I will get to the bottom of this but I want you to stay here, try and find Raphael if you can, he will keep you safe from harm, but be mindful young one, you are vulnerable here and I have dark feelings about the source behind these events. Find Raphael and get him to contact Pepsy, she will take you to safety. Trust no-one bar myself, Raphael and Pepsy ok?"

"Erm yes ok, where are you going?" Chance asked, although she wasn't entirely that interested in the answer.

"I am going to see your father" he replied and walked off.

Chance watched him disappear into the distance and she stood there playing over the last parts of the conversation to herself.

'I'm going to see your father...I am going to see YOUR father..I am GOING to see your fatherrr' she repeated over and over. Changing the subject in the sentence each time she said it to change the dynamics of the statement.

"Find the chimp boy and he will keep you safe...pffft ill crack the funnies here old guy" she said quite openly.

'Why are they all so serious here' she thought 'you are vulnerable' she thought again. 'blablabla I don't feel vulnerable' she said to herself as she began to make her way slowly out of the street and entered into the market area of the city. Her mind was easily distracted once again by all manners of new experiences that unfolded before her.

She weaved her way through the busy crowds admiring all manner of strange devices and artefacts, everything she came across seemed new and exciting and she felt the need to satisfy her curiosity at every turn by touching and tasting all kinds of gifts and treats.

She passed by so many people and marvelled at all their differences; some were really tall and skinny with paper thin limbs and long faces, she noticed that these individual had up to seven fingers at times and it puzzled her as to their genetic purpose.

Others she saw were short and stout with one little man bearing four, very muscular arms.

This place fresh to her, it seemed new and it seemed AMAZING!

She wandered on awhile more and came to rest on a small round stone pillar that was positioned at the top of a small narrow staircase that led down into a dark alley and off into the side streets. There were multiple possible routes that she could take from here and so she paused and battled with her subconscious as to which route would bear the most fruit. Which route would be the most exciting and entertain her the most.

The noise of the busy city had almost become a jumble to her now and she was able to block it out and focus once again on individual sounds.

Upon resting she thought she could hear the sound of sobbing. She turned around and scanned the area but she could see nothing. She hopped up from the stone pillar and cocked her head slightly, trying to pinpoint the sobbing and determine its location.

She heard it again, the definitive sound of sniffing followed by more sobbing, but where?

She was very patient; standing on sentry she listened hard and waited. With each similar sound she was able to home in on its position. She concluded that it must be coming from down the small set of stairs and into the alley.

Fearless and with a newfound sense of purpose Chance slowly made her way down the stairs, keeping her head cocked to one side and her ear straining hard.

As she turned a small corner she could see a little girl with her head in her hands. This little girl has the most beautiful long blonde hair, she looked very young by Chances estimation and she was wearing a little pink dress with pink slide on shoes. The sobbing was undoubtedly emanating from her.

Chance made her way up to her and began to speak.

"Hey little girl, why are you crying?"

The girl instantly stopped, she lifted her head and peered into Chances beautiful blue eyes. The little girls face was streaming with tears and her eyes were bloodshot. Through the bloodshot teary eyes, though Chance could make out a set of green peepers peering directly at her. The girl said nothing and just watched her.

Chance moved a little closer and placed one hand on the little girls back for comfort and then sat down beside her.

The little girl sniffed really hard and cleared her nose as best as she could, she then took her left hand and wiped it across her face to clear her tears. She finally spoke.

"Are you an Angel?" she asked "an Astorian Angel? You look like one"

"Well babygurl, from where I am sitting it is you that look like an Angel" Chance replied.

A huge smile filled the little girl's face, her eyes smiled too.

"Really? You think so? One day I want to be an Angel and live in Astoria" the girl said this with true conviction and Chance realised that she was in fact hearing this little girl's life ambition.

"What is your name little girl?" Chance asked

"My name is Jessica, what is your name?" the little girl replied. It was clear to Chance that life here in Sanctuary had been tough on this little girl, and she was certainly far from shy.

"My name is Chance, although I seemed to have misplaced my memory today so that is all I can tell you about me"

Jessica's eyes widened so bright, as if she had just been told she was sitting next to the very rich or the very famous.

"Oh oh oh..." she became too excited to speak "THE Chance?? Oh my goodness it is you" Jessica said.

"Surely there is more than one Chance in this sorry sand ravaged world?"

"Nope nope, names are unique here, there is only one Chance same as I'm the only Jessica, oh wow it is you, the Allfathers daughter" Chance cut her off

"How do you know so much about me?" Chance asked. "nobody seems to be able to tell me anything today" she added

"I have a painting of you in my room fighting the bone men, I want to be like you when I grow up" Jessica said, her face then fell sullen once more "but they are going to cut all my hair off" she began to sob once more.

"WHAT? Why? You have beautiful hair" Chance exclaimed

"Because of the flies, they are getting worse and the King makes us low serving people shave our heads so he can smear them with jam to attract the flies and keep them away from his fancy rich friends." Jessica said.

'So that's what chimp boy meant when he said jam heads' she thought.

"That is madness babygurl!!! I will not allow anyone to cut your lovely hair do not worry, what a strange notion, surely there are other ways to deal with the flies?"

"Well I used to have my little pet Misty" Jessica's face began to stream with tears once more "she was a little kelpie and she kept the flies away. But the king sent her away to live on the plains, he said she had gotten too big and fat." Jessica rubbed her eyes.

"I miss her so much, I sometimes call on her, and she comes to see me, but she can't stay long or ill get into trouble" Jessica added. She continued to sob. The loss of her pet had clearly been a major part in this young girl's life, the loss of her pet and then the potential loss of her beautiful hair, this poor girls life was tough Chance thought. She remained quiet, a little saddened by the story that was unfolding before her.

Jessica suddenly became excited and hopped up.

"Hey Chance, you could meet her for me one day? You could take her favourite biscuits to her and tell her I miss her and still love her, would you do that for me? Would you?"

"Of course I will darling, but how will I find little Misty?"

101

"Oh that part is easy, here take this, it's a kelpie kiss, one toot on that and she will be right with you" Jessica handed Chance a small, shiny little artefact. It was about the length of her finger and along one side had intermittent holes that must have been relevant to different notes. It looked like it was a form of musical instrument. It was very lightweight and would fit easily into her pocket. As Chance turned it over in her hands a strange green shimmer ran the length of the instrument. At first Chance thought she had imagined it, but she turned it over again and once it had caught the light it shimmered again. It was fascinating.

Jessica sat back onto the wall next to Chance and then cuddled into her. Chance was a little taken aback by the sudden embrace but then placed her arm around Jessica regardless.

"I am so glad I met you today" little Jessica said.

Meanwhile, near the main gates to Sanctuary, Ganon scratched his chin as he considered the implications of the situation he found his niece in. She had, in all manners, lost her memory which was alarming enough on the best of days. He walked along the castle battlements and thought long and hard about the meaning behind this.

'Lost her memory? Or had it taken from her, and for what purpose?'

Ganon was always a logical man and would think through every possible outcome to every possible situation. As a general of an army he was really quite something, putting his gift aside his mind could easily engineer a victory from certain doom, making full use of logic engines to work his way through problems. He was now using such logic in an attempt to understand the nature behind this trivial event.

'By taking her memory, what would she forget, who she was? What she could do? Her happy memories, her...' Ganon paused; a sudden realisation had kicked in. His old eyes widened at the new found possibilities that this logical chain of thought had taken.

"Oh dear" he said aloud, and at that he suddenly found purpose in his actions. He had to head to Astoria to see his brother; he had to float the idea to him that the whole land could be in very grave danger.

With that, Ganon raised both his hands up wide, magnetic power began to flow through his arms, reflecting off the old metals that were buried deep beneath the land he was able to project himself high into the sky.

He angled his body slightly and then manipulated the magnetic fields to propel himself at great speeds toward Astoria.

The land was passing by very quickly beneath him and he noted that far below there was unmistakably the Phoenix guard jogging across the plains. Raising his head he powered on, a newfound urgency in his actions.

His magnetic bubble was capable of travelling at great speeds so long as there was metal beneath him to project himself along. Luckily for Ganon that the old disused oil pipes ran the lengths between Sanctuary and Astoria and so he was able to make good time. He would arrive within the hour.

On the far side of Sanctuary, Angel Pepsy searched in and out of each of the drinking establishments that she had found in this sector. Most of them were fairly empty and so a simple peering in through the door was usually sufficient enough to determine whether he was in there or not.

She was having no such luck and had searched through at least seven bars already.

'*Seven bars*?' she thought, Sanctuary certainly had enough places to drink away ones problems, although she did believe that the drink ITSELF was part of the problem and this area had seven times as many problems as an Astorian street would.

She continued on as quickly as she could and she came to yet another bar and by this stage frustration really was starting to kick in. She didn't know why exactly she felt so protective of Jeremy, was he the only real link she had left to her beloved Lucas? Was that why she did her best to keep him healthy and try getting him back on the straight and narrow?

She knew deep down that Jeremy still hadn't learned how to cope with the death of his friend. Even after all these years he was still using slogan juice to ease the pain.

Pepsy thought back to that fateful day, out in the tribinium fields.

She could remember 'shifting' in to a small clearing between the toxic purple crystals. The rain was pouring down hard and the distinct sounds of epic weapons clashing could be heard. The wind was violent and the entire world seemed to be erupting from the carnage that was unfolding.

She remembered that she had done her duty; she had focussed on the task that had been set. She had followed her instructions to the letter.

She was not to get involved.

She had to get the others to safety, and it was clearly obvious why.

The rescue had almost been complete. Just before she 'shifted' them back to safety she had made the error of looking up, looking directly at the source of the clashing.

What she saw will stick with her for all her days.

She had never found the words to describe it, although she had read a scripture once about ancient titans clashing in a time long forgotten and she imagined it to have been similar, an epic hero taking on the might of a titanic warlord. Each strike and slash of their famous swords was parried with sparks and concussion blasts that shook the earth.

Pepsy shook the thought clear and focussed on the present. The drifting thought though had left a deep feeling of concern in her stomach, the same concern she had felt that fateful day for her love Lucas, but now the concern lay there and she hadn't noticed that she was now frantically making her way toward any passersby.

"Have you seen Jeremy, he is this tall, looks like" she asked

"No was the blunt reply"

She moved on to the next person whom she stood directly in front of.

"Have you seen Jeremy" she blurted out.

"I don't even know who you are lady!" the man replied.

"Did I ask you if you knew me? No! I asked if you'd seen Jeremy!" Pepsy found herself being very snippy now and the man just shook his head and walked off.

Pepsy stopped briefly for a moment, realising that she had lost her cool and wasn't thinking straight. She took a few deep breaths in and allowed herself to clear her mind. She hadn't slept in almost thirty hours.

It had been a long day.

Wallace was standing on the edge of a market stall in Astoria investigating the meats that were hanging there, waiting to be sold. There were all manner of animals that had been caught out on the desert plains and brought back to the city and smoked. Wallace was particularly interested in the leg of wildagoat, a huge wild animal that roamed the plains in herds and yet were incredibly fast and difficult to catch, making it a delicacy amongst the city goers. The leg hung there looking delicious and just recently free from the smoking rooms. A huge grin had crossed his face and his gleaming white teeth shone in the day's sun.

"Oh if you need that sampled for quality testing id be more than happy to help" he said to the vendor. The vendor was an old and very friendly man. He was very well liked and had worked the market for longer than anyone could remember and could often be found playing dice games with the children once the market had closed. He ran his market stall not for profit but more for quality of service, which he then of course made a huge profit as his reputation had soared for having the tastiest meats around. A humble man that even on the quiet weeks, he was more than happy just to get by.

"Of course Wallace, I always respect your opinion on my goods, ill cut you a slice and let me know what you think, I smoked it along with some wild onion and even threw in some dungleweed for extra flavour, let me know how it tastes"

"Oh Jim, you always know how to put a smile on my face" Wallace exclaimed and then rubbed his hands together in eagerness of the tasting to come. As he did so, four of the market dwellers stopped and looked on.

"There he is...that's the fat Angel walks around this market eating everyone's produce...quality testing he calls it" one woman started to exclaim. At first Wallace ignored it, he wasn't entirely sure they were talking about him and was a little bit surprised if they were. He thought his playful nature had always went down well, he couldn't imagine any bitterness toward him.

"Yeah that's him, fat waste of space if you ask me, shouldn't he be up in the palace eating their supplies; damn Angels think they own the place." The little man next to the woman added.

Wallace stopped rubbing his hands and turned; looking directly at them he drew them a smile hoping it would diffuse the negative situation.

"Oh look, he is sizing you up now for his next meal" the woman said. The two men behind them laughed along with the mouthy woman and the little man in front of them.

"Is there a problem here?" Wallace asked, deciding to be upfront about it all and addressing the problem head on.

"The only person that has a problem here is you...a problem with food!" the woman said and looked down at his oversized belly and the two men behind burst into hysterical laughter. Wallace looked down at his belly and then back at the group of four. His smile by this point had dropped from his face and he was a little dumbstruck as to what to say or do. Never before in all his years had he found such maliciousness by an Astorian civilian. He remained silent.

"Oh look he is lost for words...maybe his mouth is full of food!! Ahahhaha" the little man jested and all four of them burst into a fit of giggles.

Wallace felt really hurt by the whole encounter. He suddenly was not hungry any more.

Jim made his way out from the sheltered part of the stall with a few slivers of the wildagoat meat ready for tasting but Wallace had already turned and headed off, away out the market. His shoulders rounded and shrugged. Behind him he could hear Jim shouting

"Wallace... what's wrong are you not hungry?" with genuine concern in his voice. This statement was then followed up with jibes from the four nastier people.

"Oh he is always hungry...That's clear!!!" the woman shouted after him.

Wallace walked on and out of the market. All the people that he passed stopped to try and converse but he kept his eyes down and kept walking. He suddenly took stock of his general behaviour. Every day he came down to this market, everyday he would converse with all the vendors and sample their food, taking notes on the quality and then signing off their advertising boards, confirming that what they were selling WAS delicious. Who was HE to be grading food, who was HE to say what is tasty and what was not.

He suddenly felt really stupid and wanted to shut himself away from the whole world. Did everyone think as those four people did? They obviously felt strongly enough about it to have made such a display. He felt like he has been making a fool of himself all this time. Wallace, the big fat food taster!

He started to drag his feet along the ground; his motivation to enact a simple movement like lifting his feet was gone. By the time he had reached his domicile he had already worn away part of the front of his shoes.

With his big brown thundering hand he bashed his door open and then slammed it shut behind him. He shut his blinds and fell into his large hammock that hung by the window. He shut his eyes and a small tear ran down his face.

Quincy sat on the wall ledge at the top of the stairs feeling a strong sense of boredom. For the last ten minutes he had been staring up at the clouds and trying to make shapes from their white, bubbly appearance. There were quite a few of them up there and it had entertained him for awhile but he had quickly grown tired of it. So here he sat, watching the people of Astoria go about their daily business.

He had helped clear the blockage at the recycling centre with relative ease, much to his delight. When he had arrived there he had expected much worse but had found that it was a simple piece of wood that had been too large to fit through the conveyor belt gap. Once removed, the recycling went on as normal and he made his way back to the palace right away.

Boredom had sunk in again and he was filling this void with more people watching which, on a normal day, wasn't very exciting but today, well today he did notice something strange about them, a strangeness that he couldn't quite put his finger on. Earlier he noted that, as a lady passed by the market, her makeshift bag burst and the contents poured over the market floor. Instead of naturally helping, the nearest vendor began to curse at her for the mess and how it would ruin his custom for the day. It was a simple quarrel and yet one that Quincy had not seen in Astoria for many years. He actually could not remember the last time he saw any quarrel in Astoria except those play fights between the Angels.

He pondered this thought further, swinging his legs on the wall top. A voice startled him from behind, not because it was loud or sudden in any way, but because he knew all too well whom the voice belonged to and so instantly he had to jump to alert and posed a respectful stance.

"Good day to you Quincy" the Allfather said

"Good day to you Allfather" Quincy replied and kept his eyes on the Allfather at all times. Quincy had learned over the years that to show respect, you look into someone's eyes at all times when conversing with them, giving them your full attention. Today would be no different.

"I see you are at a loss as to your purpose today" the Allfather said, indicating the bored state upon which Quincy had previously sat.

"No sir, I was merely lost in thought" Quincy countered

The Allfather said nothing for a few minutes which Quincy did note as being strange as it was never the Allfathers way to try and intimidate anyone or leave uncomfortable silences. Today was very strange indeed he thought.

"I have a task for you Quincy, I require you to head to the glow valley and..."

"Is this punishment sir?" Quincy cut in

"Punishment?" the Allfather questioned, a little puzzled as to what he meant.

"Well for what I did to Wallace at the banquet?" Quincy replied.

The Allfather paused again before replying

"Yes I guess it is punishment, I require you to take a platoon of troops up there and energise the worms and then bring them back to me, a bag a man"

"A full platoon??" Quincy exclaimed "wow that's an awful lot of worms, which will take hours, maybe even days"

A smile had formed across the Allfathers lips.

"See to it you are swift in its commencement then" the Allfather stated and then slowly walked off, placing one foot in front of the other as he walked.

 Quincy shook his head as he obeyed his orders.

The Allfather never gives punishment; this really is a strange day he thought.

As soon as the Allfather was out of sight and into the shadows, his visage instantly changed to that of a dark seductress. She opened up her cloak and then produced a very small blade that was no more than 7inches in length. It was a curved blade and the sharp edge was tipped with a purple sheen that she wielded perfectly in her left and sliced thin air, tearing the fabric of reality itself. She sliced it big enough so that she could fit through and then stepped into the gaping hole.

"Oh wow well done, that's four in a row" Chance exclaimed as Jessica landed yet another little pebble into the makeshift hole they had constructed at the bottom of the stairs roughly 10ft away.

"And left handed too" Jessica gave a little burl and then a smile, trying her best to impress her new friend.

She thought Chance was amazing, with every trick she would show her, Chance would have an even better one, and yet Jessica never felt like she was competing, it felt like Chance was giving her these tricks to play on others, to help her to win in future. She decided that she wanted to be like Chance when she was older, kind and caring, funny and willing to help the little people.

As chance stood up to collect more pebbles, her small heart pendant fell out from inside her top. It hung there on its marvellously shiny chain and Jessica's eyes were instantly drawn to it.

"WOW!!!" SHE EXCLAIMED "that's a beautiful necklace, who gave you that?"

Chance at first had no idea what she was talking about, but then she remembered the pendant that she had fondled in the dark and realised that she had completely forgotten to examine it in the light. She took it in her hand and pulled it nearer to her face.

Jessica was right, it WAS a beautiful necklace. It was heart shaped and made from, well she was not entirely sure what it was made from but it looked rare and shiny, very shiny. Chance instantly felt a smile cross her face.

"Who gave me it indeed?" she pondered aloud. She kept her eyes on it and examined it further. Around the edges of the heart there were numbers. After following them around she realised it was in fact a set of clock numbers and yet there were no hands to this clock.

'How very curious' she thought.

"I have never seen a necklace like that before, the metal, its, its enchanting" Jessica said. "Whoever gave you that must really think you are special"

"Hmm yes very special" Chance muttered and then pirouetted on the spot, her thoughts lost on the puzzle of the situation. Chance found herself now staring at the ground as she played with the necklace in her hand, turning it over and over and feeling the smooth surface of the rare metal that it was made from. She became acutely aware of a set of heavy footsteps that were making their way toward her position. Jessica sat in the same spot near her, quite happily throwing the pebbles into the target hole.

The footsteps grew closer and more aggressive and before Chance had a moment to look up she heard Jessica scream.

"No please I don't want to" Jessica yelled at the unknown aggressor. Chance eyed up the person from head to foot, the man was fat and bald and wore an old overall that was worn and dirty. His shoes were brown and worn and his teeth were...well they needed some work done on them.

"What are you doing? Take your hands off her now" Chance said with a modicum of authority.

"Mind your own business Blondie, this one's for the chop, she has a duty to perform" the dirty bald man replied.

"I wasn't asking you...I was telling you" Chance said and with that she grabbed the man's wrist, twisted it down sharply which forced him to release his grip on Jessica, she then used both hands and pushed the fat man backwards where he was sent tumbling over an old barrel landing straight on his bottom. Chance stood there over him, a little bewildered at the martial art she had just performed without a second thought.

"You've made a big mistake there Blondie" the dirty man said and got up and began to yell

"GUARDS!!" he shouted, and at his call, six guards came rushing down the alley towards them. They were dressed in full battle armour and looked rough and ready. They ran together in military unison, each taking their first step with their right leg as they ran towards them.

Chance grabbed Jessica up in her arms and turned to run

"I've got you babygurl" she said and turned to make her way up the alley. She had only gone about ten steps before more guards appeared at the top end of the street blocking their path. She was amazed at the coordination of these guards given they had no clear communications device other than the fat mans yell. Clearly that bald man held some kind of power here in Sanctuary that the guards were always on patrol to protect.

Chance looked back at the way they had come and then up again at the blocked exit. She shook her head. With nowhere to go she placed Jessica back down and stood her ground.

 The first three guards ran towards her as she stood calmly waiting for them. When they got nearer she sprang up and ran her feet against the wall, pushing her up and off where she swung her leg around sharply and caught the first guard straight across the chin, knocking him clean out on his feet. He was sent crashing into the second of the three guards and they both tumbled into a heap in the alley. The third guard swung his armoured fist towards her face which she quickly caught between her two wrists; she twisted them downwards, forcing him to bend and then drove her knee straight up into his face, knocking him up into the air where he then fell and landed, slumping against the alley wall. The second guard by this stage was back on his feet and Chance ran at him, jumping, she wrapped her legs around his neck and spiralled down toward the ground taking his upper body with him. His head crashed against the floor and he was instantly unconscious.

 She stood up and turned to little Jessica

"Woo babygurl check me go, I'm ninja" Chance said smiling. She actually impressed herself here. These moves seemed to come naturally to her, the entire time though she felt this nagging, itching feeling all over her body. Almost as if her skin wanted to split or, well she couldn't explain it, it was all very peculiar.

Jessica smiled up at Chance and then frowned instantly as her eyes fell down the alley to where they had originally came from. The first six guards were standing on the ready.

"This is going to be very painful...for them" Chance said rather coolly and turned to face them.

The alley itself was fairly narrow and so was the ideal place for her to fight them given that she was outnumbered. The narrow walls meant that only two guards could engage her at any time, which immediately took away their advantage they had in numbers.

The first two swung for her with hard and high punches that her reflexes saw coming. She leaned back to dodge and then followed up with a few punches straight to their faces. She quickly realised that her upper body strength needed a little work and so opted for kicks instead, ducking another two high swings, she then performed a massive back flip up into the air, trailing her leg as she went and then spin kicking it upwards at great speed. Her foot followed through and connected with one of the guards chin and he too shared the same unconscious fate as his friends as he landed.

The other guard was a little more ferocious with his attacks and began to force her back with the sheer volume of strikes.

Chance had to keep her arms up and flexed to block each swing as it came at her with thundering malice. Every block she made she felt shockwaves shudder through her entire body and she wondered how long his stamina would keep this up for before he got tired. He continued to swing hard and wild and Chance kept her guard, walking slowly backwards up the alley.

She caught a glimpse of an opening in his attacks; an opening that would allow her to return fire and so took it, ducking under a high swinging punch and then dropping down and spin kicking his legs out from under him. He landed flat on his bottom which she then followed up with a straight boot to his face.

She turned and surveyed her position, she was almost out the top entrance to the alley which opened up into a small plaza, Jessica was keeping a safe distance behind her and the other four guards advanced on toward her.

Out in the open expanse of the plaza, all four guards could now surround her at once and she instantly realised the folly of her judgement from leaving the narrow alley. She had to call upon every ounce of her speed to duck and dodge and weave away from each strike that the four men were sending towards her. She managed to block one large strike, duck another and then took a hop step off the ground, placing her other foot onto one of the guard's thighs as a ledge and using it to push off as she performed a perfect round house kick that caught and felled all four guards at once. She landed in the middle of the carnage and looked rather impressed with herself.

"Wooo" she said "I don't half kick ass!!"

She was barely catching her breath when more shapes came looming out the darkness of the alleyway. In her tired state she had begun to realise that she had perhaps bitten off more than she could chew here. The new shapes were easily twice as big as the previous guards and once they entered the light it was clear to Chance that these heavily muscled warriors were not to be trifled with. Six walking behemoths made their way into the plaza, their faces filled with grim determination to neutralise what they saw as a threat in her.

"This is going to be very painful....and probably not for them" she said aloud.

The six large warriors casually circled her, flexing their massive muscles and cracking knuckles. Chance swallowed hard. Was now the time to play the little blonde girl card? She looked around at all the unconscious guards she had felled moments before and shook the thought away. They would never buy it. Looking closer at their faces, she concluded that these brutes can't have been very clever, they looked like they had been bred purely to fight and their eyes were burning with a passion to unleash their barely contained anger.

They were flexing their muscles, crunching their knuckles and grinding their teeth. There was barely an ounce of fat on these warriors and Chance started to pre-empt her wincing at the pain that was about to come.

Just when she thought her beautiful face was about to be mangled, a figure dropped down from above and landed directly in front of her, putting themselves between Chance and the six looming meatheads.

Chance had to lean back slightly at the proximity of the new arrival to see who it was.

"I've got this" the voice said and she instantly recognised it to be her chimp boy. He turned his head slightly and she saw his dark brown eyes looking at her.

In that moment a strange metamorphosis occurred, a creeping white light crawled all over his body and he was suddenly dressed head to foot in this bright white shining armour. It had white studded shoulder pads and white, light armoured plates running the length of all his limbs. The armour looked lightweight but durable and it seemed impossibly white in colour, shining in a shade of brilliance that she never thought possible. Chance looked at him a little surprised at how fast he had changed and also a little amused that he was wearing shoulder pads.

She looked him up and down and realised his new attire made him look very clean. She had to admit he scrubbed up well and fought back the urge to compliment him, instead she played to her side of wit.

"One chimp against six gorillas, I don't fancy your odds there" she said rather mockingly. "loving your outfit though....not"

Raphael frowned and then turned to face the oncoming behemoths who were now growling feral like angry wolves waiting to pounce. He held his arms up in a boxer's stance and then moved forwards to engage.

All six guards swung in unison and struck him hard into his guard, he had to hold his arms tight against his head to absorb the sheer force of the shot. For their strength they lacked speed and Raphael took advantage of this instantly by ducking and weaving, sending uppercuts straight up and through the chins of the hulking meatheads.

It was over in a matter of seconds, all six guards were now lying flat out on the floor around him, their threat had been neutralised. In the same moment, Raphael's eyes were drawn up to a stairwell that led down into the plaza where ten more guards came advancing down, armed with long staves that bore electricity stunners on their tips. These guards bore similarities to the first guards Chance had fought and yet looked slightly taller and leaner.

Raphael held his ground and flicked a switch on his left gauntlet, he quickly pressed a few buttons and then suddenly his arms from the shoulders to the tips of his fingers completely vanished, cloaked using some special device within his armour.

Chance looked on rather confused.

Her chimp boy in all respects looked like he had disarmed himself...literally but she very quickly made sense of his apparent madness as the first of the guards swung their stave toward him. It was deflected by what seemed like thin air and suddenly the guard was then dumbstruck as an invisible force made contact with his face and sent him sprawling. Another two guards stepped in with their staves in a spear stabbing motion; both staves were deflected by thin air as Raphael's armless body twisted and then came about hard and fast sending an invisible strike into the first guards face and then performing a spinning back fist into the other guard, knocking him clean onto his back.

With his arms cloaked, his attackers could not see his strikes coming and so Raphael was faring well against the seven remaining guards who had by this point changed their tactic slightly, circling him slowly and synchronising their attacks on the basis that he can't deflect them all at once.

As chance looked on, slightly impressed by her chimp boys antics she suddenly got this silly notion that she should perhaps help him out. Although he had already felled the six meatheads in a matter of seconds, and although he was dealing with this new threat with relative ease, Chance had still somehow come to the conclusion that she should do her part. Much to the misfortune of Raphael as she picked up a large stone from the ground at her feet, she turned, aimed quickly...a little too quickly and then threw it as hard as she could.

The rock sailed through the air toward the eight participants of the fight in the middle of the plaza.

The rock went high and then came down hard...right into the back of Raphael's head.

Chance turned to little Jessica "wooops" she said and then gave a small remorseful giggle as she turned back to see the carnage that then unfolded.

The rock had hit Raphael clean in the back of his head and pushed him forwards, straight into the stabbing strike of one of the guard's electric staves to his face. The blow was enough to make Chance cringe on the spot in relative pain. The other six guard then followed up with strikes of their own, both with the electrics tips, that were sending jolts down Raphael's body and also with the sides of the staves like clubs, beating him down to the ground before all seven of them set about him on the ground, holding their staves by the tail end and swinging them down hard upon his gleaming white armour much like an axe man chopping wood. All seven guards continued to swing down hard and fast, repeatedly smashing their weapons against his armour. After a few seconds his arm portion re-materialised as the cloaking device must have been damaged through the ferocity of the attack.

Chance watched on with a small amount of guilt. Jessica tugged on her sleeve

"Is he ok?" Jessica asked. Chance decided to lie as she wasn't entirely sure he was ok.

"Erm yes babygurl, he is just resting and is gonna come back stronger you'll see"

Chance laughed on the inside at how convincing she was and looked back over the beating that was occurring in the middle of the plaza. It looked by all means barbaric and very one sided. The guards were swinging their staves down hard and fast, repeatedly battering their foe to the ground and trying to ensure their blows kept him there.

But just as she had said to Jessica moments earlier, he slowly began to fight back. First off he swung his leg around in a sweeping motion, knocking two guards off their feet in one swoop; he then stood straight up, grabbing one of the guards by the throat and picking him high up into the air in a rage. One handed he threw the guard backwards and into some barrels that lay strewn toward the back of the plaza. Two more guards swung their staves toward him which he caught in each hand, he held them tight, and they too held on tight

117

and so he hauled the staves together forcing the men to run in tail, both men then colliding abruptly in the middle.

Raphael turned and walked straight towards the next guard who performed a stabbing motion with the electric tip of the stave. Raphael was so angry and rage-fuelled up that he didn't even bother to block the blow as it connected into his stomach and the shock was sent through his body.

 He merely grimaced, gripping the stave, and through sheer anger he held himself in check and then swung a straight punch right into the guards face knocking him clean onto his back, still holding onto the stave he then spun it around in his hands before re-addressing the guards he had swept to the ground. He spun the stave around twice in his hands, a display of sound dexterity on his part, he then made a tripping strike towards one guard's leg, connecting perfectly and taking the guard off his feet. He quickly hopped over the falling man and then performed a stabbing motion down into his chest with the electric tip as he passed over him, electrocuting the guard out cold. Raphael spun the stave in his hand again and faced the last remaining guard, he eyed him closely, switched his grip on the stave into a javelin style grip and threw the stave like a spear which stuck straight into the man's leg sending a constant stream of electricity through his body and effectively immobilising him from the fight.

Raphael stood there in the centre of the plaza, blood pouring from his nose and lip and looked over to where Chance and Jessica were standing.

 He looked back to the stairwell that the stave wielding guards had come from and immediately his eyes went wide, he turned and made a run toward Chance and Jessica, bounding as quickly as he could in their direction. He could see their faces light up in horror at the shock of his action and unsure of what he was going to do but he didn't have the time to explain, he reached them in a matter of a few large bounds, just in time before the new arrival of armed guards raised their rifles and started to fire a massive hail of projectiles in their direction. Raphael felt a good six or seven rounds strike his back as he placed himself in harm's way to protect the girls, he was instantly thankful that they were rubber tipped rounds otherwise he may have been in need of an apothecary.

He reached out and scooped both Chance and Jessica up in his arms and spun around into the safety of the wall as rounds peppered off its surface, sending dust and small pieces of rock spraying down the alleyway. He turned and looked down the alley and could see that more armed guards had been advancing slowly on their position from that angle also.

He flicked open his gauntlet once more and pressed another few buttons quickly, a small compartment opened on the back of his right hand which held four little holes. Still holding Chance and Jessica in his arms he turned and squeezed his right hand, clenching all fingers in towards his palm tightly and pressing down upon the hidden trigger within his gauntlet, sending a torrent of bright flash flares down into the alley way, he then turned and fired again up into the plaza.. He then jumped up, with the girls still in his arms he made a run back into the plaza, under the cover of the flash flares he had just launched. Once into the plaza he turned immediately to his right and made toward the cover of a small domicile.

"What was that?" Chance asked him, looking at the smoking section of his gauntlet that he had just fired from.

"That was our saving grace!!" he replied.

"What, pathetic little fireworks? I was expecting more" she said, a little unimpressed at the lack of damage it caused to their aggressors. Raphael raised his eyebrows at her latest jibe, finding it all too ironic that she was jesting him on the same power that she herself had been gifted.

"Oh I really cannot wait until you get your memory back" he replied, giving a small smile at a joke that only he was enjoying.

"You say that like the joke is on me??" she replied.

"It is!!" he responded. Chance merely scoffed.

'Stupid chimp boy' she thought.

Raphael looked behind him and realised that although they were now in cover, they were in fact trapped. Chance looked around her and came to the same conclusion as the armed guards quickly filed their way into the plaza and took up firing positions.

"Oh good one chimp boy, no banana for you this time! I knew I should have left you at this port" Chance said.

Little Jessica cuddled into her side, feeling the fear overtaking her now.

"You did leave me!" he barked back

"Yes and you keep following me around!" she shouted

"Well aren't you glad I did!!"

"Not really...you've got us trapped!" she called back. Raphael rolled his eyes. He didn't have an answer to that as he HAD basically got them trapped. He cursed himself for not opening his eyes to his surroundings and finding a suitable escape route as he had been taught during his training. Instead, he allowed his rage, from his beating in the plaza, to cloud his judgement and lead them into this boxed in position with nothing bar a painful way out.

Jessica gripped Chances leg tighter.

"Don't worry babygurl, I've got you, I won't let them hurt you" Chance said and embraced her closer, keeping her as safe as she could given their predicament.

Raphael turned his body so that his torso covered both of them safely behind him, and awaited the armed guards stalking closer. They came on slowly and meticulously and with military precision and as soon as five of them came into view, they raised their rifles to their shoulders, took quick aim and began to fire on full auto.

 The rifles were standard automatic issue capable of firing over 10 rounds per second when unleashed fully. Upon firing, Raphael now had 50 rounds sailing toward him at blistering speed with nowhere left to hide. He had to stand his ground and brace for impact.

He braced for an impact that never came, the rounds never hit their target.

 At the exact moment that the guards fired, the Phoenix guard of Astoria swooped into the plaza and unleashed a full torrent of flames that instantly melted the rubber rounds before they could hit home.

Fired from their promethium fuelled flame rifles, they easily engulfed the space between the guards and the three that were trapped, creating a shield made from hot flames for protection. This was then followed up with large, fist sized power balls of pure ice, hurtling towards the faces of every guard in the plaza, knocking them all flat in the same second. As the men hit the ground, Raphael looked up to see two faces he recognised, belonging to Angels Fern and Crystal, followed closely behind by the distinct orange armoured Phoenix guard.

Raphael gave them all a smile and breathed out.

He scuffed his boots along the white stoned rubble that littered the way to his destination, this was not the kind of rescuing he needed from his boredom, and this was going to be a tedious task on the grandest scale.

'A full platoon?' he thought to himself.

'A thousand men, each could then carry perhaps a thousand glow worms back, that's a million glow worms, what on earth could he want with a million glow worms?' Quincy thought to himself.

The idea was all very strange to him. The glow worms, which his gift of electricity would empower, are for the sole purpose of lighting. The street lamps in Astoria are lit up by these creatures and each creature lives for at least a few months. A million worms would, well it would certainly keep the shadows at bay he thought.

The men behind him walked on. This trip was usually completed in smaller task groups where Pepsy could teleport them the distance in a matter of seconds. On foot this journey was easily a six hour hike and that is if they were travelling empty handed. The sheer size of the demand the Allfather has asked for could take days and so extra supplies had to be carried along the way.

Quincy hated being in command of so many men, a thousand men doing a thousand silly things that would need a thousand orders barked at to fix them should it all get out of hand. This was definitely not his day.

He thought back to the prank that he played on Wallace; it was rather funny he thought especially because he was so hungry. Ha and then his dinner had gone cold by the time he returned.

That was definitely a prank to go down in his all time best. He was sure Wallace wouldn't hold a grudge, he never did. He was such a friendly chap and loved by all. He pretended to be mad about it, but really, deep down he would have respected the genius behind it and would only have wished he'd have thought of it first. Nonetheless, Quincy made a note to apologise to Wallace on his return.

His thoughts then wandered to the strange encounter he had with the Allfather. He couldn't recall a time when he had ever left the Allfathers presence carrying such a burden of doubt. He had this strange feeling inside him, an old feeling, from long ago but he couldn't quite put his finger on it. Perhaps the Allfather was growing weary in his old age, perhaps he missed the counsel of his dear brother or his late wife even. Quincy had never been married nor had he ever concerned himself with the opposite sex so he wasn't sure he could fully understand the feeling of loss that the Allfather must bear.

Quincy then began to consider the possibility of courting. He ran through in his mind all the possibilities of available Angels in the city. He considered Fern, and then burst out laughing to himself. That girl was a hothead for more reasons than one. He couldn't remember a single time when he had seen a smile cross her face as she was most certainly not the smiling type.

He then considered Harmony; she was a little older than he was but beautiful all the same. He then remembered her infatuation with Spanners and how he doubted such a spell could be broken even if he could prove there was 'electricity' between them.

His thoughts drifted to Crystal.

'Ah crystal, the darling of Astoria' he thought, she really was something. Wherever she walked she would turn heads with her slender body and platinum hair. What he liked most about Crystal was her warm, caring character to all that she met. She was soft spoken, empathetic and would never be heard saying anything less than positive things about anyone she came across. Quincy concluded she was just simply lovely.

He then began to wonder how it was that Raphael could ever resist her charms or her attention. *That boy must have strong morals* he thought, or a deep strangeness.

'Hmm' he thought. For as long as he had known Raphael, there was always something lingering there that could not quite be explained. It was like an unsaid truth followed him around that some higher members of the Astorian council were purvey to but not him. He liked Raphael, oh yes he liked him and would call him one of his closest friends, mostly because Raphael was never one to play pranks on anyone, never one to play the macho character or draw attention to himself, and yet somehow attention WAS still drawn to him.

Quincy thought back to his first day of school when Raphael had joined their class. He was a quiet boy then and didn't speak for the first three months. Some tragedy had befallen his circumstances and all the children were pre-warned to give him time. He was always polite and went about himself without a care in the world. Quincy remembered naturally being drawn to him purely on curiosity alone, they knew Raphael was not of Astorian born and so the questions of WHERE he had come from were rife. But again there was this 'unsaid' truth.

'That was an intense year', he thought, topped off with the frightening bone war. A battle that truly brought him and his classmates together as all of Astoria were called upon to defend their city. They had no choice and yet still, children of eight years old should not have to see the horrors that they saw during that time. They should not have had to see their heroes fall.

His mood dropped again slightly as his thoughts fell once again upon the great Lucas. His thoughts remained on his late hero as the ground before him changed from the white stone pebbles into harder, coarser strewn rock that would require his full attention to ensure he didn't injure himself. He paused for a moment, took a deep breath and then persevered onward toward the glow valley.

Crystal ran over to where Raphael leant, half slouching against the wall. She placed her hands on his face and made eye contact, a sincere look of concern in her eyes. She could see he had been involved in quite a scuffle. His face looked bruised and beaten and his armour had black scorch marks on it that she could only conclude came from the electric tipped weapons the Sanctuary guards were armed with.

"Raph are you ok?" she said

"I've had better days" he muttered and wiped a little blood from his nose. He remained slouched against the wall and his breathing remained heavy. He still hadn't shaken the cold he had been fighting for the last few days and so his lungs were in a right mess, well more of a mess than normal.

All around him the Phoenix guard had fanned out and secured their location. Fern remained on the high ground ledge, keeping an eye on the swarm that lay high in the sky above the city.

Crystal rubbed Raphael cheeks gently and then helped him to his feet.

"What happened here?" Crystal asked as she was a little confused as to why such violence had erupted between two Angels of Astoria and the personal guard of Sanctuary.

"Ah just Chance doing her usual..." Raphael trailed off as he looked around trying to locate her. Chance was over by the travel vendor, chatting away to the man that worked there and Raphael found himself relaxing a little more knowing she was safe.

Crystal remained silent, refusing to make comment on the Allfathers daughter, her caring frosty blue eyes never leaving Raphael's face. She hated seeing him beat up like this, it stirred deep feelings inside her, genuine and caring feelings.

"What are you all doing here?" Raphael asked. "Although I am glad that you are"

"The Allfather sent us here to deal with the swarm. He believes it will help strengthen relations between the two cities." Crystal began to look around at the prone forms of the guards before speaking more "Relations that definitely need repairing" she added.

"We will need to explain this to the King" Raphael said, his eyes still lay in Chances direction.

124

"I will talk with him and smooth this over don't you worry. Just focus on feeling better" Crystal replied and she stroked his cheek. Her beautiful blue eyes were still focussed on his face, longing for him to just turn his head, turn his head and allow his eyes to meet hers. They never did.

Raphael's focus was clearly directed toward Chances location. A puzzled look overcame his face as he watched the next few moments unfold before him. He watched as Chance casually shook hands with the vendor, having struck some unseen deal, head over to one of the balloon wicker baskets and hop in.

Raphael's eyes began to widen as he then saw her unhook the anchor tie and allow the balloon to raise high into the sky, with her comfortably inside it.

"Chance noooo" he shouted as he started to run toward her. The balloon was rising fast and he calculated that he would need to get to higher ground if he had any hope of reaching her.

He scrambled his weary body up the stone steps and hopped up onto the roof of a small clay domicile. He turned his run into a sprint and tore off toward the roof edge. His entire body felt exhausted and drained but he had to push it on further or he would never make it.

Crystal still stood where she had before and witnessed the whole action unfold before her. Her frosty blue eyes pinpointing the exact location required to help her friend. It wasn't the first time in her life that he had left her company so abruptly to go chasing after Chance, and it certainly wouldn't be the last time but she stayed true to herself, placing her feelings aside and calculating the best way to help him achieve his goal of reaching her.

Raphael reached the end of the roof edge at blistering speed. Just as he jumped, he reached out with both hands, desperately trying to reach the rope that was dangling beneath the wicker basket. He felt the weightlessness of air beneath his feet as they left the buildings edge and was sailing through the air. He had gathered quite a lot of speed on his run up and his forward momentum was impressive, however he quickly realised that he was going to fall short, his jump hadn't been high enough, his run up had not been fast enough.

Just as he thought gravity would have its wicked way with him, he felt a sudden purchase beneath him, a platform beneath his foot that allowed him to push off in a second bound, a bound that would take him even higher. This time his hand caught the rope! And he held on tight.

 He had made it.

As the balloon sailed high into the sky he looked back and realised that the helpful platform was in fact made of ice, a giant stalagmite of ice from the ground up to where he required it.

His eyes met the beautiful frost blue eyes of Crystals, she winked to him and he smiled back.

Chance sat on the steps watching her saviours in orange securing the perimeter. She found their choice of uniform quite amusing, bright orange armour with shoulder pads and vambraces. This really was a strange world she had found herself in and she wondered if she too owned such a ridiculous outfit. She laughed to herself, 'as if' she thought.

From where she sat she could see all the newcomers before her and she noticed that one of the orange saviours looked slightly different to the others, and also that this particular one was staring at her rather maliciously. Chance refused to be goaded into a staring contest, a contest that she of course would win but that she didn't have the time nor the interest to secure the victory. She had so far concluded that, although she had lost her memory, that was all she was going to lose today.

She looked away, choosing to ignore the situation and focus on more important issues like finding her memory. She gazed around and down towards the bottom of the stairs where she could see her chimp boy was sitting, looking very much beaten up. A blonde girl whom she had not noticed previously was next to him and nursing his wounds. She seemed, overly caring Chance thought.

'How cute, chimp boy has a girl friend' she thought to herself and then she climbed back to her feet. She stretched up onto her toes and reached as high into the sky with her hands as she could. This place was starting to bore her now and it was about time she dropped off chimp boy as she had promised earlier.

She walked further up the stairs and could see a small vendor up ahead with a collection of large, single carriage balloon baskets floating above. She made her way over to investigate.

"Good afternoon lassie, what can a get for ye" the friendly vendor spoke with an accent that she could barely discern. She took a moment to unscramble the jumble of words that had been hurled at her and then gave the best reply she could based on her estimation of what was said.

"Hi, I am interested in your balloons, how can I acquire one?"

"Well lassie are ye after wan balloon or tae? It'll cost you, although I see yer Astorian, shall I pit it on yer tab?"

Chance stood bewildered for a moment. She wasn't quite sure if he was threatening her or trying to genuinely help her, he was speaking so quickly and his hands were flailing all over the place in his strange manner of communication.

The vendor began to recognise her, as most of the civilians eventually would, and instantly offered her a deal.

"I know you lassie, you're the princess tae be, tell ye what, tack this balloon on me, tell yer daddy Jacob gave ye it" He reached forward and shook Chance's hand and then led her to a balloon that was sat just behind her. It was a single balloon with barely enough room for one. She had no idea what just happened, she had gone from listening intently to his jumbled garble of words, to shaking hands and now she was being led to the very thing she had come asking for. She decided to play along anyway, believing herself to have struck some deal.

"I take it ye flown wanna these before lassie?"

Chance just smiled and giggled, she had absolutely no clue what this man was saying to her but he seemed friendly enough and so she returned his warm smiles. The vendor seemed happy with the response and waved her off, turning on his heel and making his way back to his stall.

Chance peered over the edge of the basket; it was still firmly set on the ground. She peered down to her feet in the base of the basket and found there were two large sandbags to one side, a large box on the other side and other than that the base was bare, no chair, no mechanics and nothing visible to keep her warm should they reach the withering cold heights.

She looked up into the balloon and saw there was once again nothing, just the inside of the balloon canvas itself with no contraption, no metal engine, nothing.

There was a large thick rope that hung over one side of the basket and she followed the line it took that led over the edge and onto the ground below. Attached to the thick rope was a heavy anchor which she concluded was holding her transport in place. She reached over and carefully undid the anchor; the rope was extremely thick and tied with a well held knot. It took a few moments of straining but she eventually unravelled the knot and low and behold the balloon immediately began to rise into the sky, the thick dangling anchor free over the edge.

A small sense of excitement overcame her as the balloon started to drift higher as it was taken hold of by the winds current.

 She could smell the fresh air that lay above the city looming closer. She had risen about twenty feet into the air by now and she could see a large swarm of flies over on the west side of the city, high above the buildings. She shuddered and remembered their close call predicament on their journey to the city and how very near to suffocation they had become.

 Watching the blackness of the swarm as it slowly became a distant event on the horizon, the basket suddenly tipped violently to one side, throwing her body hard against the edge of the basket with her right shoulder taking the brunt of the force against the hardened wicker side.

Although she had no memory of flying one of these balloons before, she very quickly realised that there wouldn't be such turbulence from the low heights she had thus far climbed to. Concluding that something physical must have been caught on the balloon, she peered over the edge, looking down hard but couldn't see what was causing the problem.

The basket then tipped again to the other side, sending her tumbling hard once more and this time it was her left shoulder that collided with the hard wicker side.

'something must have got caught on the rope she had left dangling, Perhaps it had caught something heavy as it left the city's edge' she thought.

As she peered over the edge of the basket once again, she now looked upon the same side as the rope was attached. She felt her blood boil as she could see that someone was in fact holding on to HER balloon.

'That just won't do' she thought and dipped her head back in to the safety of the basket.

She looked around her feet and saw the two sandbags lying there. She picked one of them up in two arms and was shocked at just how heavy they were. Cradling the sandbag closely to her chest she tiptoed to the edge of the basket, rolling the sandbag up higher on her chest and onto the tip of the box, she then peered over and could see her pirate intruder clinging on and trying to climb the rope.

She took careful aim and then launched the first bag down toward him.

Raphael was fully airborne now and hanging on for dear life. The rope was thick, dry and was burning his hands in the exertion of holding on.

He swung his other hand around to grip the rope and began to climb, arm over arm up the rope. The rope itself was very long and his muscles were still aching from the fight in the plaza and so scaling the rope was slow and painful.

The balloon had now ascended to a great height and Raphael could see for miles in every direction and had it not been for his perilous situation he may have enjoyed this. He could see everything and it all looked so bright and beautiful. He couldn't remember a time that he had ever been up this high before. He always liked to keep both feet on the ground so to speak and so avoided unnecessary dangers like heights or vast drops.

He climbed a few more feet higher, still placing one arm over the other and hauling himself further up the rope. The skin on his arms had become almost red raw with the friction.

Having made good progress he decided to look up and see how far he had to go. The rope was swinging wildly and at times it swung him directly under the basket and out again, making it difficult to truly determine the height he had left to climb. He knew that with this level of swinging, that the last part would be difficult and dangerous and he only hoped he would have the energy required to make it to safety. Still looking up to the task above him, he began to notice Chance was moving around inside the basket. Then he saw a large brown object being laboured to the lip of the basket and that's when Raphael eyes widened in shock

"Chance...don't it's me..." his shouts fell on deaf ears as the brown object came hurtling towards him and struck him square in the head. The force of the blow was worse than any he had received in the scuffle earlier and he was reduced to a single hand gripping the rope, his legs dangling precariously into the air. His vision had become littered with stars and a strong wave of dizziness overcame him. Black spots covered the gaps between the stars in his vision and so he was basically blind. He desperately swung his other hand up again and took hold of the rope, bringing his legs in this time and wrapping them around the rope to hold on tight until he recovered. A recovery he never had the liberty to make as another heavy object struck him hard again, luckily more on the back of his broad shoulders this time. The impact was still enough to send a deep shudder through his body.

 His grip loosened slightly and he slid further down the rope, burning his hands in the process. Once again he stopped himself by wrapping his legs tightly around the rope and hanging on with everything he had. He began to feel sick, he wasn't sure if it was from the exertion of the climb, the pain of being struck or perhaps even a little vertigo from the sheer altitude that they had now reached. He started to scale the rope once more, hand over hand and had barely made it two feet up when he heard a strange sound which made him instantly look up again, a move that he regretted as soon as he had made it as a large and very heavy spanner struck him straight in the face, striking him in the right on the cheek between his eye socket and his nose. He felt like his whole face had shattered, he shut his eyes and grimaced in the pain as he then could feel more shrapnel, smaller pieces this time, peppering off his head and bouncing down into thin air below. There was then another large thump, this time to his shoulder that he could only imagine had left a bruise the size of his fist on there.

From the pain he was now in and the stupid situation SHE had put them in, Raphael had enough!

"Grrr Chance you are really pushing me this time" he growled and he then produced a grapping hook from almost thin air.

'ah well needs must' he thought. He tried to look up but again his vision was blurred and disorientated, taking rough aim he fired the grappling hook. A lucky shot as the hook sailed directly up toward the centre and pierced right through the bottom of the basket. He then hooked the device to his arm and started the auto reel in, relaxing his muscles slightly as he allowed the mechanics of the hook to do the scaling for him.

Chance threw the second sandbag and scored another direct hit. She made two fists with her hands and pulled thin air in celebration, A Huge smile crossing her face.

 Looking down into the basket she noted a large box that sat in the opposite corner. This looked slightly bigger than either of the sandbags, being slightly longer, made from reinforced steel and filled with various tools and scrap metal. *'Curious'* she thought, *'to have tools for a balloon with no engine'*. She knelt down and scooped her arms underneath it and used all the strength in her legs to hoist this box up. It was definitely a lot heavier than the sandbags had been. She waddled across to the baskets edge and rested the box on the lip once again, wasting no time in sliding this box to the edge and tipping it over. The contents of the box came pouring out and down toward her intruder and from her position she could make out spanners, hammers and bolts of various sizes all falling like deadly shrapnel toward her intruder. A smile crossed her face when she realised that nearly all of the contents had hit. Her smile faded slightly as she looked around the basket and realised she had no more ammunition to throw.

'Hmmm' she thought

A moment or two passed and she kept peering over the edge to see if her pursuer had progressed any further. To her shock, a large metallic bolt came piercing through the bottom of the basket, tearing through the wicker base and locking itself in place to the base.

'That nearly got my foot...arghg this just won't do' she thought and began pacing back and forth within the basket, her anger slowly beginning to brew. She felt her hands growing warmer as she clenched her fists. She also feet this strange sensation in her stomach, a build up of what could only be described as butterflies, but she wasn't falling in any way. The itch had returned once again and she could feel it all over her body, it took everything she had to resist the urge to scratch it. Her hands grew warmer and warmer as she felt her choler grow greater and greater. She stared at the metal bolt that could have put a hole in her foot. Her lovely little feet!

'Damn that intruder' she said to herself and suddenly had the urge to point her hands at the floor. To her absolute surprise bright sparks began emitting from her hands and blew a hole clean through the wicker floor next to the bolt.

'wow' she thought 'where on earth did that come from' she looked closer at the burned edges around the hole she had blasted and became amazed that the force had come from her own hands and brewed from her own anger toward the thing that nearly took her foot. She had missed the bolt entirely but, as realisation set in, she could now get a clean shot down to her pursuer and she felt angry.

Raphael was feeling a little more relaxed as the grappling hook began to do all the work for him. It was slow progress but effortless progress nonetheless. He was finally able to look around and actually enjoy the scenery below him.

He noted that they had drifted miles from Sanctuary by now and were also extremely high up. The colours of the land were incredible. He could see the menacing deep purple that surrounded Astoria and travelled for miles in every direction, the purple mass that forever imprisoned Astorians to this section of the world for fear of its toxic qualities. When the sun shone at the perfect angle it would reflect off the purple crystals and send bright and amazing spectrals of light in every direction. It was a truly magnificent sight that he was enjoying.

This enjoyment was cut abruptly short as he heard a loud blast directly above him. He looked up and he could see a hole had been burned clean through the basket and he instantly knew what had happened. He began to call out

"Chance, don't hunni. It's tribinium gas that powers this thing…it's flammable!!"

He strained his eyes upward and he could just about make her out through the hole she had fashioned. The grappling hook was reeling him ever closer and keeping him far steadier than the manual scaling of the rope had and this allowed him to concentrate fully on getting her attention. He watched on as she peered through the hole and then disappeared out of sight. He then saw something that he couldn't quite understand; her hand was now poking through the hole.

'Surely she isn't trying to reach to help me up, I'm still ten feet away' he thought. He watched as her hand fumbled around and then paused, palm directly toward him.

"No hunni don't!!" he tried to shout as a hail of fireworks began to pour down on top of him. He did all he could to shield his eyes but there was nowhere to hide.

Chance felt like she was unleashing some aggression as she hurled her newfound power down through the makeshift hole in the basket. This power seemed to flow without end and she enjoyed the release as she continued to pour fireworks down upon her intruder.

Suddenly, and without warning, the balloon canvas caught fire.

"Ooops" she said aloud. Chance became amazed next at just how quickly the flame spread through the entire canvas. Within a few moments the whole balloon had become a ball of fire.

She was now aware that she had butterflies in her stomach again and this time it was because she actually WAS falling. The balloon, with its flammable gases alight, was coming down hard and fast. The fire spread quickly to the wicker basket itself and she found herself trapped in an inferno of raging flames.

Thinking fast she hurled herself over the edge of the basket, gripping tightly to the thick rope that her pursuer had used to try and commandeer her vessel. She slid down the rope and could feel it burning through her hands with the friction, the pain quickly became too much and she let go. She began to freefall from the sky for a brief moment before a strong arm swung around her waist and pulled her in close.

The balloon continued to fall.

CHAPTER 6

The march to the glow valley was very long and boring.

 Leading a thousand men was never his thing and he had grown bored of it already. Every now and then a soldier would come up to him and question the orders which Quincy, of course, would have to respond to and act as if he truly believed in the purpose they had been set. A bold lie and one he was growing tired of telling.

They had walked for many hours now, carrying a lot of supplies and equipment over the harsh desert plain. They had now reached the copper mines that led out into the glow valley. The copper mines were more like caves really, set into the mountain side and had been hollowed out a long time ago, a time when copper was still a desired and sought after ore. With the need for electricity slowly dwindling, the need for the conductivity of the copper was also dwindling.

The insides of the copper mine were secured with large, and very old wooden beams that were scaffold against the walls to prevent the natural stone from giving way and burying the miners within the mine. The mine was very tall and each footstep made by Quincy would echo around its expanse. There was a slight green tinge to the wall indicating that the main section was very abundant in copper ore. Quincy looked at these sections carefully knowing full well that his gift would be multiplied exponentially in such a room.

*'Oh the trick he could play on Wallace in here '*he thought.

Hundreds more men made their way into the mine which led to a hundred more boot steps creating a hundred more echoes. Quincy stopped and noticed that a small piece of rubble began to tumble down the wall, the piece was no more than a fingertip in size but it tumbled on with increasing acceleration until it struck the cave floor and scattered amongst the rest of the rubble. He observed the mine walls with an added sense of apprehension, unsure of just how stable the mine actually was.

More men filed into the mine, each of them marching in perfect military unison. By now there must have been at least half the platoon making its way through the mine and rubble began to tumble off the walls quite freely now, hundreds of small, fingertip size, pieces of stone came tumbling down the wall face and scattering along the cave floor, some of the pieces struck the sides of the men's boots as they soldiered onward. The mine itself was apparently around a mile long and its exit led straight into the glow valley. The glow valley had no other possible route around and back to Astoria as on one side there was the mountainous face of the mine, and on the other side there was the sea of purple and very toxic crystals blocking their route, without proper climbing gear, or safety bio- suits, the mine was the only route back and so Quincy kept a close eye on the walls that were dribbling with stone precipitation, knowing that to risk a cave in would trap them all.

Quincy stood to the side and allowed the front lines of the men to pass him and continue on toward the valley. He looked further down the lines and estimated that his full platoon was now in the mine, their marching step was in perfect synchronicity and he noted that all his men must have been right side dominant, as every time they all placed their right foot down, the mine would shudder from the enhanced echo, every soldier must have been placing their full weight down onto their right legs as with each step, more rubble was raining down from the walls quite freely, scattering across the path they were treading. Quincy had now begun to consider the possibility that this mine cannot withstand the vibrations of a thousand men. Almost on queue with that thought, a large rock dislodged itself from the wall, coming hurtling down toward the men on the path. Luckily it did not hit any of the men that were marching in that area, but the impact did cause a massive panic as it smashed all over the treaded path, sending thousands of stone shards scattering in all directions. Another rock from the other side of the mine fell, its impact was impressively loud as it echoed through the confines of the mine and instantly created a pandemonium of panic within the men. Fearing they were going to be buried alive, they started to run toward the far end of the mine. The extra footsteps and increased footfalls from the running only added to the vibrations that were disturbing the wall face, these vibrations echoed all the way up the walls to the ceiling, dislodging any loose rocks to pour down into the mine.

Quincy stood immobile on the spot and watched as the route they had just come from completely collapsed in on itself, sealing them into the mine and trapping them on the far side of the mountain. Almost immediately the stone rain stopped.

The men stopped in their tracks and looked around, suddenly realising that their route home was now completely blocked off. They all remained silent, allowing the severity of the situation to slowly sink in to their minds.

"Well that's very inconvenient" Quincy stated to break the silence. He stood there looking at their blocked route and remained calm. They were not trapped completely within the mine as the path behind them would lead out into the valley, but he knew all too well that without climbing equipment, the men would not be able to scale their way over the valleys edge and take the long route home to Astoria. They were effectively cut off. One of the men came to Quincy; his face was awash with apprehension and unsure of his purpose.

"What will we do sir?" he asked wearily. Quincy looked him up and down with an emotionless face. The man was a good bit older than he was, as most of the guard were. Quincy was given command at such a young age purely due to his Angel status, it seemed strange to him then, that the man before him, who was clearly a good ten to fifteen years his senior, would need to seek reassurance from the ideas of a young one like himself.

He cleared his throat and put strength into his purpose before he spoke.

"We will complete our mission, on toward the valley" he replied and started to walk out the other end of the mine. The men, this time, taking careful steps followed in behind.

After a few hundred yards there was a light that could be seen at the far end of the mine. The men cheered at once and rubble began to tumble once more from the mine wall. Quincy merely raised his eyebrows as he looked at the men, then toward the walls, then back to the men. They all got the message without him having to open his mouth and fell silent instantly.

They all marched on carefully to the glow valley.

The balloon had come down hard, much to the dismay of Raphael who was forced to use his battered body to break the fall for the both of them.

Chance landed softly, having been safely secured within Raphael's arms, she cheerfully hopped off her improvised human crash mat and turned, regarding her would be pirate and realised all too quickly that it was in fact Raphael, her irritating little chimp. *'Damn, doesn't that guy give up? He is like a bad penny'* she thought.

"Oh it's you" she broke the silence with an exclamation of statement. "You could have got us both killed there chimp boy, what's the matter, you see a rope you gotta climb it??" she shook her head with a small smile, a smile that she always brought on whenever she felt she had conjured up a witty insult. She began to survey her surroundings and as with much of the scenery she had encountered thus far, there really wasn't much to see.

The open expanse of desert stretched as far as her eyes could see in all directions, the sun was beating down hard sending sharp beams searing in all directions. Chance looked over to where the wreckage of the balloon lay burning itself out.

"Wow that fire really got out of hand fast hey" she said rather amazed at the events that had unfolded. She heard a grumble followed by the scraping sound of disturbed rubble, turning her head she saw that it was her chimp mat, climbing to his feet and complaining as always. She shook her head with a small giggle.

"What?" was the stern response to her laugh.

"Nothing" was her soft reply, coupled with another giggle. He grumbled once more and turned away, making his way down to a small collection of rocks that were piled unevenly on the desert floor. He sat down on one of the rocks with the pace and exertion of an old man. Chance giggled again, this time mostly to herself.

'*Poor chimp boy is in pain*' she thought.

The sun continued to shine painfully bright and Chance had to shield her eyes from its glare.

'*This is going to give me a headache*' she thought. Standing tall and on the point of her toes, one hand on her hip and the other shielding her eyes, she continued to look around, looking for anything of the smallest interest. The land was bare, painfully bare. At least back in that Sanctuary place there were people of interest, and interesting people. Out here there was, well nothing really.

As she looked around, she tried to see if the scenery would stir any old memories. She thought hard briefly, about her situation. If she had been born and brought up here, then she would surely have some kind of memory of perhaps, building little castles out of the sand or digging some holes in the mud.

'*Digging a hole?*' she questioned her own thought. '*That sounds more like chimp boys department, he'd probably be dumb enough to dig himself so deep that he couldn't get out*.' She giggled at the thought of him trapped in a hole of his own making. She wished she could remember more and Chimp boy had been no use, he didn't give much away. She suspects he blames her for their predicament although she doubted it would truly have been her fault.

'*He does seem like a grumpy chap*' she thought '*could I really have caused this*?' she disregarded the thought almost as quickly as it formed.

She began to pirouette on the spot when all of a sudden; something struck her in the back. She turned sharply and looked around.

There was nothing. Bare land, glaring sun and chimp boy sat there on the rock holding an ice pack to the back of his head. His face was pathetically solemn as he stared into space.

'*Just where on earth did he find that ice pack?*' she thought to herself. '*I wonder if his little blue girlfriend gave him it*' that same thought trailed off as something caught her eye. A small black box no more than seven inches long and three inches in diameter sat on the ground barely a foot from where she stood. Against the empty nothingness of the land, the box stood out quite dramatically.

A little dumbstruck, Chance stared a little longer, trying to discern not only what it was but also where it had came from since it had not been there when she had looked moments earlier. She crouched from where she stood and looked a little closer. The box looked more like a small satchel and made of leather too by what she could discern. It had a small Lastic stud to the centre of the case that evidently unravelled the top layer. She reached forward and picked it up; it felt light in her hands, very light. She flicked open the Lastic stud and she suddenly became very excited. She remembered what THESE were immediately as she pulled her favourite sunglasses from their case and placed them onto her head, the suns glare was instantly dulled.

"Headache be gone" she exclaimed as she laughed and completed an elegant little back flip.

"Wish mine would go away" Raphael grumbled. He still sat on the rock nursing his wounds.

With her vision now protected from the light, she was able to fully look around the land before her. As she did so, a massive light burst from the sky and came hurtling down towards the ground. It was truly a magnificent sight and one that she could fully appreciate now that her eyes were shielded from the glare.

"WHAT IS THAT?" she exclaimed.

"What is what?" Raphael answered, still holding the icepack to the back of his head. With his eyes facing the ground he had no idea what she was indicating to.

"THAT!" she repeated and pointed up into the sky as the huge energy surge came down towards the earth.

"Oh...that is the halo" he answered and lowered his head again nursing his wounds, seemingly disinterested in the magnificent event that was occurring above his head.

"Well what does it do?" she asked, feeling absolutely amazed by what she was seeing. It was by far the most overwhelming display of brilliant light she had ever seen.

"It doesn't do anything" Raphael said, remaining unimpressed by the spectacle.

"A big bright light like that and it doesn't do anything? How can you know so little about something so great?" she countered. Raphael looked up at her and held her gaze for a moment longer. Something about the look he gave her told her that he had tried to pursue knowledge in this area before but to no avail, she sensed some irritation in the words he used next.

"Because...YOUR father banned all methods of analysing it, so we have no way of knowing where it comes from or what it does!!" he held her gaze a moment longer, keeping a stern look upon his face before eventually looking down again and nursing his sore head. Chance felt a little bit stumped once again for information and not for the first time today. This lack of supply of knowledge, coupled with her memory loss was becoming all too inconvenient. A moment later and the halo light vanished, leaving Chance once again bored and with a newfound need to create mischief. With nobody around but chimp boy to play with she felt compelled to wind him up.

"You really should learn how to fight you know" she said as she made her way slowly down to where he sat, carefully placing each foot between the small pieces of rubble that littered the floor.

"Oh" he exclaimed, raising both his eyebrows in unison. She looked at him hard,' *he really has bushy eyebrows'* she thought to herself and made a mental note to pluck them if he ever fell asleep. He continued to hold her gaze, clearly not impressed by her statement.

"Well..." she continued "you don't see me all battered and bruised...we were in the same fight after all" Raphael shook his head in a dismissive and bewildered manor.

"Clearly you remember the fight, very differently than I do" he returned, continuing to hold the ice pack to the back of his head. Chance moved herself closer, kneeling down next to where he sat. She lifted her left hand and placed it gently onto the side of his face. She watched as his stern gaze instantly diffused and was replaced with a softer look from his dark brown eyes.

'His eyes really were dark' she thought, there was something warm and familiar about them, something deep and caring. She realised she was now holding her breath and for what reason she did not know. She slowly exhaled and gave him a playful slap across the cheek and watched as the disappointment grew in his face.

'Dream on chimp boy' she thought and stood up once more. "You were lucky I was there to save you" she jested further, trying to goad him further.

"Lucky?" he raised one eyebrow. She was determined now to pluck those brows of his at some point, as they definitely needed it.

"Go on, just admit that you needed my help" she pushed further. Raphael laughed in patronising amusement.

"It'll be a cold day in hell..." Raphael trailed off, something far in the distance had caught his eye and he stared intensely at it, a look of sincere puzzlement crossing his features. All of his focus had now centred on the distant black dot that seemed to wave and swift its way across the sky line, almost as if it was swimming through the air itself.

"Oh like that is it...hmm I'll bet you need my help before the day is out" Chance countered. She was now hop stepping her way between the stones, ever graceful in all her movements, balancing barely on one big toe she then jumped and spun a full 360 degree before landing softly on another narrow rock. She turned to see if chimp boy had witnessed her manoeuvre and to her disappointment, he hadn't.

"Don't you think your gambling had got us into enough trouble today" Raphael said, his eyes still trying to analyse the enigma that was the black dot in the sky. He turned his head slightly; much like a small dog might do when trying to make sense of what it was seeing before it. Chance thought about the words he had just spoken and realised this must have been a reference to whatever had brought them here, stranded once again on the desert plains, but she refused to take blame, instead she opted to deflect the conversation.

"You'll get wrinkles screwing your face up like that" she said. Raphael was straining so hard to make out the object he was focussing on in the great distance that he had created thick, burrowed lines across

142

the whole of his forehead, screwing his face up in the glare of the afternoon sun. Whatever it was on the horizon, it had really caught his attention and he was struggling to make sense of what he was seeing. He continued to hold the same look.

"Did you not hear me? Wrinkles!!" she pushed further. Doing whatever she could to get a rise out of him.

"Well lend me your glasses then" he said

"Not a chance, they are designer....Besides that would mean you needed my help, it's not cold and this place, as much as it's boring me, is not hell" Raphael shot her a scowl. "Just ask me for help and I'll tell you what you are looking at" she said, playfully dancing around on the rocks.

"As if you can see that far" he scoffed.

"I can" she returned

"Can not!"

"Can so!" she came back sharply, giggling as she then completed a cartwheel between the small space in the rocks. Raphael shook his head, unwilling to be drawn into such playground theatrics.

"Well what is it then?" he asked, amusingly awaiting an answer. He had the utmost confidence in his own vision and given that he could barely make out any details on this black dot, he doubted she would fare any better.

"It's a dragon" she said quite calmly and matter-of-factly.

"A WHAT?" Raphael exclaimed with a look of extreme panic that crossed his face.

"You heard" she said, holding herself upside down in a one handed handstand.

"You ARE joking right?" his panic was plain to see. He might as well have had 'FEAR' written straight across his forehead.

"You do realise its coming this way" he said

"Yup" Chance replied.

"Great!! Just great!! Can this day get any worse" he said and ran down a small slope. Chance climbed up onto a large flat rock and sat cross-legged, she looked down and saw Raphael bustling around in preparation and upon looking closer she realised that he had completely changed his attire.

"Ahahahahaha" she almost wet herself laughing.

"What?" he shouted up to her.

"Ha-ha you look absolutely ridiculous" she was now laughing so hard that she nearly fell off the rock she was sat upon. Raphael screwed his face up at her and then continued rushing around. He was now fully kitted out in a suit of white and gold armour, with hard metal plating covering the vital areas of his body, gold and blue trimmings completed each shiny plate and a long blue cloak hung down his back. In his left hand he held a large metallic shield, complete with gold trimmings and in his right hand he held a long straight sword with a golden hilt. This armour looked similar to the suit he had worn earlier that day although the plating looked much firmer, thicker and heavier.

"My knight in shining armour" she jested, giggling away on her perch. She did wonder where he had kept such a suit all this time, although where that boy had sourced anything today had become a mystery to her.

"Sir Chimpalot, please fight for my honour" she giggled. Raphael muttered under his breath something that only he could hear. To her it sounded nothing more than a mumble so she giggled again anyway.

By now the dark shape had drawn closer, its shape was no longer a mystery on the horizon but had clearly become the dreaded outline of a fierce dragon, and it was no more than 100 yards away, approaching fast. It was massive even by a dragon's standard. Each claw was easily the size of a man, its huge green wings flapped violently through the air and the sheer size of the wings was daunting. Ten men could stand with their arms stretched out and it still would not be as wide as the dragon's wingspan. It had bright yellow, demon eyes and teeth the length of your arm. This reptilian myth was built for one purpose and Raphael was about to bear the brunt of it.

"Chance, quick, find somewhere to hide" Raphael shouted up to her, genuine concern in his voice. By now his panic had gone and had been replaced with a braver resolve, at least on the outside anyway, on the inside he felt awestruck with terror.

"Oh sir Chimpalot, your concerns speak truths to my heart" her theatrics were award winning and it caused Raphael to look at her with intense confusion; her absolute calmness was unnerving him slightly. 'Was *she that intent on winning the 'ask for help' challenge that she...'*

To say Raphael's thought trailed off would be inaccurate, his thoughts had been violently shifted quite suddenly, toward the dragon!

It had landed, growled and swung its tail all within the flash of a second, the speed of its attack belying its bulk. Raphael was struck to his ribs and hurled twenty feet through the air where he landed heavily, crashing through some rubble strewn across the desert.

'That must have hurt' Chance thought to herself. She watched on as Raphael slowly picked himself up from the ground just in time for the dragon's second swing. This strike battered straight through his armoured legs and hurled him a further twenty feet through the air where he landed heavily once again in the dust of the desert floor. He didn't move this time.

For a moment, Chance found herself holding her breath again. *'was it concern*?' she questioned herself. She slowly allowed herself to breathe out, relaxing slightly as she saw signs of movement from him as he began to haul himself to his feet.

The dragon was toying with him as it swung its massive talons, each claw easily the height of Raphael, at half speed which allowed Raphael to meet and parry with his sword. The dragon swung once more, only for Raphael to deflect this again with his sword. The dragon pivoted and flapped its massive wing, the wind force created by the swift movement blew Raphael clean off his feet and he was once again airborne, sailing through the air before landing heavily, for a third time, on his back.

'Poor chimp boy' Chance thought. She realised that he was actually a little bit cute in his attempts at heroics. Dressing in full knight's attire

and facing this reptilian foe head on, ignorantly believing he was protecting her. She giggled and pulled out a nail file, carefully she filed her nails to perfection, all the while considering her association with him. She watched as he was once again hurled across her view, landing hard on his back and then narrowly rolling out of the way of a massive stamping claw before pulling up his shield just in time to absorb a massive ball of fire that had been hurtled toward him. She blew gently on her nail and examined her work.

'Well I guess I can't get rid of him...he just seems to find me and follow me around...I guess I should learn to look for his qualities.' She thought. Another large thud as more broken rubble is scattered around from the battering Raphael was receiving at the claws of the dragon. She sat and observed him in his ridiculous armour, his bushy eyebrows and his constant grumpy demeanour toward her. She shook her head; she was going about this all wrong.

'Think of something positive' she said to herself. Her mind drifted back to the swarm when she pretended to be scared, well she WAS scared, but she thought about the instance when she had allowed herself to show it. In her moment of fear he really cared for her safety, he had pushed himself on further and sacrificed his limp little lungs to get her to safety. She smiled. 'Chimp boy is a good egg' she concluded. 'Ill cut him some slack'

"Oh sir Chimpalot...do you need a hand?" she called out. There was a thump where he landed, followed by a roll.

"Sir Chimpalot???...what's with the..." he couldn't finish his sentence as the dragon had pounced on him again so quickly, biting down deep into his shield, wedging its massive fangs on the metal. With neither party letting go, Raphael was lifted clean of his feet as the dragon lifted its long neck into the air, he was stuck dangling in mid air, desperately hanging on to his shield. He turned his head and shouted

"Any ideas?"

"What hunni? Is that you asking for help" she said, and instantly scolded herself for using the term 'hunni', she was clearly taking this new association a bit too far. Raphael was swung left and right as the dragon attempted to dislodge its prey. He was literally holding on to the shield for his life. Through gritted teeth, the dragon attempted to

146

breathe more fire onto its prey but it deflected harmlessly against the shield that remained trapped within its bite, the flames dispersing harmlessly out from the sides of its mouth. The dragon then snapped its head sharply to the left again and this time sent Raphael hurling away from his life saving shield. He landed neatly into a forward roll and came about, keeping his eyes firmly fixed on the dragon.

The dragon spat out the shield as it would have spat a tasteless piece of bone, spitting it far and away from Raphael's reach and then, taking large menacing steps, the dragon faced him square on, knowing full well that he was now defenceless. It stalked its way closer, its massive form looming over him in the most menacing way possible. It leaned its head back and snapped its tail across its front, a long swiping motion that came straight for Raphael who was standing, knees bent, and waiting for it to pounce. He had foreseen this attack coming and neatly jumped over the incoming tail, landing into a small crouch and holding this stance, balanced and unsure of what to do, he called up to Chance

"Can you see my sword?" he asked her.

"Nope" she replied.

"How far is my shield from me?"

"Ah...hmm nah you'll never make it to that either" she said, still maintaining a modicum of calm in this perilous situation.

"Are you enjoying this?" he asked, although he was not entirely sure he wanted to hear the answer.

"A little bit" she giggled. He was right; he really didn't want to hear THAT answer. The dragon swung for him again, this time throwing its tail across its front once more but then following it up with a swipe of its claw and then a snap of its teeth. Raphael jumped the tail, side stepped the swipe then rolled away from the snap. His legs were beginning to feel really tired now. Chance sat, perfectly at peace on the rock looking at her nails and bobbing her head. By this stage, Raphael had weighed up his odds. He was tiring and not faring well against this obsidian beast. He needed a new solution and he concluded that perhaps Chance, in her calm and casual state, may just have the answer. He was about to lose the bet but he had no other choice.

"Okay okay" he yelled, "if you have any ideas please help" he shouted, his eyes never leaving the reptilian beast in front of him.

A massive smile crossed Chances face, she stood up slowly and cracked her neck to both sides, she then stretched up as high as she could and started to perform some side bends to nimble up.

"What on earth are you doing?" Raphael shouted, his irritation now clear in his voice as he was tiring, constantly being forced to leap out the way of yet more vicious, life ending attacks by the dragon.

"Now now, I must do my stretches, don't want to pull a muscle" she said as she then started performing a few lunges to either side. Calmly and carefully, she then made her way down from the rocks, on to the sand, and over to the battlefield that was once the desert plain.

The dragon instantly turned its evil eyes upon her and slowly began to turn its body slightly to size her up. This did nothing in the way of concerning her as she continued to walk bravely before it, stopping about five feet in front of the dragon with her hands behind her back. Raphael could feel his heart beating in his chest, he had no idea what her plan was, but she was certainly well within biting reach of the beast and he knew all too well the power in those razor sharp fangs. His concern for her grew exponentially.

The dragon by now had sized her up, leaned its head back and was about to breathe a cavalcade of fire right over where she stood, had it not been for what she did next; it might have completed the task. Chance very swiftly pulled a small silver artefact from her back pocket, placed it to her lips and blew. To Raphael's ears nothing happened, he heard but not a single sound, not even the sound of the air that she had blown into it, leaving it, nothing.

 But to the dragon its ears perked up, its tail dropped down and it instantly became obedient. It brought both it's from paws together, retracting its human size sharp claws and then sat down on the spot, bringing its massive, hurricane creating wingspan to rest at its sides. Chance smiled, and then produced a small cookie from her other pocket. The cookie was roughly the size of her hand, brown and smelled very sweet. The dragon carefully and gingerly leaned forward; looming massively over the tiny form of its new master and with its front lips alone, picked up the cookie and ate it. The dragon instantly enjoyed this treat and began to rub its huge head against Chances legs, displaying its pleasure and then gestured with its wing, safe passage upon its back.

Raphael walked over slowly toward Chance. His face was an expression of a person outwitted and yet respectful in defeat. She gestured to him with her arm in a little curtsy, to climb aboard the dragon, which he reluctantly did. As he passed by her shoulder he said simply "very clever"

"Why thank you" she replied, taking centre stage after her amazing taming performance.

"Could you not have done that earlier?" he asked.

"Wouldn't have been so funny, it's all about the build up" she then winked at him. He shook his head as he climbed on.

The Allfather paced back and forth at the entrance to the palace, his hands were fixed firmly behind his back and his irritation was clear for all to see. From his position on the palace steps he could quite easily hear the shouts and roars of raging arguments emanating from the market area. These shouts were clear disagreements that seemed moments away from becoming physical fights and it would only be a matter of time before somebody loses it completely and throws the first punch, once that happened he had no doubt that a full scale riot would break loose.

 His thoughts drifted toward his Angels and their lack of attendance here in the city. Right when he needed them all the most, none of them could be found and he cursed them for choosing such a time to disappear.

He turned sharply as his eye caught the outline of Spanners jogging across the plaza toward the palace steps. Spanners himself was always very composed in everything he did. Slow and meticulous, careful and logical was his way, and so seeing him performing a simple act as running depicted the severity of the situation. After a few long strides Spanners was before the Allfather, a data slate in hand as always.

"Did you find anyone?" the Allfather asked sharply.

"Sir it seems you have sent them all away. According to my investigation, YOU were seen ordering Fern and the Phoenix guard toward Sanctuary earlier today. Quincy has been sent, along with a full platoon of guards, off toward the copper mines. Your daughter I have no idea as to her whereabouts or Pepsy's although Jeremy did storm out at dinner last night, so I believe it may have something to do with that"

"The Phoenix guard In Sanctuary?" he asked.

"Yes sir, the sentry guards at the main gates confirm it, very early this morning you were seen ordering them away"

"Oh Fern, what I wouldn't give to have Lucas here right now, he wouldn't have fallen for any doppelganger trickery which is obviously what has occurred here. Somebody is going around the city pretending to be me and sending out orders, I thought she would have been wiser than that"

"In Ferns defence sir, Lucas lived in a time of war, where paranoia was high and such trickery would have been spotted a mile off, we live in a current time of peace and so suspicions are lower."

"Well it may not be a time of peace for much longer if this continues, look at them Spanners, the good people of our city fighting over anything and everything, irritation is high and I can almost sense the bad feelings emanating from the locals." He paused "we need to get the Angels back here to restore order and as quickly as possible. Spanners, I need you to reactivate the ACG"

"The ACG has lain dormant for eight years sir, it may take some time"

"See to it that it is done as quickly as possible, I need the communications grid up and running immediately so we can call back our Angels for I fear the situation here is about to get much worse"

"It will be done sir" Spanners responded and turned to make off, down the stairs toward the lower levels of the palace itself to where the main communications grid is located.

The Allfather shook his head grimly. He had no choice now but to use technology. After all he had tried to achieve here by eradicating its uses and purifying the people, here he was with his work being undone before his very eyes. His eyes dropped to the floor in disappointment.

Fern launched a few fire bolts high into the sky which caught some of the lower flying parts of the swarm, incinerating them almost instantly. It was but a small dent in the ever growing mass that was gathering really high up, its mass was beginning to black out the sun. She cursed as she realised it was just out of her reach. Her Phoenix guard were fairing no better, their flame launchers had not the power that her natural gifts could wield and so were basically useless unless the swarm dared hover lower into the city limits.

Crystal stood near Fern, keeping a respectful distance as she could sense her fiery friends' irritation. Fern stopped and turned.

"This is hopeless, we need to reach higher ground" Fern said rather frustrated with the current situation. Should the swarm keep amassing in the numbers it has, when it finally swooped it could suffocate the entire population of the city within minutes, there would be little the Phoenix guard could do to stop it. They were basically a deterrent for now.

"I could make an ice bridge? Although I don't know how long it would hold under the heat of your power" Crystal replied.

It was a strange pairing putting Fern and Crystal together. They were opposites not only in their gifts but in their personalities too. Where Crystal had a cold gaze coupled with a warm heart, Fern had a fiery gaze complimented with an icy heart. Where Crystal was full of care and empathy, Fern was brutal and to the point. Perhaps they worked well in balancing one another out.

Fern considered Crystals idea for a moment and then nodded,

"It's worth a try" Fern said. Just as Crystal began to turn and walk into a free space to unleash her gift, Fern stopped her in her tracks and their eyes met. What Fern was going to ask next she clearly did not want her Phoenix guard or any other ears to hear.

"Did you notice anything...strange about Chances behaviour?"

"Strange in what way?" Crystal returned.

"Well you know that she and I have never seen eye-eye, but she usually takes every opportunity to stare me down or win some point in her childish games, today she did no such thing. It was, unnerving" Fern said. Crystal was a little shocked that anything could unnerve Fern, she was always so stern and battle ready. She thought about this for a moment and then nodded.

"Something about today doesn't feel right I'll admit" Crystal said. "I feel Raphael was protecting her from something, it was as if he knew something that he didn't want us to know."

"His loyalty has always been with her" Fern agreed.

"I'm not sure what it was, I know Raphael, and I know him well enough to know when he is trying to hide something. He is an honest man, and this can only lead me to believe that he is hiding it for her benefit"

"Do you think she led him here on some wild goose chase, for her own begotten games?" Fern asked rather brutish and with no love lost toward Chance.

"I just don't know, I just don't know" Crystal repeated and then walked off toward a small clearing.

Meanwhile, over near the walls of Astoria, Ganon arrived at the great city to meet his brother. His gravitational bubble approached at a much slower pace as to not cause any panic or alarm to the Astorian guard. Much to Ganon's pleasure, the Allfather was out on the palace balcony awaiting his arrival. He lowered himself slowly, uniquely manipulating the magnetic flow of his powers, and then placed a careful foot onto the large stone balcony. He placed his eyes on his sibling and instantly they rekindled their brotherhood.

"Ah brother, it is with a warm welcome you arrive back in Astoria" the Allfather stated.

"It has been a long time Jonas" Ganon replied. They both stepped forwards and embraced. Both brothers could feel just how much either of them had aged through their bonier physiques.

"How was your journey brother? The deep lines of tunnelled iron still sufficient enough to project you at great speeds across the plains?" the Allfather asked.

"Ah yes, scavengers have yet to dig that deep to salvage their precious metals, so for now my transit was no more than an hour. I am however troubled if I try to go west, as the roots between here and there have been stripped, it leads to a ...precarious journey and not one I like to make too often" Ganon replied. Both brothers laughed slightly as they imagined such a peril.

"Much has changed here Jonas" Ganon said.

"For the good I hope" replied the Allfather.

"Naturally" Ganon responded "although I feel there is...some difficulty in there ambience here"

"You are not wrong there brother, there has been a strange cloud descended over Astoria today, a cloud that eyes cannot see and yet its effects are....disturbing" the Allfather said.

"Indulge me" said Ganon

"I feel embarrassed to say but the streets are in anarchy, there are fights all over the city, quarrels, bustles and a general sense of unease and I cannot explain what has brought it on"

"Corruption?" Ganon queried.

"It is hard to tell, but I fear the worst"

"And where are your Angels?" Ganon asked.

"I have searched high and low, and with every corner I turn, I hear that I in fact sent them away on errands, errands that I do not recall making."

"Hmm   I can tell you that your Phoenix guard were en-route to Sanctuary today and that I also saw Chance today, IN Sanctuary"

"What? What on earth is she doing there? We need her here; now, in this moment of chaos we need her shining light to bring order, what on earth has she headed off there for?"

"It gets worse brother, when I conversed with her; she had no idea whom I was. It seems she has had her memory wiped"

"Her memory? What, why?"

"I do not know brother, but now that you have mentioned the 'disturbances' in the streets, I fear the worst"

"Do you think Mobeus is at work here?" the Allfather asked.

"No I do not. Mobeus is not subtle, his mutants would come direct. No this seems more sinister, perhaps the Sarfan lord may be at work here?"

"Surely not, he was banished a long time ago. His return is mere rumours, hearsay. His dark touch cannot breach the psychic shield"

"Perhaps he has found another way, another method? Chance leaving the city is a bad omen, you know of her importance, her importance in keeping the balance" Ganon stated

"I know of the importance, but I also know that she has never been forced, she follows her heart in all things...she always has" the Allfather replied.

"If the Sarfan lord does return, you know what he seeks, it has never changed and you know who he needs to get it." He paused a moment before continuing "He will target her specifically, he will try to upset the balance"

"And she is away in Sanctuary just now with her memory wiped? And out of the protection of the psychic shield? She is vulnerable."

"The boy is with her"

"The boy always ensures she is safe" the Allfather said.

"Yes, a fact that is known to all...even the Sarfan lord...where she leads...he will surely follow, a weakness that may be exploited" Ganon said.

"I had never considered this" the Allfather said, standing now with his back to Ganon and scratching his chin. He was trying to make sense of everything that was unfolding before him.

"I have asked Spanners to reactivate the ACG, it will take time but I must find my Angels and return them to the city, their mere presence should bring an element of calm"

"Make the perfect city bleed, and the people will stop believing" Ganon said.

"What?" was the Allfathers shocked reply.

"The Sarfan lord told me this long ago, before he had revealed himself as the dark lord, he said that if you can make the perfect city bleed, the people that live there will stop believing. I think he intends to destroy Astoria from the inside out. Consider this brother, the Angels are all posted elsewhere, by your hand nonetheless, there is anarchy in the streets and nobody to turn to and nobody to take charge. It will bleed the street dry"

The Allfather remained silent, thinking everything through clearly.

"And what of the Astorian guard?" Ganon asked.

" A full platoon no less, that I apparently ordered off on a long march to the glow valley, the rest garrisoned here have succumbed to the madness, and they are as much spreading the nonsense as they were trying to contain it.

"This is like a game of chess brother, strategically moving all of your assets out of reach before striking at the heart of the city, we may not have time, you must declare martial law and activate the Lastic drones"

"If we declare martial law it will make the situation worse"

"We don't have a choice brother!!" Ganon raised his voice.

"THERE IS ALWAYS A CHOICE" the Allfather shouted. His choler had risen higher than it had in many years. He no longer had the wise council of his late wife and he was only just digesting the information that his darling daughter could be in serious danger. The Allfather was certainly not thinking clearly. Ganon remained silent at the sight of his brother losing his temper, an occurrence that rarely happened if ever at all.

"It has occurred to me, Ganon that all of this madness plays into your hands, and wishes of ruling with an iron hand! How do I know this is not your doing??" the Allfather said. The hurt was evidently clear within an instant as Ganon's eyes went vacant in sorrow; he chose to remain quiet for a moment. The hurt sank deeper at his brother's comments and he took a moment to choose his next words carefully

"Lastic drones and rubber bullets, I lie at night and wonder, brother, why it is that both cities see me as such a great threat. I have always been loyal to you; I do not always share your views or your ideals. Your dreams and visions differ from mine but I would never seek to undo your own work just to please mine. You are my brother Jonas and I have never forgotten that...even if you perhaps have" Ganon turned to make his way off the balcony. His shoulders had sunk a little at the sheer impact of his brother's hurtful comments.

"Wait brother, I am sorry. I did not mean those words" Allfather shouted. Ganon continued to walk to the edge of the balcony.

"Where are you going?"

"I am going back to Sanctuary; at least there, the people don't pretend not to fear me. I am going to get my niece; I fear she is in grave danger"

CHAPTER 7

Misty took them soaring to incredible heights in the sky. Chance was sat at the front, just behind Misty's neck and held onto her thick leather studded collar. Raphael sat reluctantly behind her, gripping her waist. From her position she could see far across the land. Never before had she felt so free, she felt like the world was at her fingertips. To the north she could make out the tips of the high mountains. She could see individual mountain habitats suspended from reinforced wooden beams, a symbol of the engineering marvels of old. If she turned her head she could see all the way south, as far as Sanctuary and the dust plains beyond. To the west, where they were heading, was unmistakably Astoria, its grand city walls looked perfectly white and sheen and stretched almost as high as the clouds in some places. She marvelled at its magnificence, its beauty, it was aesthetically pleasing to the eye. Her eyes were drawn up and beyond the desert planes where all she could see was miles upon miles of purple, solid purple with hardly any gaps or breaks. She found herself staring intently at it.

What could that be? She thought.

"Oi, Monkey business, what is that?" she asked Raphael. She had turned her head slightly and realised he was leaning his against her back and didn't reply. He either couldn't hear her or perhaps he was too scared from the heights to respond. She looked back to the purple land which seemed to shimmer in the light.

They flew on for awhile longer before she heard something, something different. It was a strange sound, soft, light hearted notes that seemed nearby and yet far away. Each note she heard spoke right into her heart and made her feel warm and welcome. She felt her skin tingle and the tiny hairs on her arms went up. Completely unaware that she was doing this, she had in-avertedly started to squeeze her right thigh in against Misty's side forcing her to turn her trajectory toward the source of the song. Misty took a wide arc that now placed the grand walls of Astoria squarely on her left and they soared on directly north toward the mountains.

The song was beautiful. At times she could hear it clearly, each word in decipherable and yet she still understood it. She still felt its touch on her soul. She looked down at Misty and pondered if there was a way in which she could make her fly any faster, she reached forward and tapped softly on the long reptilian green neck. It was difficult to tell if it had worked but it certainly made Chance feel better that she was at least trying.

They flew on further north and the mountains were becoming clearer now. The song was most definitely coming from there and she just had to get to it, she had to find out what it meant.

As they neared the mountain edge Misty started a slow descent by circling downwards in big wide arcs. It was the only way that she could drop slowly and safely while keeping her passengers intact on her back.

With the ground coming into view Chance could start to make out the openings to a cave near the bottom. She was almost certain this would lead her to the source of the music. Misty took them down slowly and landed perfectly and smoothly onto the ground next to the cave. Raphael was leaning heavily into Chance's back and snoring like an old man. She had to peel him off her as she hopped down from Misty. As she turned she looked back up at him, lying there straddling Misty's neck, eyes shut and his thumb in his mouth.

 'He did look kind of cute' she thought.

"Ok misty I'm going in, try not to eat our chimp boy now." She paused for a second as she watched him stir; a frown crossed his face as he began to scratch his head impetuously and then dropped back into a sleep.

"On second thought, just be careful you don't get indigestion" she added and then made her way into the cave.

The cave was cold, dark and dusky. The sound of dripping water could be heard at regular intervals along with a few other unfamiliar sounds that she did not recognise. Far in the distance she could hear that song again, that beautiful song. She had to find out where it was coming from.

 She walked along a small path that had been smoothed clear amongst the jagged rocks of the cave and it seemed to lead deeper into the caves bowels. Every now and then, she would get a shock, as a large drip of water would fall from the ceiling and land directly onto the back of her neck. Its cold touch would send an instant and unwelcome shiver down her spine. She made a note to keep her eyes on the floor and watch out for any puddles or signs of water that could be an indicator of such drips. Further on into the cave she went.

 It wasn't long before the darkness became comfortable. It wasn't quite pitch darkness, it had become a slight dullness now and in her comfort Chance had began to skip step her way along, making good time. Avoiding the dripping puddle marks where she could and all the time listening hard for another note of that wonderful tune. She skipped on down and into a clearing. In this clearing there was an 8ft drop down into a channel. On either side of the channel there was clearly a man made slab stone of massive proportions that made up either side of the channel wall and ran the length of the room. There appeared to be no way around it so she eyed it more carefully. To the left there was a small, broken wooden sign and on it there was some writing.

"If you are not Moses then you'd better be fast" it read. She drew a puzzled look across her face. She didn't quite know what it meant but she did know that she was indeed fast. She smiled at her inner confidence and hopped down into the channel. Upon her foot touching the channel floor, almost instantly the man made slab stones began to move, grinding their way along the floor and closing the gap in the channel. Chance now realised why she needed to be fast and she broke into a run toward the opposite end of the room. Her legs moved at blistering speeds, each foot driving hard into the floor and propelling her off, further towards her goal. The walls continued to close in at their death inviting pace. She was sprinting with everything she had; her heart was pounding in her chest so hard that she thought it might actually burst right out. The channel was long, longer than she had first interpreted. It must have been around 400 yards in length and her legs were starting to wane. Each push from her legs became an effort now and she could feel herself slowing down. The walls however were not slowing down and so she had to keep going.

Out of the corner of her eye she started to judge the height of the channel. Her heart sank a little as she realised there was no way she could jump that high to get out. She would need something to use as a step and the only steps she could see were located at either end of the channel, she was going to have to run this one. She powered on as fast as she could but time was definitely running out for her. The walls were frighteningly close now, perhaps a yard away from each of her shoulders.

She had no air left in her lungs.

She had no drive left in her legs.

She had run out of fight.

She slowed to a stop.

The end of the channel was still about 100 yards away. The walls continued to close.

Was this how it was going to end for her, Squished to a pulp in some dark deep cave?

She actually wished she had her chimp boy here again, even when he carried her he was faster than she could ever hope to be. They might have made it. The walls loomed closer and she instinctively placed her arms out wide to each side. She felt the annoying itch return all over her body and she cursed to herself that now was not the time for minor ailments. She held her arms out wide but there was no way she could push the massive weight of the slabs, although it seemed natural to try.

The walls closed further and then stopped. Chance was, by this stage, squeezing her eyes shut and bracing for impact. The impact never came.

She opened her eyes slowly and realised the walls had in fact stopped. No wait, they had BEEN stopped. She looked towards her hands and realised she could feel the rock. She looked closer at them and her eyes went wide in confusion. She could actually FEEL the rock but she was NOT touching the rock. Her hand had never made contact. She was somehow holding the rock at bay. A smile crossed her face.

"I am pretty awesome" she said aloud and then flexed her arms as hard as she could. The feeling seemed natural and suddenly the force increased through her palms and she pushed the rock further apart. She flexed again and did the same, sliding it even further. She started a slow and causal walk along the channel; every few steps she would thrust her arms out and force push the walls away again. It had dawned on her that this must be some kind of gift, a power similar to the fireworks she had used in the balloon.

As she reached the opposite end of the channel there was a small set of stairs that led out of the deep drop. She turned and looked back down at the way she had come.

"Pfft, as if I needed that monkeys help" she scoffed out loud and walked on, quite pleased with herself and loving life. She made her way deeper into the cave, playing with her newfound skill and blasting chunks of rock out of the wall where she saw fit. Every now and then she would hurl some of her fireworks that would light up the room and she marvelled at the size of the open expanse, at how high the cave ceiling actually was. Her wandering took her through a narrow archway that opened out into another large expanse of a room. The ceiling seemed impossibly high and there was a huge gap that seemed bottomless that stretched between her platform and the opposite side of the room. There was a small door on the opposite side that she was sure she had to get to but she had no way of crossing the gap. She looked high and low, trying to see if there was something she could grip on to, some way that she could climb up and around it. Her eyes drifted to the wall face, the rock there seemed remarkably smooth. Getting any form of grip would be nigh on impossible. She sighed slightly, feeling a little stumped by the obstacle before her. Once again there was a small wooden sign that was protruding from the ground on the left. Chance walked a little closer and could read the words

"A leap of faith required" she laughed. She would need more than a leap of faith she thought. She leaned over the edge of her platform and looked down into the dark abyss below. It seemed to go on forever. She lifted her right hand used her gift of fireworks to light up the hole. This act proved fruitful but not in the way she had intended.

161

As the fireworks lit up the area she caught a small glimpse of platforms. It must have been the way the fireworks light reflected off their surface that made them visible, as when the light faded, so too did the platforms. She took a step back, taking a deep breath, she launched her fireworks again and then hurled herself off the edge of the platform and down onto the nearest platform that became visible. She landed hard onto the smallest of ledges. It was barely big enough for her to stand on one foot and it took every ounce of her skill to remain balanced after the momentum of her jump. She held fast, steadied herself then fired again. She caught a short glimpse again of another platform out in front and launched herself toward it, landing slightly lighter this time and on her toes. She threw her arms out to the side to balance herself. She remained on this platform for a few minutes, trying to slow her breathing down and relax. Once completely calm she fired again and then jumped as far as she could, onto the next platform. She continued to do this across the great expanse, landing as softly as she could each time. After a few more jumps she was almost there, one more jump and she would be in, she fired her power again and then jumped. But this time she hadn't given herself enough push. She was going to fall short. She reached out desperately with her hands, clutching for anything.

She barely caught the edge of the platform in her fingertips. Bashing her nose against it at the same time and grazing her face. The shock of the impact almost made her lose her grip. Her fingers were turning white and starting to slip, she tasted blood in her mouth and she panicked slightly, hoping that her teeth had not been broken in the process. She reached up with her other hand to check that all her teeth were intact. Once satisfied, she then used both hands to haul herself up. As soon as she was steady on the platform she took the last small jump and landed on the other side. She turned back and looked at her accomplishment. That was quite a distance she had covered there. Quite pleased with herself she turned and headed through the little door.

Upon opening the door, the heat could be felt straight away. She felt it warm against her face before the light of the flames had even crept into her view. Once again she had found herself in a massive chamber, a chamber that had clearly been set up yet again as some sort of a test. This one however looked far more daunting than the rest of them. She viewed the room before her.

As before, on the far side of the room was a little door that was clearly to be her intended destination. Between her current location and the door was a contraption that spat fire and looked difficult to cross. Again there was a large gap, this time the gap was filled with what looked like molten hot lava. She couldn't recall if the cave they had entered had a volcanic peak to it but it mattered not, here she was now in the thick of what was clearly lava of some description. The gap was again traversed with a corrugated metal bridge that hung on large chains. Below the bridge were dozens of little flame spouts that ran the length of the bridge. Chance calculated that every ten seconds the bridge would drop, at the same time the little flames would spit higher and ignite some sort of gas that had been spraying into the area of the bridge from the right hand side of the expanse. The bridge would land on the little flame spouts, extinguishing them, but by that point the gas from the right side would be ignited and spewing flames straight across the bridge itself. This would last for at least another ten seconds before the gas ran out and then a large cranking wheel began to turn and lift the bridge back up to the top. The small flame spouts on the ground would then reignite once the bridge was clear of them and the process would start all over again. She viewed the cranking mechanism closely, it was a large turning wheel and there was one situated on either side of the bridge. Her eyes were drawn up above the bridge where she noticed there were four bars, evenly spaced along the roof that crossed the same length of the bridge. Once the bridge returned to its starting location, Chance eyed it carefully, trying to calculate the distance between the bridge base and the handles at the roof. She reckoned her only shot at getting across this would involve some kind of gymnastics using the bars to keep her above the flames, and so off she set. She waited until the cranking mechanism had run another cycle and then she made a run across the bridge, counting in her head as she went.

"6...7...8..." she starting saying aloud and then jumped, both arms stretched out and grabbed the bar above her head. Gripping tight, she hauled herself up as the bridge dropped below her. She watched as the flames aggressively licked the bridge and the heat she felt was incredible. She held on as the bridge reclined and then she hopped down and ran again, counting as she went then jumped as high as she could, grabbing hold of the next bar along the sequence. Again the bridge dropped below her. She tried to hold on but her hands had become sweaty from the sheer heat that was rising through the chamber. Her grip slipped and she had to haul her leg up and over to grip on as her body fell upside down from the bar. She felt pain behind her knees as they gripped the bar desperately.

From her inverted position she watched the bridge fall again and yet another gust of heat came flowing up towards her. She recoiled in it and tried to use her abdominal muscles to pull herself up. She was tired she realised, and was beginning to struggle. She slung her head down and watched as the bridge started to rise again. She waiting and then rolled off the bar backwards, landing heavily on both feet. She felt her left knee jar slightly upon landing and it sent a shooting pain through her entire leg. She tried to make a dash further across the bridge, counting as she went. She hadn't run fast enough, either that or she hadn't counted correctly as she suddenly felt the bridge give way beneath her. She jumped as high as she could and barely caught the top bar. Another gust of heat rose up that was barely tolerable. Her leg was aching now and she doubted it would sustain another drop and a run. She was so close, just one bar to go and then she was in. Her grip held fast this time as the bridge dropped again for another cycle. She began to kick out with her legs, this simple motion starting to give her some momentum. She continued to do this over and over. She had generated enough of a swing now that all she had to do was await the back swing, as her momentum then brought her swinging forwards she let go of the bar and sent herself sailing high into the air.

Hundreds of thoughts crossed her mind in the second she had become airborne.

Had she generated enough lift?

Did she release at the right angle?

Would she make the distance?

All of these thoughts plagued her mind at once as her body sailed through the air, turning end over end. As her manoeuvre brought her more upright once again, she lifted her hands up and hoped she would make it. Before her, she could only see the bridge, then, as her momentum carried her more upright, she could see the opposite side's door. And then finally, as she became almost vertical she saw the other bar. Relief sunk in as she felt the cold metal against her skin. She gripped on hard and slowed her momentum, looking down she then swung slightly more and released, landing safely onto the other side. She turned and looked at her achievement, shaking her head in disbelief.

This was really turning out to be some day she thought. She turned and headed through the little door.

The next chamber she entered was different altogether. It seemed grand and well maintained. As her footsteps took her further into the chamber, she could once again hear that song, that happy, delightful song. In this room it was so much clearer now. It amazed her that the heavenly voice had managed to travel through so many chambers, from deep down in the cave and be heard miles up into the sky. She moved on, deeper into this chamber and found the temperature to be perfect, absolutely perfect. Not too hot and not too cold. A small serf ran up to her, she didn't even see where he had come from. The serf placed a grand cloak around her shoulders, made from some soft, rare animal and its touch was comforting against her skin. The serf then handed her a glass, and in it contained the most delicious beverage that she had ever tasted. She slowed her steps, enjoying the wonders of this room entirely. She then realised that it was more than a room, it was a market of some sort with stalls everywhere. Stalls filled with shoes and rare clothing. Her eyes marvelled at the wonders she was seeing. This place truly was something else. She noted that each market stall had a beautiful vendor, standing and waiting to serve. As she passed them, the vendors would curtsey and politely acknowledge her with "my lady". On she walked further and further into the room.

The song she so desperately needed to find was beautiful. Its every note sung to perfection. Chance followed it intently, a desperate need to find its source. She reached the end of the market and four little serfs ran to her. She had no time to act but they scooped her up and placed her onto a soft little bed. The serfs then lifted this bed up onto their shoulders and carried her in any direction she wanted to go. Another serf appeared carrying strawberries on a gold plate; this was placed onto the bed beside her as they progressed on, deeper and deeper.

Chance felt euphoric, she finally felt at peace. This was the kind of place she liked, calm and tranquil. No monkey business ruining her day. She was being treated like a princess and ...that song...the beautiful heavenly song. An excitement grew in her as she neared the source. The notes were definitely louder. She couldn't have been far away, and then she set eyes on it. A bright light, and at the centre of the light there was a beautiful woman singing. Singing and yet her lips were not moving. She couldn't make out the words of the song but she knew they must have been describing something so beautiful that perhaps there weren't such words to do it justice. She felt warm, she felt relaxed, she felt...

SPLASH!!! Chance suddenly had a rude awakening. She shook her head and looked around her. She was in a dark, horrible cold cave and...

SPLASH! Another gallon of water was hurled over her. The water was cold and irritating. She turned to its source and her choler grew. There was Raphael, standing at her side, he was bent over and picking something up from the ground.
"And there was me just rejoicing in the fact I had no monkey business and here you..." she didn't have the opportunity to finish as he hurled yet another bucket of cold water straight into her face. She was now dripping from head to toe in cold, wet water. She clenched her fists in anger and also from the shiver response from the coldness that was now chilling her to her core. She looked him dead in the eye.

"Welcome back" he said with a stupid smile across his stupid monkey face.

"Grrrrr" she replied.

Jessica was awestruck at being surrounded by so many Angels of Astoria, resplendent in their glorious armour, and throwing fire from their hands as simply as she would place one foot in front of the other.

Her eyes never left them for a second, watching their every move, fascinated by the way their armour glistened in the rays of the sun as they swung their flame rifles around so majestically. She found herself listening to the very way, in which they spoke to one another, communicating swiftly and boldly, making each sentence sound more like a statement, so sincere, so true of fact. There was not a hint of doubt in their words, no sliver of uncertainty, no faltering, just confident straight talking words that instantly bolstered the moral of those in ear shot.

She observed how they interacted with one another; each warrior seemed strong and defiant and yet openly displayed mutual respect for both their comrades and also the people they were protecting. They were everything she imagined they would be and more! Oh how she longed so much to be an Angel one day.

She turned on the spot, straining her arms out in front of her, forcing an action that she knew would never come and yet refusing to relent, to accept that she was normal. Flexing her arms as hard as she could, her tiny veins pulsing slightly on her emancipated arms, she continued her tautness, inviting a headache as she focused hard, willing a drip of fire to leave her fingertips, hoping that an energy force of any kind would be released.

Her sadness slowly returned as nothing came, she sighed and relaxed her arms, allowing her shoulders to sag, once again accepting that she was simply just normal, she returned to observing her Angels.

One Angel in particular caught her eye; she was adorned in baby blue armour similar to the others except that she was creating ice from her fingertips. Jessica's eyes widened as she realised it was Chance. She hopped up and ran as fast as she could over toward her friend. She hopped over the legs of a street beggar who had refused to move even for the Phoenix guard. She ran with all her might. So fast that she then realised she could not stop herself and ran straight into the legs of Chance. Jessica fell straight onto her bottom, a little dazed, the sun shone directly down into her eyes as she gazed up.

"Chance, wow you remembered your power" Jessica paused and suddenly felt really embarrassed.

The face looming over hers, although similar, was not Chance. Jessica bowed her eyes suddenly and realised the mistake she had made. A soft sweet voice made her look up

"Hello little girl, and what's got you going in such a hurry?" the Angel in blue said, her eyes were a dazzling shade of icy blue, something cold and yet warm about her demeanour. Jessica was helped to her feet by a blue gauntleted hand that she instantly realised felt very cold to the touch. She dusted herself off and curiosity began to grow exponentially within her.

"You look a lot like my friend" Jessica said,

"Oh yes, I heard you say Chance, I too call her a friend. My name is Crystal, I am an Angel of Astoria, and what is your name?" Jessica was instantly charmed by this Angel, like Chance she was absolutely beautiful in every possible way and it amazed her just how much they looked alike.

"My name is Jessica, although I am not an Angel" Jessica's head dropped, feeling a little sadness that she had yet to display any real power, power that would allow her to join the ranks of Astoria.

"Well that's ok, you are still young, what are you, seven maybe? Gifts don't become apparent until after the age of eight" Crystal said and placed a gentle hand under her chin, lifting it slightly to peer into her eyes.

"You are a beautiful little girl Jessica, gifted or not you will be an Angel to somebody someday" she added. Jessica went red with embarrassment. She decided she liked this lady; she almost immediately began to determine whether she wanted to be more like Crystal than Chance, a tough notion?

"Are you scared? Is that why you are in a hurry?" Crystal asked.

"Scared?" Jessica replied. Crystal then merely looked up toward the swarm high above, then back down to Jessica.

"The flies don't scare me Angel Crystal" she said slowly, "it's what comes before it that does"

"Oh?" Crystal asked, a little intrigued by the little girls chain of thought. Crystal turned and knelt down to her height, making sure she gave her full attention.

"It's the panic, the people will go crazy and it will be infectious, the panic will spread and innocents will get squashed, just like a flock of wildagoats when startled" Jessica said. Crystal was a little impressed by this girl's insight into the situation. She was spot on, the initial panic and resultant stampede would crush thousands. The pandemonium would create chaos and in the end, by the time the swarm hit and sucked the air out of the area, the worst will have already been done. Crystal began to ask a few very specific questions, trying her best to determine the true potential of this young girl.

"And what would you do if you had the power to help?" Crystal asked, and watched Jessica closely as she answered.

"I would keep an eye on the swarm and order everyone to the other end of the city, keep everyone orderly and away from harm. I would shout at them, my father always taught me fear can be controlled through one act of bravery, I would be that act." Jessica replied and folded her arms, completely believing in herself and her desired purpose.

"That is very insightful of you Jessica, you must be pure of heart to think of others the way you do. And if I then told you there was a way I could Give you the opportunity to help these people, what would you say?" Crystal asked.

"I'd say, let me do my part" Jessica responded.

Crystal stood up having heard all she needed to hear. She pulled a long satchel from her back compartment; the satchel itself seemed old in design and yet spoke of futuristic technology.

"I Crystal, of the Astorian Angels, hereby deputise you, Jessica of Sanctuary, into the Astorian guard with the sole purpose of protecting the people of Sanctuary from any harm that may befall them. With this Boomer, I hereby grant you the power that you require, for the purpose I have stated. Let your heart guide you always young one" Crystal handed the satchel over to Jessica who took it rather puzzlingly. It was just short of two feet long and wrapped over many times, the material was of a very strange and almost alien design. Upon taking it in two hands, the satchel became animated and she got a small fright as the satchel began to sprout tentacles that began to attach themselves to her and cover her entire body. She looked up at Crystal who stood there with a caring smile on her face, a smile that told her not to fight it. So she didn't.

Her whole body began to get covered now and she felt herself rising into the sky, rising much taller than the blue Angel before her. She looked to her arms which were now fully covered in this grey material, a material which by now began to expand and take on a more squared off look. This same process was occurring over her entire body, she looked to her legs which now resembled square, robotic pillars of power, and her body was no different. After about two whole minutes the process had stopped. Jessica glanced at Crystal who smiled and simply said "impressive" before turning and walking slowly away. The old beggar that sat, ten yards away, looked on, absolutely gobsmacked as Jessica, who had now taken the form of a 10ft robotic guardian, stood before him. Her little 7 year old body safely secured inside this massive tactical armour.

"Ah the great betrayer" Raphael said, turning his full attention toward the Siren who sat on the raised throne before them.

The Siren had long, shiny black hair that she was wearing tied up on top of her head. She was very slim with hazel coloured eyes. She was dressed head to toe in a seductive black dress that covered her feet entirely. The dress seemed to shimmer irregularly almost as if it was some illusion in itself. Raphael walked up casually, one hand in his pocket and the other hand was eating a fresh green apple. He bit into it, taking a juicy large bite.

Chance stood to his left, absolutely dripping wet and irritable from the experience. She was scowling directly at Raphael but he took no notice.

"I do much prefer...the grand illusionist" the Siren replied, making a wide gesture with her arms toward their surroundings. As she did so, the walls lit up in golden bright colours, decorating the surroundings with the image of a banquet of a grand scale. Chances eyes widened in awe at the sheer beauty of it. The glass chandeliers, the golden...

Another cold bucket of water was hurled over her head bringing her brutally back to reality. The bitter cold shock of it caught on her breath.

"I wish you'd stop doing that" she growled at Raphael through freeze chattered teeth. He merely smirked at her and turned back to the Siren.

"Grand illusionist...that figures...and what illusion of reality are you aiming to bestow upon us today?" Raphael said, standing firm and immune to her gift.

"Oh my little Raphael, if only my power had any true effect on you" she paused "you must want for nothing"

"Or have everything I want" he countered.

"A cute sentiment, although I am pretty sure it fell on deaf ears "the Siren drew a smile across her beautiful face. Raphael turned to look at Chance, who was now attempting to use her fingers to comb through her soaking wet hair. A little disappointed, he threw her a comb that he once again produced from nowhere.

It bounced gently off the back of her hand and landed on the floor in front of her. She looked at it confused as to where it had came from, shrugged her shoulders and concluded that straight hair was more important that an explanation. She picked up the comb and began using it. The Siren looked at the apple in Raphael's hand before speaking.

"Swapped your sugar cane for fruit now have you?" she asked, with an element of coyness to her tone.

"I'm just watching my waistline" he replied and took another large bite; his hand ever remained loosely in his pocket.

"Well aren't you going to share? Like you did in the...good old days?" the Siren added. Raphael looked at her for a moment and then looked down at his half eaten apple; he nodded slightly and threw her the half eaten apple. She caught it in her hand and then allowed it to drop to the floor, landing amongst the dust. Raphael shrugged his shoulders and produced another apple from seemingly thin air. He turned slightly and could see Chance was still scowling at him. He sighed, looked at his fresh apple and then tossed it across to her. With a comb in one hand, she only just managed to catch the apple in her other. Once safely in her hand she turned it over, took aim and

171

launched it straight back at his head. The apple hit Raphael to the side of his temple and bounced off, landing on a small rock next to his feet. Raphael just shrugged his shoulders again, bent down and picked the apple up, dusted it off against his top and then took a large bite. He then continued his interrogation of the siren

"You lured..." he paused, ensuring he got his facts correct "HER here, and for what purpose?" he asked

"Well you may well have all that you want dear Raphael, but your sidekick here has very strong wants and desires. There is something important to her that she seeks, I could feel her 'need' from miles away" Chance stopped combing her hair and looked up. A genuine look of defiance had now adorned her face.

"Hey I'm no sidekick sister!! I'm the main show!!" she said and then began to flick her thumb in the direction of Raphael

"This chimp follows ME around!"

Raphael merely raised his eyebrows at her. Chance met his gaze and held it there, defiant in justifying her place and therefore ensuring Raphael knew his place. Raphael gave a small laugh as he submitted and then turned back toward the siren.

"And let me guess, this 'need' that she seeks, you know where to find it?" he asked

"Naturally" she said. An entertaining playful smile crossed her face.

 For the first time in a long time, the Siren felt a genuine playful humour that took her back to her younger days, to a time when she had once been deemed an Angel within the eyes of the Astorians. She could even remember Raphael thinking likewise of her.

"This information...I assume it comes at a cost?" he asked.

The Sirens nostalgic mood was reduced slightly, the question reminding her of just how low she was now regarded by her previous comrades.

"No cost....I seek to redeem myself in the eyes of Astoria, a mere mention of my aid will suffice"

Raphael scoffed and then took another bite of his apple. The sirens smile very quickly became an angry frown as he had so willingly and easily disregarded her attempts to repent.

"Do not be so quick to judge me Raphael, I am not the only one here with dark secrets" her words were challenging bordering blackmail.

"You are the only one with a chequered past" Raphael countered quickly.

"Yes and a past that I wish to recompense" Raphael remained silent, wondering whether such a debt could ever truly be repent or repaid. Chance continued to comb her hair, pretending not to listen to the exchange that had been going on between them both. For now, they both remained silent. It was not long before the Siren broke the silence and gave up the information that they required.

"The artefact you seek is a small, red memory orb, within its spherical wonders you will find what she is longing for. This orb lies deep within a temple on the north eastern edge. If you follow the mountain line it will be six hours walk for you" the Siren then paused, a coy smile crossed her face "alternatively you could cut across the old bone yard, you'd be there within half the time"

"I'd rather not" Raphael quickly replied "we will fly there and arrive within the hour"

"Oh I hope it's not a technological flying device...you know how much Astorian law frowns on such devices" the Siren said. A frown had now crossed Chances face as she realised that, and not for the first time today, there was an unsaid truth lingering in the air.

"Do tell me, how is it that you know its location? Or in fact know anything about this 'orb' at all?" he asked, a strong feeling that the Siren was somehow involved in the events that had unfolded this day.

"I see and hear ALL things my dear little necro.." the Siren paused mid sentence as Raphael shot her a stern and sincere look, a silence descending for a few whole seconds as she chose her next words a little more carefully.

"It matters not HOW I know, it's merely important WHAT I know" she replied, once again wearing a coy grin across her face as she enjoyed the small moment of vulnerability she placed him under.

Chance was, by this stage, triply confused with the subject content being discussed before her, she chose to cut to the chase and voice her queries.

"Why are we to avoid the bone yard?" Raphael held his gaze stoically upon the Siren who met his eyes then turned to respond to Chance.

"Oh trust me my little darling, in this scenario, ignorance truly is bliss!"

Chance shook her head in frustration and muttered under her breath.

'Why was nobody straight with her' she thought to herself. Upon shaking her head, the light reflected off her necklace that was fastened and held close to her chest. The Siren instantly recognised the charm and began to reminisce a time before her fall, a time when she had been allowed to move freely around Astoria serving its people as a protector, a beacon of light. She remembered how she would stop the peasants in the street and cloud their minds with visions of a shinier life, of treasures on a grand scale to put smiles on their faces if only for brief moments. The Siren looked at Raphael and realised that he had grown into a man now, a strong, honest and good man. To her though, he would always be that little boy, that sweet little boy. Her eyes filled with sorrow, feeling the emotional strength of the emotional loss.

"Until the end of time" the Siren said "and I'll bet that sentiment falls on deaf ears also" the Siren said. Both Raphael and the Siren turned to look at Chance who was, for the second time today, filing her nails. Chance looked up and exclaimed

"What?"

Raphael shook his head again. This girl never failed to disappoint he thought. At that they took their leave of the Sirens presence and headed back out the chamber and through the wooden door.

The room they re-entered was the blazing hot fire trap room. The bridge was still performing its descending ritual, and fire was still being burst across its front. Chance stepped in front of Raphael, turned, and stopped him in his tracks.

"Now look here, you may be a little trigger happy with your buckets of water there, but I doubt they will extinguish these flames. I need you to watch carefully, as this is very tricky and dangerous. One wrong move and you'll be a burnt little monkey. Got it?" she said rather patronisingly. Raphael merely nodded, feeling her potential wrath if he was to do anything else, she seemed very sincere and for the first time this day, he thought he had best just leave her to it.

Seemingly satisfied, Chance nodded and ensured his eyes were firmly fixed on her. She turned and made her way to the bridge. Her left leg was still aching from earlier and she doubted she would look too graceful jumping and dropping like in her initial attempts, and so she opted for her latter strategy of acrobatically swinging from bar to bar, keeping the bridge well beneath her and away from the hot flames. She hopped up and grabbed the first bar and began to make her way across. She found her method easier now, as she had judged the distances between the bars perfectly, she had an audience now too so she did not want to seem clumsy or risk falling. Fortunately neither of the above occurred and she gracefully hopped down to the safety of the other platform, smiling from ear to ear, knowing full well a display of such skill must surely have impressed him. She turned, bowed and started to speak.

"Now you'll need a good run..." her voice trailed off as she watched him walk slowly over to the cranking mechanism that was located on that side. She watched him curiously, as he waited for the bridge to drop, as it did so, it extinguished the flame spouts beneath it, but not before the gas that had been sprayed from the side, had been ignited, sending a massive torrent of flame bursting across the bridge itself. This burst eventually burned itself out, and as it did so, the cranking mechanism started to turn to lift the bridge back up once more, ready to repeat the entire process.

Raphael stepped up, waited until the opportune moment, and jammed a rock into the cranking mechanism, preventing it from turning, and so the bridge stopped its ascent. The ignition flame spouts beneath it could not relight, and the bridge sat quite still, traversing the gap over the extinguished flames.

He calmly and slowly walked over to the bridge, hopped down and crossed the expanse, crossing over it completely safe and out of harms way, he then climbed up onto the other platform just in time for the rock to come loose, and allow the bridge to rise once more, Starting the whole deathly cycle off again.

Chance eyed him irritatingly, her eyes burning through him in a way that the gas flamers had not.

"What?" he exclaimed, she shook her head and walked ahead.

In the next room, she didn't even bother to help him.

"Find your own way across this one then genius" she said, clearly indicating her huffy mood. With no explanation of her plans, she jumped up into the air and began launching her fireworks down into the gap, revealing the platforms once more and gingerly jumping from step to step. It was a tedious and very risky task; she could barely catch a glimpse of the platforms before jumping. After a few precarious leaps and bounds she reached the other side and turned.

"I hope you were paying attention to where the platforms were!!" she said, a look of general dislike toward him was worn across her face.

Raphael walked over to a small gathering of rocks that lay strewn on the floor. He picked one up and crushed it in his hand, turning it to powder. He then scattered the powder across the gap, and as it stuck onto each platform, it revealed them perfectly and permanently. He grabbed a few more stones, crushing them into powder and repeated the process, revealing platforms all the way across the gap. It took little effort for him now, to hop his way across and reach the other side.

Chance immediately turned on the spot and headed for the door, absolutely fuming by this stage.

They finally entered the initial room, the crushing chamber. The large stone sliding slabs were sitting at the walls edge, just waiting for them to enter its channel and start its fatefully crushing movement. Chance turned to him.

"Well I guess you have a clever way across this trap as well do you??" she asked, although she did not actually wish to hear the answer. She hoped he had been forced to run as she had, to sweat, to work, to panic, and use sheer adrenaline to make it through. She had really felt like she had achieved something today completing these tasks, and yet, here was this irritating man, making it all look easy.

Raphael wore an anxious and worried look upon his face, knowing full well that his next action was most probably going to irritate her even further. He grabbed a large stone from the nearby wall, dislodging it from its position, and carrying it in two arms; he walked to the edge of the channel. He pushed his arms out away from his body so that the rock hovered, just over the start of the channel, he then let go of the rock. It dropped, and as soon as it hit the floor of the channel, the walls on either side of it began to slide inward. Raphael waited a few seconds, as the massive stone slabs advanced into range, then hopped onto the tip of one of the sliding walls, and started to casually walk his way across. The slab was continuing its advance, closing the gap in the channel beneath him as he was safely walking along its peak. By the time he was at the other side, the two walls had completely slammed shut in the centre, and he could walk quite freely across the room which was now simple a large, flat stoned area. He turned and could see Chance following in behind. Her fists were clenched so tight that her knuckles were glaring white. He tried to give her a small smile but she shot him a look that told him otherwise.

"You're not funny!" she stated and brushed passed him aggressively. He shook his head dismissively, he could only imagine the lengths she must have gone to, to bypass this trap. He chose to remain silent for awhile afterwards.

On the far side of Sanctuary, Pepsy followed the directions that had been given to her by one of the market vendors that seemed to have an idea where her friend may be dwelling. She had not been to this place before and so could not visualise it. Without a homing beacon or something to emit a glimpse of the place she was heading to, she could not use her gift of teleportation and so she had to do the old fashioned method of placing one foot in front of the other repeatedly. She turned down an alley and realised that she was most certainly in the grimiest area of the city, all manner of lowlifes and undesirables clearly dwelled here.

Jeremy had really chosen this spot well this time she thought. A few drunken down and outs littered the alley floor and paid her very little attention as she stepped over them and continued on towards her destination. After a few more yards she stopped, looked to her right and here she was.

'No chance saloon' figures thought Pepsy to herself. She took a deep breath and then pushed her way in through the double swing doors.

Inside, the room was dark and equally as dingy as the alley outside. There was a bar that ran the length of the room along with some stools that had uneven legs propped up next to it. In the far corner there was an old duke box that was lit up with the brightest, most neon colours and this was easily the eye catcher of the whole place. It drew your attention away from the dirt that was inch thick on the floor. The room was quite large but something felt small about it to her and she couldn't quite put her finger on it, It just sort of felt like a nullifying place and she had no idea why.

Slouched on the bar upon one of the stools was undeniably her friend Jeremy whom she had spent the last two days looking for. She took a few steps forwards and was then stood beside him, the strong smell of booze and mint was filling her nostrils and she began to try and determine just how much of that had been drunk, and how much he may have spilled in his state. She hoped more of the latter.

"Jeremy... its Pepsy, iv come to take you home" Jeremy's intoxicated eyes looked up, his head was swaying and he was struggling to focus. After a few moments he smiled and slouched his head back down into his arms. He began to speak and Pepsy had to strain her ears to make out his words through his muffled arms.

"Home is where the heart is" he said and started laughing. She was in no mood for jokes or games. She had almost worn herself out with worry the last 48 hours and here he was, drunk as a skunk and without a care in the world.

"This isn't funny Jeremy, come on lets go, I'm taking you back"

Jeremy's giggle turned almost manic and he started to repeat the same words over and over "oops...ooops...ooops" She couldn't work out what on earth he was talking about until she suddenly saw something shiny hanging from his wrist. It was very thick and shiny and trailed from his wrists down, and over the other side of the bar. Pepsy pulled Jeremy toward her and her eyes went wide in alarm. Jeremy's arms were chained to the bar with massive thick set chains and a thick lock. She panned her eyes back toward the doorway which was now blocked by four, very large and muscular men. They stood menacingly with their arms across their chests, a simple indication that they were in charge here.

Pepsy shook her head, grabbed Jeremy's arm and attempted to teleport out of there and back to Astoria.

Nothing happened. She tried again, and again nothing, she felt nullified, she just couldn't feel her gift.

"Ooops" Jeremy said again.

"What on earth is going on here?" Pepsy said suddenly realising, to her alarm, that the four very large men were now making their way toward her.

"Ooops" was all Jeremy said as the men lunged for her.

CHAPTER 8

Misty dropped them down low and slow toward the ground, landing her massive talons gently on the desert surface and allowing her passengers to climb off. Raphael had at least on this occasion remained awake for the duration of the flight.

Before them stood an ancient temple that had been built into the mountain side. Its front face was the only side that was visible as the rest of the structure looked like it was built right into the mountain rock to unfathomable depths. The temple face itself was made from a strange kind of black smooth stone that almost reflected the light at peculiar angles. There was a main set of stairs that led up into a dark doorway and on either side of the staircase there was a large statue with a symbol on its peak. The symbol looked like the number eight but on its side. Chance looked up at the temple face in awe, she found it beautiful in a dark sort of way. As she turned to Raphael she nearly choked as she found him dressed in yet another ridiculous outfit.

"Pfft what are you wearing this time?" "You look like a stupid space ranger" she said poking fun at him. Raphael had adorned his armour although this time it looked slightly different. The armour plating was denser, the shoulder plates were larger and thicker and a small optical readout device had appeared up the back of his neck that craned around to his right eye. On his back there was a medium sized pulse rifle capable of firing explosive tipped rounds rapidly. Raphael simply glowered at her, he did not appreciate her poking fun at him and at the same time he was weary at his choice of armour.

One of his gifts that he had been granted a long time ago, gave him the power of necessity. Not many people were purvey to this information as Raphael's gift always seemed a bit irregular and random. But he was very capable of producing anything that he needed at any given time from seemingly thin air. Sometimes his gift had a mind of its own and would sense what he required. In this case, it had upgraded his armour for him and given him a rifle. All signs Raphael did not like of what was to come. He continued to glower at her for a moment longer before speaking.

"I think I liked you better in the cave!" he said.

"What? When I was all doped up on the Siren's song?"

"Yep...you were all delirious and goofy looking, was refreshing to see" he said and finished it off with a smirk. Chance really did not have a comeback to that one and simply huffed and walked on toward the stairs. Raphael checked his rifles ammunition chamber and then followed in behind.

As they entered the temple, Raphael's eye optics automatically adjusted for the low lighting as he scanned around the room. It appeared they had walked into a very long entry chamber that would have probably been used once upon a time for holding an army out of the weather until ready to march, at the moment though it was bare empty.

 They crept along slowly and every twenty metres or so Raphael turned his gauntlet and fired off a small device that stuck into the temple wall and emitted a small pulsing light. He started to fire these on random walls as they progressed through the dark corridors.

"What are you doing now?" Chance asked, her face screwed up at yet another strange act from her chimp boy.

"I'm detailing the dimensions of this place, the pulse these nodes emit will eventually map the entire temple for us and give us a hololith display to work with" he replied.

"Sounds very fancy and technical" she said and immediately lost interest in what he was doing.

They made their way into a very large, dark chamber. Its ceiling was easily 100ft tall and the room carried on down throughout as far as the eye could see. Raphael trained his rifle around the room checking for any possible danger; it was quiet, eerily quiet. Chance followed closely behind and began to scuff her feet along the stone floor. She has long since concluded that her little shoes were ruined and therefore had no qualms about destroying them further. They crept quietly and slowly further into the chamber where the light in Raphael's torch began to reveal a large holding apparatus of some description. Both their eyes grew wide in awe as they realised the holding apparatus was linked to dozens more and each held rows upon rows of shiny metallic robots, hanging there lifeless on the racks.

181

There must have been thousands of them all the way down the chamber. Raphael eyed them suspiciously but then concluded that they were in fact lifeless and began to creep on slowly, Chance following behind as she began to hop step, to and fro.

"Dem bones dem bones dem dryyy bones" she began to sing.

"SSshhh" Raphael said as he continued to strafe his rifle tip from left to right as he realised that similar holding apparatus's were littered down the left hand side of the room also, complete with a full quota of robots attached.

"Don't sssh me chimp boy, it's my new song" Chance replied, keeping her eyes on the floor and doing her best not to step into the cracks on the stones.

"That song has been around for years" he replied and surveyed the area further, refusing to turn and give her any notice.

"Well its new to me" she continued to sing it much to the frustration of Raphael. Rather than address the song once more he piped up regarding another comment

"And what's with this chimp boy stuff all the time?"

"Well you do look like a monkey, I actually find it hard to believe we are friends really" she said.

"That stings" he replied, creeping ever deeper in the temple. By now they were about halfway down the large dark chamber and the torch on his rifle was revealing a stairway at the far end of the room some 50 ft away.

"I'll bet you work for me, I reckon you are my bodyguard!! Although I'd have thought I'd be able to afford someone far better" she eyed him up and down slowly with an unimpressed look. Raphael stopped and turned, returning her unimpressed glare.

"The quicker we find your memory the better" he said

"Or you could just tell me?" she asked. Raphael remained silent. She spoke again

"I think you DO work for me and you aren't telling me in case I boss you around"

"You boss me around anyway" he replied sharply.

"Huh" Chance said a little hurt by the last statement. She decided to make a little defiant stand and crossed her arms across her chest, refusing to move any further. Raphael turned and instantly recognised such a mood and cocked his head to one side with a small smile.

"Oh come on, you can give but not take it?" he asked. She remained silent this time, unwilling to give in until she had some form of apology. He slung his rifle and walked closer to her, placing one hand on her shoulder which her eyes were drawn to with another unimpressed look.

"Look I am sorry" he said with eyes that said he meant it. She tried to remain defiant but there was something about his eyes that stirred old memories. She tried her hardest not to smile but the more she fought it, the more she lost.

"Ok ok you are forgiven she said, but I am singing my song and no more complaints from you...chimp boy" she added the little jibe in the end. Raphael tried to take no notice.

"Hip bones connected to the...." she paused to think.

"Thigh bone" he said

"I knew that...and the thigh bones connected to the..."

"Knee bone!" he cut in.

"Hey you are good at this, and the knees bones connected to the" she continued to sing as Raphael cut her off with a question.

"What's got that song in your head anyway?" he asked, genuinely interested in her answer.

"Duh all the skeletons, do you think I'd just randomly start singing about skeletons when in a deep dark temple?" she replied quite calmly.

"I'm not sure what goes through that head of yours, but I'm sure it's pink, sparkly and completely useless!"

"HEY!! Easy there chimp chops, don't take your grumps out on me, I'm only little teehee" she placed her hands behind her back again and began to sway from side to side in an attempt to look cute for him. He stopped and turned, eyeing her closely and then shook his head with a small smile.

"Ok fair enough, but if you do see a skeleton you let me know yeah, haha skeletons" he shook his head dismissively.

"Are you not listening? I CAN see skeletons!!!"

"What??? Where?" Raphael asked, his eyes suddenly wide with panic, blurting out his response just as quickly.

"Duh look around you donkey kong, they are hanging from the ceiling" Raphael looked up and around him, shining the torch of his rifle into all the corners of the room. All he could see were the robots that were hanging from their racks. He furrowed his brow slightly as he regarded the robots a little more closely and realised that she was in fact correct. The robots looked like perfect skeletons made out of a very shiny metallic alloy. They hung there lifeless, each with two arms and two legs and bare shiny skull. They were quite simply metal skeletons. His eyes panned up slowly around the room, craning his neck around in a wide arc as his mouth lay open in awe. His eyes remained wide as he took in all the information that this new discovery meant to him.

"I really shouldn't be here" Raphael started to say, his demeanour had changed altogether and now his eyes were fully focused on the robot skeletons hanging from the walls. Realisation had set in to the perilous predicament that his proximity to such things had now caused.

"I've been trying to tell you that all day but you keep following me around" Chance rolled her eyes; this chimp was borderline stalking her. Raphael trained his rifle upon the skeleton robots that continued to hang lifeless; he continued walking backwards and his eyes were focussed like never before. Chance observed him slowly and started to shake her head dismissively at his newfound seriousness. She just couldn't work this boy out, he seemed brave and yet fearful, cautious and yet reckless, he truly was an enigma to her. If only she had her memory back she could perhaps make sense of this entire situation which, in her opinion, seemed to grow stranger by the minute. This strangeness grew even more as a gust of whispering air began to circle within the large chamber. At first she thought it just the wind, but she could definitely make out the hint of voices within it. She watched as Raphael's eyes began to widen, his rifle that was previously being expertly harnessed and directed with precision now hung at an angle toward the floor as his eyes looked on at the next few moments in awe.

"YOOOOO!!!" Raphael exclaimed.

The eye sockets in all of the robots instantly turned to a dark shade of purple. The metallic hands, all in unison, curled and the legs began to kick. Within minutes, thousands of metal robots had started to hop their way off the hanging harness, un-shouldering they long black rifles that had slung unseen on their backs and form up into long straight lines. Raphael gently took hold of Chances arm and pulled her softly towards him, being careful not to make any sudden movements or draw any attention to them as they crept backwards towards the stairwell that featured the top end of the chamber. They both watched on as more and more robots hopped down, slung rifles and then turned toward their location. They all stood there, in perfect straight lines a hundred robots across, staring at the duo like mindless drones. Raphael looked back and could see they were about 20 ft from the door by now but still refused to make any sudden movements like running. So they crept slowly backward.

As if an unheard voice had spoken, the drones raised their rifles in perfect unison, thousand of battle ready metallic skeletons all coming to attention at once. They all took a step forwards and immediately opened fire on Raphael and Chance. Raphael wasted no time and hooked her up in his arm, turned and made a run for the door way. A hail of green coloured bolts sailed past his face and sizzled into the wall in front. He ran with everything he had and when he reached the stairwell his feet slid along the stone wall and into the cover of the stairway. More green bolts, presumably fired from the metal skeletons, sailed in through the door way and sizzled on the wall behind.

"Oh not again today, why can't we ever meet anyone nice" Raphael said as more bright green bolts passed by their vision and fizzled harmlessly against the far wall.

"Why can't we ever meet anyone that can shoot straight" Chance replied, as always the severity of the situation never failed to sail above her head. Raphael turned and looked at her, shaking his head and recalling the bruises his back had sustained protecting her from the rubber bullets in Sanctuary. This had probably gone unnoticed to her, mostly because he didn't complain much at the time; well he never had the time to as the fight had been on him so quick after that.

The bright green bolts continued to pass through the opening to the stairwell as they hid safely in cover, guarded behind the wall next to it. It was as if the drones were programmed to fire a constant stream in their direction regardless of whether they had a direct target or not. Raphael looked down the stairwell with his rifle, using the torch to light the way down. The stairs went down quite a depth however he didn't like the prospect of going back out into the chamber, face on with the platoon of drones marching toward them, firing a green bolt that could deliver any untold amount of harm upon them. He weighed up the odds and then directed Chance toward the stairs. She bounced along quite happily.

Raphael began to wonder about her behaviour, did she have genuine belief that he could keep her safe and out of harms way or had her memory loss included the emotion of fear, because to him she seemed fearless and disinterested in the obvious dire situation that they had yet again found themselves in today. He pondered this further as they made their way down two flights of stairs. Chance was following slowly behind, her slow progress mostly due to her examination of the walls as and she ran her hands along them. Everything she came across today seemed fascinating and new and she was going to make sure she took in and enjoyed every moment of it.

"I think I am going to call them 'Skelemets' since I did see them first" she stated, her thoughts had drifted to the metal skeleton drones that were pursuing them.

"Well since you are claiming ownership can you tell them to stop?" Raphael replied.

186

"Why? They don't seem to be aiming at me" she said. Raphael scoffed before replying

"I think I'll write a book entitled 'perils of a human shield'" he said.

"I'll write mine first, called 'dealing with a whining sidekick" she countered. Raphael tried to ignore her comment and turned, and was just about to make a gesture to hurry her up when a bright green bolt struck him square in the chest and knocked him flat onto his back. He immediately began to convulse and shake all over.

His armour began to smoke from the heat that the bolt had poured into him. His hands were clenched and Chance stopped in her tracks, almost dumbstruck as to what to do. She watched as he climbed to his feet quickly and staggered, seemingly disorientated. He turned and threw his armoured fist straight into the wall and smashed through the stone, sending small pieces of rubble bouncing down the stairwell.

"Aargghghgh do you have any idea how much this stings!!!" he growled, picked up his rifle and leaning into the centre of the stairwell, firing up toward the advancing drones that had now entered the stairway. He fired off a few rounds and felled a few more drones before another green bolt struck him again, this time in his shoulder. The bolt itself, upon looking closer, resembled a large stream of green electricity.

"AArghgh ouch, it's like that frustratingly sore feeling you get when a limb goes numb...and the tickly feeling resulting from the blood flowing back in..." he said and slid himself against the wall and out of a clear line of sight of the enemy.

"Oh stop being a baby, I thought you were genuinely hurt there" she said. She looked up and saw that the robots were now marching slowly yet relentlessly down the stairwell about two floors up.

"Would you care if I WAS hurt?" he asked, looking for some level of sympathy from her

"Not really" she shot back quickly. Raphael shook his head in disbelief.

"I'll be glad when this day is over" he said.

They started down the stairs at a much quicker rate, taking the stairs almost two at a time with Raphael directing his rifle and torch light into every dark corner or any open corridor that presented itself to them on their descent. They were now a good four floors ahead and the stair way ended into another large chamber although this time slightly narrower, almost like a corridor except of larger dimensions. Raphael's torch was barely reaching all the way to the sides, the corridor was so big.

As he stepped forward, a purple beam of light beamed down hard from above him. It ran its way all over his armour and down every contour of his body. It covered him and yet was causing him no harm whatsoever. A curious thing he thought to himself and then walked on, after a few steps the light shut out but then came back on as soon as Chance entered the vicinity of its range, she too marvelled under its light and wondered as to what purpose it stowed as the light ran its way down her entire body, almost as if it was scanning her in some way to detect for weapons or perhaps to make note of her dimensions, its purpose was unclear. Likewise as soon as she lost interest she walked forward and the light shut out. She had to hop step to catch up with Raphael as the corridor was really dark and she did not want to become lost or be trapped in the dark for a second time today.

Had it only been a day? She thought,

Between dark caves, swarms, rubber bullets, burning balloons, fire breathing dragons, enchanting Sirens and now freaky, tickly firing skeleton robots, hell chimp boy was right, she will also be glad when this day is over. They continued on through the temple cautiously, the sound of the metal skeletons could be heard looming closer from the stair way behind.

They emerged into another tall dark room. In front of them there was a very large gap that ran the expanse of the room itself, too large for either of them to jump across even on a good day. Raphael quickly looked around and could see there was a contraption to his left that bore a great wheeled handle that was easily as tall as he was. The contraption was attached to a group of pulleys that when he followed their origins, found that they were linked to a hanging bridge that sat twenty feet above them in the air. The bridge itself was very wide and looked like it was made from the same metallic material that the

188

pursuing drones were constructed from. Raphael slung his rifle and gripped the large wheel in both hands. It didn't budge at all under his initial attempt. He turned slightly to look over to Chance who had a less than impressed look upon her face. She didn't have to say a word and yet he got the message loud and clear. He turned back toward the wheel, dropped his hips and put his every ounce of strength into trying to shift this wheel. Very slowly it moved and with it the bridge started to lower toward the expanse it needed to traverse. Raphael gripped tighter and a bead of sweat ran down his forehead. Inside his gauntlets he imagined his knuckles were bright white with the exertion of gripping the old metal wheel. He wondered just how long this contraption had lain dormant for, or perhaps its workings are made for stronger, more metallic hands.

Chance remained at the stairwell looking up at their slow pursuers as Raphael continued to labour at the wheel, turning it painfully slow and using up all of his energy to do so. His breathing had increased and by now, sweat was flowing freely from his head and dripping down onto the floor in front of him. He laboured on like this for some time until the Bridge had been lowered about halfway, by this stage and he was running out of steam. He paused for a second to catch his breath.

"Erm chimp boy, I don't think you have the liberties of a break today" Chance said, her eyes were wide and contra sending. Raphael looked at her as his lungs heaved up and down in his chest and his hands rested on his hips as he tried to recover slightly.

"I'm serious, there are at least a thousand drones 4 floors away" Chance added.

"What?" Raphael was shocked. He thought they had made good progress down the stairwell and had placed a good bit of distance between themselves and the drones. The metallic robots didn't seem to move with any real pace and he was slightly bewildered at the progress they had made. Four floors away meant they had perhaps 2 minutes at the very most before they would be in range to start firing. He immediately jumped back to the wheel with a new found sense of urgency, hauling all of the strength that he had left into the mechanics of the wheel. One turn more had brought the bridge down within 6ft of their position. Raphael began to grumble.

"After the day we are having, running, fighting, jumping, lifting, pulling and falling, I'm trying hard here to get us to safety and you go and give me news like that... could you not have lied?" he grumbled to her.

"I was lying" she said matter-of-factly "they were only two floors away...one floor now"

"Arghghg" he growled and then kicked the handle of the wheel with such force that it was sent spinning, bringing the bridge down to bear in the gap. It landed with a clank and then sealed into place. Chance made her way over and as she passed him she gave him a patronising pat on his cheek. He shook his head and followed her across the bridge and deeper into the temple.

Jessica, safely wearing the large suit of boomer armour, stood an impressive ten feet tall and was using her full bulk and stature to direct the panicked crowds away to safely. She estimated that the swarm had gathered mostly above the northern quadrant of the city and so redirected as many people as possible toward the southern edge of the city, ensuring that they followed a strict code of conduct, no running, no shouting, and always keeping orderly lines. Her voice was projected at a far greater volume which helped in posing an element of authority from a seven year old girl.

Crystal was hovering around watching on, rather impressed by the work of her newly deputised member of the Astorian guard.

"You are taking to the job excellently Jessica" Crystal praised.

"Why thank you ma'm" they both laughed at Jessica's use of official terminology to a higher ranking personnel in the guard. Jessica looked at Crystal closely, whose eyes were on the sky but not directed toward the swarm, her mind was elsewhere. Jessica took a rough guess as to what was on her mind and decided to angle her conversation toward the subject, to see if she was right.

"So THAT was Raphael?" Jessica declared. Crystal's eyes lit up slightly at the use of his name and turned toward her. She drew a smile and then looked back to the sky.

"I had heard many stories about him but had never seen him before, he is quite something" Jessica said. For a seven year old she was very much on the ball with such things.

"He is indeed...he is...unique" Crystal chose her words carefully, trying her best not to give away too much. Jessica decided to cut to the chase.

"You like him don't you?" she asked.

Crystal turned fully around this time and smiled at Jessica.

"You are a funny little girl aren't you, what makes you say that?" Crystal asked. Jessica continued to direct the civilians of the city as they spoke, her eyes darting between the people and then back to Crystal.

"I've seen the way you look at him, the way you cared for him when he was hurt"

"I will always care for him, I have known him a very long time" Crystal replied. Jessica considered this and knew that if she pried deeper she would get what she was looking for in the truth. Crystal continued and opened up a little more "he became my friend when all others wouldn't, he has always been there for me and he always makes me smile" Jessica considered these words and then replied

"The jester in the market always makes me smile, I've known him all my life too but I don't look at him the way you do at Raphael"

"You are an observant little girl aren't you, seems I was spot on to deputise you. A guardian must see and hear all things" Jessica smiled at the recognition that her observances was receiving. Never before today had she been praised as much as she was being now.

"Does he know how you feel?" Jessica asked, keeping the conversation on the hot topic and not allowing it to be diverted onto some tangent.

"I have tried to tell him many times but he is always so...distracted.." her voice trailed off, almost as if she was in deep thought as to the volume of incident in which she HAD actually tried to tell him but couldn't.

191

"Distracted...like with Chance? I've seen the way he looks at her, he cares for her very much" Jessica said.

"Raphael cares for all his friends, that is what makes him so special. There is no boundary or length he won't go to help a friend out if needed" Crystal responded.

"But you want his special attention?" Jessica shot back

"It is a selfish notion yes, to be his special someone would be a fairytale, but not one I would indulge at the cost of other peoples happiness"

"He seemed relaxed around you, it looked natural, perhaps if you told him..."Jessica started but Crystal cut her off.

"Jessica darling you are sweet and I do appreciate that you wish to see me happy. But some dreams are best left as dreams for if you make them a reality and they don't work out, they can quickly turn to nightmares" Crystal said.

"Chance said that IV to follow my dreams" Jessica said.

"Yes darling and Chance is correct, I said 'some' dreams must be left as dreams. Now focus on your flock my little deputy as a few stray sheep have escaped" Crystal indicated to a small family that were going against the flow of traffic in Jessica's movements to safety. Jessica smiled and took her leave and went to solve the problem.

Jessica's line of questioning had scored deep into Crystals mind and as she turned to walk along the causeway, back toward the Phoenix guard, she couldn't shake the thoughts that had plagued her since childhood.

Tell Raphael she thought, such a simple notion and yet it had been all too difficult over the years. She had tried so many times, and on each occasion something would go wrong or she would lose her bottle. She thought back to her youth when she was still at school.

She was lonely at school for the other children stayed clear of her. They had heard some stories of how her parents had been killed and how she had been given a gift that she couldn't control. This gift was the power to control the weather and it seemed, at least to Crystal, to

192

be so random. In her first few weeks at school she had made it snow so heavily that the ground became frozen and the crops and vegetables could not be harvested. Each day that the snow remained, she was shouted at and jeered at to make it go away, that it was all her fault. Some of the children had taken her jacket from her, in the aim of making her feel the cold so badly that she would somehow warm herself up and so melt the land. What the children hadn't realised was that she was dual gifted, and her second power was ice, so she didn't really feel the cold. This angered the children more.

Although she couldn't feel the cold, a small boy came to her, weaving his way through the crowd that were playing in the school yard. He sat down beside her and took off his straggly old jacket and wrapped it around her. The jacket did nothing to warm her up, but the gesture itself melted her heart. The same boy then produced a sugar cane from thin air and handed it to her; he sat there on the wall with her and never said a word as he too crunched his way through a sugar cane. She remembered looking at his arms and seeing he was covered in goose bumps as he was clearly feeling the chill and yet he never let on. He sat there beside her, swinging his legs on the wall as happy as could be.

That small boy was Raphael and their friendship had grown every day since. It took a few months of sitting in silence before he spoke and she learned that he too had lost his parents. That he too was not from Astoria. She found they had a lot in common and each day at lunchtime, they would sit on the wall and he would give her sugar canes and they would swing their legs together in unison. It was a simple act and yet she found it made her happy.

Crystal remembered the time of a bad storm. She had been in school and minding her own business when she received word that Raphael had been hurt. The word on the street was that Fern had burned him for some unknown reason and that his hands were covered in deep blisters. He had been apparently held at the medical bay. She recalled the level of worry she felt, not knowing if her friend was ok, how badly he was hurt, if he needed anything, *if anyone was with him to care*? All these thoughts had begun to cross her mind. And then it had started to rain and rain heavily. Large plumes of thick heavy rain that smashed up the dirt as it landed.

Since the world had been ravaged by technology, it rarely rained anymore and so this rain was clearly manufactured. All blame was placed upon her. The other children became irritated at her, telling her she had better stop the rain before the floods damaged the crops and nobody would be able to eat. With each hour that passed, the people around her grew concerned. This concern grew greater and greater. They began to turn on her in a very aggressive way. The older children of the school were called down to orchestrate the safe evacuation of the school and get the children safely home before it got any worse. Upon exiting the school one child turned to her and told her it was all her fault and that she should just leave. She became so upset that she ran, out into the rain as fast as she could. She ran through the streets, tears streaming from her eyes. Within a fraction of a second her clothes were absolutely soaking and were becoming very heavy. She ran to the river which had, by this point, burst its banks and started to flood the surrounding grass areas. There was an old rotten bridge that traversed the river and so she ran to it, ran to its middle and put her head in her arms and sobbed. All around her she could hear the splashing of rain and the ever increasing aggressive flow of the river below. She stood there, soaking wet and sobbing, the tears pouring down her face almost as quickly as the rain that hit it.

After about five minutes, she was holding her head in her hands and she heard strange sounds followed by the deeper sound of water hitting something Lastic. It took her a moment to realise that the rain was no longer hitting her face. She looked up and there was Raphael, standing with an umbrella to shield her from the rain. He was simply smiling at her like he always did. She succumbed instantly to her emotions and lunged herself into his arms and sobbed.

"This is my entire fault" she sobbed into his little chest. She could hear that his breathing was weathered; he must have run here to get her. He simply held her head and stroked her hair.

"I can't control it IV tried, I can't make it stop" she sobbed further. Raphael continued to stroke her hair slowly, holding her close to him. When he spoke he didn't say much. "some things are beyond our human control, but our conduct is always within our own power" She looked at him rather bewildered. He added "what a man's mind can create, his character can control"

She actually laughed a little and wiped some tears from her face. Never before has she heard Raphael be so profound.

"Did you read that on your cereal this morning?" She joked, still wiping the tears from her eyes. He returned her smile and laughed also.

"ha-ha no no, the Allfather has been teaching me things, ways to control my..." he paused" "other gift" Crystal merely smiled and felt so happy that he was her friend. He was the only one that had come to find her.

 Just as she was about to embrace him further, a large wave came crashing over the bridge, knocking them both into the river which was flowing very fast. The current was violent and both of them were tumbling end over end down the river. After a few hundred yards the river poured into a large lake basin that had also burst its banks and its depth was unmeasured. She shook her eyes clear and swam to the edge of the lake to climb out. When she looked back she couldn't see Raphael.

 Panic started to set in, her eyes started to dart back and forth, left to right. Still she couldn't see him. She glanced back up the river but still could see nothing. Her heart began to race even faster. Her eyes were suddenly drawn to a thrashing shape in the middle of the lake, arms and legs were flailing everywhere.

'Oh bless him' she thought 'he can't swim'

Keeping completely calm, she dipped her hand into the water and focused all of her thoughts. Her hand went super frozen cold and the water around it froze instantly. This effect spread straight across the lake and froze it all solid instantly. She yanked her hand clear and then skated her way across the ice to where Raphael was stuck, almost fully submerged within the ice. His head was protruding from one part, and a stray hand was poking out the ice a length away. He was stuck in place but safe nonetheless.

Crystal slid down onto her belly and came face to face with him.

"Hahahaha I really wasn't expecting that to happen" he said and laughed on the end of it as he referred to the events that had happened only moments before. She shared his laugh. They were both smiling and gazing into one another's eyes. It had taken her a few moments to realise that they had in fact both fallen silent. Her face was a mere three inches from his and she could feel her hand toying with his trapped hand. She couldn't even remember reaching for it. She turned her head slightly and looked closely at her hand; Raphael's eyes followed hers as she interlaced her fingers through his. She took her time doing this, each finger meticulously making contact with his. From his position he couldn't move and so she had to make all the movements for him. She now had all her fingers laced around his and there was a strong sense of comfort from his touch. She turned back slowly towards his eyes and looked deep into them. It had not occurred to her that the rain had in fact stopped, and the sun had started to shine through the clouds that had polluted the sky previously. The sun beamed down on a section of ice around 5ft feet away from where they were lying. It was still cold and with each breath they took, they could see it powder into the air.

Her eyes dropped onto Raphael's lips which had gone a slight shade of blue but were otherwise tempting her in. She looked back to his face, gazing deeply into his brown eyes and could see no sign of him rejecting her. Her heart began to race faster and faster. She had longed for this moment for some time now and it was almost upon her. She took her other hand and placed it carefully onto the side of his face, his eyes never left hers. She was no more than an inch away from his face by now. She felt him grip her hand a little tighter and she smiled on the inside at his show of nerves also. She moved just a little bit closer so that their lips would touch...

"WELL WELL WELL...quite the frosty predicament you've found yourself in this time hey chimp boy" Chance said it her usual mocking tone.

Crystal hauled herself to her feet, unsure of how much Chance had witnessed from the angle that she had approached.

"Do you want me to give Fern a call to come melt you out?"

"I think Fern has 'melted' me enough today" was Raphael's simple reply.

"Hmm yes I suppose she has, and what was that all about anyway, you never play games and yet you run on mid way and get in a fight with miss inferno" Chance said as she began to skate slide around Raphael's trapped head.

"Never mind" Raphael said, his heroics that day had obviously gone unseen by her as always. Chance turned towards Crystal and smiled

"Mr. Ganon would like to see you in his office right away" Chance said matter-of-factly. Crystal nodded and then said "what about him, how will we get him out?"

"Oh you leave chimp boy to me, I'm going to have a little fun with him first" Chance said and giggled on the end. Crystal turned and headed back up toward the school.

That was the closest she had ever come to doing anything about her feelings for him.

Pepsy dodged out of the way just in time as the first muscle thug lunged in with a flying fist to her face. As she retreated, she left her front foot where it was, stretched out before her, and sent the attacker tripping straight over the bar as he followed through on his missed attempt, smashing the glass contents of the beverages that hung there. The second thug swung a high kick straight toward her face, a move that she had anticipated, and so she ducked underneath it and then followed it up with a perfectly executed sweeping kick that took the muscle thug straight off his feet and crashing down and through the rotten wooden floorboards. She made a note, of just the kind of dive that Jeremy had been found in lately.

The last two thugs came charging at her, at full speed, aiming to tackle her to the floor and render her useless. Transferring all her weight onto the balls of her feet, she spun on the spot while holding her elbows high. The bony point of her elbow caught each thug perfectly as she spun around at high speed, catapulting the men spiralling on toward the bar like some expert bull fighter. Their desperate attempts to grasp her led to nothing as her rotating form made her difficult to touch.

"Yo lay" She exclaimed as she celebrated her triumph. Jeremy still sat slouched on the bar and grumbled something, it was quiet and burbled as his arms still lay cradling his aching, and drink induced sore head. Pepsy had to walk closer to make out what it was he was saying, as she got closer she heard him repeat himself.

"It's not them that you need to worry about" he said, dribbling at the mouth from his drunken disposition. She stood up straight and turned; from there she set eyes upon somebody entirely different and all the more menacing. The fifth thug stood calmly in the doorway; he was around 5ft 10 inches tall but was heavily muscled. He had a bald head that was littered in inked decoration of unknown origins, a dark patch covered one eye and from his smiling demeanour she could see that his teeth were encased in some shiny metal. His arms were as thick as tree trunks and his thighs even bigger, upon his arms he wore some kind of intricate armour, very high tech from Pepsys point of view and this stretched from the elbows right down and over his hands. Its legs were similarly strapped with this hi-specification armour.

She held her stance and awaited him to make the first move. She watched him closely to analyse his stance, try and find some weakness. Was he overcompensating on one side, was he left or right handed, was he truly uni-optic with that eye, would he be able to judge distance? All these thoughts now filled Pepsys mind given that she could not escape with her gifts nullified.

The large ink-decorated thug took a step forward, swung his massively built arms backwards and then lunged, a full length whip that appeared from nowhere. The whip wrapped itself around Pepsys leg and swept her to the floor. She landed hard; surprised that she too didn't fall through the boards as the other thug had. She looked up at this new thug as he approached her, the whip nowhere to be seen. He then raised his palm toward her and a large cargo net catapulted outwards and wrapped her up. It began to screw itself tighter around her, squashing her into a little ball.

"How...are you gifts not nullified?" she tried to say as her legs were squashed up to her chest. The large thug started to laugh, an evil deep and arrogant laugh.

"Because my little lady...I am not gifted...I am skilled. A token of technology...oh the wonders that you're All...daddy hides from you by banning tech" he said and continued to laugh.

Once she was completely pressed into a tight ball, trapped within the cargo net, the thug then looked down at her with utter hatred in his eyes and disgust; he threw his palm towards her and a bolt of what she could only describe as electricity fired down toward her.

The severe jolt of pain was the last thing she felt before she blacked out.

The Allfather stood in his observation chambers high up in the palace. The observation room was large enough to easily accommodate the entire Astorian council should the occasion ever arise. The room's shape and structure naturally directed its occupants attention toward the main viewing windows which were easily 20ft tall and three times as wide, letting in an abundance of light into the room. The Allfather stood there, a strong sense of solemnise in his mood. His eyes were fixed on the streets below and from his position he could see all the way down the entire city to the gates themselves, it was not difficult now, to see the madness and anarchy that had overtaken the city. Small skirmishes and fist fights over seemingly trivial matters were breaking out everywhere. The sheer volume of shouting and angry screaming, had filled the streets and the Allfather shook his head in disbelief at the sight of his life's work being undone in a mere chaotic few hours.

High above him in the sky, the second halo pulse of the day shone down upon Astoria. Its massively bright, slightly blue tinted ringed pulse rained down from the heavens towards the ground at a steady pace. As it hit the ground it fizzled into nothing and vanished almost as quickly as it had appeared. It truly was a thing of beauty and the Allfather adjusted his attention back to his people. Usually the halo would bring about a moment of silence and to those that worshipped it as an act of god would drop to their knees and pray, giving thanks to the gods they held faith with. On this day, with the anarchy in the streets, not a single civilian paid the halo any attention whatsoever. It was very alarming to him and a clear symbol that Astoria had lost something very important today.

The door behind him slid open and Spanners made his way quietly into the observation chambers, taking his steps carefully as always so as not to disturb any chain of thought the Allfather may be in. He walked forward a few more steps to a small circle on the floor marked into the marble decoration. The circle had no significance whatsoever but Spanners always felt the need to occupy this space when addressing his Allfather, a habit that he did plan one day to try and break, but felt he needed to be focused and on an afternoon like this one he opted to stick to his routine. The Allfather broke the silence, his voice was soft and spoken calmly, almost as if he was pre-empting the answers and had already felt defeat.

"Have you managed to locate the tech- signals that entered the city?"

"Not yet great one, it is a puzzle even to myself. There was a definite reading late last evening, a mass of devices that could easily have had a hand in what has occurred today. But all my searches have thus far come up short." Spanners replied.

The Allfather breathed out slowly in a sigh. If they did not get to the bottom of this quickly, the whole of Astoria could be swamped under this madness. He shook his head in sadness and remained quiet once more, thinking through other possibilities. As he did so a small white and beautiful little bird flew in through the observation window and hovered just in front of the Allfathers eyes. It was a small bird, no bigger than the size of his hand. It was a beautifully perfect white colour and the Allfather marvelled at just how pristine and clean it had maintained itself. On its little chest was a slightly red coloured set of feathers that made the perfect shape of a little heart that stood out amongst the contrast of the white. The Allfather lifted his right hand and held out his index finger and allowed the little bird to land on it as he examined the bird further. He continued to speak with Spanners as he did so

"And how is the progress on the ACG?" he asked.

"The ACG should be active within the hour. It took a bit of dusting off but should work efficiently once reactivated"

"Good...that's a little bit of positive news at least. It does, however concern me that we needed to activate it at all. I sense an old foe has been...lingering around our great city and causing her mischief wherever she sees fit" the Allfather added. He began to stroke the little white bird on its head gently, fixing his old wise eyes on its own. The little bird began to push its head into his finger as he stroked it, indicating it was enjoying the act.

"It is quite logical that she has had a hand in this, it would explain the misappropriation of our troops and Angels." Spanners added. The Allfather nodded. The little white bird flew off from the Allfathers fingers and landed straight onto Spanners shoulder, cocking its head to look into his eyes but he paid it no attention.

"Logic...hmm if only logic would enlighten us as to the location of our missing tech...Perhaps then we may have the answers we seek." The Allfather said.

"I have followed all logical steps. Our tech sensors picked up a signal passing into the city last night, our sensors did not pick up the devices leaving the city nor did they then pick up any readings of them INSIDE the city. I ran a check again both inside and outside the city walls but nothing. The missing tech, by all manners is no longer inside or outside the city walls." Spanners concluded.

At that the little white bird started to chirp erratically. Its squeal was very loud and ear piercing as the little avian beauty started to hop up and down on the spot frantically. Spanners turned his head slightly to look closely at the little bird as it continued to create a scene in the otherwise calm chamber. The Allfather remained facing the window as he spoke next.

"My dear little Harmony, how many times do I have to tell you that I do not speak bird, Spanners doesn't speak bird, and none of the Astorians can speak bird. So if you have something to add, please do so in a dialect we can understand." The little white bird fell silent. It flapped its little wings and glided off from Spanners shoulder and landed onto the floor next to his feet. In that same moment the little bird morphed and almost instantly took on the form of the Angel Harmony.

"What about the city walls themselves?" Harmony said. A level of excitement had entered her voice as she felt she had something useful to add to the problem. The Allfather turned almost instantly, took a few steps forward and pressed both his hands onto her cheeks.

"How blessedly clear is the mind too small for doubt" he said and smiled.

"It is very possible, that thought had not occurred to me, the pheromone readings were highest around the perimeter edge" Spanners added, suddenly aware that this could well be the answer they were seeking.

"See to it immediately" the Allfather ordered Spanners.

Over in the glow valley, Quincy and his full platoon of men were busy gathering up the glow worms. The worms themselves only glowed ever so slightly in the days light, when darkness would fall they would glow even brighter having charged up their glow cells from the suns energy. Quincy's task was to super charge their cells by adding in a little electricity, this part was fairly easy and yet was very tedious work. He would have a bag of glow worms gathered up before him, he would stretch out his hand and unleash a small torrent of electricity on the bag for around 5 seconds before stopping. The bag would glow brightly for a few moments until the energy was absorbed into the cells and then dull slightly, he would then move on to the next bag.

He felt grumpy and bored and his mind kept wandering to the blocked mine and how he was going to get through it, or worse how on earth he was going to get around it? His eyes were drawn up the cliff edge that rose up and over the copper mine, the rock face was ragged and dangerous and he did not fancy his men's chances scaling that. They had not the equipment for such a task and even if they had he doubted it would be an easy journey. His eyes were then drawn across the glow valley to the other side where the distinct purple glows could be seen creeping into the valley, the tribinium fields, the purple glowing matter that had ravaged this world so many years ago. Very toxic to touch, it also exhibits mutative qualities. Some rumours over the years have insinuated that it was the tribinium that gave birth to the Angel's gifts, an idea that may have some truth about it.

Quincy looked down at the equipment bags that lay strewn about the valley floor; none of them had re-breather equipment or even the correct bio-suits to navigate their way through the purple fields without risking severe mutation. In all essences of the word they were trapped between a rock and a hard place.

He continued to energise the glow worms when he heard some footsteps make their way up behind him. He turned and found one of his sergeants looking rather embarrassed; Quincy looked him up and down slowly before addressing him.

"Is there a problem sergeant?" Quincy asked, ensuring he kept a level of authority over his men. *His men* he thought, oh how he hated being in command, it was such a large responsibility.

"Sir, we are doing our duties as instructed, but, well it's just the men are concerned"

"Concerned that we are trapped here?" Quincy asked

"Yes sir, they have families they cannot contact, they are worried that they may be stuck here for some time, that they may not make it back?"

"I see...well you can tell the men that I will see to it personally that we will find a way out of this mess." Quincy stated and gave the sergeant a long hard stare. The sergeant then nodded, saluted and then walked away. Quincy shook his head. He hadn't even begun to formulate a plan and now he had a thousand men's concerns on his hands. A thousand more worries than he had this morning; this day was certainly not going his way.

He walked off through the glow valley, completely at one with his thoughts. He stepped his way carefully along a small track, ensuring that he didn't step on any of the worms, the risk of squashing one single worm could jeopardise everything here as the squeal would be heard for miles around and the worms would migrate to a new valley, perhaps one beyond the reach of the Astorians. He walked on and on the tip of his view, the purple mass of the tribinium fields shone brightly. He walked ever closer, still pondering the trapped conundrum he was in. He shook his head; it's not even as if he could call for help as they were carrying no tech that would allow a signal to be transmitted. The Allfather had banned such devices long ago. There was method to the madness then, but here and now, with a thousand men trapped he wished the ban had been lifted.

He had walked on a good few hundred metres and realised that he had in fact left the glow worm gathering behind, and now, all around him was just brown dirty rocks. He sat down on a larger rock and looked toward the purple masses that were no more than 40 yards away. From his position he could make out the intricate purple crystals, the crystals that, when oxidised with air, grew exponentially out of control and had swamped the entire planet like a fatal weed. The sad part of it all was that tribinium had been in fact man made once upon a time. It was designed in a laboratory somewhere far away and its purpose had been to power massive air ships that could leave the solar system. Little did they know back then, what they were unleashing upon the world, this very toxic fuel source. It did however serve its purpose, it was as they had originally promised it would be...unlimited. He laughed a little at the scientists being so right and yet so wrong.

 He looked far out into the fields and wondered just how many corpses lay strewn amongst the purple matter. It was never clear what happened to the entire population, to Quincy there was a lot that had not been said. Questions that he asked that were never fully answered. One simple question was why the tribinium never entered the Astorian realm? Why it sat on the outer edges like a perimeter of death, trapping them all in, keeping their world small. He was sure that someone had an answer and yet would probably not share it with the likes of him. He knew he could be childish at times. He never felt the need to take life too seriously and yet here he was, suddenly responsible for a thousand lives and being forced to tell the same lies to his men as he was probably told once by his superiors, white lies that kept the morale in place, but lies nonetheless.

As his eyes remained on the purple fields before him, his mind drifted back to when he was very young, and had found himself trapped within that terrible field, trapped between the toxic purple crystals, and the blade of a terrible 'iced aggressor' of a man hell bent on destruction. He remembered the heroics of his champion, swinging in to save the day, the Fireblade in hand, clashing with the ornate katanas of that Frost-king. Blow after blow, his fire cancelling out the ice, a show of power of epic proportions, screaming from each parried crash of their swords.

He shook his head; a feeling of sorrow had sunk into his heart. He had no doubt in his mind that the loss of Lucas, HIS idol, his HERO had definitely changed his views on posts of command, of authority, of taking responsibility of people's lives. He knew then that he was not capable of being self-sacrificing like Lucas had been, to put his own life ahead of others, and yet here he was, now responsible for so many lives and in such a predicament. He buried his thoughts deep and longed for the strength of a solution.

He began to flick his fingers and sent little shock of electricity out into the area before him, a pastime he enjoyed when in his state's of boredom. Looking back down to the valley he could see the men were still working hard and had stacked up a good number of bags for him to energise. His part of the process took a matter of seconds and so the backlog of work bothered him very little. He continued to flick his finger as his agitation grew.

He didn't ask to be responsible for all these men, he had never liked command and he had always made this very clear. Punishment or not, this had been a mistake and now a thousand lives were going to pay the price for it. His guilt was ever growing. He began to flick his finger even harder this time, gritting his teeth slightly as he held his choler in check. When he, if he, ever got back to Astoria he was going to have a meeting with the Allfather and declare himself not worthy of command. He had thought this through over the course of the day and he had come to the decision that he preferred to follow than lead. He would make his argument clear and point blankly refuse another command position again, irrespective if he was to be punished for such a refusal. He gritted his teeth more in his frustration and sent off a larger bolt of electricity.

Suddenly there was a massive explosion that knocked him clean off his rock and sent him tumbling down into the rubble. He landed hard against the stone and was completely bewildered as to what had just happened. His vision dazed and his heart pumping wildly from the adrenaline, he felt to the back of his head and realised that it was slightly wet, he brought his hand round to his eyes and could see that he had in fact cut his head against the rock, not a bad cut but the blood was flowing slightly and had covered his hand. He climbed back to his feet and heard the sound of 30 sets of boots making their way toward him. He turned and regarded his men, armed and readily alert as ever. They had no idea what had happened either but were coming straight to the aid of their Commander.

He looked around at the area before him. There was rock dust floating in the air and a lot more fresh rubble strewn around the ground. He looked closer and could just about make out tiny purple shards stuck into the rocks around him, thousands of tiny shards.

'*Strange* he thought, *how did they get all the way over here?'*

Realisation quickly sank in and he instructed his men to stand down as he walked over slowly toward where he had been sitting, his eyes firmly on the tribinium fields that were quite a bit out in front of him. As the dust began to settle he could see that there was now a patch of bare ground amongst the field that had not been there before. The 30 men stationed behind him watched on warily, unsure of what happened or what to do next. They could see no apparent threat and yet the explosion had really been quite something.

Quincy lifted his hand and aimed it toward another section of the field; he spread his fingers wide and focussed hard, unleashing his gift of electricity once more, straight into the purple mass.

This explosion had twice the power of the first one and knocked him clean off his feet again and sent him sprawling a good 40 yards back. His men had similarly been felled and sent tumbling back down into the valley, dropping their rifles in the process. Quincy slowly climbed back to his feet.

"Sorry guys...I had to be sure" he said, feeling slightly awkward that he had blatantly set fire to something explosively flammable and at an unsafe range, luckily none of the men were hurt as it would have been clearly his fault for not taking the necessary precautions, yet another reason that he shouldn't be in command as he acts before he thinks.

He waited for a few moments as the smoke began to clear, his eyes firmly fixed upon the new bare patch that had been created within the tribinium field. A smile formed across his face as he started to formulate a plan, a possible way out.

"Sergeant Do we have any thick tox-gloves in our inventory?" Quincy called out.

"No sir, we are not equipped with such protective wear today"

"Oh that's a shame; I'll just have to do this the old fashioned way then"

"Sir I must stress, if I'm thinking correctly to what you are planning, that tribinium is very toxic, the effects on you could be.." the sergeant trailed off, mostly unsure of what the effects really would be on an Angel. He was well aware that it was toxic but he was merely human, an Angel was already in some respects mutated.

"I told you sergeant, I'll find a way out of this for all of us, this is our way" and with that he stepped forward into the tribinium field.

Once inside he immediately felt a strange sense of lightness overcome his entire body. The gases being released entered his nostrils and gave an almost euphoric effect. Quincy, playing on the side of caution activated his re-breather kit which popped out from the collar section of his armour; it hooked up automatically around his nose and mouth and effectively would filter the air of any toxins before allowing it to enter his lungs. He took a few steps further into the field; a purple haze now clouded his vision. His muscles all felt tense and yet relaxed at the same time, he felt like something deep down in his body was changing, but he couldn't quite put his finger on it. He made a note that he wouldn't want to stay in the field too long, the strange sensation he was feeling was quite powerful and he was unsure of what exactly it was doing to him, and so he reached down toward a grouping of the purple crystals that lay sprouting outward from the floor next to him, and plucked them from the ground. He immediately was surprised at just how easily they came free, almost expecting them to be rooted deep underground. He lifted up four large shards and cradled them to his chest before turning and making his way out of the field. He took careful steps on his way out, the sensation he had been feeling was quite intense now and he was finding it difficult to focus. Once free of the field, he had thought the strange sensation would leave him, but it didn't. The proximity to the crystals was having a very strange effect on him; he now felt butterflies deep in his stomach and his vision had almost tunnelled from the strain. He walked carefully back down the valley into the glow worm area and noted that the glow worms shuffled laterally, clearing a definite path for him to pass. It was as if they could feel the same presence that the crystals effect was having on him and he wondered if he was perhaps being poisoned by the crystals, the effects being a negative factor that the glow worms did their very best to avoid. He questioned his theory on being poisoned, he certainly didn't feel that way, he actually felt good.

The men following kept their distance, knowing all too well from their teachings, the dire effects these purple shards could have on their health. Quincy continued on and had almost walked clear of the glow worms. His fingers and toes began to tingle and he felt like his vision had somehow improved, he could see much further and clearer now, the tunnelling effect had seemed to have subsided; it was all very bizarre for him.

 He walked on carefully and into the copper mine, taking care not to activate his gift and risk setting off the crystals, especially when he was cradling them so close to his body. Even his great Angel armour would not be able to deflect such a blast.

He walked on awhile longer, taking very careful steps until he reached the section where the walls had caved in on themselves. He gently placed the crystals down onto the floor and slowly crept backwards, keeping his eyes on the shards the entire time, almost anticipating them going off without a warning. He crept back to about 40 yards, the limit to his gift. He was feeling apprehensive, as he knew that this was this same distance he had been from the blast earlier, and it had still sent him sprawling. He decided to take another few steps back just to be sure, then lifting his arms; he took aim toward the crystals.

Something felt very different about his gift this time, almost as if it had changed in some way but he couldn't be sure, he followed through regardless as he normally would and unleashed his electricity onto the shards. His gift flowed at an even higher rate, exponentially higher and instantly ignited the tribinium shards.

The explosion this time was even greater than the previous two. A massive concussive blast wave erupted from the point of contact and shuddered the entire copper mine. The fallen rubble that had previously blocked the path was cleared instantly and blasted out the front entrance to the mine and scattered across the desert plains. All of this happened so quickly that Quincy had forgotten to disengage his gift. The higher rate of electricity conducted along the copper walls had begun to spike at anything that was conductive along the mine. It struck the poor 30 men that were waiting, all the way at the far end of the tunnel. It shocked them with so much force that their bodies were burned black almost instantly and they fell into a crumpled heap.

Quincy tried to stop his power, he tried to focus and shut it off but it wasn't obeying him at all. With nothing else to target now, it began to spike towards him, conducting off the walls and then flowing freely through him, lighting him up so bright that it seemed like a solar sun was going supernova in the tunnels. His eyes went white with the extreme power as it flowed through him. He could feel all his fingers and toes energised with such potential power, it was incredible. He felt like a god.

He managed to find focus, his vision became sharp and he once again felt in control of himself, he closed his hands and the flow stopped. The excess electricity bounced around the tunnel for a few moments more before grounding itself out. Quincy stood there in the middle of the open tunnel smiling, his body felt brand new and he felt like he was coursing with untold levels of potential energy. He had never felt this way before, he felt unstoppable. He turned and began to jog along the tunnel; an element of excitement started making his heart race. He had done it, he had kept his promise to the men. Perhaps command WAS for him after all.

He ran on faster and before long he reached the end of the tunnel. A group of men were gathered around what looked like a pile of charred carbon, the men's faces were full of grim sadness. Quincy stopped in his tracks; a cold feeling of dread overcame him. His heart almost stopped, his eyes dropped down to the carbon and as he scanned over the remains he began to make out arms and legs...hands...skulls, lots of skulls. He suddenly felt sick.

The smell of burnt skin was now stinking out the tunnel, a cold breeze was pushing it further out of the tunnel and even the men stationed outside began to screw their noses up at the smell. Still looking upon the remains, he naturally started to count the skulls, but tears started to flood down his face before he could get past 20. He was in command and he wasn't supposed to show such weakness, but he couldn't hold it back any longer. The men that stood over the remains looked on warily, 30 of their comrades had just been killed in what could only be described as an electrical attack and before them stood the only person, the Angel, with the gift of electricity. They were all a little dumbstruck as to what to do.

Quincy dropped to his knees next to one of the remains; the smell was terrible and pungent. The bones were still hot to the touch and smoking where they lay. He reached forwards and pulled out a white, hot piece of metal that instantly began to burn his hands. He cared not; the metal was one of the men's dog tags and had belonged to his sergeant, the same sergeant that had queried him earlier. He clenched his fist hard around the tag and his flesh started to burn. He felt nothing of the pain, all he felt was nauseous, dizzy and sick from the massacre he had just inflicted upon his squad.

Everyone fell silent.

The moment was so extreme, so out of this world that a catastrophe of this nature could happen in Astoria, that all the men around them were speechless. Tears were now flowing freely down his face, he had caused this, he had killed 30 innocent lives, he should have commanded them to wait in the valley, he should have thought this through. He was too busy enjoying the euphoric high that the crystals gave him that he forgot about the safety of his men, HIS men...and now HIS guilt a burden to bear.

"Lieutenant, I want you to take command and gather the remains, the route has been cleared and we make for Astoria. This mission is being aborted and we will return home. I take full responsibility for what has happened here, Ensure that your reports are as accurate and honest as they should be" Quincy said. His remorse was clear for all to see. The lieutenant nodded and started to quietly give orders to his men, being respectful of the dead around him. Quincy stood up and walked slowly down the tunnel and back toward Astoria.

CHAPTER 9

The large ink-decorated thug knelt down on one knee before the purple cloud before him. His head was bowed in supplication, daring not to look upon the being that was speaking to him.

"You have done well....Fasterix....now see to it that you attach the device to her armour...we must see and hear All that goes on behind the walls of Astoria" the cold voice said.

"My lord, the nullifying device will not allow her to activate her armour, we..." Fasterix was abruptly cut off by the cold sincere voice.

"Do what must be done...your task here is simple...Do not let your pride allow you to fall.."

"This device, wont the tech-sensors in Astoria detect such a thing?"

The cold voice laughed "this is not of technology based. This is unique in origin...I shall doubt they will find it" the voice ghosted off.

Fasterix nodded and stood to his feet. Turned and headed back into the saloon.

Once inside, Fasterix could see his thugs nursing their wounds at one end of the bar, in the middle of the room, next to the damaged floor, sat two chairs back to back. On one chair, closest to the bar sat the pathetic whelp; on the chair facing the door sat the Astorian Angel, His target. Both prisoners were tied together by a thick rope. He gritted his teeth in an attempt to control his anger. If he had his way, he would be done with this Angel now, destroy her where she stands and remove her from the board of play altogether. As it is, this is not his way and he was serving a higher power. For now he would follow those orders exactly, even if that meant doing things he did not like. He walked closer and then gave a sharp kick to the shin of the imprisoned Angel. She awoke sharply and with an irritation in her voice.

"What? Where am I?" she asked as her eyes darted around the room. Fasterix slowly took his massively muscled form, and stalked his way around her as he spoke. He was going to make sure he enjoyed this part as much as he could.

"You are in the 'no chance saloon' my little lady, and for now you are my prisoner until I see fit to set you free" he said.

"Who are you? Do you work for the king, when Astoria hears of this outrage..." Fasterix started laughing really loudly and Pepsy was immediately taken aback by his arrogance and self assurance.

"Oh my...you really have no concept of what is to come do you...the king, ha, he is but a mere pawn and will be removed from the board when the time comes." Pepsy took a moment to absorb everything she was hearing, it seemed all a bit bizarre that yesterday she set off to rescue her friend from his usual drunken disappearances', and now there is grand talk of secret plots to remove the king. Had Sanctuary really harboured such lowlifes all this time? It didn't make sense.

"And what are you exactly, A soldier for hire? What is your name?"

"A soldier for hire, hmm yes I guess you could say that, mercenary of destruction sounds far more appropriate. You may call me Fasterix for now, but there will come a time when you will call me 'lord'"

Pepsy really had no clue what was going on but she had quickly concluded that the thug in front of her liked the sound of his own voice. She longed so much to have her powers handy to get them out of there, she wasn't entirely sure if this creep was getting above his station or whether there was some truth in what he had to say, she decided it was her duty as an Angel, to probe further to make a better assessment.

"Hmm, and what is to come exactly? You look like you have friends in low places, planning a rebellion?" Pepsy put a small smirk on the end of her statement, not entirely ready for the answer she would receive.

"Ha-ha, a rebellion? Rebels, hmm a curious thought, and what does a rebel do exactly? Overthrow a constitution, re-instate their own leader, make things the way they want them to be?"

"Sounds pretty close for someone of your obvious IQ" Pepsy returned.

"And what if... WE just want everything to burn? Is that rebellious?"

Pepsy began to feel a small pool of dread begin to fill up inside.

This guy was crazy, she thought. It had been many years since she had come across anything sinister and yet this guy, this Fasterix, already topped the all time craziest. She reckoned that on the crazy scale he was at least nine and a half chainsaws. She chose to remain silent, a little shocked at how his story was becoming all the more believable.

"There has only ever been one Angel that has betrayed Astoria...in its entire history...One...That really is quite something don't you think?" Fasterix said as he walked menacingly around the room.

"We strive to better ourselves; we make a safe and fair environment where people can live at peace both in their bodies and in their minds. There has never been another betrayal because we are pure of heart, so NO, i don't find it strange at all" Pepsy returned, her resolve stronger after remembering what it was to be Astorian.

"Ah yes...Pure of heart...now isn't it chapter 2 in Astorian law that states 'even the best of the good can turn to bad'?" Pepsy remained silent, unsure of where he was going with this.

"It's almost as if your All-daddy is giving you permission to betray...for treachery...It's right there in your book, be pure of heart and yet he 'accepts' that even the best can go bad.."

"Nobody will betray what we have built, we are a family we..."

"WELL I AM HERE TO TELL YOU THERE WILL BE!!" he shouted almost directly into her face, she could feel his spit hit her cheek as he yelled his heresy at her. "TWO betrayals in Astorian history and this one will break the hearts of its entire people. Your perfect city will burn in the chaotic fires of wave space"

Pepsy held her tongue. She had to get out of here and fast. Whether this guy was crazy or not, he had used a phrase that she had heard only once before, and a long time ago, she instantly needed to make the Allfather aware of it. Talk of 'wave space' unnerved her and added some sincerity to his crazy ideals. He was perhaps corrupted and so there may be some truth in a plot to overthrow and destroy Astoria. She pulled in her chair and felt the tightness of the ropes around her.

She watched Fasterix, her eyes never leaving him as he walked across the room, taking a tribinium fuelled lamp in his hand, and then smashed it against the floor. His thugs made for the door as the room erupted in flames. Fasterix turned and spoke

"Everything will burn" he stated, an evil grin across his face before he walked out the doors.

The room was quickly filling up with smoke and she started to cough as some of it entered her lungs. She couldn't quite see the flames and yet it was obvious what had happened. She turned her head slightly and realised that Jeremy was in fact asleep. She kicked her leg under her chair and hit his draping leg.

"Hey what?" he said rather startled. "Woooo the bars on fire Pepsy.....aaannd the chair" he said as his predicament worsened almost instantly. She could hear him stamping furiously at the floor and she could only imagine he was trying to put out the flames.

"We need to get out of these ropes" she shouted over the noise of the burning bar.

"We need to get out of this bar" Jeremy countered

Pepsy just rolled her eyes at him stating the obvious. She looked around the room and could see no obvious sharp instrument that she could use to cut the rope, no clear sharp edge nothing. She would have to use good old blunt force trauma to break the chairs they were on, and hope to slide out from under the rope.

"Jeremy, we need to tip the chairs, we will go to the left in three" she said.

"Wait, your left or my left?" he replied.

"My left!" she shouted. Jeremy paused for a second as he thought about what she said.

"So my right?"

"That's right!" Pepsy shouted.

"That's right or my right?" he questioned again. She rolled her eyes yet again. They were in clear danger here, the air was slowly being sucked out the room and he was arguing over the smallest of details.

"Doesn't matter, in three yeah?" she shouted.

"What's IN three mean? On three or after three?" he asked again much to her frustration.

"Argh never mind" and with that she hauled her weight over to her left, sending both chairs crashing to the floor. She heard the distinct sound of snapping and hoped that it was wood, and not bone that had burst beneath the pressure of the fall. She quickly felt around her hands and realised the rope itself had become loose from her wrists. She rolled to one side and to her satisfaction concluded that the plan had actually worked. Jeremy picked himself up grumbling

"That had nothing to do with three, that wasn't even on one!" he said, genuinely annoyed at not being served the appropriate notice before such a tumble. She let his comments flow in one ear and out the other, grabbing him by his shirt sleeve and hauling him out toward the door. The heat of the blaze could be felt burning against their backs as they made their escape. They stumbled out and into the bright light of day that blinded them for a moment before their eyes could adjust.

Once outside the nullifying effect of the saloon, and still under the pressure of potential danger, Pepsys Angel armour automatically concealed her body. She adorned sleek red armour, with red plated shoulder pads and a red armour plated body protector complete with red boots. She was squinting in the bright light but could just about make out five shapes standing in the small clearing out front. The shape most probably belonging to that of Fasterix began to laugh.

"I don't know what it is you keep finding so funny but you are in big trouble now" she said with a newfound defiance and stronger resolve. Jeremy slouched to the ground to one side, clearly opting out of this fight. She merely shook her head at him in disapproval.

"Ah of course, a red knight...Always the aggressor, your armour betrays you"

"My armour tells nothing of my fighting ability" she countered, again upholding her defiance against such arrogance.

"Ha-ha true, but it does pre-tell me your fighting style. Another weakness your all-daddy bestowed upon you Astorian fools. Red – aggressive, green submissive, blue defensive..." His knowledge of Astorian military protocol was quite astounding and unnerved her even greater than she had already today.

"What about white?" she questioned as she began to circle him and his four thugs, deciding, as always, to take the fight to them.

"Creative" Fasterix responded... "and black destructive" he smiled on the end of that comment, a coy and creepy smile that screamed arrogance from lip to lip.

"Well perhaps I'll have my Allfather repaint mine red and black after this encounter with you" Pepsy said.

"Ahahaha, oh my little lady what a thought...you know your all-daddy has it all backwards...only in Astoria could green mean stop...and red mean GO!!" and with that he lunged his arm forwards, throwing a long coiled whip, lightening quick toward Pepsy shoulder. She estimated it was going wide by about an inch and so she stood her ground, keeping her cool. The whip did exactly as she had thought, although, when it then whipped back, it made light contact with the back of her shoulder before recoiling back and disappearing into his armour. She found herself feeling a little confused as it appeared to have done no damage whatsoever to her.

She cocked her head to where it had struck her, just to make sure and then looked back at him rather puzzled.

"Not so skilled after all" she said. She then watched his smile grow wider and that's when she decided to play to her armour and be aggressive. She jumped high into the air and started a corkscrew dive down toward her targets, after spiralling for around 4 yards lengthways, to gain their attention, she then 'shifted' and reappeared behind one of the thugs and swept him cleaned off his feet with a low spinning leg swipe. She moved swiftly and jumped high into the air with a spinning roundhouse kick, catching the other thug clean through the jaw and sending him straight toward the ground,

216

unconscious before he had even landed. The third thug had swung for her head, so she 'shifted;' away quickly and reappeared a few yards back, only to have Fasterix launch an electrified net towards her new position. It was bright green and buzzing with energy, giving her the distinct impression that this particular net would hurt a lot more than the net he had used to capture her earlier. Ensuring she never fell for the same trick twice; she quickly shifted again and appeared miles away in an orchard, somewhere on the far side of Astoria.

"Arghg wrong place" she said angrily aloud but grabbed three apples from the trees anyway and shifted back to the fight, launching all three apples at the third thug who had swung for her earlier. All three apples hit him straight in the face, exploding instantly with the force of the throw and sending handfuls of the squashed fruit into the vision of her attacker. She landed down into a crouch and grabbed her left vambrace, from there she pre-set some co-ordinates into her suits projectiles and then completed a perfect backwards roll to avoid a slashing whip from Fasterix, a whip that was laced with a purple matter that she could only hazard a guess would have hurt. She flipped up onto her feet and aimed her left arm toward the third thug, a small compartment opening up on the back of her knuckles and four small projectile holes could now be seen. She waited until the thugs' eyes met her and then she squeezed her hand into a fist, firing one of the projectiles at him and then, quickly re-aiming, she fired again, this time at the fourth thug.

The projectiles were small darts, no more than an inch long but were pre-set with teleport technology, to any destination she had programmed them to. Both shots found their targets perfectly and instantly both thugs disappeared.

"Enjoy the walk" she said with a smile, as she knew where she had sent them would be a long and hazardous journey to get back to civilisation. Both thugs' re-materialised far away, finding themselves slap bang in the middle of the desert plains, miles from anything remotely useful for survival, they grunted as they realised their predicament.

Pepsy walked casually forwards as Fasterix eyed her cautiously. The first thug, whom she had swept from his feet, was groggily clambering his way back up. Pepsys eyes never left Fasterix as she casually pointed her left arm down toward the thug and squeezed, sending him to accompany his friends into the desert.

Now it was just the two of them and they sized each other up carefully. They started to circle one another, eyes locked and hands trigger happy for action. Pepsy took her index finger of her right hand and began to make quick incisions into thin air. At first Fasterix ignored it as some distraction quirk, but it wasn't until he realised he had now circled around to where the first incision had been made that he was in danger, Pepsy wasted no time and threw her fist into her most recent incision next to her, and watched as her fist emerged through the first incision like a portal, punching him straight in the face. She then turned and kicked down into another incision she had made lower down, and her leg came through another portal and smashed into his knee, causing him to grimace and show his metal encased teeth.

Fasterix however was a fast learner and was by no means a slouch in combat, he quickly turned the tables and threw his electric whip straight back through the portal, emerging at her end and striking her straight in the chest, sending a deep shock through her entire body. She stumbled backwards, all her muscles tensing and before she had time to evade, Fasterix had jumped and landed a punch clean onto her face, knocking her to the ground and reeling in pain.

 Fasterix was vicious and dangerous; he ensured malice was hurled into his every movement. He had no plans to maim what he couldn't kill and so he followed up her felling with a stamp towards her head. As his boot was descending, large spikes protruded from the base of his boot that were intended to end her life, Pepsys eyes went wide in terror as she couldn't shift while still convulsing from the electric whip. She could feel the voltage still pulsing through her body as the boot was descending ever closer to her face.

At the last possible second she felt the voltage clear and she shifted out of harm's way and landed some 10ft away from him, crouched and panting heavily. Fasterix turned in annoyance, his eyes were now a solid black and she began to wonder if he was entirely human or if he was perhaps possessed in some way, his visage was certainly changing as the fight went on and she doubted anything truly human could have eyes as black as those.

Fasterix flicked a switch in his gauntlet, and then turned his attention back towards her as he hurled his massively muscular arm in her direction. At the last possible second he too clenched his fist, and sent four spiralling bolts from the end of his arm, spinning out of his advanced armour with menacing speed.

Pepsy turned to run and could feel the bolts homing in on her location. She shifted, appearing in the air high above and then shifted again, landing on ground level some ten yards away, but the bolts followed her through the gaping portals that were always left open in her wake and continued to pursue her, forcing her to dive straight out the way as the bolts sailed past her, she landed face down in the dust and rolled only to see the bolts turn on a large axis and were still heading toward her. She shifted again and this time cleverly put herself directly in harm's way by shifting in front of Fasterix himself, who immediately swung his massive fists toward her. This she had counted on, and held both of her arms tight to her head in a perfect boxing guard. The force of the strike knocked her back a few steps where she shifted again and landed behind his location. The bolts sailed through her initial portal, recalculated her position as being behind Fasterix and so tried to take the shortest route possible...through Fasterix to get to her. The bolts exploded against his massive armoured form.

He roared in anger as the bolts payload was of incendiary, and the flames engulfed him. Pepsys just watched on as the flames swallowed his entire form up in a fraction of a second, his body became a massively bright avatar of fire, his arms were thrashing and throwing the flames around. After a moment he dropped to one knee and the flames still burned white hot. She breathed out, allowing herself to regain some composure.

"That was a close..." she didn't have time to finish her sentence. She looked up and could see his menacing dark eyes focused on her. His armour was smoking but no longer alight, his face was slightly charred but apart from that, he was relatively unharmed. He was still kneeling but then he slowly made himself vertical once more, his jaws muscles clenching in anger from the obvious grinding of his teeth.

"Argh what is this guy's problem" she said aloud, perhaps hoping Jeremy would have an answer to her problem but he didn't. He still lay slouched against a barrel next to the saloon entrance, apparently oblivious to the danger SHE was in and also oblivious to the fact that the saloon was completely in flames by this point and would soon also be a danger to him with his proximity to it.

Fasterix growled and began to walk toward her.

"Very clever little lady...I say everything will burn and you think I am part of that everything..." he said through gritted, metal encased teeth.

"Well I didn't want you feeling left out" she countered with raised eyebrows. She had almost caught her breath by now but was clean out of ideas on how to beat this guy, if he was even human.

"This is the part when you realise that running is your only option" his eyes were pure black and demonic. She had never encountered such evil in one being before but her pride was refusing to let her run.

"What was it you said...green means stop...and red means go?" she watched him briefly as an sadistic smile crossed his face. She took that moment and began her attack. She shifted directly in front of him and unleashed a flurry of punches and kicks straight toward his face. Fasterix didn't even attempt to block a single strike and simply backhanded her with his left hand, sending her flying, heels over head, backwards onto the floor. Just before she hit the ground she shifted, reappearing on his right shoulder and started again, punch after punch after kick after....

Another swatting strike from Fasterix sent her sprawling to the deck.

This one had made her head ring a little and she was struggling to see properly as black spots were clouding her vision. She shifted away again and this time appeared up on the building top, four standard stories above ground.

Fasterix shifted his view and directed his black demon eyes straight upon her. Realising she had the high ground, he then headed straight for the bottom of the building. He played with his gauntlet for a brief second then fired a few shots that instantly stuck to the buildings base. When the bolts landed, five little legs sprouted from each of them, the legs expanded and spread out against the stone, planting itself firmly onto the buildings surface. A small descending bleep could be heard and then the bolts exploded.

At first nothing appeared to happen, the building remained perfectly still, and then after a few seconds, as the foundations started to give way, the building started to rock from side to side.

Pepsy made a run for the buildings edge, her right hand fiddling with her vambrace and presetting some co-ordinates as quickly as she could. She increased her speed, realising the building was about to crumble under its own weight, she powered on, reaching the buildings edge and jumped clean off, twisting her torso mid way, and pointing her left gauntlet toward the building she just left. She squeezed her hand into a fist four times, depressing the hidden firing trigger within her gauntlet, and launching her armours projectiles off at great pace. The inch long darts sped toward their target as she 'shifted' and reappeared next to Jeremy, down by the barrels at the saloon entrance. As the bolts reached their targets, they too expanded and stuck firmly onto the four corners of the buildings edge.

The entire building, foundations and all instantly vanished.

Fasterix was in no way gifted; his powers and abilities were all generated through his suit, which was technologically superior to most armour in all ways. Advanced as the suit was, it could not predict the future or pre-empt attacks made by his opponents, it could not tell him where each strike would come from or how best to deal with each attack made, this part was mostly down to his own instincts, his gut feelings and mostly down to his own, logical line of combat reasoning. It was with this line of reasoning then, that made him naturally look up as soon as the building vanished, and it was with this line of reasoning that made him brace for impact before he had even set eyes on the building once more. He was not in the least part surprised then, as it reappeared directly above his head and dropped down hard, crushing him into the ground with all its weight. He was not surprised as, had he the power; he would have done the same.

Pepsy was breathing heavy, very heavy. She could feel her heart beating hard through her armour, harder than she had ever challenged it before. She watched the mass of rubble for a few moments; the dust was still heavy in the air as the entire contents of the building, and the building itself, had come down hard and ended into a crumpled heap.

 A few more moments passed and still nothing moved. Her heart began to slow. A little calmer, she turned toward Jeremy who was stirring slightly.

"Ahhh how bright is it, my head hurts, and what's that burning smell...have you been cooking again?"

Pepsy looked down at him; her vision was only just clearing from the black spots she had been harboured with earlier.

"You my boy have got us in a lot of trouble today!" she said with a sincere look upon her face.

"Trouble?" Jeremy looked around and could see the burning saloon, the remains of a demolished building and a random thug lying unconscious on the street floor. "I did this?"

Pepsy thought she would tease him a little and let him believe he had.

"Yes you did! And you are going to be in big trouble" Jeremy looked around the carnage again, and then back at Pepsy with a look of mischief in his eyes.

"You're only in trouble if you get caught" he winked. She knew what he meant, she had known him long enough to know of his constant desire to escape situations rather than face the consequences, she went to grab his arm and teleport him back to Astoria.

"No wait...not teleport please...I'll be sick...can't we.."

Pepsy eyed him carefully giving him a look that said she was done with his nonsense today.

"Can't we find another way" Jeremy said. She grabbed him by the scruff of his collar and hauled him to his feet.

"Fine! But you owe me big time"

"As always" he mumbled as they made their way back toward the main market.

A few more moments passed and the rubble began to stir. At first just a few small stone were displaced, and then a few more.

The vibration really began to pick up and with a ferocious roar, Fasterix burst through the debris, all of his muscles pumped and his eyes darker than black. He was breathing heavy from the force he had just exerted freeing himself, and his anger was beyond simmering point. He looked around and noted that his targets were now gone. A smile crossed his face, an evil conspiring, and arrogant smile. His breathing slowed and his eyes returned to a modicum of normal.

The Skelemet Commander differed from the standard drones in that it had a voice box built into its cybernetic structure coupled with a cognitive 'thinking' chip in its CPU that allowed it to process thoughts on a much higher level than the standard drone. The Commander unit was given the liberty to move freely about the lines of drones and adapt the strategy where it saw ineffective routines; it was in effect, a combat general and had proved very useful over the years. Its main torso was made from a standard drone so that in the event of damage being sustained, only the chip needed rescuing and placed into a fresh surrogate where it could retain all of its memories. This was vital to the drone's method of war as they worked from adaptation, trying one method and learning from mistakes. The very bold nature of the way in which they waged war meant that mistakes were accepted, and yet never the same mistake made twice.

There had been a few occasions when the Commander unit would have sustained excessive damage beyond that of salvageable repair. It mattered not as there were always thousands more units ready to march through previous routines to re-highlight errors and compile a fresh set of perfect routines.

The Commander received a coded transmission from the drones on the front line. The transmission came in and was displayed across his retinal display in the top left hand corner of his view.

It read simply 'PROCESS COMPLETED'

Immediately the Commander straightened its cybernetic form, turned and headed off in the opposite direction. It moved with a speed belying its shape. It passed many corridors before arriving at one such large opening. The room was dark and tall, with an alter at the far end. The Commander made its way there and knelt before it.

A purple cloud of energy began to coerce into existence above him almost immediately. A cold and calculated voice spoke

"Excellent work Commander...." there was a severe lack of emotion in these words of praise "the clones will be with your shortly...now bring me their bodies, you know which one I need alive, and for the other... dead or alive it matters not" the voice ghosted out towards the end.

The Skelemet Commander nodded its head in affirmation and rose to its feet; placing its metallic-alloy finger to its temple it immediately sent a relay message across the drone network.

Further up on the front line, where the drones were marching defiantly toward their intruders, six drones in unison stepped out of line. Each drone simultaneously flicked a switch on its rifle and almost instantly the power crystal, from where the energy blasts originated from, turned from green to a shining bright blue. These drones then began to march their way to the front line.

Meanwhile, in the dark chambers in the temple below, Raphael and Chance made their way down the long corridors, trying as best as they could to put some distance between themselves and their pursuers.

 The drones moved slow and particular, keeping in strict straight lines wherever possible and would advance as one. It was not difficult for Raphael and Chance to run ahead and keep a safe distance between them. It was not difficult that was, until they turned the next corner and ran straight into another mass of drones that were marching from the inner sanctum of the temple outward. They both ground to an abrupt halt, their feet sliding slightly along the stone floor, the metallic skeletons automatically raising their rifles and started firing straight at the pair. With no obvious cover in sight, Raphael had no choice but to grab Chance and turn his back to the drones, holding her in close to him and protecting her from harm as twenty or more green electric bolts struck his back and forced his muscles to convulse. Though his vision was shaking from the shock, he spotted a small alcove a short jump away and pushed Chance safely into it. He then ducked his head as best as his cramping muscles would allow and made a dive for the alcove and into cover. His whole body was still shaking and reeling from the pain. He leaned out slightly and took aim with his rifle, his vision was slightly blurred and he found that his aim was wavering quite dramatically, making it difficult to gain any sort of accuracy, it mattered not he concluded as there was enough of a target in the mass of drones that he was sure he couldn't possibly miss. He fired off a short burst and destroyed a few more drones that marched toward them.

Under heavy fire from the drones, Raphael continued to use his rifle to send bursts of fire down the corridor. The drones continued to march toward them, completely unfazed by the carnage that he was creating by destroying their ranks, expertly using the small intermittent alcoves that lined the corridor for cover and continuing their advance towards their goal. The alcoves were shallow but covered enough of his armoured bulk to protect him from the frustratingly painful green shots that the drones were sending his way. They were making slow progress and Chance was becoming impatient.

"Are we there yet are we there yet? Are we there yet?" she giggled as she realised that she was beginning to annoy herself with her childish behaviour. She giggled even louder when she concluded that she was annoying him even more.

"Are you paying attention?" he snapped "there are hundreds of them, thousands even, and shooting might I add" he said with a level of sincerity and frustration in his voice.

The severity of the situation was lost on her.

"You said it's like a tickle...so man up!" she said.

"LIKE!! I said, like a tickle but a thousand times worse" he barked. Again this was lost on her. She wasn't really tickly, in fact she wasn't tickly at all so she figured her tickle score was zero. She calculated that zero times a thousand was still zero and so decided to take charge.

She summed up all her strength through the palms of her hands as she thought back to the Siren cave; she took a deep breath and pushed...

Her soft little hands never made contact with Raphael's back. Instead they hit thin air about two inches short. A force nothing short of exponential made the final contact and hurled Raphael's armoured form out into the corridor and into a hail of green bolts. She hopped out gracefully behind and sheltered herself behind his body, her hands falling gently onto his derrière just as the green bolts landed. His whole body tensed and seized under the trauma and she felt his bum muscles go extremely tight in the seizure, she smirked.

"Someone's been doing their lunges" she said. Through grimaced teeth he tried to reply but she never gave him the opportunity.

"Now chop chop, we don't have all day" she said and conjured up another force push through her hand. She was amazed at how natural it was becoming. She unleashed it softly on his bum nudging him forward. He was pushed, once again, directly into a hail of green bolts that stung him to his core. Speaking clearly in pain he said

"I'm not Wallace!!"

She had no idea what he meant nor did she care, she merely smiled and forced pushed him again. Accepting his fate as a meat shield, he raised his rifle and began return firing.

They made much faster progress along the tunnels. Destroying drones by the hundreds. Their metal alloy bodies dropping to the floor as carefully placed snap shots through the eye sockets felled them instantly, the purple lights fading from their eye sockets.

Raphael absorbed a score of shots, with each new wave of drones that appeared there was an automatic hail of bolts, snapped off in unison upon setting their eerie optics upon the duo. These bolts, he found, he had no choice but to absorb with his body. The pain must have been incredible but anytime it nearly overcame him, Chance was there with her 'encouraging' little push.

They fought their way along three large corridors and at the tail end of the third there was a staircase. Chance had by this stage, placed her hands on his hips, playfully dancing her way along safely behind him.

"Follow the banana, follow the banana, follow the banana"

"STOP STOP STOP" Raphael exclaimed "please, I need a rest"

Chance paused and looked at him; he was bent in two with his hands supported on his knees. His armour was emitting smoke, possibly from the heat and volume of rounds he had taken face on.

"Awww...is my space captain needing a rest" she pouted her bottom lip while simultaneously giving him a patronising rub to his head. He didn't answer; his breathing was heavy and weathered.

The marching clanking sound could be heard from behind them and also from the stairway ahead. They had managed to clear a little rest bite from the enemy for now but it was clear they were slowly being surrounded.

Raphael stood up straighter and then leaned into the stairway. Down below he could make out the form of hundreds more drones making their way up the stairs. A hail of inaccurate fire sped towards him but fizzled out harmlessly against the wall.

He was getting tired.

"I think we need a new tactic" he said

"I don't" she exclaimed "this one works fine for me" she finished her sentence with a giggle and then began to examine her nails; she hadn't done them properly since this morning.

'Hell I'm really letting myself go' she thought

"I'm getting pulverised and all you are concerned about is your nails" Raphael barked in. She was taken aback.

Had she said that out loud or had he read her mind? Can he read minds? She wondered. She looked at him for a second before replying.

"You are sounding all pathetic oh grand space marine" she gestured to his attire "it's just a little tickle hee heee...look" she said "green really isn't my colour otherwise id respectfully take my turn at the front.

"What about blue?" he asked

"Blue?"

"Well, baby blue" he countered.

She considered this for a moment. "Blue, hmm baby blue, yes that might work" she replied. Raphael nudged her attention towards the corridor behind as a searing bolt of blue energy was sailing down the corridor toward them.

"What...like now?" she asked

"No time like the present" he said

"But I don't have a fancy, kickass suit like yours" she pulled a little sad face, placed her hands together and began to rotate her shoulders. He couldn't resist her cute moments, and smirked.

"Just a tickle" he said. She scoffed, turned around and faced the blue bolt that was nearly upon them.

"Alright" she stated rather boldly, she was a team player after all. She planted both her feet, screwed up her face and braced for impact. She could feel the sheer heat of the bolt approaching; it was about three seconds away and all she could think about was how much it was going to hurt.

Two seconds to impact.

Once again she could feel that itch over her entire body, she could feel it against her skin from head to toe but she just couldn't quite understand what it was.

One second to impact.

"sod this" she screamed and hurled herself to the floor. The bolt impacted on the wall behind. The wall section exploded quite dramatically and sprayed them both with dust and stone shrapnel, the hole that was left in the wall itself was enormous. Unlike the green bolts, these blue shots certainly dealt damage.

She glanced at Raphael and met his gaze. His face, like hers, shared the same look of shock; she then looked deeper into his eyes and saw instant sorrow. Within a second he had picked her up in his arms and turned into the stairwell, his free hand barking off rounds from his rifle as he descended deeper into the temple, a strong sense of urgency in his movements. She felt so safe in the crook of his arm; the shock of the moment was beginning to pass.

They began to make swift progress with Raphael's newfound aggression. Electric green energy zapped passed their shoulders as Raphael stepped out from the corners edge and returned fire, hitting a Skelemet straight through the eye socket, its purple light flickered out and its metal frame sunk to the floor. Two more drones immediately stepped out from the corridor to replace the fallen drone and began firing, the shots hitting Raphael in his shoulder guards and instantly causing mini seizures throughout his body. He sunk back into cover grimacing.

They were fighting a hopeless battle here. For every drone that dropped, two or more would take its place. There must have been thousands of them marching through the complex on a mission to capture them. They were now holed up in a small room just off the main staircase. The Skelemet drones seemed to be coming from everywhere at once. Raphael held fort at the corner of the doorway, snapping off shots when he could and doing his best to avoid the hail of debilitating shots that were fired back.

"Which way?" he asked, Chance became suddenly alert.

'Which way he asks, hell I'm following him' she thought.

"erm…" she said hesitantly "I don't know if you'd noticed but it's hardly sign posted" Raphael leaned around the corner and snapped off a few more shots, felling another two drones before ducking back into cover. He quickly slung his rifle over his shoulder and then reached for his left vambrace, flicking it open revealed a small computer inside.

"That's my boy, you call star command for backup" She said. He looked up and met her eyes, she smirked at him, and he couldn't help but return the smile. Her quick wit was always charming, he would never admit it but it was this same wit, while in the face of certain death, that had attracted him to her in the first place.

He turned his attention back to his wrist where he flicked a few switches and a small holographic display was emitted in 3d. It depicted the pyramid and then their current location.

"What do you think?" he asked her, the clunking of metal on stone could be heard marching closer.

"It's nice but can I have it in pink?" she replied. Raphael merely looked toward the doorway where the ever growing sound of animated alloy could be heard; he then looked back at Chance. "Okay okay, now's not the time I get it" she said and then turned her attention back to the hololith protruding from his arm.

"I reckon it'll be in this big room in the middle" she guessed "that's where id keep it". Raphael took in what she said and nodded.

"Look, there are stairs leading right to it" she exclaimed, suddenly feeling very useful. She looked for some appraisal from him but none came, instead he was rapidly switching his attention from the hololith, to the far wall in the room they occupied, and then back to the hololith.

"Ah...there is a snag" Raphael started "your staircase is through that wall and I don't have any dynamite or explosives to get us there, the only other way is down those stairs and through the drones to the adjoining stairway" Raphael made his opinion on the latter part of the task clear with the sceptical look that crossed his face. The clanking sound was very near now, a few stray green bolts started to come peppering through the doorway. No sign yet of the deadly blue bolts but they were surely only a few staircases away. Raphael swung his rifle to bear and using his free hand, he edged Chance slowly behind his armoured bulk to protect her. They were running out of time and were very short on options. He looked back towards her, standing there looking all cute and tiny. His job had always been to protect her and keep her safe, he was about to let her down in the worst way possible. Two green electric bolts sailed through the doorway and struck Raphael square in the chest causing him more excruciating pain.

"Any ideas?" he said through gritted teeth as he fought back the urge to drop to the ground adopting the foetal position. The drones had made steady progress in their advance and were almost at the door now.

"You're the one dressed like a juggernaut, run through them" she said and giggled at the end of her remark, once again she looked at his choice of attire, never failing to put a smile on her face.

Raphael paused for a brief moment, turned his head and looked right at her.

"Okay bad timing I know I get it...again" she muttered. He pushed passed her and moved swiftly toward the back wall, pressing both his hands against the cold stone for a brief moment before turning back to face her.

"You know...that might not actually be a bad idea" he said, Chance drew a puzzled look. What he did next made her burst into hysterics.

Raphael picked up his rifle, took aim, and then fired an entire clip of rounds into the wall. He then dropped his shoulder, adopted a crouched position and looked directly at the wall section that he had just wounded.

"Oh well whyyy not!"He exclaimed as he charged head first toward the wall at full speed.

Naturally he bounced off, landing hard onto his back, rebounding almost as far back into the room as where he had started. Chance also ended up in a crumpled heap on the floor, although her felling was one of hysterical laughter, laughing so hard that her legs gave way beneath her and toppled straight down. Her stomach became a knot of absolute comedy, laughing so hard that she nearly wet herself. She became suddenly aware that she couldn't breathe; her hysterics were taxing her natural ability to breathe in and out. She was fairly sure she had just witnessed the funniest moment in her life. As she sat in a fit of giggles, Raphael clambered back to his feet, muttering angrily to himself as his world became dark and dizzy. His shoulder was a modicum of pain and his head was ringing so loudly that he was struggling to balance. He stumbled back, took aim and charged again.

To Chance it felt like there was a hand deep in her belly squeezing tight, She was trying so hard to breathe but couldn't, when the fool hit the wall the second time she was nearly sick.

The third time he hit, she WAS sick.

Had it not been for the noise of the wall crashing down on the fourth attempt, then Chance was pretty sure she would have blacked out completely.

Meanwhile, in Sanctuary, Fern was focussing on the black mass that was ever expanding. By now it had covered the entire skyline and only small beams of sunlight were able to pierce through the small gaps in the swarm.

"It's moving" Fern exclaimed.

"Where?" Crystal asked?

"Down!! Phoenix guard, re-breathers on!!" Fern shouted. At once all of her guard including herself activated their facial re-breathers and a mouthpiece popped up from the collar of their armour, covering their faces up to the bridge of their noses. Ferns eyes began to burn a very bright, orange colour and her armour seemed to be coated in a seething mirage, a sign that made her seem like she herself was actually on fire.

She had been right; the swarm had now started its descent into the city, in mere moments the streets would be engulfed and the inhabitants would not be able to breathe. Visibility would be nigh on zero and pandemonium would be everywhere. The swarm must have been at least 3 miles in width and she could only imagine how thick. Whatever had caused such a thick swarm to mass she could not understand, although she no longer had the luxury of time to think that particular puzzle through, as the swarm was almost down upon them.

"Crystal, can you make a channel; keep it away from the market?" Fern called out

"Of course my lady" Crystal shouted and stepped forwards, her eyes turning completely blue as she conjured up her gift. She raised her hands from her sides and with it came a mass of ice that appeared from nowhere. She then thrust her hands high into the air and began to pour the ice from her hands 20ft above them in a constant flow. The ice was forming a protective roof layer along the market top, supported at each 20 yard juncture by ice stalagmites from the ground up. The protective layer now ran the entire length of the market and stood as a platform for the Phoenix guard to climb up onto and unleash their torrent of flames upon the swarm. They did so immediately under the barking orders of Fern.

The swarm was amongst them now and it was difficult to see. Everywhere Fern looked, she saw blackness followed by bursts of tribinium flames and then more blackness. It was impossible to tell the flow of either the swarm now, or how well they were fairing against such a tide of darkness. She looked down toward a group of gathered civilians that were hiding next to the ice shield; a part of the swarm headed straight for them and engulfed them almost instantly. They flailed their hands in desperation but after a few moments the swarm moved on and the bodies lay there lifeless, suffocated from the encounter.

It seemed strange to Fern, this swarms behaviour. The flies themselves were sugar hunters, why they were deliberately attacking humans for the sake of suffocation made no sense. She sensed something else at work here but from her darkened disposition she could not see anyone controlling them. She decided to clear the path, conjuring up massive flames from her hands and hurling them upwards into the dark mass. The smell of burning protein could be tasted all around as millions of the flies burned up under her touch. The flames cleared a small gap in the mass that was quickly filled within a fraction of a second; she shook her head and continued to launch her fire.

All along the ice platform the Phoenix guard were garrisoned and launching their flamers into the swarm. The flies were now at a low enough height that they could feel the Phoenixes wrath. This swarm seemed different; it was almost as if it was thinking. One unfortunate member of the guard had been targeted by the mass. It had lunged, as one, for the man's face and headed for every little orifice in the re-breather mask. At first nothing seemed to be bothering the man as he continued to unleash his flaming fury. But then suddenly, as some flies got into his mask, he began to writhe and panic, gripping his face and trying to remove the mask, pulling and tugging and choking all at the same time. He eventually freed the mask from his face which was then his fatal mistake as more flies swamped in and suffocated him within seconds.

Crystal remained under the ice shield pouring a constant flow into the shield, the heat from the Phoenix guard's weapons was very quickly melting her work and so she had to maintain a constant stream to keep the advantage. She craned her neck around and could just make out Jessica in the distance, using her boomer to direct the people away. There were a few stragglers or civilians that had lost their way in the panic. One straggler was a little boy clutching a teddy bear. He was calling out to some unknown parent which Crystal could only hazard a guess had lost him in the confusion. His tears had attracted the attention of the swarm and a large mass separated from the group and headed towards him. Crystal watched on in horror at what was to come. The young boy must only have been 4 years old at most and had his whole life ahead of him, she had to help him but she also had her duty to the Phoenix guard, maintaining the platform so that they wouldn't fall through. Focussing hard, Crystal took a large step toward the boy, angling her body now so that her left hand kept a constant stream on the ice platform and allowed her right hand to be freed up and take aim at the boy. She raised her hand up, with the palm facing down and started to throw off some ice. As she did so, she started to contract her fingers laterally in a scissor motion as the ice came out; this separated the ice in tiny little shards and was sent hurling towards the open space a few feet in front of the boy. The timing was, as always, perfect as the ice shards smashed into the swarm mere inches from the boys face in a constant flow, each tiny shard was no bigger than a fly and so the flow acted almost like a bolter gun, neutralising the threat almost instantly. The boy looked over in surprise, he smiled and waved. Crystal smiled back but knew she had to get the boy out of danger. She then looked further down the street and could see that Jessica was no more than a hundred yards away. She had to get the boy to safety and yet she couldn't leave her position. Instead she turned her right hand slightly, closing the fingers together and began another constant flow of ice, constructing a large and yet narrow ice section that ran from the boy's location down toward Jessica's boomer. The structure started high but was made into a perfect descending slope.

"Sorry little guy" she said, mostly to herself as she then created an ice stalagmite beneath his feet that started to lift him into the air. He instantly got a fright as the platform was unstable and he was shaky on his feet, he knelt down and placed one hand onto the rising stalagmite and the other hand clutching his teddy. The stalagmite grew to the same height as the ice slope and then a fraction higher, Crystal then tipped the stalagmite and sent the boy hurtling, feet first, all the way down the ice construction, sliding at very high speeds further down the street to safety. The boys screams could be heard all around although she smiled, as she realised they were not screams of pain or discomfort but in fact pleasure. She just hoped that when he hit the bottom he didn't turn and say 'again again'

Fern grimaced in anger as she watched another two of her guard fall to the swarms thinking mind, again they had swarmed their re-breathers until they found a gap and then choked them profusely.

"Don't let them near you" she barked loudly. She looked all around and felt a sense of hopelessness. She could barely see bar the sections she had burned out. Civilians were being picked off as well as her guard. This swarm definitely had a thinking element to it and she needed to get to the root of that if they were to have any hope of victory here.

Crystal climbed up to her side to hold conference, her left hand holding an ever constant flow of ice onto the platform to keep it stable.

"We need a new tactic, any ideas?" Fern asked. This was the first time that Crystal had seen Fern stumped in combat as to what to do, she was normally so bold and forthcoming, barking orders and remaining defiant in the clear face of danger, and yet against this swarm she seemed a little baffled.

"Why don't we, 'whip' it into shape high up, and give us some room to breathe?" Crystal said. A smile now crossed Ferns face, a rare occurrence for the fire Angel.

"I can always rely on you for the good ideas" Fern said to Crystal. Fern then barked at one of her guard to throw them a torch. The guardsman took one from his back satchel and launched it across to them; Fern set the tribinium wick alight and stuck it down hard into the ice platform, wedging it deep so that it sat upright. Crystal then focussed hard and once again a protruding ice stalagmite grew from the ground upon which the torch sat. She raised the platform a good 40ft into the sky, the torch burning bright at its peak. She had judged the distance perfectly as always, to be just at the tip of Ferns gift reach. Fern crouched and focussed both her fiery eyes on the torch, she took her right hand and began a small circle at first with just her fingers, and then her hand began to circle, and then she was swinging her full arm around like a lasso. From the tip of the torch a massive fire tail had trailed out and was spinning like a long fire whip in the air, burning all in its path and clearing out a portion of the blackened sky. Millions of flies were dying with each turn it made around its apex, the day sky shone through brightly, it was a warm welcome from the blackness that had covered it for so many hours now.

Crystal and Fern watched on and caught a glimpse of something, something slightly larger than a standard fly, somewhere quite a bit larger it seemed, perhaps the size of a small ball, it was flying too, hovering menacingly over the swarm.

"Can you see that?" Fern asked, Crystal's beautiful blue eyes never left the object.

"Yes...although I am unsure as to what it is, it's certainly too high for us to reach" she replied as Fern turned to her with a small smile

"You were always good at javelin no?" Fern said, Crystal laughed.

"I'll give it a go, but that will take two hands, I won't be able to sustain this platform for long without a constant stream onto it" Crystal said, Fern considered this and then said

"That thing has something to do with this, all of this, if we cannot disable it we are lost anyway. We will retreat beneath the platform, hopefully as it melts it will wash my armour" Fern smiled. Crystal was amazed at how often Fern was smiling today, she rarely smiled. Perhaps it was in the face of defeat that she found her comic relief.

The fire Angel and her Phoenix guard hopped down the 20ft drop and safely stowed away under the ice platform. Without their gusts of flame melting it, the platform was actually quite stable. Crystal knelt down and placed both hands together; expanding them wide and creating a long ice spike the length of her arm. She stood up and looked high up into the sky, the fire whip was still spinning although without Ferns touch it was starting to slow down, its flame arc was shortening and the clearing it had made was shrinking. Crystal took her left hand and aimed it towards the black, strange, hovering device and held it there. Her accuracy was always remarkable, almost as astute to Jeremy's although her skill came mostly down to her patience; she would wait as long as it took, for the perfect shot and not be in a hurry to make it. She slowed her breathing down and could feel the cacophony of carnage going on all around her. From the corners of her eyes she could see the Phoenix guard flaming the low flying swarm, there was only 7 members of them left. She could see Ferns fiery gaze locked on her, a look of anticipation from her flaming friend.

From her other eyes corner, she could make out in the distance the large flow directing hands of Jessica, looking powerful in her boomer armour. She smiled inwardly at the success that young girl was having. She then focussed squarely on the hovering object; holding her breath she then swung her arm as hard as she could, making sure she released the ice shard at the last possible second. It sailed through the air at great speed and tore a massive gaping hole through the swarm as it travelled on towards its target. Crystal's eyes watched on intently, she could feel Ferns doing the same from down below. The ice javelin soared onward and upward.

Closer and closer, and then.

It struck.

It hit the object clean in its side and instantly shattered. Tiny shards of ice fell from the heavens as the weapon had found its target, and yet the target was still there, still hovering, but had now turned its attention towards her. There was a sudden increase in the tone of the buzzing and the entire swarm now turned toward Crystal, clearly sensing an immediate and actual threat.

"Oh dear" Crystal said aloud and turned to run. From her raised platform she threw her hands out in front of her, running as fast as she could she could still feel the swarm tight on her tail. As she came to the edge of the platform she jumped and immediately started to spray ice from her hands towards her feet. She was now effectively sliding through the air on her makeshift ice platforms and at very high speeds. She had excellent balance as she surfed her way through the street, the swarm buzzing dangerously close behind her.

Fern had also taken off down below, careering down the street after her, frantically launching fire into the air to thin the swarm. From her position on the ground she could only guess that the entire swarm was now pursuing Crystal, this was not good.

Crystal was surfing at great speed but she could feel it was still not fast enough, she could sense the swarm getting closer. Up ahead, on the tip of a raised building she could make out a water tower in the distance. She slowly raised one hand, being careful not to upset the flow she was creating on her slide, she made a large ice spike with her free hand and held it ready, waiting for the opportune moment. Her slide was getting ever closer and yet so was the swarm. As she passed the tower she hurled the ice spike into its side and watched as it tore the contents of the tower out, spilling onto the rooftop. Thousands of gallons of water came tumbling out instantly and splashing out all around it, Crystal hop stepped and flipped around so that she was now sliding backwards, using her right hand again to hurl ice cold air, into the water, and then continue to blast it with force. The water instantly froze and shattered into millions of tiny ice particles that tore into the pursuing swarm, millions more of the flies were annihilated in that simple movement and yet they continued on relentless.

Fern had fallen way behind by now; she was not nearly as fast as the swarm or her sliding ice friend, but she continued to launch her flames regardless, doing whatever she could to thin the herd.

Crystal turned back toward her ice flow; she was running out of time. The swarm was relentless and unending, it would catch her within minutes, she had to think.

Her gift? Her 'other gift?' she hadn't quite mastered that one yet and so it was a very risky plan, although she really didn't have much of a choice.

Continuing to slide on, her eyes went completely white as she called upon the skies above and brought rain down over Sanctuary. The rain came down heavy and hard but was serving nicely in making her ice slide, allowing her to gain a little bit extra speed from the easy accessible ice. The next part was the tricky part; she called upon the lightening to strike the rain, and with a bit of luck, the swarm. This was the part that she had never quite mastered, and upon failing usually left her feeling a little bit 'shocked'.

The swarm was ever nearer now, the buzzing she could hear creeping closer all the time. She realised that the buzzing had become frantic and almost angry; she had no doubt in her mind now that the object she struck with the ice javelin was somehow connected. She focussed hard and called upon the lightening to strike the swarm....

Well, at least half of what she asked for occurred, the lightening did indeed come down, although not on her intended target.

"Oh no..." she said "not again" The lightening came down hard and fast, and struck her clean in the chest. Her whole body convulsed under the shock and she could no longer hold the flow to her ice slide. It came to an abrupt end and she was sent tumbling head over heels, down onto the street floor, landing with a crash. The pain from the fall went unnoticed as she was still shaking from the electricity that she had called upon herself. She landed hard, rolled a few times before coming to rest on her back. Her armour was smoking from the scorch marks and her head was ringing. Her lips felt tingly as did her fingertips and she felt paralysed, unable to command her limbs to move. She was given no time to lie there and contemplate her failings, the swarm swooped down instantly and engulfed her. The black mass swallowed her up almost instantly and she couldn't see anything, she could barely hear and she realised that she couldn't breathe either. She wasn't sure if this was her natural instinct, not to open her mouth, or if the flies themselves had swallowed up all the oxygen in the area creating a vacuum. She tried to thrash her arms around in all directions, throwing out ice shards and ice air where she could. She felt frozen flies peppering her armour as they fell, frozen winged from where they had been.

The seconds were passing like minutes, the minutes like hours. Just blackness, solid unforgiving blackness was all that she could see. She continued to fight, she knew she had to, but for how long she was not sure. It was strange she thought that in her moment of certain death, her thoughts had drifted to Raphael. Inwardly she smiled, as she would not dare have smiled to the swarm and face instant execution.

She could visualise him, when they were young, sitting next to her on the wall, his little cheeky smile he would wear as he would swing his legs in unison with hers. Did she wish she had told him? Told him how she really felt, what he meant to her, perhaps now it mattered not, It was most certainly too late now. She just held her smile, with him in her thoughts. The swarm ever aggressively swamped her location.

Fern fought her way through violently; a strong sense of urgency had overcome her as she launched her flames even harder into the grounded swarm. She could barely see but followed the trail of flies to where it was thickest. Millions upon millions of them, she tore through them angrily, shouting with each burst she made, engulfing masses of the pests with her gift, trying to reach her companion, her friend.

Fern didn't have anyone she could call a friend, she had always been so blunt and brutish in her life that she knew she was disliked by many if not all. Respected and yet disliked. But with Crystal, her apparent opposite, she felt she had a genuine friend there, a friend whom was almost going to meet a dishonourable end at the hands of such insects.

She fought on hard; each step she took was laboured. The flies had now started to target her too as a threat and she could feel them crawling around her re-breather mask, looking for a way in. She looked around and then felt she no longer had a choice.

"Don't let me down now Lucas" she said aloud as she pulled the Fireblade from her back and ignited it with her gift. The blade burned furiously and it seemed to Fern, that it enhanced her in some way, she felt stronger, more powerful. She swung the massive sword that was almost the height of a man, the flames followed it in its wake, massive swipes of superhot fire, hotter than any tribinium fuelled flamer could produce and she hurled it around with anger in her purpose. Burning her aggressors by the millions and clearing a path where she could, with a few large swipes she had cleared a massive gap in the swarm and high above she could see the larger fly hovering, almost surveying the scene below. She growled and wished there was a way to reach it, she battled on. At her feet she began to see pools of water, small puddles littered around the floor that would quickly evaporate under the heat of her armour, she must have been close, she swung harder and faster, the swarm falling and burning out by the tens of millions now. The smell of burnt hair was stinging her nostrils but she fought on, her heart beat was racing; she had to get to her friend before it was too late.

After a few more steps, she cleared the path and saw Crystal lying there, barely moving, her fingers wearily scraping the ground. Fern stood over her and swung the Fireblade around her head, its flaming touch was keeping a clear gap for a ten yard circumference around them, and the swarm couldn't enter its death circle without burning up.

"Crystal, I'm here, you can breathe, I'm here" Fern said. Crystal could hear Ferns voice, and hearing her sounding concerned seemed alien to her, perhaps Fern really did have a feminine side to her after all. She opened her eyes and was thankful to see Fern standing over her, looking magnificent in her orange blazing armour. Crystal looked up and slightly behind her, their predicament was now very apparent to her. They were completely surrounded by a black buzzing wall kept only at bay by Ferns constant patrol swings of her Fireblade.

"Still not mastered that other gift yet no?" Fern asked

Crystal laughed "no not yet""and I see Lucas has saved the day yet again" she indicated to the Fireblade in Ferns grasp, it seemed strange to be making jokes in clear perilous danger and yet was somehow appropriate. Crystal stood and kept a small slouch so as not to get in the way of the swings of the Fireblade. She looked around and could not work out the best route to go.

The two antagonist Angels stood huddled together amongst the swarm, at a complete loss as to what to do. Crystal looked behind Fern and then hurled some strong ice air in that direction, a small clearing of flies froze and fell to the ground; she caught a small glimpse of the bottom end of the market before the gap filled up.

"We don't want to go that way, as that's where Jessica sent the civilians, we need to lead the swarm to the main gates and hopefully outside the city" Crystal said.

"Well which way is that?" Fern asked.

"Good question" Crystal returned. The buzzing of the swarm was emitting an even higher pitch tone now, almost as if it was frustrated, stopped in its task of destroying them. Fern continued to swing their saving grace of a sword and Crystal stood close to her, holding onto her waist and keeping her head low. Every now and then they would catch a glimpse of daylight, of the city buildings, of anything other than the darkness of the swarm which was buzzing frantically now. Both Angels began a precariously slow sidestep motion toward the only direction they deemed must have been the correct way although in this mess it was beginning to be difficult to determine even which way was up or down.

Amongst the high pitched buzzing, both Fern and Crystal then started to hear an entirely different kind of buzzing sound altogether. This sound had a faster and more constant stream, as if it was emanating from some energy source rather than the wings of the flies. They both tried to look up and around them but that were no use at all. The new sound grew ever closer to them.

"Do you hear that?" Fern shouted over the noise to Crystal

"JUST" Crystal shouted back.

"Be ready" Fern commanded. Although both Fern and Crystal shared the same rank, and although they were both respected and considered great warriors and Angels of Astoria, it was always Fern that would assume command in most situations, a position that Crystal never felt the need to challenge. The new sound grew ever closer until the swarm above them cleared slightly and they saw this large sphere of crackling energy surrounding a man in robes at its centre, the sight was truly magnificent to see and both Angels felt hope once more as they recognised the new arrival instantly.

"GANON" Crystal shouted up as the electrically magnetic field slowly lowered him down toward them, expanding slightly to accommodate both Fern and Crystal into the safety of its field.

"Ah more Angels to the great Sanctuary today, what a pleasant surprise...yourselves I mean and not your" he looked up "choice of company"

"Well we are glad to see you old man, as you can see we are in a bit of a pickle" Crystal said, Fern choosing to remain silent. Inside she was joyous at his arrival but joy never came easily to Fern and more often than not she chose to remain quiet instead of openly expressing her feelings.

"Yes that you are...It seems there is anarchy all over Astoria today...hmmm curious it has spread this far also" he scratched his chin as the swarm buzzed angrily just outside the safety of his magnetic shield.

"Something is controlling the swarm, I am positive of it" Crystal declared and indicated high up into the swarm. The gesture was in fact hopeless as there was a thick black mass of flies coating the outside of his shield, but she pointed nonetheless.

"Man made you believe?" Ganon asked?

"Without a doubt" Fern piped in.

"Hmm, then let's see if they had taken my gifts into consideration upon unleashing such a plan" Ganon said calmly and then raised his hand into the air. He closed his eyes for a moment and held his hand there very still. A few more moments passed and then he suddenly pulled his fingers into a fist and kept his arm held there for a moment longer.

Fern and crystal looked on, a little unsure if they should be aiding him in any way but could see no method in which they could. High above them, the tide of the swarm parted and a black object approached, descending slowly and on a direct path toward them. The tide of the swarm continued to part before the object and then closed up behind it as it descended further. A mere few seconds later and the object passed through the magnetic shield and landed right into Ganon's hand and sat there. It was in all manners a mechanical fly; it was a hundred times bigger than the flies of the swarm, sitting neatly into the palm of his hand, desperately trying to flap its wing and fly off but the metallic nature to its construction was powerless against Ganon's gift of magnetism. They all looked on with curiosity.

"It seems this swarm was in fact generated by this little...thing" Ganon said "emitting a high pitched frequency no doubt that would attract and control the swarm" he added.

"The question is who is controlling the device?" Crystal asked. Fern as always looked on with a stoic fire in her eyes and remained silent. Ganon simply closed his fist ever so slightly and the mechanical fly crumpled into a tiny piece of scrap metal. Instantly the high pitch buzz of the swarm dissipated and the flies headed for high altitude, hundreds of billions of flies simultaneously ascending to the high reaches of the city and massing again higher up. Crystal looked on in amazement at how simple the swarms demise had been, had they only been able to get their hands on this one mechanical fly in the first place they could have stopped the chaos far sooner.

Ganon's eyes scrolled around the area and he could see the decimation that the swarm had created upon the inhabitants of Sanctuary. Bodies littered the street where they had been choked and unable to breathe. The market stalls that once bore fruit and exotic vegetables were harvested bare, mauled by the ferocity and satiety of the swarm. The buildings themselves even looked weathered, the stone work having been peppered by millions of tiny strikes, as stray flies hit into them from the sheer density of the swarm.

"Who was controlling the device indeed" Ganon said aloud.

CHAPTER 10

Meanwhile, deep down in the temple, dust was still settling from the wall he had just crashed through. The stone work had been held together with some ancient, sand based cement which broke easily enough under pressure. Rocks lay strewn across the ground and Raphael knelt on his knees still recovering from the ordeal.

The room they had entered was enormous and sphere shaped. In the centre of the room there lay a stair case that led to a raised dais and a level platform with some ornate contraption resting on the platform. The staircase itself came down and toward where they were, having fashioned their own way into the room, and then turned and led down to the right where a dark corridor adjoined it. All around the staircase there was simply blackness, an indication of the depths this room must fall to. Chance's eyes fell onto the raised dais and the wonder that sat upon it. Raphael's eyes similarly looked up and around the sphere shaped room that they had burst into and began to wonder its purpose.

"Sure is a BIG round room" he said aloud, but Chance had taken no notice, she had run all the way up the stairs to the platform, her eyes now fixed directly upon her prize, as before her was undoubtedly the artefact that she had been longing for all day, the artefact that could answer all of her questions in one swift go. Her prize was within her grasp and yet frustratingly out of reach.

The orb that contained her compressed memories was bright red and filled with a peculiar mix of reflective shiny pieces. It could have been no bigger than a golf ball and it sat encased within an intricate maze puzzle before her. The maze sat upright and hummed with some unforeseen energy, its wining pathways were perfectly shaped to carry the small red orb through them and it was clear that this puzzle would have to be unlocked in order to release its secrets.

At first, she tried to simply place her hand into the maze and take her prize, opting for the most direct route possible. Each attempt made by her was met with a jolt of electricity, striking her from an invisible force field that only revealed itself upon activation and therefore electrocution.

Her fingers recoiled in shock and she stamped her foot in frustration. Raphael slowly made his way up the stairs and stood a few steps behind her, his body still ached from the pain of smashing through the wall. He scanned his eyes back down toward the hole he had made but it showed no sign yet of their pursuers, he then turned his eyes toward the official entrance, or what seemed a more suitable method of entering the room compared with the barbaric and destructive plan he had enforced. He allowed his eyes to linger there for a moment, ensuring there were no signs of movement, happy that they were alone for now, he turned back and looked upon the puzzle.

"This is really bugging me, give me your gun" she said, without even turning to look at him.

"I'm not giving you a gun" he replied simply.

"I wasn't asking, I'm telling you, give me your gun!" this time she had turned to face him to show her sincerity.

"I'm not going to give you a gun" he said again simply.

"Just give me your gun, I am going to shoot it out"

"For the last time, I'm not giving you a gun" he said.

"No you are absolutely right" she said, almost in defeat "give me a grenade"

Raphael just looked at her and raised both eyebrows, his armour was still dented, battered and covered in dust from the wall he had broken through moments before.

"If I had a grenade do you really think I'd have run head first through a stone wall?" she looked him up and down and took note of the state his armour was now in and then felt annoyingly silly at her last comment.

"Argh you are so irritating" she said.

"You like a good challenge, what is so difficult about this one?" he asked. She chose not to respond to his last comment.

She took a deep breath, calmed her mind and examined the puzzle before her once more. She placed a hand on the raised dais upon which the puzzle sat and looked closer, tapping her finger on the surface edge. She noticed that the orb was bobbing in unison with the tapping of her finger. She rested her hand and the orb became still. She tapped again and it moved.

"And once again, my awesomeness prevails" she said as she rejoiced in the discovery of her special powers from earlier that day. Leaning back, she cracked her neck to both sides and then focused the power through her hands as she began to move the orb very slowly around the intricate puzzle.

It was slow and tedious work, at any point that she lost concentration; the orb would touch the puzzle edge, sending a jolt of electricity straight into her, the shock would stall her momentarily and as she lost control, without her gift manipulating its movements, the orb would slowly begin to reverse, back the way she had made it come. At times she made good progress; at others she made countless errors that sent the orb almost back to the beginning.

Raphael stood just off her right shoulder, watching intently, much to her frustration.

"I can hear you breathing" she said rather irritated.

"I can hear you breathing too" he replied, unsure of her demeanour but sensing irritation all the same.

"You are breathing heavy! It's annoying me" she said

"What do you want me to do? Stop breathing?"

"Now that WOULD make my day" she snapped.

Raphael remained quiet, a little put back by her snap comment. She could now hear him trying his best to hold his weathered breath, he had been badly beaten and his lungs had taken a lot today, he was struggling as he tried to slow the release of air, minimising the sound of each exhalation, it was taking a great bit of effort.

Bless him he is trying she thought, her choler lowered slightly at his exertion.

"Oi!! Limp lungs!!.. my back pocket" she called to him.

He stepped up slowly and made his way over behind her, removing both gauntlets from his hands and standing directly behind her, softly placing his left hand on her waist.

His touch at first made her jump; she felt what could have been electricity pass between them. His hand felt warm and completely at one at her side and she now found herself smiling on the inside and she didn't know why. In the cold confines of the dark pyramid she suddenly felt warm and comfortable. It had been a very long day and until this moment she hadn't realised just how tired she had become. His right hand came to rest on her other hip and she felt herself drifting somewhere far away, somewhere warm, somewhere happy. She could feel his breathing pass her neck and it made her tingle, a small smile passing her lips as she found herself leaning back dreamily into his arms, sinking into him, enjoying his touch.

She turned her head slightly and from the corner of her eye she could see him moving his head closer, she could make out his lips nearing her ear, he had such big lips; she began to wonder what they would feel like against her own. Very softly and calmly he spoke into her ear

"Which pocket?"

She heard his voice but had no idea what he had said; she felt very far away, she felt at home. She could feel her lips move but what she replied was a mystery even to herself, she was suddenly aware of the weight of the necklace around her collarbone, its delicately rare metal felt like it was glowing warmer against her skin and she felt this overwhelming sense of fulfilment, like she had everything she could ever need in the world and the necklace was a symbol of this. She felt his left hand move but had no idea where. Her world had been numbed. She turned her head slowly and watched him produce the blue item Pepsy had bestowed to her earlier. She watched, her eyes all dreamy and drugged from his touch, as he shook it in his hands and placed it slowly to his lips, those big, soft lips...

He depressed the top of the inhaler; the noise burst the bubble in dramatic fashion.

Instantly she had returned to the here and now, the cold and the dark, the frustrating puzzle before her. She looked at the puzzle closely and realised that in her dreamy state, she had allowed the orb to slowly drift back almost completely to the start.

'Damn him' she thought, suddenly annoyed at how vulnerable she had allowed herself to become. A moment passed and he still remained behind her, one hand remaining on her hip.

"Erm huh" she coughed and regarded his hand that still resided on her waist. "No freebies on this ship" she said and bum nudged him backward slightly, out of her personal space.

"Charming" he replied, his sarcasm irritated her further.

"Can't you go play with the curtains or something?" she asked. He chose to remain quiet after that, his breathing had vastly improved and yet he still chose to control it quietly as to not irritate her further.

The next seven minutes passed frustratingly slowly. Chance was forever muttering words of frustration as she continued to navigate the orb around the obstacle. Raphael continued to scan the room.

A dark shape flittered past his vision, instantly catching his eye. He trained his eyes further and could make out a little figure ghosting its way through the dark corridor that led to where they stood. He watched as the figure emerged into the half light, his eyes going wide with shock, he almost couldn't believe what he was seeing, the figure looked exactly like Chance! Her absolute double, she was identical in every way except that her hair was jet black.

The figure stalked menacingly closer, a look of malice was worn across its face and for once Raphael did not know what to do.

"Erm..Chance hunni" he said

'Who is he calling hunni' she thought *'one cheeky hand on the hips and he thinks he is getting my lips'* she giggled to herself at how she made that rhyme.

The figure loomed closer. It was now fully inside the room and stepping carefully toward the stairs.

"Not now" Chance finally replied

"You might want to take a look at this" he said.

'Argh' she thought 'he is so annoying, who does he' her thought trailed off as she turned and saw what he had been fussing about.

"OH MY WORD!!" she exclaimed, pausing between each word, "I really WOULD look hot with dark hair" she exclaimed, she then giggled and went back to focusing on the puzzle. Raphael rolled his eyes.

"What should I do?" he yelled as the figure got closer.

"Just do what you do best, get beat up hee hee" she didn't even look up; her attention was completely on the puzzle that she had almost completed. Raphael raised his guard, he had no intention of hitting this thing, how could he? It looked like her. Before he could form a plan, the dark clone had lunged itself straight at him, throwing a flurry of lightening fast strikes from both its hands and its feet. It took everything he had to match her speed, blocking each strike before it landed and evading her kicks.

The dark clone was fast and it was relentless, swinging ten fast punches to his head, following up with a spinning kick to his ribs. Luckily he blocked each punch and then caught her leg before the kick had landed; he hoisted the leg up, taking the clone fully off the ground and then hurled it across the room. Chance glanced over to see him throwing her darker self. 'hmm' she thought 'he definitely knows how to take charge' she smiled to herself before calling out

"Doing a great job there champ"

Raphael held his position but the thing was on him again in an instant. It moved so fast that a blur actually followed in the wake of where it had been. The fight continued on like this for another few minutes, Raphael blocking strikes and then grabbing the dark thing and hurling it out of harm's way.

To Chance, all she could hear was the constant thump of strikes followed by an air of exertion, the sound of something sliding along the floor, fast footsteps and then more thumps. She focussed harder on the puzzle, the puzzle that she had almost completed, two more turns and she was in.

She suddenly heard this extra large, single concussive thump, and then there was a short silence, broken once more by the sliding sound again, except this time it wasn't sliding, more like dragging.

"You ok there monkey?" she called out; she glanced slightly but couldn't see a thing. The room seemed slightly darker as she had been staring at the bright red orb for so long now that it was hard to make out every little corner of the room, through her light scarred view she could see nothing.

She also heard nothing. No reply nothing. She turned her attention back to the puzzle. Navigating the orb around the last bend, she became aware of a presence out the corner of her eye. She turned and began to recognise the person as Raphael.

"There you are, I'm just about..." she trailed off as she realised it wasn't him, it looked like him, it looked a lot like him but it wasn't him.

All in the flash of an instant, the red orb popped out of the puzzle and into Chances waiting hand as the being swung its massive arm up in the air, Chance hopped out of harm's way just as the large arm came thundering down, smashing explosively through the puzzle force field, through the puzzle itself and also through the raised dais table upon which it sat. Such raw power in one swing was incredible.

Chance landed lightly on her feet as always and adopted an athletic crouch, her eyes fell on to the being before her.

This being was dark, dangerously dark. Its hair was straight and combed forward, it had pale skin and its eyes were a vicious black that screamed horrors of malice. At first glance its features were all identical to Raphael, Unmistakably; only with proximity would one notice the subtle differences. Its armour was menacing, all clad in black with shoulder pads studded with protruding spikes of incredible sharpness. It bore no weapons and yet its sheer presence screamed power, dark power.

She quickly took note of her surroundings, on the floor next to the dark being lay the prone form of Raphael, limp and unconscious. It had clearly been his body that had been dragged when she had heard that sound. She felt a strange sense of concern for him, a feeling that

251

was alien to her. She tried her best to focus but she couldn't pull her eyes the sight of the souls of his feet, a clear symbol of his felling, rooting concern deep into her.

The dark Raphael being lunged toward her and came crashing down with a thundering fist where she had stood moments before, had she not back flipped to safety in time, then she would have borne the brunt of the fate of the rock beneath her as it cracked under the sheer force of the impact. The whole attack screamed violence of epic proportions.

"Ok Raph-hulk...Clearly you put the anger in danger!! But I feel we have got off on the wrong foot here" Chance tried to make light of the situation as always. She felt her hands begin to grow warm again and she felt she had better control of such a weapon now. She kept her eyes firmly on the dark-Raphael approaching menacingly toward her. The brief thought did cross her mind as to what had happened to the other thing, her double, but she didn't have much time to dwell on it as another thundering blow came down toward her. Once again she flipped back to safety. She was running out of space to jump to, and her evasive manoeuvres, although life saving had now put her even further away from her little chimp who was still very much unconscious.

Was he unconscious? She thought *or worse?*

A deep feeling of concern was manifesting inside her, made all the worse each time her eyes fell upon the souls of his shoes.

The dark-Raphael loomed closer and by now her hands were white-hot with power. She recalled the last time she had unleashed such a power and hoped it would create a similar hole, this time hopefully in this dark being. She pulled both her palms up to chest height, aiming towards the dark aggressor and unleashed a full torrent of bright fireworks, all streaming towards the menacing dark Raphael. They all struck it directly in the chest, although, apart from the apparent dazzling to its vision; it seemed to be relatively unharmed.

'Arghg' she thought '*I really thought that would have been awesome'* she said to herself, she then thought back to Raphael's remarks back in Sanctuary when they were fighting the rubber bullet guards, his comment about the joke being on her with useless fireworks.

"Oh you are just TOO funny chimp boy" she said aloud as a smile crossed her face from his earlier humour. Before she could enjoy the joke, she felt a strange feeling like she was being stalked, as if answering an earlier question she had forethought, the dark being that resembled her came bounding down towards her, almost as if it had been crawling along the walls itself like some demon spider. The dark-Chance led with a flurry of super fast strikes toward her face. Acting purely on instinct, she began to grab the back of her head in her hands, almost in a monkey grip, and began to repeatedly flex her elbows upward, expertly deflecting each strike made by the dark being. She realised that she too was capable of moving at blistering speeds.

"Bring it girl" she said to the dark- Chance "I love a good..." she suddenly felt the need to cartwheel completely down to the side and toward the stairs. In the same moment the dark-Raphael smashed down again where she had stood and made a massive crack appear along the pyramid floor. The intensity of the fight had been set and she now realised that she was going to have her work cut out for her here. All the while she could feel that annoying itch once more, she could feel it from her shins up, all the way across her chest and down her arms. It was almost distracting her.

"So that's the kind of fights its going to be" she said aloud. Just at that the dark-Chance flew toward her again and began a lightning fast array of kicks, she raised her knee up and checked each kick, ducked and then returned with the full swing of a spinning back punch, landing square in the face of her doppelganger and sending her sprawling toward the floor. Before she had the time to follow up the wounding strike, she suddenly was forced to bend back double, her knees now flexed at 90 degree angle to avoid a perilous punch from the larger and darker clone. She returned to vertical and began to deliver twenty fast punches into the beings ribs followed by a kick. Each strike seemed to do nothing in terms of damage and the dark-Raphael grabbed her by her little face, hauled her up and then hurled her towards the far wall. The impact was concussive and she lay there, face down, for a few seconds before slowly pressing herself to her feet. From her position, her hands were spread out on the cold floor, fingers wide and she could see all her manicured work undone.

"Oh this will just not do" she said, realising that her nails had been mangled into something resembling her chimp boy's hands. She stood up slowly, cracked her neck to both sides and strengthened her resolve. She had a brief moment to formulate a plan and she was going to take full advantage of it. She needed to escape, that much was clear. She was, after all outnumbered here and she doubted she fancied her chances against the dark-chimp alone. She felt into her back pocket and remembered the piece of tech that Pepsy had given her earlier, a homing beacon she had said. Perhaps if she can activate it, help might arrive.

She glanced over to Raphael, still lying there lifeless on the cold floor, she couldn't leave him behind, she felt the need to protect him and she wasn't sure why. Perhaps she owed him a debt from today, he had been there for her after all. She dug in deep and conjured up all her remaining strength in her legs, she waited for the opportune moment, for the dark beings to pounce, their aggression being their weakness that she would exploit to her advantage. She waited.

Closer they came.

She waited still as they neared closer and closer. Once in range, both dark beings did as she had expected they would do, and lunged in violently, throwing powerful strikes that were intended to fell her in one shot. She leapt with all her might up and kicked off against the wall, performing an amazing high back flip, up and over both her attackers and landing squarely behind them. She then performed another perfect back flip and landed by her bodyguard's side. Without wasting a moment she unhooked the device Pepsy had given her earlier and depressed the top, a red light began to pulse on its top surface and along its edges, the lights remained permanently on this time instead of the pulse they were emitting earlier. She spared a moment to look down at her chimp boy, he was clean knocked out but she could see his chest moving up and down, he was still breathing.

Something stirred in her again but she couldn't quite put her finger on it, she felt it every time she looked at his prone form, lying there helpless and clearly hurt. Something deeply bothered her about his and she couldn't understand why. She moved her eyes away from his body and viewed the dark beings creeping back up the stair. The dark Raphael was truly something, he looked very menacing and it struck a

254

cold feeling through her heart to see her chimp boy filled with so much dark angry energy. She watched and waited, hoping that help would arrive soon.

Pepsy was speeding across the desert plains in her mechanised technology vehicle. It was a simple design and fuelled by tribinium through compression chambers that blasted the energy out from under the vehicle giving it the ability to hover. It had cost her quite a bit of credits, much to the dismay of her credit balance.

"I don't know why we had to use tech, you know how the Allfather feels about this" she said, letting her annoyance show at having to fork out HER credits to save his sorrow soul yet again.

"I swear if we teleport I'll be sick I am sure of it" Jeremy replied. He was lying slouched in the passenger chair holding his stomach. He had really overdone it this time on the drink front and was reeling from the overdose.

"You really need to sort yourself out Jeremy, I mean this, it's just not on" She began to scold him and she had every reason to. She had spent the best part of the last two days looking for him and worrying. She had travelled many miles and not all of those were gifted. Jeremy began to mouth some profanities in defiance, unwilling yet to accept that he truly had a problem. Whatever he was mouthing, he was leaving his mouth really wide open in doing so. Pepsy took full advantage of this and instantly teleported back to her domicile in Astoria and straight into her washroom where she grabbed a bar of soap, she 'shifted' back to the where she had been previously and stuck the bar straight into Jeremy's gaping mouth, doing this all within the blink of an eye.

He instantly began to gag and spit out the large glycerine bar from his mouth, she just sniggered at her quick action wit. As she watched him continue to gag and spit, she burst into a fit of hysterics, she couldn't stop laughing, all she could think about was how much running around she had done for him that day, in which he disregarded and unappreciated, and now, in his moment of soapy enlightenment, she had retribution.

Just as she was beginning to saviour the moment, her homing beacon locator began to bleep, she looked to her wrist and could see it had been activated by Chance and she immediately set to go and collect her.

"Here take the wheel, I'll be right back" Pepsy said to Jeremy.

"What?" he saw through soap bubbled mouth "I've been drinking I can't drive"

"You also had a dirty mouth up until 2 minutes ago and I solved that one for you" she countered. Jeremy considered this and shook his head. "Just hold it" she said, rather more sincere this time.

Submitting to her wishes as he grumbled "you are setting a really bad example" she gave him a long look, raising her eyebrows before 'shifting' away.

She arrived straight into what could only be described as a rumble. She crouched next to Chance who was standing guard over Raphael's body. Chances focus was clearly on the stairs before her, Pepsy did not care to look at whatever had captured her attention and instantly grabbed a hand onto Chances leg, one onto Raphael's leg and then shifted them straight out of danger and back to the vehicle. Pepsy landed straight on top of Jeremy's lap as Chance fell into the passenger seat, Raphael dropped into the rear seats.

As Pepsy tried to un-straddle herself from Jeremy he immediately muttered

"A very bad example!!!"

Pepsy jumped straight into the back seat to see to Raphael, Jeremy then realised that his driving task was not complete with her arrival and scoffed at having to use his head aching mind to focus.

"Darling are you ok?" her question was almost reciprocal as it was clear from his battered visage that he was far from ok. She quickly checked him up and down, he was covered in bruises all over and his eyes were almost spinning in their sockets. "He looks very concussed" she said aloud, but the other occupants of the car seemed disinterested. Chance sat in the front seat, desperately playing with the small red orb, turning it over in her hands and attempting to pry it open to no avail. Pepsy drew herself nearer to Raphael and spoke loud into his face "Raphael, can you hear me, its Pepsy?"

Raphael mumbled something that Pepsy took as confirmation. "Raph hunni, I need you to give me some smelling salts so I can help you focus, okay, SMELLING SALTS" she said, increasing the volume of her voice in an attempt to make him focus, his eyes were still spinning within their sockets. Raphael grumbled again, rummaged around in his pocket and then produced a large piece of clothing; she took it in her hand and was instantly repulsed at the smell, she pinched the cloth between her two fingers and lifted it up to examine it, her other hand pinching her nose. Upon looking closer she realised that the cloth was in fact a pair of shorts, and judging by the pungent aroma, a smelly pair of shorts.

"Oh dear we are in a bad way" she said.

Spanners could feel his eyes slowly drying out; they had been strained beyond the hurting point and now all he could feel was the gentle, crisp breeze that was flowing throughout the draughty chamber. He had been staring intently at the data screen before him for what felt like hours, refusing to move until he had fulfilled his task; its completion was of the most utter importance. Deep inside the lower levels of the palace in the main communications room, he stood in front of the main control tower and had been down there since the Allfather had ordered him earlier, jostling around and connecting old wires and cabling.

A small drop of water fell from the low ceiling, splashing hard against the plating of his green Angel armour, the sound echoing theatrically around the small confines of the stone walls but he paid it no attention, it was of no concern to him.

He watched as the progress bar on his data slates completely filled up green, indicating to him that the process had now been completed and all that was required to do now was to turn the machine on.

This part he had been dreading. The room in which the main communications hub was stored was not very well maintained; drips and leaks were often sprouting from the walls and giving the room a very damp feel to it, although the vital systems were protected behind a thick, clear Lastic panel, Spanners was not sure how the damp would affect the running of the system. He walked over to the secondary system tower and eyed its control panel precariously. There was a large black switch in the top right hand corner of the tower, it was currently sitting at 'o' for off. He took a deep breath, closed his eyes and flicked the switch to '1' to turn it on.

Instantly the sound of a great fan firing up could be heard around the room, the sound easily drowning out the noise of the dripping water. The whole control tower lit up with various coloured flashing lights and Spanners stood and observed it for a moment. A small smile of success crossed his face. It was a very rare occasion to see a genuine smile from Spanners, He had his 'polite' smile that he would use to fit in with others, this was but a small flex of his jaw muscles, splitting his mouth ever so slightly to show his teeth and hint at his heightened spirits, but this was usually forced through habit and didn't feel genuine. This smile that now crossed his face was a little more gratified, upbeat and he now felt genuine happiness with the fruits of his labour.

He turned his attention to his gauntlet where a small light had started to flash, his smile grew even bigger as he turned sharply and headed for the door.

Once outside the door he started to run up the spiral staircase and out toward the main Plaza where he had left the Allfather earlier. This was the second time that day he had found himself running and yet this time, he had a genuine spring in his step, and each bound propelled him up the stairs with an element of excitement. He ran on.

Down in the market place of Astoria, there was a full scale riot taking place.

Punches were being thrown by anyone and everyone; the stalls were being over turned as the products that had once rested there were being hurled as weapons. There was no rhyme or reason to the fighting, just the compelling need to unleash their pent up aggression, their barely contained rage that had been manifesting within them from the chemical inhibitors of the pheromone devices.

One woman was simply taking small valuable vases from one of the stalls and smashing them against the stone floor. The sound of breaking porcelain was sending thrills up her spine, working her way along the shelf with an intense look of passion in her eyes; she continued to satisfy her destructive urges. When she had reached the final vase, she gripped it tight within her manic hands and hurled toward the ground, watching it smash into hundreds of tiny pieces. She then looked up and around her, a deep sadness had filled eyes as she realised there was nothing left that could recreate that smashing sound. The feeling of loss running deep within her intoxicated soul, she turned on the spot and went looking for something else to break, feeling the insatiable need to destroy something beautiful.

All over Astoria it was the same, needless fights and vandalism, pent up aggression being unleashed on any unsuspecting soul.

The Astorian guard fared no better. Those that were trying to maintain order and control were doing so in an aggressive manner, grabbing and throwing civilians around with all their might, grinding their teeth in anger at the events unfolding before them.

Just outside the market in Astoria, Gregor stood with his credit token placed neatly on a stand and his bagpipes under his arm. He took a big breath and started to play yet another tune from his repertoire.

He had done well financially today and his mother was going to be so proud of him when he got home. He hadn't checked his token in the last hour or so but he was pretty sure he had earned a lot of credits, perhaps even enough to purchase the Superfuse gloves he so desired.

He had worked hard today, playing tune after tune and truly testing his playing stamina. He had noticed however, that in the last and most recent hour, there seemed to be some commotion going on in the market that he was not purvey to. It was quite frustrating as he had set himself up in such a way that he would catch the passersby as they went to and from the market, but he noted that fewer and fewer passersby were actually paying him any attention now.

Continuing to play on regardless, he worked his way through to the end of his song, holding the last note for as long as his little lungs would allow before letting it wail out. He then stopped to catch his breath.

Upon resting, he looked up and could see that the sun had started to descend, bringing in the evening sky and he decided he should probably get home for his dinner. He hated nothing more than trying to take down his equipment while dusk was falling so he thought it wise to stay one step ahead of the game today.

Just as he placed his pipes onto the ground a small man stopped and turned to him. Gregor looked up and met his eyes.

"Would you like me to play you something sir?" he asked very politely. Gregor had been brought up well and always ensured he was polite to others, especially strangers. He was not, however, always polite to his mother which sometimes led to him going hungry at nights as punishment.

"You shouldn't be playing those pipes boy! Those are war pipes!! Can't you see what's happening here, it's a riot!!" the man said.

A riot? Gregor thought. He didn't think he even knew the meaning of the word. He assumed it meant a disturbance of some sort but here? In Astoria, he very much doubted it.

The man's nature suddenly changed as his eyes were drawn to the credit token sitting on the stand next to the grounded pipes.

"You boy, Are making money by instigating a riot with your damned musical instrument of war!!!" it was a statement more than a question, and it was delivered with a newfound aggression in the man. His demeanour changed altogether as he started to walk towards Gregor and the token card.

"No sir, it's just bagpipes, for entertainment" Gregor replied

"Those damn things are for marching to war!!! And now the very sound is irritating me also!"

Gregor looked confused. The pipes had been laid on the ground since the man had arrived, no music could be heard playing from them any longer and so how could he still be annoyed.

"But sir I'm not playing anything?"

"Don't be cheeky with me boy...The noise is still ringing in my ear from earlier. Now give me that token card. In fact give me your noise polluting pipes also!" the man reached forward but Gregor displayed excellent speed by snatching his hand out quickly and taking the card from the stand, he then wedged his left foot under his pipes, flicking them up, and catching them in his other hand.

Standing firm, his credit token safely in one hand, his pipes cradled in the other, he now found himself trapped between the man and the wall he had chosen to busk from.

Gregor as always tried to negotiate his way out of this.

"How about I give you 20% of my takings to leave me alone?" Gregor said.

The man crept further forward. His eyes had gone an angry dark, with bloodshot lines straining through his eyeballs.

"Erm, ok angry man, 30%...and I'll throw in some ear plugs for you next time we play" Gregor tried again. The man ignored him.

By now he was almost within reaching distance. The angry man seemed very daunting but Gregor held fast, he was a brave little boy and wouldn't be intimidated by anyone. He weighed up his options, His credit token was full from months of busking and so he could easily buy a new set of pipes with it and still have credits left over. The pipes themselves would be awkward to carry and he knew he had to think fast here.

Having weighed up his options, Gregor launched the pipes up into the air space just above the angry man's head.

The man's automatic reaction was to reach up and grab them, much to Gregors' delight, as the second part of his plan was to kick this man where it hurt, and make a run for it.

Half of the plan went well.

As the angry man reached up, naturally throwing his arms towards the incoming bagpipes, he left his entire mid-section of his body exposed giving Gregor the opportunity to drop his hip and swing a high kick up and toward the man's groin.

He missed.

He more than missed, he missed so badly that his momentum carried him forwards and he fell into the man, knocking them both crashing to the ground. The bagpipes landed in the man's face and he began thrashing to free his vision.

Gregor tried to climb to his feet but the man's thrashing was throwing him off balance. He managed to roll off the man's stomach and onto the stone floor, arm over arm he started to crawl free, scraping his knees along the floor as he went. Just as he was about to push himself to his feet, he felt a strong hand clamp around his little ankle, he looked down to see that the angry man had grabbed him and wasn't letting go.

Gregor screamed.

Pepsy mopped Raphael's brow with a cold towel, his eyes had stopped spinning in his head and he was starting to make a little more sense in his speech.

Jeremy looked back at him in the rear view mirror.

"You are in a bad way son" Jeremy stated the obvious, the intoxication of the booze he had consumed earlier had worn off and he was beginning to resemble something more like himself. Raphael's eyes met his but he said nothing.

Chance sat in the front passenger seat, still attempting to gain access to her orb and release her memories. It was perfectly sealed shut and made of a very thick glassy material. She attempted to tap it hard against the side of the vehicle but that didn't work either. She sat there feeling very frustrated and her thoughts started to drift elsewhere. Something about that whole encounter had struck a nerve with her and she felt it deep within her heart. She remained silent for the first time that day, something as simple as seeing the souls of his feet had set it off, set off an emotion that she was pretty sure she did not want to feel again if she could help it. She continued to chew on her nail and her eyes drifted towards the rear view mirror and met those of Raphael. She became locked in a soundless conversation with him, bouncing unsaid words through reflections' in the glass. Something about his gaze told her he cared for her, cared for her very much. He appeared to have a worried look, almost like he had let her down in some fashion, that he hadn't protected her properly. She looked deeper, finding she just couldn't look away.

There was a lot of emotion in his eyes, a look that said a thousand words; she just wished she could remember who he was.

Were they brother and sister? He looked nothing like her, did he have to? Is he her bodyguard and is his look of care based on his dedication to his duty? She thought back to moments throughout the day and she was convinced it was more than that. Well at least for him it was. She could tell by the way he had looked at her, the way he had protected her and put himself in harm's way regardless of the situation. He really did care about her on a much deeper level than she had given him credit for. She started to feel a little remorse at her treatment of him that day, she had been slightly cruel and yet he had taken it al,l and stuck by her. If only she could remember. Her eyes remained on his and she could see how tired he was, he had black rims around his eyes, although she wasn't entirely sure they were not in fact bruises. She felt something touch her, a soft, light touch just above her chest. She continued to gaze at him and realised that the touch she had felt, the soft and gentle touch, was in fact her own hand as it had naturally been drawn to the necklace. She must have done it instinctively as she played with its intricate design between her two fingers. She held his gaze for a moment longer, realising that his eyes were smoulderingly caring for her, she could feel the intense feelings he had for her, feelings she couldn't return, she had to look away. She couldn't remember him; surely if he meant something to her she wouldn't have forgotten him.

She shook her head and continued to turn the necklace over in her fingers. If only she could remember.

The vehicle sped on.

Pepsy's gauntlet began to bleep, and at the same time so did Jeremy's and Raphael's. Chance heard a bleeping on her body but she could not see where it was coming from, she tried to home in on the sound but found herself distracted by the re-occurring itch that was irritating her skin once more, unable to resist it, she began to scratch.

"It's the ACG...strange it has been activated" Pepsy stated.

"ACG?" Chance asked, screwing her face up in confusion as she continued to drag her nails over her own skin.

"Audible Communications Grid, it was deemed tech and therefore frowned upon and eventually phased out, strange now that it's been activated." Pepsy answered. She brought her gauntlet to her mouth and pressed the switch, instantly a hololith sprung up from her wrist and showed the form of Spanners.

"My lady, you are to bring all available Angels back to the palace immediately. This is a code red" Spanners stated in his usual mechanically emotionless voice.

"Spanners what has happened?" she exclaimed.

"No time to explain, shift all Angels here immediately, imminent threat to Astoria" he replied again.

"Spanners! Quickly, you must inform the Allfather that I encountered something today that spoke of 'wave space' I know such terms are deemed heretical and so I thought I'd let you know right away" she added.

"That explains a lot of what has occurred today thank you Pepsy" he replied and then cut the feed.

Everyone in the car looked shocked and bewildered. Jeremy turned to Pepsy in an effort to resist the inevitable, he hated teleportation at the best of times, and with a hangover, he hated it even more. He tried to protest but she cut him off before he even had the chance to complain, placing a hand on all three passengers in the car, she instantly shifted them all to the palace.

Upon arriving, Jeremy bent in two and hurled the contents of his stomach onto the floor.

"I told you so" he said as vomit dribbled from his mouth. Nobody took any notice of him as he sprawled himself across the cold tiled floor. Raphael lay on the ground, still a little concussed; Pepsy was already on the move and went straight to Spanners.

"Where is everyone else?" she asked

"You must seek Quincy firstly at the copper mines, his men are making their way back now but we need him immediately" Spanners responded.

"It will be done" she said and 'shifted' away instantly.

Chance stood there and gazed around, amazed by the size of the palace and feeling strangely at home. She had remained quiet since her time in the car and listened on intently. All day she had went, not truly knowing who she was or what she was doing. Now that she had her memory orb back, she was almost at her goal and yet frustratingly, she couldn't unlock it, the method was beyond her and so she felt like she was still no further forward. Knowing whom she had to seek, to end this stupor, she turned and made her way toward the stairs.

 Raphael scrambled and tried to regain his feet.

"Chance, please don't" he called to her. She stopped dead in her tracks, his voice cutting through her resolve instantly. She turned and met his eyes once more, He looked helplessly weak and it hurt her to see him like this, but she had to get her memory back and work out how to unlock the orb and he looked in no fit condition to follow her.

"I'm sorry..." she said softly "I need to remember" she turned and left him there, lying on the palace floor, and headed down the stairway and out into the main courtyard.

CHAPTER 11

Meanwhile, out on the desert plains, Quincy and the 970 troops trailed their way back to Astoria.

Quincy walked alone and at one with his thoughts. He was two thirds of the way back in the troop line and from the corner of his eye he could make out the large stretchers that were carrying the remains of his...mistake.

 He was doing everything he could to hold back the tears but every time he closed his eyes he could see their blackened bodies, all charred and burnt and still smoking from the carnage he had unleashed.

He shook his head and attempted to free his vision of such images. He thought back to the bone war, where he could freely use his gift, openly charring the bones of the advancing army and being commended for doing so, the smell had been the same and yet back then he was somehow righteous in his purpose. This today, this massacre of innocents, this was far from righteous. What saddened Quincy the most is that he knew it would be labelled an accident; these poor men's lives had been taken without any hope of justice. It would be said that, an Angel makes margin calls every day, and that the lives of the 30 was just that, a margin call, an unforeseen loss, but to Quincy this was 30 lives, 30 families that he would have to face.

He suddenly felt sick, and not for the first time today he bent over and heaved the contents of his stomach onto the ground. As he did so the men carrying the stretchers, who had been a few paces back, had now marched by him. Upon passing he noticed that one of the body bags had not been fully zipped up, he stared in at the ghostly dark, burnt out socket of one of the men. No horror he could ever face again could out do the fear that image struck deep into his heart. He dropped his eyes in shame.

He continued to walk on, each step he took was laboured with guilt and his eyes never left the ground in front of him. He started to feel this gnawing sensation deep within him. At first he ignored it as perhaps a hunger pang or fatigue, but the feeling grew. It felt like a great power was crawling beneath his skin and it wanted to be unleashed. He could feel his fingertips begin to tingle with the anticipation of using his gift; he quickly placed both his hands under his arms in an attempt to null the sensation. This act did very little except take away the tingle in his fingertips, the feeling in his stomach remained however and continued to grow, he had to focus on his breathing to take his mind off the power growing within.

He felt his heart beating irregularly, unsure as to whether it was to remain calm or beat fast in excitement. This further sensation made him feel a little nauseous, well a little more nauseas than he was previously feeling. What was happening to him he was not sure, he only wished he was closer to Astoria so that he could meet with the Allfather, perhaps he had an answer, or even a cure.

It had finally dawned on him that he had underestimated the potency of the tribinium crystals and had also, to his own misfortune, not heeded the clear warnings from his sergeant, of the dangers of coming into contact with such a substance.

A foolish move and one he now wished he could undo.

For that he would need the gift of time travel.

Now there was a thought...

A few moments had passed before a bleeping sound distracted his attention. It was emanating from his gauntlet on his left arm and he was a little puzzled as to its origin. He flicked open its panel and discovered that it was in fact his in built ACG device calling him. It had been many a year since he had used the ACG system, so long that he had forgotten it was even there.

He pressed the pulsing red light and answered.

"Quincy this is Spanners, we have a code red emergency in Astoria, all Angels are being 'shifted' immediately back to the city. Pepsy will be with you shortly to retrieve you"

"Spanners, I can't, I can't leave the men, something has happened here and it would be unwise..." Quincy was not allowed to finish

"Orders come direct from the Allfather. Immediately" and then Spanners cut the communications.

Quincy sighed and let out a deep breath, this day just could not get any worse.

Lying in his hammock, over in his dwellings, Wallace rested his eyes and replayed the events from earlier that day. He just could not understand it, for years he had hung around that market, right through his school years he had helped the local vendors with deliveries, sampled their foods, and covered their stalls while they took their lunch breaks. When there was a flood he had been the first man there to help and the last man there to leave. It was only 5 months ago that he had graduated from school and all the market dwellers had come to cheer him on. They were like his family, they were his friends and here they were, casting him out with the rejects and the wasters.

He rubbed his eyes and could feel the crusted remains of tears on his face. He turned slightly, rolling out of his hammock and onto his feet. He stretched his arms up as high as they would go, feeling his back crack all the way up the spine, and yawning as he enjoyed the brief moment of levity, it was the best feeling he had felt that day.

He walked over to his small chilling cabinet and gripping the cold steel handle, he opened the door. There wasn't much in the way of food in there, there never needed to be, he would normally have his fill of food for the day from the market, sampling all the foods as he went and eliminating the need to stock food at home. The Allfather was forever holding banquets in the main hall for a variety of grand occasions, from simple gift day celebrations to anniversaries of important events. Wallace wasn't a greedy man, his bulk was an unfortunate side effect of his gift and he did whatever he could to minimise his portions and remain as slim as his gifted genetics would allow. One of his food sanctions was to abstain from eating anything after working hours and that meant foregoing the storing of food at his domicile, a sanction that he was now regretting.

He looked to the back of the cabinet and could just about make out a spicy sauce condiment bottle, it was half empty and pressed into the far corner where it had lain forgotten about for some time. He reached in and took it, flipping open the lid and pouring the remainder of the contents down his gullet, tasting its spicy consistency and quickly realising that it was not meant for consumption in the manner that he had chosen, he cared not.

He finished the bottle and then threw it at the recycling belt. It landed hard and the conveyor belt immediately started to move. He watched as his discarded bottle was taken out through a sliding door panel and away off through the underground pipes to the recycling centre. The thought crossed his mind to go after the bottle, to hop on the belt and be 'recycled', let the vendors at the plant find another use for him besides food sampling. He dismissed this thought as he concluded he wouldn't fit through the little sliding door.

He turned on the spot, completely at a loss as to what to do. He had never spent this much time awake in his domicile before, he was quite literally bored. Outside he could hear all kinds of shouting, he was even sure he could hear random sounds of smashing glass which made him wonder Just what really WAS going on here today? What brought such nonsense to his peaceful city?

He lingered on that thought briefly as he heard a scream. This wasn't a joyful scream nor was it a short scream either, this was a scream laced with dread, Wallace wasted no time in heading for the door.

The Skelemet Commander knelt before the dark alter as a purple cloud of energy began to coerce into existence above him. He turned his gaze to the floor.

The Commander waited a few moments longer to ensure the rift had been fully opened before delivering his message.

"My lord, our plan has failed. The clone does not possess the gift you seek"

There was a silence and a growing tension of anger that could be felt emanating from the gaping tear in the continuum.

"Your failures today....Commander...have been noted..When I instruct you to capture...you ensure you capture...and when I tell you to kill...see to it it's done.."

The Commander stood weary, unwilling to give a response for fear of retaliation of the grimmest kind.

"Luckily for you....Commander....the clone not possessing the power was as I had forethought, the dark clones will however serve another purpose. We will follow the alternative solution; eliminate all that we do not need!" The purple cloud slowly ghosted away into nothing.

Gregor struggled with the angry man.

"Get off me!" he kicked and shouted, defiant to the last. The angry man was still at Gregors' feet but was holding on tight, so tight that it was actually hurting the little boy's leg.

With each kick that Gregor sent to the man's face, only angered him further, tightening his grip, turning poor Gregors' foot almost blue with the lack of circulation. The angry man would not relent; he just seemed to get angrier with each second.

Gregor began to lose his own temper.

This was HIS money and HE had earned it! THIS stupid angry man was going to TRY and take HIS money from him.

His anger also started to rise.

This STUPID man had FORCED him to nearly break HIS pipes. HIS pipes!!

Gregors' anger grew exponentially, and so too did this strange feeling in his stomach. It wasn't butterflies, like he would have felt at the

270

funfair, it wasn't a nauseous feeling either, like if he had been ill. It was something else entirely.

His eyes began to turn a fiery orange, his core body temperature started rising dramatically. His fingers became sweaty but then dried instantly from the heat, and his skin took a colour of red, then orange, then white...Then...

The strange sensation built to a climax, he felt his blood actually boiling within his veins and his eyes dried out instantly as raw heat exploded from his sockets.

He immolated dramatically into a boy of flames.

The angry man instantly recoiled, his hands burning from Gregors' touch. He rolled away in a panic.

Before his very eyes, was a young boy, covered head to toe in flames, He was completely on fire, blistering hot and unrelenting fire.

The man, his choler now extinguished by what he saw, tried to offer some help, trying to encourage Gregor to roll over and douse the flames, he fell silent as he watched Gregor stand up quite calmly, not a single burn mark on his skin or an indication that he was in pain. He the realised that, not only was the boy unharmed, he looked angry, very angry.

Just as he was about to turn and run, he felt a massive hand land on his shoulder, its sheer size easily wrapping around his shoulder cuff, gripping tightly and immobilising him immediately.

A little startled, and with a newfound fear seeping through his body, the man slowly lifted his eyes, creeping up the massive hulking form of an Angel is blue armour. His eyes finally reached the peak and found he was now staring at none other than the Angel Wallace. Wallace stood there an impressive sight, massive blue shoulder pads with a silver tinted lining and white leg guards and gauntlets. His gleaming white smile, as always, was spread across his face.

"I think it is time for you to leave little man" Wallace said to him. The man quickly nodded and ran off. Wallace started to laugh, a deep and friendly laugh as he eyed Gregor carefully.

"Hahahaha I came to your rescue and yet you seemed to have handled it yourself" he said.

Gregor looked on, a little confused as to what was happening to him. He peered at his hands and realised that they too were on fire, panic started to creep into his mind.

Was he going to be stuck like this. How what? How?

Having gone through a similar ordeal when he too was just a young lad, Wallace immediately recognised the anxious look in Gregor's eyes.

"Relax boy, you have finally found your gift, it is a privilege to be one of the few to be born with such. Immolation hey..One day you will lead the Phoenix guard of that I am sure. You can even wield a fire sword..THE fire sword. You can use the sword of Lucas!" Wallace said and laughed a little more.

"But...but how do I turn it off" Gregor said as the panic subsiding slightly, Wallace's calming demeanour and approach relaxing him.

"Until you master it, you might not be able to turn it off willingly, but for now.." Wallace walked over to him and placed a hand on his burning shoulder, he instantly began to grow in stature as he absorbed the boy's power into himself. After a few moments, he was easily 9ft tall and super charged with flaming energy, his physique had expanded to a great size until eventually it stopped, the flames around Gregor sizzling out.

Wallace raised his hand into the air, stretching it as high as he could, flexing his muscles as he did so, and unleashed a massive fireball toward the heavens, a huge spherical spectacle of flames was sent hurtling into the evening sky, and as the energy left his body, Wallace shrunk back to his regular size.

"But for now boy I can help you out" he said smiling. Gregor stood before him now, light steam rising from his body as he slowly cooled down in the evening air. He looked at both his hands, which had now returned to his regular colour of peach.

"This is awesome!" he exclaimed.

"The targets are...... en-route toward you now...see to it personally that I get my prize....alive!!...fail me and suffer the consequences..." the cold dark voice said, the words left the purple cloud like an incandescent whisper.

"If they come to face me, I will need an honour guard...I have not the strength to fight them alone" the old man said.

"Your weakness is...pathetic...but so be it, I will tolerate no more failings" the voice trailed off as the purple cloud slowly dissipated.

The old man ground his teeth in anger. He was growing weaker by the minute; another encounter with that particular duo would most certainly drain him to his very grave.

He attempted to clench his claw fist, to squeeze the emancipated fingers into his palm in anger, but had not the strength to finish the task.

'Obedience or vengeance' he pondered. 'The latter definitely seemed more appealing given his ageing predicament' he thought.

The old man smiled a cunning and devious old smile.

His attention was suddenly drawn to the four little servants that held sentry at the edge of the room, their weak, skinny little bodies began to convulse and shake violently. Their muscles began to flex and then grow violently out of proportion.

Each slave grew in stature by at least three feet and their shoulders broadened before his very eyes. The eyes of the servants became sullen, black and lacking emotion. Their faces changed in colour from white and half-healthy, to a deathly purple. Contusions began to bubble out of them all over their bodies. Some of them burst and some of them turned to bone. Their nails grew three times in length and turned a dirty yellow colour, the tips became razor sharp as their knuckles too grew extra bone over them. Their muscles became denser and black veins flowed quite visibly through them, pulsing with a darkness that was just waiting to be unleashed. Their jaws became

273

thicker and harder, squarer, and their neck muscles grew twice as big, like thick tree roots holding their disfigured heads in place.

The old man looked on at his honour guard, grinning from ear to ear.

"Go now! Find him, and bring him before me! The girl must not be harmed, her I will deal with myself" the old man said.

Raphael had to muster all his strength to haul himself to his feet. His head was spinning, his world was spinning. He felt aches and pains in places he didn't think was possible.

His left leg was damaged somehow, he couldn't recall when but pain shot through his body every time he tried to place some weight on it. He could taste blood in his mouth and he had to swallow hard to remove it. His throat was raw and bleeding.

He limped over to a small post that stood a few feet away and he used its length to steady himself. He felt nauseous, struggling hard to focus. Every breath he took had become an effort, as if his lung itself was punctured and bleeding air into his body with each inhalation. He leaned hard into the post, his eyes focussed on the stairs that led out of the plaza and down into the market area, he HAD to go after her, he had to try.

Leaning heavily on the post, he flipped open his gauntlet, pressed a few keys and brought up Chances locator on his mini map. He could see that she had now made her way down to the gaming arena. He flipped shut his gauntlet and pushed himself up off the post. He staggered sideways slightly, limping each time he placed weight on his left side.

After a few strained steps, he felt his ribs begin to ache. He held an arm across his front to cradle them, holding the bones in tight which helped to ease the pain slightly.

He had reached the top of the stairs and his descent was extremely painful. Each step he took shot searing white pain through his entire body. He nearly blacked out with each step. His eyes dropped to the floor where he saw a small red spot appear against the white stone floor. A tiny red spot, and then another, and another. After a few seconds he realised that the spots were in fact blood and dripping from his nose. He took his right hand and wiped it across his face.

He had to find her fast. His girl was in danger and he had to protect her.

He limped on down toward the market where he took a sharp right and headed straight toward the gaming arena. His breathing was suffering now, each breath felt like he was inhaling small tacks, deep into his lungs. The sharp pain had returned to his ribs now regardless of his attempts to cradle them. He battled on, keeping his focus on simply putting one foot in front of the other repeatedly.

His entire body wanted to stop, it was screaming at him to sit down, to rest but he fought on. His muscles felt like they were filled with battery acid and burning him to his core but he drove onwards. He had to get to her.

He turned a corner into a wide channel passageway; his vision was badly blurring and to look up, brought about the nauseous feeling again. The light was hurting his eyes and he was forced to squint.

He paused suddenly; aware that there were four, massive figures making their way toward him. His eyes remained on the ground but the evening sun was casting their shadows out before him.

The four figures were massive, bigger than anything he could have ever faced before and they were moving aggressively fast toward him. He knew of no-one or no-thing in the whole of Astoria that could host a shadow as big as these and so immediately he felt the threat.

He spread his stance as he slowed, lifting his head was an extreme effort now, and as he did so he realised that the four monstrosities had now circled him, they were most certainly not friendly's, not by their behaviour now.

His arms were tired and he could barely lift them, his armour was battered and dented. He managed to lift his right gauntlet slowly and took rough aim; his head was spinning faster now. He unleashed a full torrent of flares into the eyes of his aggressors, blinding them with their bright brilliance. The act was fairly useless as he had not the strength to follow it up with anything useful, he was merely delaying the inevitable.

One of the monstrous aggressors swung for his face, and it took every bit of his energy to dodge the brunt of the incoming fist, bring his left arm up to parry the shot, and striking the thing straight back in the face, knocking it back a good few steps.

His vision was so blurred that he could not even make out the faces of his attackers but he could just about discern that they were disfigured in some way. He didn't have the time to make a further evaluation as one of the beings struck him straight in the ribs with a thundering punch.

Raphael felt the life being sucked out of him, he felt light headed and almost euphoric, a feeling he would have enjoyed had it not been for the next strike, aimed at his damaged left leg, that sent him reeling in pain and straight to the deck.

He landed hard, his leg having given way from his previous injury. He felt the wind of another strike coming down towards him but he had not the strength to move. It was a stamp from one of their massive feet, straight down onto his chest. He felt bones crack under the sheer barbaric force of the strike.

His eyes became droopy. There was a pause, a gap in the attacks. Raphael used this to roll over onto his front.

 Still no finishing blow came.

He used everything he had left, to push him up onto his elbows and drive his knees along the ground. Crawling painfully slowly and in the direction of his love, he hauled his right arm over, then pulled himself along, hauled his left arm over and dragged himself along. He had barely the strength to move.

He spat to clear his mouth and bright red blood struck the ground before him. He could feel the four monstrous things watching him; he could feel their eyes on him, watching curiously.

It was only a matter of time, he knew it was coming.

He heard it first, the deep inhalation, the sucking of air before the great exertion. He then heard the wind as the velocity of the incoming strike gained momentum.

He never felt the finishing strike, it came hard and fast across the front of his face, the sheer power knocking him out cold for the second time that day.

Raphael's eyes peered towards the doorway of the gaming arena, looking long fully at how close he had come to being there for her, his vision became tunnelled, and then his world went completely black.

At the north end of the palace, near the city walls stood the Allfather alongside Spanners, Quincy, Harmony, Pepsy and Jeremy. Their attention was fixed solely on the devices attached to the surface of the wall. They were spread out at 5 yard intervals and went all the way around the perimeter wall as far as they could see.

"And you are sure these devices are causing all this pandemonium" the Allfather asked Spanners.

"I am positive of it" he replied.

"Good, Jeremy, please make yourself useful and take it out" the Allfather said.

At that Jeremy suddenly became very alert, followed the order instantly and picked up a small stone, throwing it directly at the device on the wall. It instantly destroyed it with the sheer accuracy of his shot.

The Angels eyes all furrowed in unison at the strange event that unfolded next. The devices either side of the one that had been destroyed sprouted long spider like legs, stretching across to the gap where a device had previously been. Within a few seconds a new device had been installed, and the whole system was working to full potential again.

Jeremy grumbled, picking up another pebble, aimed slightly and threw it. This pebble sailed at a slightly different angle, struck the first device and bounced, catching the second and third device on its ricochet and destroyed all three in the same throw.

He smiled.

And yet once again the devices further down the wall stretched out with the spider like legs, and within a few moments all the broken devices were repaired and replaced.

"Arghgh, there must be another way" Jeremy growled in frustration as he went to pick up another pebble. The Allfather stepped forward and placed a hand across his chest to stop him; with a simple look he had excused him from the task.

"There is another way, a way in which we can destroy all the devices in one go and not allow them to repair" the Allfather said, he turned to look at Spanners who nodded in agreement and they both turned towards Quincy.

Quincy had remained strangely sullen and quiet since he had arrived. His eyes had remained on the ground in front of him and only under the intense glare he felt from the Allfather did he look up and meet their gaze.

"No please I can't" he said.

"Cant what? Don't be stupid Quincy" the Allfather said.

"No really I can't, I'm not in control, I can't I won't" "I'm not in control, people will get hurt"

"People are already getting hurt and you can stop this!"The Allfather shouted.

Quincy began to back away, his grief could be read across his face and the Angels present were shocked to see him in such a way.

"have you succumb to this madness as well?" the Allfather asked, completely unaware of what had happened in the copper mine "pull yourself together boy" the Allfather deliberately used the condescending phrase 'boy' to bring a little sharpness back into Quincy's resolve.

It worked, as he immediately straightened up, tears welling up in his eyes along with a distinct look of fear in them, which spoke of his obvious apprehension to the task.

Pepsy saw this look and stepped forward, always the one to look out for others.

"Are you ok darling?" she asked him, he merely looked at her with his deep teary eyes, saying nothing. He then stepped forward slowly, raising both his arms out to the side, preparing to conjure up his gift.

 The tears had begun to run down his face now as he looked toward the gathered Angels before him, he mouthed the words 'sorry' and then unleashed his gift.

Enormous amounts of electricity flowed from both his arms and were sent in opposite directions along the perimeter wall. The flow was powerful and streamed massive voltages, higher than Quincy had ever conjured up before. Both beams made contact with the devices along the wall and instantly began to fry the intricate circuits within. His eyes went white as his gifts output grew exponentially. The Angels before him eyes lit up in wonder. They had never seen him so powerful.

Tears were flowing freely now down his face and his muscles along his arms were flexing violently under the force.

Every one of the devices along the wall had now been destroyed and yet the flow of energy continued to be forced along. By now, both beams had connected at the far end of the perimeter wall, and had begun to spark and spike inward toward the city. They were attracted to the high conducting metals of the light posts, and immediately made contact, frying the glow worms that were nested inside. The electricity crept its way further and further into the city, attaching itself to anything that would conduct it, and burning all carbon it came across.

Fires erupted at various points around the city and the people who were already in pandemonium, grew into an even greater panic.

"Quincy, stop this now!" the Allfather shouted.

Quincy was openly crying now, the sheer power flowing from his arms that he had no control over. He tried to pull his arms inward; this only switched the flow of electricity through him. He was lit up brightly, and still the strands of lightening sparked out in all directions. His gift was lashing like storm lightning and attaching itself to anything and everything.

"I ..I...I can't" he shouted.

The Allfather looked to his Angels; they were all at a loss as what to do next. Jeremy had even taken a few sensible steps backwards; his sense of self preservation was always his highest priority.

"Pepsy, can you shift him out the city limits?" the Allfather suggested.

"I'll try" she replied, stepping forwards quickly, trying her best to avoid the strands of lightening that were violently leaving his body.

Quincy had by now folded his arms under his arm pits in an attempt to stop them directing the flow, it was doing very little but to bubble the electricity into the one spot, and in higher voltages.

Pepsy got closer, reaching forwards to touch him, but as soon as she made contact, she was instantly electrocuted and sent hurtling backward.

Quincy's face had a look of great remorse and sorrow. He stepped backwards and away from the gathered Angels, his power output was definitely increasing and he had no way of controlling it.

It was just too much.

He could feel it inside, a mass of energy just waiting to explode, it took everything he had to release it this slowly, and even at this it was causing damage.

Harmony ran straight over to Pepsy's smoking form, she lay there, still shaking off the aftershocks. Harmony placed both her hands onto Pepsys chest and activated her gift. A bright white light flowed from her hands and in an instant Pepsy was healed once more, her eyes met Harmony's and she smiled, Harmony then helped her back to her feet.

Quincy was delirious now, his gift was dangerous and he now saw himself as a direct threat to Astoria and all it stood for. With tears still streaming from his face he called out.

"You have to kill me"

"Don't be stupid" the Allfather called back "we will find a way"

"There is no other way, I don't know how much longer I can hold it..It's getting worse" He yelled.

He was correct though; his entire body was turning an extremely bright colour of white and was buzzing dangerously with potential energy.

Jeremy was almost a good 40 yards back now; his natural instincts had continued his steps backwards. He suddenly felt an abrupt bump, his heels hitting it first before his back too, hit the obstacle. It was something soft and yet firm, turning slowly, he found it to be the massive belly of Wallace.

"Looks like my boy is in a spot of bother" Wallace said, a big grin covering his face, his white teeth spreading ear to ear. He brushed past Jeremy and made his way toward Quincy, as he neared, he too could feel the immense build up within his friend.

"Well my boy, what's has got you all wired up today" he grinned and grabbed Quincy by both shoulders.

At the mere sight of his friend, Quincy's eyes dropped, tears flowing freely, he broke down in a mess of tears.

"I've got you little guy" Wallace said comfortingly.

As was his gift of absorbing power, he instantly began to grow as the electricity flowed straight into his body. He could feel Quincy sink into his massive form in comfort, sobbing into his massive belly, which was in fact growing bigger by the second.

He continued to grow, bigger and bigger and bigger.

Wallace's smile quickly faded as he had now grown bigger than he ever had before, his clothing ripped and his Astorian blue armour had to activate to keep him decent.

"Erm, guys, any ideas...I don't think this is going to stop" he said as he did in fact continue to grow, he was now easily 30 ft tall and getting bigger by the second. The Angels stood back in absolute astonishment.

The Allfather took charge instantly, recognising that they needed a new solution before Wallace himself grew so big that he would crush Astoria under his weight.

"Spanners, your thoughts?" he shouted.

"We need to insulate him somehow; something to ground the flow, a boomer may do the trick as it's made of Lastic"

"Where?"

"The armoury has one" Spanner replied.

"Pepsy go!" the Allfather shouted.

"I've never been there, I can only shift as far as the palace cellars" Pepsy replied.

"THEN GO" the Allfather yelled, urgency was clearly in his voice.

Pepsy grabbed Spanners and 'shifted' away, the Allfather turned his attention back to Wallace, who held Quincy in his arms a good 50ft up in the air now, and from his position, it looked like Quincy was still sobbing in his arms, the electricity flowing out of him and directly into Wallace.

"This had better work" the Allfather said aloud.

Deep Down in the cellars, Spanners and Pepsy teleported in.

"This way" Spanners said and indicated to Pepsy to follow him. They ran down a long cobbled passageway that had dripping water at each junction, Spanners turned left about halfway down and then descended down a flight of stairs. Pepsy kept close tail behind, feeling rather impressed by Spanners speed; she had never seen him move so fast before. Perhaps the situation of urgency had never required it, but here they were now, in a great rush and he was by no mean a slouch, she had to give it everything she had to keep him in sight.

At the bottom of the next stairwell there was a short passageway followed by another set of stairs, this time a spiral set. They quickly made their way down them. Every twenty or so stairs, there were small doors in the side of the walls and Pepsy counted that she had passed four of them already, she started to wonder just how far down underground they had travelled.

Her thoughts caused her distraction, she lost focus and hadn't noticed that Spanners, had in fact made his way into one of the doors that lay concealed into the wall. She was moving quickly and tried to stop, it was too late; she tripped and started a humiliating tumble further down the spiral staircase.

Her world was being flipped upside down constantly. She was actually amazed at how much her armour was minimising the impact as she felt next to no pain at all, just the embarrassment of the fall itself.

After falling for what seemed like forever, she hit the bottom of the spiral staircase and crashed through a wooden door, rolling into a massively dark room. She lay there on a grilled metal platform and allowed herself a few moments to recover before standing up and taking in her surroundings.

The room was vast, almost indescribably vast. She couldn't believe that something so big could exist underground nor to what purpose it had in being here.

Her eyes panned left and right through the darkness. She felt a newfound curiosity overcome her.

She took a device from her gauntlet and dropped it off the platform and down into the darkness below, she began to count.

"one *** two ** three**" she continued like this for a few moments more. So long in fact that she started to doubt whether she had missed the sound she was looking for.

"32 *** 33**" clink...she heard the distinct sound of her gauntlet indicate that the device had now hit the ground.

33 seconds she calculated, that surely cannot be correct, 3.5 miles to the bottom, the room must have been MASSIVE she thought. Just as she was about to activate the homing element of the device, she heard a noise behind her, she turned to face Spanners who had made his way down to collect her. In his hand he held the boomer satchel they required.

"What is this room?" she asked, acutely aware that Spanners was not shocked by the room's presence and so was clearly privy to its purpose.

"This room is off limits to most" Spanners said coldly. "We must go" Pepsy merely nodded, concluding that her curiosity would have to be satisfied later; the safety of Astoria was of a higher importance. Placing her hand onto his, she 'shifted them out of there.

They arrived back outside at the north end of the palace; their eyes grew wide in shock.

Wallace was now a towering avatar, standing like a mythical god, easily 100feet tall, above the city. In his gargantuan hands, he still clutched Quincy close to him, the electricity continuing to flow freely from him.

"Ok now how do we get it up there?" Pepsy spoke aloud what basically was on everyone's mind.

Jeremy finally made himself useful and stepped forwards.

"Please, must I do everything" he said and then turned to Pepsy "take me high, but please...don't let me freefall for too long, I've already been sick today"

She smiled, grabbed his arm and then 'shifted' him up into the air.

They teleported into the space just above Wallace's head, hanging in mid air, she held onto Jeremy as they both started to fall.

Jeremy took the satchel in his right hand and very quickly hurled it toward Quincy. As with everything Jeremy did, he did it with expert accuracy, the satchel struck him, and not only hit him perfectly, but also started to unravel.

The satchel instantly took hold; long strands sprouted that attached to Quincy's body, long Lastic strands then crept their way across his entire body.

Within a short moment, Wallace had stopped growing, and he held his position as the boomer took full effect on the electric Angel, encasing him in Lastic technology and perfectly insulating his gift. The electricity eventually stopped, Quincy's sobbing however did not.

Jeremy and Pepsy were freefalling now directly toward the ground.

"Any time...now Pepsy" he tried to say, Pepsy however, was enjoying the thrill of the fall a little too much, leaving it to the last possible second before 'shifting' again and appearing back where they had started.

Jeremy hurled the content of his stomach onto the ground once more.

"Not again" he grumbled.

Wallace, standing an impressive 170ft tall now, slowly bent down and placed Quincy onto the ground.

Quincy, twice as tall in his boomer armour, sunk to the floor in defeat. He was dreadfully ashamed of his actions today; his uncontrollable gift took many lives and had nearly destroyed all of Astoria, his guilt was undeniable.

Wallace stood there grinning, awaiting the order he desperately needed. The Allfather gave it.

"Release it into the sky Wallace"

"With pleasure" Wallace said and raised his hand high into the sky, unleashing a 40ft wide beam of super potent, high voltage electricity straight into the sky. It flowed strongly for a good ten second before wearing itself out and returning Wallace back to his usual, overly fat size. He breathed out a heavy sigh of relief.

Chance made her way down from the plaza and toward the market area of Astoria. As soon as she turned the corner she could see the chaos that had unfolded there, a mass riot had erupted and all manner of objects were being thrown around. The mess was incredible and it was very difficult to see a clear route through it all, without risking being drawn into the fighting.

She looked around her and saw a sign that pointed towards 'gaming quadrant' she turned and quickly headed in that direction.

She had no idea where she was heading for, she only knew that she had to find and confront the one who had taken her memory, find him and demand he unlock it once again for her.

The noise of the riot from the nearby market stirred her adrenaline and she found herself running quickly in her chosen direction. Before her came a large set of double doors that she almost burst through with great speed.

"At last she returns" came an old voice from inside; she took a moment to scan the room to determine where it had come from, looking briefly left and right but could see no-one, just rows upon rows of gaming tables, filling the depths of the room. Each table had its own set of bleachers, positioned for the viewers she presumed, ten yards back from each table.

"Aren't you going to greet me with a warm hug?" the voice spoke again, this time she was able to hone in on the voices exact location. About halfway down the hall, on the benches opposite the respective gaming table, sat an old frail man. He sat hunch backed and wearing a dirty dark cloak, looking almost like he was cold and curling up in an attempt to keep warm.

She edged her way forwards carefully, keeping her eyes on him at all times. For once she thought carefully before speaking.

"Are you the one that took my memory?" she asked.

"I am indeed, and if you want it back you are going to have to beat me once more" the voice added.

"What is your name?" she asked, having completely no memory of the events from earlier that day. In all respects she felt like she was meeting this person for the first time although she knew otherwise.

"Haha, well I guess in your condition, I can now tell you my real name...I am Kane" the old man responded, Chance remained silent; the name meant nothing to her.

"Well Kane, it seems I already have my memory back" she had by this point lifted the red orb out from her pocket and held it between her thumb and forefinger so that he could see it. "why would I need to beat you now?"

"Because my little lady, as is clear to me, you have not succeeded in opening that orb, and in effect, you have not achieved anything. Face me once again at your pathetic *Superfuse* game, and I will unlock your orb for you"

Chance slowly, placing the orb into her front pocket which, compared with her back pocket, was half as shallow, leaving the orb sitting only half submerged.

"From what I gather, you played dirty on our last encounter, how do I know I can trust you?" Chance asked.

"You can't!" Kane replied, a coy smile crossed his old face. She had little choice in the situation and he knew it, he was her only opportunity of remembering who she was.

"Let's not stand on ceremony then!" she stated and they made their way to the table.

"I have one small rule to add....if you leave the table before the game is done, then you LOSE!" he stated.

Chance merely smiled at him, she had no intentions of leaving any table without a victory and therefore her memory. Picking up the small Lastic ball, she popped it into the hole and the game began.

She started off fast, making swift passes between her players and getting the ball forward as quickly as she could. Once the ball had rolled into range of her forward line, she gripped the handles tightly where she was then immediately transported, down onto the board itself, where she then made the shot, scoring with a perfectly booted strike to the top corner of the goals. Kane could do very little to stop it.

She popped the next ball in and off they went again. She used the same tactic and made short, sharp passes that were difficult to defend. On this occasion, she played it to her midline, where she then gripped the middle handles, zoomed into the board and struck a long shot from mid table; it took a strange bounce and hit the back of the goal.

The score was now 2-0 and the game was going smoothly for her. She had a little memory of this game, enough to know the rules and yet she seemed to be able to play it naturally and with a great amount of skill. She lifted her eyes and viewed her opponent; something about him had changed since the start of the match. She wasn't quite sure what it was but somehow, the old man looked even older, frailer, his claw hands had began to shake more and his breathing sounded even worse than her chimp boys had been earlier. Her eyes met those of the old man and he drew a grin across his old wrinkly face.

"Perhaps now is the time we should up the stakes, and do not forget the rules my little dear" Kane said, and at that, his attention was drawn behind her. With no ball currently in play, she followed his gaze, craning her neck around to see a large tank filled with water. Upon its peak there were five shapes, four very much larger than the fifth. She screwed her eyes up to look closer and realised it was in fact her chimp boy, held captive by four of the most hideous looking beasts she had ever seen. They were hulking monstrosities, with pale purple skins and bubbling contusions on their faces. Their veins were pulsing with a dark fluid and their feet looked like oversized animal paws with long yellow claws on each toe. Raphael looked in a bad way, a worse state than she had left him earlier in the plaza. His left leg was slightly bent and he was leaning heavily on the beast to his right, his head was slouched and he was struggling to remain vertical. He lifted his eyes slightly and met hers; he had a look of deep sorrow and regret, her heart sunk a little to see him so badly beaten. She turned her gaze back to her opponent.

"Slightly distracted now are we little lady?" Kane said.

"Not in the slightest" she replied quickly and calmly.

"Oh well that IS a shame" he countered, and then nodded to his honour guard who, in turn, launched Raphael down into the ice-water filled tank.

The water was cold, so cold that its shiver sharpness cut deep into his lungs like a knife.

He had never felt a cold like this before. To Raphael it felt like two icy hands had reached into his chest, and began to compress his weak lungs, he was in deep trouble and never before had that phrase been more literally accurate to his perilous situation as it did now.

He became acutely aware that his arms and legs were thrashing, violently kicking out in all directions with no sense of order or rhythm. None of this did anything to disperse the frost that was seeping deep into his bones. His fingers were numb, feeling only the thrashing, panic stricken movements of his wrists.

Although he couldn't see them, he imagined his lips will have turned blue, he part-swallowed, and then spat some water. His throat was instantly frosted and the terror began to soak its way through his skin.

He was drowning.

His time was running short and there was nothing he could do about it.

He thought back to all the time Chance had spent trying to teach him to paddle; she had been very patient with him he recalled, taking her time with him, and helping to control his fear.

He hated water, or more he didn't understand it. It was a medium where he had no control, no strength, in water he was vulnerable, but she had made it bearable.

He loved mostly to watch her, her beautifully slender body sailed through the water like an exotic fish. She could hold her breath for what seemed like an eternity, weaving her way along the bottom of the pool, navigating along the pool base before shooting up like a torpedo back to the surface to ensure he was still ok.

His eyes had become bloodshot, the tension and the straining had burst the tiny vessels in his dark brown eyes, littering his vision with red streaks, he was pretty sure his nose had started to bleed, as the strong taste of iron coated the inside of his mouth, it was a taste he loathed, and he screwed his face up as he attempted to spit it out, his attempt failing as he realised his head was now fully submerged into the icy cold water.

He reached out with his mind and focused on his legs that were beginning to tire.

On land he was as strong as life would ever need him to be but in this elemental medium, this fluidly moving surface, he was as weak as they come.

He reached out again with his mind, mustering all his strength and willed his legs to push, to kick out with all their might, his legs answered and propelled him above the water line with one huge push, the sheer exertion of the effort emptying his lungs of what little air remained, and his eyes were once again clear of the fateful fluid. He caught one last glimpse of his girl, before gravity returned its grasp on him.

Without time or thought to inhale any life, he slipped under.

Chance played on, keeping to her hard and fast tactic, she was now 3-0 up and could not understand how this old man had supposedly beaten her earlier that day. It was a strange notion, as his hands were lacking the speed required to beat her nimble hands, and yet that was what she had been told, that he had secured victory. She chose to remain cautious.

As she moved around the table, shifting her weight from one leg to the other, the red orb slipped out of her shallow pocket and fell to the floor. It cracked slightly upon impact, and started to roll slowly away from the table, gathering speed as it followed the slightly sloped contours of the floor, coming to rest against the edge of a stone pillar that overlooked the gaming tables, the cracked edge striking the stone and smashing completely open, the contents of the orb floating freely from the broken container, drifting its way back towards Chance, toward her face and entering through her nose. Her eyes lit up as she processed all the information in the blink of an eye.

The ghostly red contents crept further up her nose and into her mind, reactivating the dormant memory cells and bringing her old self back online.

She could remember EVERYTHING!

She remembered her powers, her capabilities and also her limits. She remembered how she had lost her memory in the first place, how she had been outsmarted by the old man who had cheated, possibly using his gifts during play to display such blinding speed.

She remembered her first day at school; she remembered her gift day and what she had done to celebrate it every year. She remembered her mother, her dear mother and her passing.

She remembered her father and what he meant to her, the times they had spent together, and the laughs they had shared. She remembered when she had customised her armour, decorating it to make her stand out from the rest; she even remembered how she had to explain herself to her father for doing so.

She remembered her necklace, the clock less face and what that stood for, she remembered who had given her it and what he had said to her that day, she remembered how she had felt, as she had heard the words leave his lips, feeling like all her dreams had come true, as he told her that he would love her until the end of time, she remembered how he...

291

She paused and panicked at the same time, her heart stopping in her chest, her breath held as realisation sunk in.

She remembered he couldn't swim!

She turned her head toward the tank; her gloriously customised armour immediately began to form across her entire body, realising that all this time, that annoying itch that had plagued her all day, had actually been her Angel armour calling, demanding to be worn.

A bright light shone, all around her body, a uniquely set of pink shoulder guards, studded with shiny diamonds and finished off with a gleaming white trimming to finish, formed across her shoulders, her limbs were now covered in the same decoration of pink and white with diamonds, making her look absolutely Angelic as the light shone off her gleaming attire, casting sharp beams in all directions. On her feet she wore a set of pink boots with long stiletto heels, making her easily a few inches taller than before.

She made to run, as quickly as she could, toward the tank. She made it there within a dozen long stridden steps, before she jumped, with all her might, and sent herself sailing high into the air, turning mid flight, and spiralling down and in towards the tank. Her hands above her head, she performed a perfect corkscrewed dive, straight into the icy cold water.

Right away she could see Raphael's lifeless form, sunk to the bottom of the tank and she wasted no time in swimming down to him, taking his athletic frame in her arms, she click flicked her stiletto heel on her right foot, loading a small explosive cap onto its tip; she then kicked out hard into the side of the tank and allowed the tip of her heel to plant the explosive round into its thick glass. Grabbing Raphael under his armpits she swam back to the opposite side of the tank before clicking her heels together. The heel tip exploded and immediately the tank burst its contents out into the games area, the flow of water slid them both out into fresh air and Chance now lay directly on top of Raphael, hopping straight off, she then knelt down at his side and checked if he was breathing.

"Please Raph" she pleaded but there was no response. She checked for a pulse and found there was none so she leaned back slightly, brought both her hands together and shut her eyes, she focussed hard and then raised both hands above her head, held them there for a second and then drove them down towards his chest, adding in the force of her gift and struck him square in the chest. The impact point was perfect, and kick started his heart right away while at the same time sent enough force through his body that he jolted upright, and spat out all the water from his lungs in one large exhale.

"You're ok thank goodness your ok" she was genuinely so happy to see him and held his face in both her hands. Her memory had fully returned now and there was no longer a mystery as to what he was to her.

She pulled his face close to hers and started to kiss him repeatedly, over and over, pressing her lips as hard as she could into his. Deep down she was so happy he was alive, a close call, as she kissed him over and over she replayed all the events of the day, everything they had been through, she felt so relieved that he had stood by her through all of it. She kept kissing him and refusing to let up, he started to mumble but she couldn't make out a word he said, she was just so happy he was ok.

He mumbled some more before finally bringing his hands up and pushing her back slightly.

"Chance hunni...I ...I...I can't breathe" he said, his eyes were bloodshot from the whole experience and his lips were a distinct colour of blue. She looked at him long and hard, his deeply brown, wounded eyes gazed into her newfound fiery blue eyes, she smiled, grabbing his face and gave him another big kiss.

"I am so sorry I forgot you" she said.

"Well..It happens I guess" he responded, attempting to help excuse her actions.

"No really I am truly sorry, I know you'd never have forgotten me" she said. Upon hearing those words, he gave her a deeply loving look, a gaze that her words had touched him to his heart.

"Obviously because I'm UNFORGETTABLE" she said and smirked, giving him another short kiss. Raphael rolled his eyes, knowing the idea of her being sentimental wouldn't have lasted and that a joke couldn't have been far on the horizon.

Chance stood up and turned, changing her caring demeanour into one of vengeful defiance. Her amazingly pink, sparkly, and yet advanced armour shone brightly even in the days receding light. The water from the tank had all but dripped off its proofed surface, and she stood there in all her mighty splendour, her eyes darting between the old man and his four deformed bodyguards. She turned her shoulders slowly, putting herself between the foe and her love, she carefully cracked her neck to each side, nimbling up for the carnage she was about to unleash.

In the blink of an eye she launched herself at them, taking on all four bodyguards at once, with a lightning fast combination of attacks, Swinging punches and kicks, at least ten thrown every second. Her arms became a blur. The deformed guards blocked what they could and absorbed much of the rest, their sheer size made them mountains of meat, her physical attacks were doing very little to upset their day.

Kane took a few steps back and automatically concluded that his time here had come to an end. He turned and made for the alleyway that lay at the bottom of the clearing. Chance watched him leave but was powerless to do anything about it, as she ducked and weaved her way between the bodyguards return shots.

Her eyes dropped to the floor, toward Raphael, who by this point had turned onto his front and was crawling his way toward her position.

The first bodyguard swung its huge, vein pulsing pink arm toward her face which she dodged so perfectly, that it enabled her to duck under his attack and throw four punches straight into its side. She immediately felt the solid impact of the muscle bound guard, her fist recoiling under the shock. She took a step back and lifted her hands, unleashing her gift of fireworks straight into his face, temporarily blinding him, and allowing her to jump, evading the other three guards strikes, and land behind the first guard, keeping all her attackers in front of her.

By now Raphael had crawled his way across the floor and was within reach of the guards, Chance eyed him precariously and unsure of what he was planning to do. Her concern for his safety grew as one of the guards turned towards him and began marching across the clearing to attack the fallen Angel. Chance denied him the easy opportunity by bounding in front, jumping with a spin kick, digging her heal into its side, she tore her stiletto away, leaving the small tip behind which immediately began to send electricity up through the guard, forcing his mutated body into a pulsing frenzy.

Before she had time to react, another guard was on her, swinging hard and wild with all its might. Each strike fortunately missed her, but even the wind that dragged along with it was enough to force her back. She felt her choler rise inside as the ferocity of the attack increased, she still couldn't see an opening in its fast swings, and with each swing, the deformed guard seemed to gain momentum, his power was increasing along with his speed. If he kept this up, he would land one of those strikes eventually and she was sure it would send her head spinning.

Just before she had the misfortune of such an outcome, the big guard paused and looked down, almost dumbstruck. At its feet lay Raphael, his hands gripping onto its ankles. Raphael looked at Chance and shouted.

"Now"

She instantly knew what he meant, taking a deep breath she hopped off her right foot, landing on the toe of her left and spinning her right leg around, she then hopped off the left and onto the right, gaining momentum..she repeated this at least 20 times all in the space of 3 seconds. Her legs were now spinning dangerously fast, creating a small tornado with the sheer velocity she had generated. She hopped up off her back leg, and directed the full force of the spinning leg attack toward the deformed guards face; spinning at un-recordable speeds she must have struck his face 100 times in a second. There was a small explosion and a burst of purple light and matter. The light was blinding and the other guards covered their eyes in recoil. Raphael was forced to do the same as he still lay there, holding tight onto its legs. Chance landed softly, after virtually hovering on the spot for a further ten seconds from the sheer velocity of the move she had just performed.

Raphael opened his eyes and found he was still clutching the feet of the deformed guard, his face furrowed into a puzzled look, as he then

295

realised that the legs were ALL he was holding, from the knee up there was nothing, completely obliterated. He looked to Chance and nodded his impressed approval, she looked down at the purple remains of the guard and realised that they were not in fact human. She couldn't discern what they were, but she knew one thing was for sure...this had changed EVERYTHING.

She flicked open her left gauntlet and played with a few buttons, Raphael watched her closely.

"So you got it in pink after all" he said, a smile across his face. Chance looked down at him and smiled, blowing him a kiss and then flicked shut her gauntlet, turning just in time to meet the attack of the other three guards who had just recovered from the blinding light of the attack.

She met the first swing with a block, parried its massive arm to one side and then blasted him with a force push which knocked the muscle bound beast onto its back. She turned and launched fireworks from her hands into the other guard, again blinding his vision before turning to face the last guard. Lifting her right hand, a small compartment popped open on the back of her fist; she took careful aim and then fired! A stream of diamond projectiles came bursting out of her right gauntlet and were sent straight into one of the guard, shredding his muscled body and bursting purple matter all over the area. She kept the flow of her attack up and within a few seconds his entire form burst into a purple cloud of vapour.

The other two guards stood to attention, one was rubbing its eyes and the other had just climbed back to its feet. Chance stood there all calm and serene. She dropped her hand to her side and slowly clipped her heels together, preloading a particular tipped round into her stiletto heel. She turned her hips fully now to face her two opponents, swung her arms back and burst into a run. With every bounding step she took with her lean muscular legs, she gained momentum, faster and faster and faster. Both guards stood their ground and lifted their arms ready to strike. She boomed in closer and closer and then, at the last possible second, she jumped high into the air.

Raphael watched on in awe. He loved nothing more than to watch his special girl in action. He loved how she majestically and calmly dispatched of the first two guards, and now watched on eagerly for the grand finish. He watched her advance at full speed toward two massive and towering hulking beasts. She bounded on, completely fearless and with purpose, he watched as she jumped impossibly high into the air, everything seemingly going in slow motion as she twisted and somehow managed to kick both enemies, in their ribs, at the same time and then land perfectly with her back to both guards, with no intention of turning. He watched as both guards were bent over double from the attack. He watched eagerly as she stood there, waiting for the perfect moment, the perfect finish, always about a show his girl was.

Chance turned, gave both guards a wink and then clicked her heels together... Suddenly both guards were completely encrusted in a massive, smoothed edged perfect diamond. Their whole bodies were encased in the perfect glassy surface, created by the small stiletto heel tip that she had planted upon kicking their ribs. In the same second that both guards became one massive diamond...they then shattered into a thousand tiny priceless stones. The pieces fell to the floor and scattered across the ground instantly.

Chance walked over carefully, turned her heels where a small compartment opened up, a small vacuum, it then sucked up the small diamond pieces back into her suit and she smiled, she then made her way over to Raphael.

He was by this stage sitting upright and leaning against the small wall by the edge of the clearing. A smile creased his face as she arrived; she too couldn't help but smile at him.

He always had that effect on her and she loved putting on a good performance for him, this one she knew, would stick in his mind for awhile. She knelt down beside him and kissed his forehead gently.

"The way you fight your armour should really be red" he said, his eyes wide and matter-of-factly.

"hee hee I'm specially customised... you aren't going to tell on me are you?" she said playfully, his smile grew as he gave in to her charms. She returned the smile and for the first time that day she gave him a look to let him know she genuinely cared. She lifted her hand slowly and then brought it near his face. She watched as his breathing slowed under his nervousness of the action, she held his gaze a moment longer, trying her best to give him her smouldering eyes before she then patronisingly patted him on the cheek, smiling on the inside as she saw him breath out in disappointment.

"Now don't think iv forgotten our wager from yesterday...LAUNDRY!!" she said.

He smiled and rolled his eyes.

CHAPTER 12

A few hours later, and all the people of Astoria had been rounded up and calmed down by the presence of the Angels.

They had all been directed to the main plaza at the front of the palace where the Allfather stood on a raised platform, waiting to address them all. Thousands upon thousands of civilians had now left their homes and were tightly packed all the way from the city's main gates, up through the mess of the market, and all the way up to the plaza itself.

Each civilian adorned a look of shame upon their faces at the carnage that the majority of them had invoked; some held their heads low, unwilling to meet the eyes of the Angels.

The Allfather waited briefly before then addressing the crowd, his voice was being amplified through the speakers that were littered about Astoria and had long since been forgotten about. The Allfather deemed that today, of all days, that tech would be required.

"Citizens and loyal servants of Astoria, it seems today we have befallen a grave chain of events. Some of those among you have followed actions that you are not proud of, said things that you did not mean, committed crimes you now regret. Well I am here to lay the truth out before you, to shed some light on the cause of this anguish that you felt in your hearts." The Allfathers words had been listened to intently, some of the Astorians raised their heads in curiosity.

"A dark cloud found its way over Astoria, it was brought in to our great city and allowed to manifest itself in the very walls that we built to keep us safe. This darkness was designed to bring out the very worst in you all, to corrupt you, to stain your pure hearts. Well I am here to commend you ALL! For Astoria still stands and this darkness did not prevail! Let us not hold our heads low in shame but keep them high, and be mindful for the future. For never again will we allow ourselves to be lowered as we did to day. No go!! Celebrate! Be thankful of what we have and what we have built!"

The crowd were roused and cheers went up. Their actions, although not condoned, now had reasoning. Each person turned to one another, clasping hands and making vows to keep one another straight and pure of heart, to never again allow the anger and stress into their lives, and at the first sign of any of these routes to darkness...to inform the Angels straight away.

For all, it was very enlightening and they all set off, without instruction and made their way to the market areas to clean up the mess. Thousand upon thousand of civilians, some of them whom were not even involved, were all mucking in and helping to fix what had been broken that day. Working together they were reminded of what it was to be astorian.

A few hours later, and the streets were bursting with crowds of excited people.

Fireworks were being set off from the roof tops, the skies were filled with colourful explosions of every possible shade, and cheers could be heard after each bang. It had been but a few hours since Chance had returned, and yet the whole city was buzzing as if the party hadn't even started.

Kane staggered and fell into a dark side street, his body was old and his condition was worse now that he'd been using his powers to escape. He was breathing heavily through his old lungs, and a spell of dizziness had begun to swirl in his mind. He leaned against the cold brick wall and tried to regain some level of composure.

He looked down at his hands, they looked older and more claw like than ever, he cursed his father's sorcery. He didn't choose this and yet here he was, bent over double in some dark alley with this terrible affliction. He tried to remember a time where his life was his own, a time when he had free will to choose a path that suited his own. He couldn't, all of his days he had been part of this plot, groomed and manipulated by his father for his own begotten gains. All of his days he had been tied to this fate, he was far too young to feel this weary and yet here he was, personified to any stranger as a raggedly old man.

He became angry and attempted to stand up straight, his old knees gave out from fatigue and he slumped to the floor, landing in a puddle. The water began to soak through his clothes but he had not the strength to move anymore.

From his position on the wet ground, he could make out the bright flashes as each firework exploded high into the sky. Some blew up into large flares of multiple colours; others had multiple explosions leading to a cluster of bangs and crashes coupled with cheers from the crowds.

He smiled to himself. There had been a time when he foresaw his desired future, he foresaw himself crowned as a ruler of such lands and that the people would worship him, setting off fireworks in his name. He would have been powerful, his gift allowing him to rule without question, making things the way he wanted them to be, that dream was gone now.

His powers had waned over time, an unfortunate side effect of his condition.

'Damn my father' he thought

"Damn me?....my boy Kane....I am already damned" the cold ghostly voice had returned. He hadn't even sensed the usual shift in temperature this time; perhaps it was his cold disposition in the puddle that clouded his senses.

"I did all that you asked of me father, now please reverse this affliction" the old man gestured with his clawed hands; his face had become one of weakness and pleading.

"I warned you Kane... that I would not tolerate weakness..." the voice trailed off

"But I did all that you..."

The ghost voice cut in before the old man could finish.

"Your sibling rivalry nearly cost me.....nearly.." it trailed off again "your brother will become...powerful....more than you can imagine...you were always the weak one...and I....will tolerate you no longer..."

Before Kane had a chance to open his mouth, his entire body started to convert into a shiny metallic alloy. It started from his limbs and worked its way inward, he had not the strength left to resist it. Just as he was about to yell out in pain, one final defiant cry and anguish, his lungs turned to metal and he lay there, a frozen, cold, metal carcass.

Jessica, still encased in her boomer, was redirecting the civilians of Sanctuary into the western quadrant of the city. The swarm was now down to an acceptable level and yet was still looming too high for the Phoenix guard to reach. It was too difficult to determine if the swarm was growing again, if it was, it was expanding in such a small way compared with earlier when that device was drawing millions of the pests from all around.

With her left hand pointing the way, and the right hand waving everyone in the correct flow, she stood there controlling the traffic expertly. From her heightened positioned inside her armour, she could see well into the distance, and began to make out a shape that she instantly recognised, approaching toward the city limits. A smile crossed her face and yet she continued to do her duty and direct the flow.

With every moment that passed, the shape loomed even closer and Jessica's smile grew even bigger for two reasons, the excitement of the shape itself, and also the possibility that it would be carrying a special someone toward her.

The shape was moving fast, it was very big, very wide and it was clearly reptilian of nature. The sun was shining bright and coming from the same direction so she had to shield her eyes to make it out clearly.

Within minutes the shape became clearer as her pet misty, flapping its massive wing span into the city limits, it flew straight toward the swarm of flies that still congregated high above the reaches of the Phoenix guard.

Misty stopped mid flight and held its position by flapping its wings rapidly on the same spot, she then fired a massive burst of flame that incinerated the entire swarm in one massive burst. The civilians broke out in a cheer that could be heard for miles all around.

Misty slowly began to descend until she hovered a mere 30 ft above the city itself, on her back sat the Astorian Angel Chance, resplendent in her pink armour with shiny studded shoulder guards and pink stiletto boots coupled with 'dangerous' heels.

Chance pulled her sunglasses from her head and shook them free of her hair, she cracked her neck to both sides and then hurled her glasses over the back of her shoulders and down toward the ground below. Jessica's eyes followed the demise of the sunglasses as they fell, end over end, toward the hard stone floor. About a metre from the ground, a hand reached out and caught them softly, this hand then folded the legs inward and the glasses were placed into a small lastic satchel which then vanished from sight. Jessica's eyes looked closer and realised that the hand belonged to none other than the Angel Raphael, who also wore his gleaming white Angel armour.

Raphael looked up to where Chance sat on the back of misty, she looked right back down at him and winked; she then carefully took her little hand, brought it up to her mouth, and blew him a kiss.

Raphael smiled.

The next day, the party and celebrations continued throughout the city. Something about the actions of the day before had hit deep into the hearts of all who dwelled in Astoria, and once freed of the darkness, they felt an overwhelming urge to be joyful and thankful that their minds were once again pure. Fireworks remained to be set off regularly. There was dancing in the streets and singing too, the sheer happiness of the situation was lost on nobody, not even the Allfather who stood in the palace plaza looking down into the market place. He stood there in his white robes, arms folded across his body and watched on, very thankful that his work had not been undone.

A curious little sight caught his attention, and drew his eyes instantly to it. He saw six, perfectly white little ducklings, making their way up the steps from the market and across the plaza. Their tiny little orange feet padding along against the white stone, all following in a perfect straight line towards his location. From his position, he noted that the lead duck was slightly whiter than the following five and bore a little red heart in its feathers upon it chest. The Allfather smiled as the duckling came nearer.

"well my little Harmony, you have surpassed your powers capabilities this time, how on earth have you manifested more of you" the Allfather said as he loomed over the lead duckling. Upon hearing his question, the duckling at the front cocked its head and began to communicate back.

"quack quackquququack" it said. The Allfather merely rolled his eyes. In all her brilliance, she still hadn't grasped that he couldn't talk to animals. There was a pause and then the little duckling morphed straight into the Angel Harmony. She was wearing a tight little black dress that showed off her voluptuous figure perfectly, she wasn't wearing any shoes and her bare feet padded along the ground as she drew closer to the Allfather.

"Its not me" she exclaimed and turned to regard the ducklings that followed her. All five of them were perfectly white like her shape was previously.

"I wanted the children to feed me some bread, so I turned into a duckling, and now these five started following me...I cant get rid of them" Harmony said, a genuine sense of puzzlement on her face from her obvious predicament.

"hmm... curious that they are white and not yellow for ducklings" the Allfather said as he had crouched down to regard them closer.

"they have been following me about all day..i cant shake them off" she said. Her face was slightly panicked as she clearly did not know what to do. The Allfather chuckled at her misfortune.

"oh Harmony, our city walls nearly fall, our people went crazy, our armies were sent away and an Angel nearly burned us all with his gift...through all this you seemed unfazed, and yet here you are now...with your five little pursuers, and you are panicked and at a loss as to what to do" the Allfather said.

304

"err..yes...i really do not know what to do, It's quite an issue for me. I tried becoming a fox to chase them but they thought it was a game and chased me back. I tried becoming a worm but..well that didn't end all to well for me..and no i don't want to talk about how i got out of its belly!"

The Allfather began to laugh as he walked away, giving her a gentle pat on her shoulder as he passed her. She raised her hand and scratched her head as her eyes remained on her five little puzzles before her.

He made his way over to the palace stairs where Spanners stood there waiting, a data slate in hand. He gave Spanners a small smile and then took the data slate from his hand and stood beside him, Spanners, from his position on the stairs, was watching Harmony trying to chase the little ducklings around. A smile ACTUALLY crossed Spanners face when he saw Harmony's poor attempts at being stern and mean to the little birds. Her attempts were in vain as the five little birds chased her around in a circle.

"it is a good day today Spanners" the Allfather said. "seems all traces of the madness were obliterated along with those devices"

"Yes oh great one, It seems Quincy made a good job of that task"

"And how is our Quincy, last I heard he was held up in his room and refusing to talk to anyone?"

"nothing has changed. He remains in his Boomer for his, and everyone else's safety, I have yet to determine a solution to his problem but i shall get on the case." Spanners said.

"good work Spanners, i shall try and drop in with him very soon, i feel he has some issues he needs to get off his chest" they both fell silent. Watching and listening to the cheers around the city. Large fireworks were blowing off into the skies, cheers could be heard from down in the market placed and the whole of Astoria seemed to be smiling.

"Yes it is a good day" Spanners said.

"Yes...but have you noticed there hasn't been a single halo today, nor last night" both their eyes rose to the heavens, contemplating the absence of the halo. They both fell silent.

Over in eastern quadrant of Astoria, Pepsy was playing cupid. She stood in front of Wallace and adjusted his bow tie as he stood there in an outfit made from so much cloth, that he had virtually spent his entire week's credits to attain it. In his other hand he held a beautiful bunch of flowers, most of which were white lilies, there was no guessing who had picked these flowers for him.

"Ok you are almost ready, now remember just be yourself" Pepsy said to him as she could see the nervousness growing in his big round face. He pulled his usual smile and yet it was not as wide as normal. She play slapped him and returned the smile. She then stood up straight, gave him one last look, and once satisfied she grabbed him and shifted him to the other end of the city.

There they appeared just outside a little bar called the 'Pepper pott'

"Ok now just walk in, sit down...erm actually stand, I don't want you breaking anything, stand but be charming. You'll be fine" she said.

She turned Wallace's shoulders and then gave him a playful push in the direction of the doors, he took quite a few careful steps forwards before the bar doors burst outwards, and Paulina exited the bar to meet him. She was wearing this magnificent long purple dress that, although it hugged her round her figure, it gave her voluptuous curves and made her look her best. On her feet she wore delicate cream little shoes finished off with a cream little handbag. Her eyes lit up once she saw Wallace had brought her flowers and she instantly embraced him and kissed him on both cheeks. She certainly wasn't shy. Upon hugging Wallace she looked over his large shoulders and gave Pepsy a wink and mouthed a thank you for helping her pick out such an amazing outfit. Paulina turned to walk down the street, Wallace gave a weary shy look back to Pepsy who returned it with a push of her hand to indicate he should get going, and get in there.

Pepsy watched them walk off down the street together making small talk. She watched them walk further and further until she could no longer make them out at all. As soon as she found herself alone, Pepsy activated her armour, which coated her body instantly in her red protective plates. She then flipped the control panel on her left gauntlet and found that the red bleeping light was still pulsing from the homing device she had dropped the day before. She took a deep breath and then 'shifted' back to that big dark room.

She had teleported into pitch darkness, lit only by a small, pulsing red item on the floor next to her. She knelt down and picked up her homing device and deactivated it, flipped open her gauntlet once more and returned the device to the appropriate slot. She then flip shut her gauntlets' and turned her attention to her right hand where she depressed a section on the inside of her wrist and a small panel protruded from the back of her fist. She squeezed her knuckles and four bright torch beams shone out from the holes there.

Pepsy stood up straight and started to explore her surroundings.

The room was as she had expected, epically huge. So big that her torch light couldn't even illuminate it all. She turned around slowly and could make out the main wall which, further up, would have the gantry attached to it that she had found the day before. She looked closer at the walls and realised they were not flat but in fact slightly angled, giving the huge room a rounder feel to it. She wondered just how big the dimensions of it were.

She walked on a bit, shining her torch around in all directions. There was definitely a centre piece to the room that she couldn't quite make out. Her torch was just catching the tip of something as she walked closer. At her feet, she felt an incredibly straight grooved line in the rockcrete below, and she wondered if the floor was capable of moving in any way, perhaps to reveal an even larger chamber below?

She drew even closer and her torch began to make out a large cone shaped object protruding from the floor. It was easily 20ft tall and gradually got wider as it went down, and into the floor. Pepsy now realised that the floor she was walking on, was in fact a false bottom and she had no doubt that it had a mechanical function to open. She drew even nearer, her torch shining on a shiny metallic plate that was attached to the side of the cone object. As the torch highlighted its every detail, Pepsys eyes grew wide in shock as she ran over the symbols on the plate. Her heart stopped beating in her chest, her eyes furrowed in confusion and she was absolutely baffled by what she read.

The plate read simply 'Arc 137- the 'Astoria'

WWW.MRSHIELDS.CO.UK

Made in the USA
Charleston, SC
05 February 2013